IVY BAYGREN

Downington Avenue

The sound was only mildly alarming, a persistent non-menacing scratch like bare branches against thin glass on a blustery December night. But it wasn't winter, the covers had been kicked to my ankles, and the house was July-muggy.

I reached over and tapped the mattress near my husband's head to wake him, knowing without opening my eyes our raccoon was back and nesting in the attic. Typically, it took both of us to triangulate her stealthy movements among the rafters, then come morning, we could easily locate her cozy mound of shredded cloth and insulation. We had a routine. With elbow-length gloves and face protection, Adam would catch the hissing female and lock her in our old puppy crate. If there were babies, I would hand him a towel I'd heated in the dryer, and he'd bundle her masked kits for transport. Together we'd drive them back into the foothills of the Wasatch Mountains near our home. There we'd shake the mama out of the cage (again), run for cover, and admonish her through the open windows of the minivan to stay in the woods where she belonged, or the next time we'd be forced to take more drastic measures.

I leaned closer to his sleeping form and whispered so my voice wouldn't muffle the sounds of the creature in the attic. "Adam, she's back. Listen."

The response was a lolling lick, wetting me from finger to forearm. Recoiling, I gasped, "Oh, God, Chloe. What are you doing on the bed?"

Wiping dog slobber onto the quilt, I foggily tried to recall Adam's whereabouts. Was this the bar convention in Sun Valley? Or that deposition he'd scheduled in Denver? And then with a nauseating punch I sat up in bed, hand to my mouth. Knowing. I glared at Chloe, willing her night-blurry canine silhouette to be my husband. But it wasn't. Her fringed tail thumped once against the mattress in response to my flinty stare. She sighed, perhaps in sympathy, and laid her head back on the pillow.

Sliding from the bed to the floor, moaning lightly with each breath, I reached under the skirt for the box I knew was there, all the while pleading it into nonexistence. But the tips of my fingers found the cardboard container my brother Stephen used to bury the items I couldn't look at, not even for a second. He was certain I'd want them someday. But I didn't. I didn't ever want them to be there, because if they were under the bed it meant—

"No, no, no, no, no," I whispered softly, my voice quivering as I tugged at the lid. "Please be empty, please be empty." I willed it with my words even as I recognized the intimately familiar contents. Lifting the red T-shirt, threadbare at neck and hem, I breathed in the lingering smell of laundry detergent and sweat, swiping at my cheeks with my shoulder so tears wouldn't tarnish the precious item. My heart was pounding behind my forehead, blurring the remaining contents as I groped inside the box with shaking hands. His gym shoes had been placed at the bottom, as free from impact as the morning he last tied them to his feet, and his socks, still crunchy from his run, were tucked inside. Holding the crumpled pair to my nose, they smelled antiseptic, like the floor of a hospital, but I inhaled until my lungs groaned with the effort.

"Where are you?" I whispered into the dark, imploring him to respond. Silence answered me. After shedding my pajama top I slipped into the worn red cotton, the last shirt he'd worn. We'd purchased it together, more than fifteen years earlier, high from cheap beer and victory after one of the best football games in all

Praise for *Root, Petal, Thorn*
by Ella Joy Olsen

"Five women. Five complicated lives. One house where they all live over a period of one hundred years. In this story, the walls talk. Wonderful, compelling saga!"
— Cathy Lamb, author of *My Very Best Friend*

"Within this captivating debut, we recognize ourselves, our mothers, our sisters, and our daughters in these flawed yet endearing characters. In reading, we are left with a deeper appreciation for our own imperfect lives."
— Sandra Kring, bestselling author of *The Book of Bright Ideas* and *Carry Me Home*

"Olsen does a remarkable job re-creating each historical era, from the days before WWI to the present time. Each time period is as vivid and true as her captivating characters. Olsen is an emerging voice to watch for in historical and contemporary women's fiction."
— Aimie K. Runyan, author of *Promised to the Crown*

"Ella Joy Olsen's *Root, Petal, Thorn* is the perfect addition to a librarian's toolkit of recommended reads for book clubs looking for a lively discussion!"
— Deborah Ehrman, Librarian and Deputy Director, Salt Lake City Public Library System

ROOT,
Petal,
THORN

ELLA JOY OLSEN

𝄞

KENSINGTON BOOKS
www.kensingtonbooks.com

KENSINGTON BOOKS are published by

Kensington Publishing Corp.
119 West 40th Street
New York, NY 10018

All Kensington titles, imprints, and distributed lines are available at special quantity discounts for bulk purchases for sales promotion, premiums, fundraising, educational, or institutional use.

Special book excerpts or customized printings can also be created to fit specific needs. For details, write or phone the office of the Kensington Sales Manager: Kensington Publishing Corp., 119 West 40th Street, New York, NY 10018. Attn. Sales Department. Phone: 1-800-221-2647.

Kensington and the K logo Reg. U.S. Pat. & TM Off.

eISBN-13: 978-1-4967-0563-1
eISBN-10: 1-4967-0563-7
First Kensington Electronic Edition: September 2016

ISBN-13: 978-1-4967-0562-4
ISBN-10: 1-4967-0562-9
First Kensington Trade Paperback Printing: September 2016

10 9 8 7 6 5 4 3 2 1

Printed in the United States of America

Dedicated to George:
my across-the-street neighbor
who inspired this book

And George: the little dog who sat
on my lap while I wrote it

ACKNOWLEDGMENTS

I want to thank my parents, Max and Susan: who taught me to work hard and pursue a passion.

My husband, Chris: who never made me account for my time.

My kids, Nicholas, Annabelle, and Jonathan: who inspire my characters and who are becoming.

My neighborhood: which is full of dreamers, acceptance, big trees, and an awesome book store.

My agent, Rachel Ekstrom: who continues to believe in this story.

My editor, Tara Gavin: who made the whole thing better.

My publisher, Kensington: who gave this book to the world.

The Utah State Historical Society: for collecting, saving, and sharing.

My readers, Bobi, Courtney, Heather, Laura, and Terri: for reading and telling it to me straight.

My book club: for believing in my Alchemist dream and helping it come true.

our years at the University of Utah. Late-season golden leaves swirled under our feet as we walked across campus to our apartment, swinging through the bookstore to buy it. Warmed from exhilaration, he'd stripped from the sweatshirt he'd worn that day and, boldly bare-chested, switched into the new shirt, his boyish abs turning to chicken skin with a rush of October air. Later that afternoon, he'd abandoned it in the corner of our newlywed bedroom, his skin smooth and warm against mine, pressed together under the down comforter.

I crossed my arms at the thought of him and crushed my hands into the sinew of my shoulders until my fingers ached. Embraced once again against the chest of my husband, I curled onto the floor and slept.

Porter was close to my face, his nose nearly touching mine, and his breath was tinged with his regular breakfast of Cheerios and chocolate milk. He jumped back as I opened my eyes, and I noticed the snail trail of slick tears across his cheeks. "Mom? Are you getting up? It's after lunchtime and . . ."

I willed myself to look at him, to answer, to stand. But his eyes, the almond shape of them, the arc of his brow, though he was only eleven, they were Adam's. I pressed my lids together, shutting him out.

"I'm calling Uncle Stephen." Naomi's voice came from the kitchen, shrill and worried.

"She moved a second ago," Porter said. "Let me shake her again." He touched my arm, fingers cold and tentative.

Naomi's voice found me, speaking loudly from the kitchen. "She's on the floor in his shirt and she hasn't moved all morning. Yes, she's breathing, but . . ." Her voice hitched the way it always did before she cried, and I could picture her bottom lip curling up in the center, like a bow, looking like it did when she was a toddler and crying was a daily occurrence.

Go to her! I screamed silently. Every impulse pushed me toward my daughter, arms surrounding her with familiar comfort before she could feel pain, but I couldn't move.

Her sobbing was real now. She hadn't cried openly since she

entered the teen years, but this morning she was sniffing like a child between words, her voice clogged with tears. "There's a pot of oatmeal on the stove. It's rotten, there's mold all over the inside. I think it's from that day!" My daughter was coming unraveled, but heaviness bound me to the carpet as surely as stones. My heart raced like it did when I was seven and my brother, Stephen, buried me in the sand at the beach, my legs and arms paralyzed, fighting against a brain begging me to *Move!*

"He says he's on his way," Naomi said to Porter, hanging up the phone. Relief swept over me at her muffled words. Stephen could fix me if I couldn't fix myself.

"Ivy." Stephen pushed stiff threads of hair from my face and, using gentle hands, he pulled me into a sitting positon. "I wondered if this might happen." My brother crouched next to me still in his scrubs. "It's been a month, and until now, I haven't seen a single tear."

"If I cried, it would mean he was really gone." I spoke quietly, telling my brother what I'd realized only hours earlier. "But Stephen, I don't think he's coming back."

"No, honey, he's not." My brother held me until I could lift my face from his shoulder. He looked older than he had moments earlier. He loved Adam too. "So what happened? The kids found the oatmeal, and you're in his shirt—"

"The oatmeal?" What was he talking about? And then I remembered pulling it from the back of the cupboard, where I'd stashed it weeks earlier. Last night, the midnight kitchen was inky black, the yellow Post-it reading "oatmeal for you" left from that morning still stuck to the lid of my red ceramic pot. "Where are the kids now?" I asked, suddenly alarmed. They shouldn't see me this way. I pulled my hands through my hair, embarrassed at the snarled mess.

"Porter has a couple of buddies over. They're in the basement playing *Call of Duty,* and I had Naomi walk over to Amber's for the evening."

"They've been so strong," I said. "But you know, I hear Naomi crying most nights after I close her door. I've tried to get her to talk with me, but she hides her sorrow because she's being strong for me. Stephen, I'm the mom. If I don't pull myself together I'm going to scare her. I'll scare them both."

Stephen stood from the balls of his feet and extended me a hand. "I think you should take a shower. Nothing like the thump of hot water to give you a little clarity. However, you're right, when you get out we need to come up with a plan. You know, I wasn't sure you'd need it, but there are medications that might help smooth this transition. I could even prescribe—"

I shook my head. "I don't want my memories dulled. I just need to—I don't even know what I need to do." Finally standing, my legs felt like I'd run a marathon. I leaned into Stephen's shoulder, a safe haven where I'd sought shelter more than once.

When we were children, my brother was usually the one to tuck in my shirt, point out Oreo stuck in my teeth, hand me a tissue and dry my tears—because Stephen was more than a regular big brother, he'd been my solid my *whole* life. More handsome than the best-looking doctor on a television hospital drama, face lined with compassion, sandy blond hair graying with gravitas at the temples—that was Stephen. Swoon-worthy, my girlfriends called him. When he came out after college, I swear there was a cry heard round the dating world. But secretly I loved that my big brother was gay because, no matter what I did, I would always be Stephen's best girl.

After the shower I put on a long cardigan and leggings. Though it was July, I was shivering. Lingering on each aspect I could recall of my husband, and torturing myself with the timeline of events on the day he died, took every drop of hot water plus at least ten minutes of ice pouring from the pipes to drive me from the bathroom. Stephen had changed into shorts and a shirt from Adam's closet and was sitting at the dining room table when I emerged.

"I thought you'd drowned in there. I beat Porter and his friends in a round of *Call of Duty* and had time for a cup of tea before I heard the water shut off."

"I think I have a fever." I pressed my thumbs into my eyelids.

Stephen put his hand to my forehead. "I wouldn't doubt it.

It's amazing what the brain can do to the body." He removed his hand. "But you feel fine to me. Now sit." He slid his luke-warm tea toward me. "And let's talk about Adam."

"I can't talk about him like he's gone. Not yet." In quiet mo-ments since my husband died, when I hadn't pasted on an I'm-doing-fine face, I'd catch myself staring out the window at the quiet street in front of my house, incredulous the ash trees canopying our front walk still held the same leaves, alive and verdant, the same ones that graced the branches the day he died. With something as momentous as his death, it seemed unfair the neighbors could drop by with lasagna and go on with their lives, backing down their drives and leaving for work like the world hadn't shifted. In every corner of our fixer-upper bungalow, abandoned tools were idle without his able hands. And the oat-meal I'd made that morning waited for him to return for break-fast.

"Stephen, help me." I slid my chin into my hands, pushing back the tears. "Tell me it's going to be fine, like you did when we were kids and I'd come crying into your room after a fight with so-and-so. Tease me, rationalize with me. Say something funny. I feel like I'm crumbling."

He was quiet for several minutes, then he spoke with a self-assured tone he'd assume when he was sure he was going to beat me at Monopoly, or he'd diagnosed the symptoms in a mystifying medical case. "Today, before I leave, we're going to make you a plan—a list to help you when you can't figure out the next step. Like the study chart you used for calculus, re-member?"

"Calculus was my worst subject." I rested my head on my folded arms.

"But you passed."

"Only because you kept bugging me to study."

"Using the chart." He was smiling now, and I couldn't help but smile back. "Get some paper and a nice pen. We're making you a chart, or an action plan, or a list, or whatever you want to call it."

"If that's what the doctor orders," I said with false stubbornness, but I was actually fizzing. My list-making skills had always been my inflatable water wings in choppy waters, and at this point my head was above water. But just barely. I could really use a plan.

I handed him several sheets of my nicest stationery, a pale green with intertwined leaves. I bought it in bulk, because it was my name paper—Ivy. I put the pen next to the paper in front of him.

"No, you hold the pen," Stephen said. "These are your words and your commitment. I can't do this for you. I can only help you with the tools."

I uncapped the pen and held it over the paper. "What's first?"

"You tell me. Don't you have some articles on grieving, some self-help books? I swear I saw a stack someone brought over after the funeral."

Suddenly inspired, and wanting to show Stephen I still had a wobbling sense of humor, I wrote: *#1: If one glass of wine isn't enough, pour another.* Stephen slid the paper over so he could see it.

"Yes, drinking is a coping skill," he said seriously. "But maybe not the healthiest. However, you should list anything you think of." Stephen stood. "I'm making more tea, do you want some? And maybe I'll figure out dinner for the kids since you're currently occupied." He cocked his head toward the task before me.

I put pen to paper as Stephen clunked about in the kitchen. The tea was taking an eternity, and I figured he had the gas on low to give me time to think. Stephen called his partner, Drew, and speaking in a hushed voice, told him he wouldn't be home for dinner. I immediately thought of all the times Adam would call me from the office, telling me he'd be late. But he always came home.

I wrote my second step, half listening as Stephen asked Porter and his buddies what they'd like on their pizza. Porter came upstairs, and I knew from their whispers my son had been deflected from looking for me by his uncle. Stephen ordered the pizza and called Naomi, who, after a few minutes of chatting, appeared to decide to have dinner with Amber.

By the time he returned with a *National Geographic,* half read, and my cup of tea, I had five steps:

1: If one glass of wine isn't enough, pour another (I won't erase this—wine does help)

2: Surround yourself with things you love (I'm thinking my family and my home)

3: Find a deeper meaning (not sure about this one, but it sounds good)

4: Get the dog to sleep on his side of the bed (Chloe started sleeping on his side after the funeral, which means I can immediately check something off)

5: Never forget (not sure if this is a step to recovery, but I must never forget Adam)

Stephen read the list slowly. "This is a good start," he finally said. "But I have at least one more suggestion."

"Okay," I agreed. Writing this list felt like reaching my arm out of the deep end of the pool and finding a ladder. Knowing I could use the rungs to hoist myself out of the water—still a little ungainly, but possible. I would write anything he suggested.

"One question first. Is 'get the dog to sleep on his side of the bed' even a skill?"

"If you've ever awakened from a dream, only to realize your perfectly alive dream-husband is actually dead, you'd understand. It comforts me to bury my hands in Chloe's fur. It's silly, I know."

"Not silly. It stays," he said. "Now, don't get offended, but I'm going to add number six, 'Get your house in order.' I can see, like always, you and Adam were in the middle of several fix-it-up projects." He swept his arm around him, palm up, indicating the dining room was a perfect case in point. "But you can't leave them half done forever. It might help you through the denial part of grief to admit he won't be finishing them."

"But I don't know how—" I protested logistics.

"Come on. You're capable," Stephen said, as he added Step #6 in pen. "I've seen you work a power drill with as much proficiency as most construction workers. You just don't *want* to finish them. And if you need actual help, call a professional."

"But if I change things . . ."

"Ivy, you know I'm not the one who will sell you a bunch of bullshit. Adam's death is one of the truest tragedies I've seen. And I've seen a few, but . . ." Stephen gazed at the hardwood under the table as he spoke, his own eyes brimming. "He's not coming home and you can't live in a shrine. First, it's unhealthy; second, with kids, it's impossible. Start by putting away the tools." He pointed to the jigsaw, a stack of sandpaper, and a level sitting in a dusty pile in the corner of the dining room. "If you clean up your house, you'll be able to see your way to the deeper issues. By the way, I like number three, 'Find a deeper meaning.' Let me know what you discover."

"Maybe I should move," I said, hoping for a reaction.

"Not a bad idea," he said slowly. "You and Adam put so much of yourselves into this place, it would be hard to leave, but maybe it would help." Stephen studied the corners of the room as he said it, likely remembering the days he spent helping Adam rewire the dining room and kitchen. He had memories here as well.

The doorbell rang. Stephen jumped up and grabbed his wallet from the pocket of his scrubs, which he had folded near the door. "I've got this. And now, grab a bottle of wine. I think we've made good progress, and it's time to work on step number one."

As I opened a bottle of no-name cabernet and collected plates and paper napkins from the kitchen, Porter and his two friends sat at the dining room table eagerly opening the cardboard box. The rich smell of tomato sauce and the abundance of voices in the room made me forget, if only for a second, Adam was missing. I took a sip of wine and felt it settle into my stomach. I could definitely master Step #1.

"I love it when Uncle Stephen comes over," Porter said, his mouth full of food. "Pizza from The Pie is so much better than Little Caesars, especially since we've had Little Caesars, like, every day." Porter swallowed and grinned sheepishly after divulging our main source of sustenance these past few weeks. My son. He still looked rumpled with worry from the day, but his shoulders were relaxed and thank goodness he wasn't biting his left thumbnail, a little obsessive behavior he'd picked up when things got especially emotional around our house.

The three young boys resumed their conversation about the video game, discussing the weapons they'd accumulated. They finished their pizza and left the dining room fully engrossed in each other. A minute later Porter returned and touched my shoulder lightly, almost as if he was confirming my physical presence. It was an "I'm here" touch, like Adam would give the kids when they were sad. The tiniest sob rose from his throat, and I knew my baby boy was aching too. I leaned my cheek against his fingers, pressing them between my face and my shoulder. He held perfectly still for several beats, then left without saying a word, his steps light through the kitchen and down the stairs. The maelstrom of eleven-year-olds away from the table and one glass of wine consumed, I reached for a piece of pizza.

Stephen and I ate wordlessly, peacefully, because really what else was there to say? After we'd both pushed away from our plates, Stephen stood and picked up the nearly empty pizza box. "Do you mind if I take this extra piece back to Drew?"

"Take it, of course." I stood next to him.

He put the box back on the table and put his warm hand on my shoulder. "You can do this, Ivy. Day by day—all right? What will you work on tomorrow?"

I rested my finger lightly on Step #6, *Get your house in order.* Stephen's physician scrawl was much less legible than mine on the first several steps. "I have to work the Saturday shift at the bank, just until two o'clock, but I'll stop on my way home and get some paint for Naomi's room. It's almost done and it's about time we—or I, finish up. I also think there are raccoons in the attic, which I'll have to deal with. Good?"

"Let's call it a good *start.*"

* * *

I was doing my best to get my house in order, because Stephen was right, a day filled with work was a day I wouldn't spiral. It was a sleepy Saturday morning a week later, the fingers of a hot July day slowly stretching into my empty rooms. Naomi and Porter had spent the night with the neighbor-friends, intent on getting an early start at the water park, and I'd intended to capture mother and kits, but frankly I was a little frightened at the prospect. Besides, the raccoons had been quiet the last couple days. For a week, I'd acted like a crotchety old lady pounding the ceiling with a broomstick to send them an audible warning, but if it worked and I didn't have to crawl into the attic (because it was Adam's job, after all), it would be worth it.

This morning, however, with the kids out of the house I felt a little out of sorts, the desire to curl up like a pill bug and burrow into the quilts overriding my sense of purpose. Having painted Naomi's room, I figured there was nothing like crossing things off a list for inspiration. If not the raccoons, then I must do *something*.

Sticking my handwritten recovery list on the refrigerator using a magnet Naomi made me for Mother's Day, I stared with laser focus at my options while eating a sesame-seed bagel, willing myself to tackle recovery step du jour. I was considering Step #2, *Surround yourself with things you love,* which, in all practicality, could be called yard work. And there was my plan.

Outside, the air was still kissed with the pink of dawn, an early summer morning fresh with the lingering chill of a starry night. Blossoms blinked in the sun, heavy with dew, their fragrance emerging—surrounding me. Despite the work, this was why I loved my roses. The wrought iron trellis signifying the entrance to the garden was draped heavily in the papery lavender blossoms of a Blue Moon climbing rose. Carefully, I grasped one of the flowers, pulled it toward me, and breathed a heady aroma resonant of lemon and spun sugar. Rows of pastel beauty beckoned me beyond the gate, calling me to a place where time paused. This quiet corner full of sunshine, color, and peace was my sanctuary.

But today the roses were rangy. Roses were a needy plant, and I'd been a neglectful gardener. Many of the flowers had already dropped their petals, exposing the naked center, the round hips swollen like crab apples. Readying my shears, I reached behind a branch of the Sutter's Gold to deadhead an aging blossom. Several peachy petals scattered on the brown earth and into the palm of my gloved hand. I touched them to my cheek, smooth and cool like the contours of my children's faces—gently cupping their tiny heads as I put them down to nap. Was it yesterday? Or was it another life?

Deadheading was a necessary but melancholy part of keeping roses, because the belle of the ball only days ago must be abandoned the moment she started to age. She no longer served a purpose. Get rid of the old, allowing the new buds to utilize the nutrients otherwise captured by the fading. A practical yet dreary reality.

And where am I in my rose life span?

Stop it, Ivy, I scolded myself. I could hear Stephen's voice. "Here's the problem with ruminating: you don't accomplish much."

With determination, I reached for the next bush. Vibrant yellow, tiny withering suns shone from Sun Goddess—a rose with a perfect name. However, it didn't stop me from trimming her dying blossoms. Next shrub—this one named Timeless. I clipped it without remorse; turns out, timelessness was a myth. Love Potion, Peace and Paradise—sadly none were immune to my blade.

The final bush: the Emmeline, the rose that inspired the garden. It was the only rosebush here, overgrown and strewn with thorns, when we decided to buy our home. Emmeline was an old-fashioned girl, her growth wild and unruly. She'd fill the yard if unattended and she stubbornly bloomed only once a season. Why not rid myself of her? Why plant more roses to accompany her? Two reasons. The fragrance: ephemeral and haunting. It changed from day to day, hour to hour—melting butter, jasmine, sun shimmering on wet pavement, or green. The second reason: She had a story.

The listing agent for this quaint redbrick bungalow on Down-ington Avenue must have seen in my face the starry-eyed notions I had about living in a historic house, attention skimming past the cracked foundation, overgrown lawn, and peeling paint, and resting instead on tiny perfect details—glass doorknobs, arts and crafts tile on the hearth (chipped but original), a covered porch spanning the width of the home complete with a white-painted wooden porch swing.

"The neighbor across the street told me this is called the Emmeline rose," the realtor said as we walked into the romantically overgrown backyard for the first time, his hand lingering on one of the snowy blossoms like it was a precious gift. "Apparently, the bare root was carried west across the plains in a handcart, and planted right here in 1913, the year the home was built."

"Was it 1912 or 1913 when the *Titanic* sunk?" I asked, mostly to myself, lost in a vision of a youthful Leonardo DiCaprio, standing proud on the deck of an ill-fated ship. The fragrance touched me, and I pictured corseted women with long skirts and feather-plumed hats. Could someone from that sepia time have planted this rose?

In that moment long ago, reflecting upon the lives spent in the house, the innumerable stories held within the walls, I longed to *be* one of those stories. Mine would be a fairy tale embraced by the little bungalow. Happily ever after.

If only.

Now, one hundred years after she took root, my Emmeline rose continued to thrive, but she'd outlived my husband. She'd surely lived decades longer than the actual Emmeline, the woman who must have carried the bare root across the plains. What might she have been like, Emmeline? Living in my house a century ago? In the years we'd lived in the time-worn redbrick bungalow our walls had seen several colors of paint, not to mention patching of wood floors, new kitchen cabinets, and updated lighting. What would the house have been like when the home was new and the beloved antique features, like push-button light switches and built-in bookshelves, were both cutting edge and modern? How must it have felt to live in new walls harboring no secrets and concealing no pain?

I was sure I'd heard her again, the elusive and evasive masked bandit. This time I was fully aware Adam wouldn't be tracking her movement with me, but that didn't mean I didn't curse at him for leaving me with raccoon duty. Ensconced in full battle gear—safety glasses, long pants, leather gloves, and a stocking cap to keep the sweat from dripping down my nose, I was ready. An old attic at noon (because raccoons were nocturnal) at the end of a high-desert July was no breeze, literally.

Porter and Naomi were stationed in the living room, phone in hand if they needed to call the paramedics to report wild animal attack or heat stroke. Why hadn't I called an exterminator like Stephen told me to? Because Adam and I liked the gumption of the old mama. He'd never wanted to kill her, instead risking claw marks and rabies to rescue her and her kits. So for Adam, I wouldn't kill this wily girl.

Like a tightrope walker without a pole, I scaled the ladder in our hall closet holding the plastic puppy crate, and pushed open the attic door. I almost expected her to be peering out at me with her wise and crafty black eyes, but initially the coast was clear.

Scanning the wood beams with my high-powered flashlight for the telltale signs of a nest, it appeared the space was empty, but I knew I'd heard familiar rustling in the attic. Bats, maybe? One knee up, then another, and I took the first anxious step in my crawling tour of the space. This wasn't a typical grandma attic, stuffed with chests full of treasures, toys, and rocking chairs. This was a utility space—steeply gabled roof strung with cloth-covered electrical wires barely secured with rusty nails, decaying insulation, and weathered lumber. I'd never been up here, but I remembered pulling bits of dusty fluff from Adam's hair when he'd descend sweaty and triumphant holding a hissing raccoon in the crate.

Behind one of the rickety wood slats, tucked near the attic

trapdoor, I spotted a wad of crumpled newspapers. Not shredded in typical rodent style. I wondered how long they'd been
hiding up here. Hoping for a headline, I pulled the pages out in-
tending to replace them with actual insulation. The newsprint
crackled with age as I smoothed it with my gloved hands. It was
a page from the *Salt Lake Tribune* dated September 6, 1969,
and I recognized several familiar comic strips: *Dennis the Men-
ace* and *Beetle Bailey*. This paper was older than me, but as
Adam would say, we'd found better Easter eggs in this hundred-
year-old house.

In the fourteen years he'd lived in our bungalow, Adam bragged
he had touched nearly every pipe, two-by-four, and outlet in the
place. He claimed there wasn't a surface he hadn't rubbed with
sandpaper or a paintbrush. He loved the weight of our old home,
the certainty someone had been embraced by these walls before
him. As he worked he always searched for clues, Easter eggs, he
called them. Together we'd speculate who had owned the house
when the Easter egg had been inadvertently hidden. Never without something in the works, Adam completed what turned out
to be his final woodworking project just two days before he
died: the window seat in the dining room.

We theorized at one time there had been a window seat in the
alcove because the oak floor had been pieced, plus, my neighbor
across the street owned a similar bungalow built in 1914, and
her house had all of the original gumwood built-ins, including a
window seat with hand-carved inset paneling. Who, we wondered, as we imagined what could fill the empty space, would
tear out such beautiful woodwork? What would possess someone to make such dramatic alterations to a lovely old house? I
had been persistent in requesting a replacement for our missing
window seat, one true to the architecture of the home, and
Adam built me one.

My brother, Stephen, was right when he said I'd been keeping
the corner behind our table an unfinished shrine, but since
Adam's death completing any project seemed to be an undoing
of him. But now, with Stephen's encouragement, I was determined to get my house in order.

Dropping the aged newspaper through the trapdoor and into the hall below, I shined the flashlight one last time into all the dark corners. What was hiding up here, if not our raccoon? As I prepared to descend, gratefully empty-handed, I spotted in the gap revealed by the missing newspaper a wavering flash—a glint of something shiny—and considered perhaps the old mama had her paws on something valuable. Didn't raccoons like shiny things? I double-checked that my glove covered my vulnerable wrist, in case the girl was waiting in the hole for an ambush, then plunged my hand into the void and grabbed at what felt like a piece of wood debris. Prepared for more resistance, I fell back as a board tumbled to the floor of the attic with a hollow thud. Naomi hollered from below, asking if I was okay, and after reassuring her I was fine, I realized what I'd uncovered wasn't wood at all.

Sitting in front of me was a little traveling case the size of an unabridged dictionary made of brown leather so ancient it was peeling and flaking in spots. The corners were squared and held together with rusty brackets. A faded monogram graced the top—an elegant cursive *E*. Now this was an Easter egg! I took off the safety glasses and stared at the case, contemplating.

I instantly wanted to call Adam at the office to fill him in on this little discovery. I almost yelled for Naomi to hand me the phone. Then, with a heaviness that sat squarely on my shoulders, I remembered I couldn't call Adam at the office, ever again.

I shook my head to clear the thought and considered the little case. What secret could it contain? Hopefully nothing gory; it was too small to hold a body, which was of some relief. Finally, no longer able to stand the suspense, I took a deep breath and flipped the latch. Folded tightly at the bottom was a piece of muslin yellowed with age. Pulling it out, I straightened the folds on a piece of embroidery.

An image of the Salt Lake City Temple, the original temple built by the first Mormons in my town, had been meticulously completed, and in an arc above the temple were the words, *Sealed for Time and all Eternity*. Below the temple were two names looped together with embroidered vines and flowers,

Emmeline and Nathaniel, and the year—*1916.* The names were written roughly in pencil, the stitches covering the script only half complete.

Emmeline! The girl of the rose—it was hers. Caressing the colored floss, I held the muslin close, marveling anyone could produce such evenly spaced, tiny stitches with needle and thread. This embroidery should have been a wall-hanging, a lovingly made memento celebrating a longed-for wedding day. But it was only half complete. Why would Emmeline hide away an unfinished statement of her love? What could have happened?

"Adam, she's the girl who planted our rosebush, I know she is." I searched the ceiling, speaking aloud now, looking for him. "I have an idea. Find Emmeline up there, wherever you are. Tell her I've found her embroidery and I want to know what happened with this Nathaniel guy."

Adam didn't answer me, yet again, but this incomplete handwork told me Emmeline had a story of her own. Relieved to take a break from the sad twist in my own tale, I was more than eager to consider hers.

EMMELINE LANSING

Downington Avenue
1913

From where we sat on the porch, we could see for miles. Gazing west toward the Salt Lake Valley, the land dropped, flattened, and rose again at the Oquirrh Mountains, a fuzzy blur of green in the distance. Our redbrick bungalow was located on the opposite side of the wide valley tucked against the steeply sloping foothills of the Wasatch Range. How could one be discouraged living on the upslope of a smile? The day was a clear one and in the near distance we could see a few structures dotting the landscape, corrals, barns, and coops, many clustered around the creeks, deep green smudges of scrub oak and maple defining the fields of brown and gold grass.

But upon closer inspection, it was clear this land was changing. New brick buildings, most two stories tall, populated a blossoming community called Sugar House. On all sides of Sugar House, the crisscross of hopeful streets divided the valley into a plaid tapestry. Wide roads empty of homes just yet were poised and ready.

My sister, Cora, pushed her toe against the floorboards of the wooden porch spanning the front of the bungalow, setting the porch swing in motion. "What a mess I've made," she murmured, drawing me from my reflection.

"Stop fretting. Things will be fine," I reassured her. "The

hard work is done. And in the end, this move will be favorable, you'll see." I took her hand. "Besides, life must be sweet in a town called Sugar House, how could it not?"

She smiled wearily at my joke, but the false happiness didn't release the furrow from her brow. "Haven't you been listening to your lessons, Emmeline? Sugar House was a failed plan. The prophet's not-so-sweet sugar beet experiment produced not a single spoonful for eating."

"The name's still nice, though, don't you think?"

"Our home is in Helper," Cora replied.

"Not any longer. Besides, Helper? What kind of name is that?"

"A name that means home," Cora whispered.

"Nothing happens in Helper." I dismissed her argument. "At least here in the city we can continue our schooling. I mean, look, I could throw a rock and hit Westminster College." I pointed west toward a steeply gabled building a couple of vacant blocks away. The clarity of the day and the prospect of change were hopeful to me, thrilling in fact. My buoyant mood would have to be enough for us both, at least until Cora could stand on her own.

"I don't know. We've left Mother behind." Cora swallowed. "Plus, the cost of the move, we'll have to take in sewing. . . ."

"Stop agonizing," I said, and brushed a stray lock of hair behind her shoulder. Gazing at Cora, it was clear she was a beauty hiding beneath a layer of unkempt hair and wrinkled dress. Though we were both work-worn from moving crates into our new house, her coiled braids hung especially disheveled, like she had simply rolled from bed, paying no mind to look in the mirror. Her wide brown eyes, though no longer swollen from tears, were still heavy, and a line of worry formed a pleat between them.

Cora was my younger sister. But really, she was so much more than that. I was seven and she was five when Mama passed. From that point forward, to one another we were mother, sister, and best friend, taking care when care was needed through the long hours our father put in at the coal mine. I would do anything, sacrifice everything, to soothe her worries. She, however, was still shaking her head, fretting over the things we'd left behind.

I stomped my foot, halting the movement of the swing. I needed her to listen to me. "Cora, what happened with Brother Redding was *not* your fault!"

She shook her head. "But it was. I dressed up, I turned on the charm. I acted every bit the coquette. It shames me to think of it." She shuddered.

"You didn't intend to attract the attention of an old man," I argued.

"But I did attract him, Emmeline, even though I didn't mean to. I need to be less—"

"No, Cora, you need to be *you*. A flirt—a beautiful seventeen-year-old girl. Fellows notice you because you're friendly and smart. And it's no crime. However, if it were, Father would have to lock you up and throw away the key."

"Very funny, seeing as how he works at the prison now," Cora said, but I could tell from her voice she was suppressing a smile.

Encouraged, I continued to tease. "Though locking you away might be nice. I might get more attention from the young men around here. Of the two of us, it's always you they see first."

She smiled at the compliment. That was my sister. "Oh, you don't really want the attention, though," Cora replied, her voice containing the tiniest hint of levity. "Most of your admirers don't know what to do with a girl who speaks so plainly. You should try being a little coy." She batted her lashes at me. "Sometimes in conversation with men, less is more."

"Less is more?" I groaned. "I want someone who will talk to me, not someone who wants me to speak less. Besides, in Helper all the men were so boring. Coal miner, coal miner, coal miner . . . I want more from a husband."

The front door swung wide. Cora and I jumped guiltily as our father stepped out onto the porch.

"There's not much coal to be mined in this city, so I guess you're in luck," my father said.

I gasped at my own words.

"Hush now, Emmeline, no offense taken. Though you may want to follow Cora's advice. Sometimes it's a good thing to watch the tongue." He smiled to soften his words.

I sighed. "I'll try to take your advice to heart."

My father tapped his pocket watch. "Now, you two should get yourselves cleaned up." He looked pointedly at Cora. "There's a fireside meeting at the church, intended for young adults. It might be a nice time to greet some of the new neighbors."

"By neighbors, he means men of marriageable age." I pinched Cora's arm playfully. It was time to stop dwelling on things that couldn't be changed.

"I think I might sit this one out," Cora said softly, her light mood dissolving.

I stood and gripped her at the elbows, pulling her to standing. "No, no. You're going with me. I'll do a lot of things for you, but I won't go to this meeting by myself. Besides, you don't want me to snatch up the best bachelor before you even get a chance to see him, do you?"

"When you put it that way . . ." Cora grinned. I returned her smile. It was sweet relief to see a tiny piece of my joyful sister emerge from her cloak of despair.

Cora and I strolled arm in arm along sidewalks that zig-zagged through lots graded for building, but empty aside from earth and weed. At the corner we were forced to step into the packed-clay road. Recently pressed into the fresh concrete of the sidewalk, and roped off to prevent damage, was the name of our street, "Downington Avenue," and the year, "1913." Power poles lined lonely Downington Avenue. We were one of the first neighborhoods equipped with electric power. In our new house, we would never have to carry a candle. And based on the number of empty lots, it was clear the builders of this up-and-coming neighborhood were hopeful many families would want to live here.

Unfortunately, the meeting house was farther away than we had anticipated, and our slow stroll made us late. The group of nearly twenty was seated in a large circle, as if gathered around an invisible bonfire. Hence the name *fireside*, I supposed. Their arrangement made our late entry impossible to miss. Several men rushed to pull up two of the wooden chairs surrounding the perimeter of the meeting room.

"Men of marriageable age," I whispered to Cora as I tucked my hat under my chair. "Father will be pleased."

Cora giggled softly and turned to view a gaggle of young men gazing doe-like in our direction. Most of them were staring at Cora, as usual. Where she was curvy, I was straight. Where she had a smooth olive complexion, I had freckles. She had eyes the color of a fawn, and I had blue. I was a bit too tall for a girl, but we both had our mother's thick Italian hair. And I did have teeth as straight as a picket fence, which made for a decent smile. Small blessings.

"All right, let's settle down. We'll have a chance to meet our new neighbors in a few minutes. I'll finish the lesson I've prepared; after that we'll open the meeting for discussion." Brother Conner, who was leading the fireside, nodded in our direction. "The topic for this evening is free agency and how it relates to current events."

"Oh, this should be interesting," I said under my breath.

For some reason, these meetings always brought out my most unladylike behavior. "Ours is not to question why . . ." the bishop said whenever I spoke out, like he was quoting scripture. I wondered if he knew the true source of the quote. Cora always told me my quick tongue would spoil my chances of finding a beau. My father said the reason I loved books so much was they never argued back. They were both right.

It's only with religion came so many rules. It seemed most of the rules, written or not, were aimed at women. And rules, very simply, made me bristle.

"Behave," said Cora.

I folded my arms and I nipped the tip my tongue whenever Brother Conner said something I disagreed with. Finally, he opened the discussion to the group.

A small, mousy girl raised her hand. "I make an important decision using my free agency, each and every day," she squeaked, "and that decision is to be happy." Several in the group nodded blandly, trying hard to stay awake.

"Oh, please." I sighed louder than anticipated. All heads swung my direction.

"Would you like to add to this discussion? What was your name?" Brother Conner shot me a warning glance.

I swallowed. "Emmeline."

"Go ahead, but keep it positive," Brother Conner said.

"Coy! Emmeline! We don't even know them," Cora hissed, her mouth hidden by her hand.

"Well, I think . . ." I swallowed, deciding what to say. Cora was staring at the floor, her perfect cheeks pink with embarrassment. Her hand covered her mouth as she suppressed nervous laughter.

I continued, undaunted. "I think women in particular . . . we've recently been given rights, for example, the legal right to vote and the right to pursue an education. But it seems this is, well, lip service. And I don't mean in just the Mormon faith. I mean in the world! Women are *expected* to get married and have children. We're expected to be satisfied with the way things have *always* been."

"Now this is more like it," said a boy three seats to my right. "A fireside discussion that actually has some heat!"

I turned to look at him, and the color rose to my face. He leaned forward in his chair. His green eyes sparked. His chestnut hair, wavy and clearly in need of a trim, hung low across his forehead.

"I figured we'd get a word or two out of you, Nathaniel, we usually do," said Brother Conner, resigned to the debate at hand.

Nathaniel smiled. "Let's start with women's suffrage, or the right to vote, as it relates to free agency."

My stomach flipped. I knew women's suffrage. I'd done an oral report on it my last year of school, but was I ready to argue my point in front of a crowd, against this disarmingly good-looking boy? How many of my new neighbors could I offend in one fireside discussion? And yet, Nathaniel was grinning, and no one, except for the girl who chose to be happy, appeared too out of sorts.

"No, let's start with polygamy," a blond boy challenged, looking directly at Nathaniel.

Nathaniel startled for an instant, then leaned back in his chair and said, "Fine, Levi, let's start with polygamy."

Brother Conner cleared his throat. "Boys, how about we stop right there. You know I don't mind lively discourse, but let's stay on topic. Go ahead, Nathaniel—free agency and the right to vote."

Nathaniel leaned forward, his hands on his knees. He cleared his throat. "Emmeline, I think you're only scratching the surface with your examples of agency. Doctrine indicates *agency* is man's ability—"

"Woman's . . ." I broke in.

"Fine, man's and *woman's* . . ."

I giggled. I couldn't help it.

". . . ability to make moral decisions based on our innate knowledge of right and wrong. Consequences follow poor decisions, which allow for accountability and growth."

"I understand your definition, but I thought your charge was to relate it to women's suffrage," I batted back.

"I was just getting started." Light danced from his eyes as he spoke. I felt we were the only two in the room.

"Did you know in the Utah territory, Mormon *women* were one of the first groups of women in the United States granted the right to vote?" he asked.

I nodded, searching my memory for the facts I had carefully researched and presented a year prior. "Yes, the federal government thought that given the vote, the women would put an end to the practice of plural marriage."

"Right, but did they? Did they use their free agency and their legal vote to outlaw polygamy?" he questioned, his face beaming.

I was silent. This argument wasn't going exactly where I had anticipated.

Levi stood. His hands were clenched. "Polygamy is against

church doctrine. We all know there will be consequences for those who still practice."

I glanced at Cora to see how she was reacting to this discussion. She was slumped low in her seat.

Nathaniel answered calmly, without indicating he heard Levi, "What happened is this . . . Women were given the right to vote against polygamy, but they used their free agency to continue the practice. Their vote was their choice."

"But the practice is wrong!" I sputtered.

Nathaniel cocked his head. "I'll grant your claim, Emmeline. But I spoke to free agency, women's suffrage, and polygamy in one argument. Beat that!" He turned and grinned wickedly at Levi, who grumbled, tipped his hat, and walked from the room.

Brother Conner took a deep breath. "On that note, I think we should adjourn this meeting. Just a reminder, the young adult dance will be held Friday, here at this church. Now, who wants to offer closing prayer?"

Nathaniel was standing at the door, holding his hat in his hands as Cora and I attempted to leave.

"Emmeline? Our discussion was enjoyable. There's nothing I like more than a pretty girl willing to speak up."

I turned away from him and slipped through the door. My thoughts were muddled. He hadn't been rude, but I felt bested, as if I had lost a game of cards. Plus, I didn't want to continue our conversation. Discussing polygamy in this jovial manner with Cora nearby would be unthinkable.

"Oh, never mind her," Cora answered for me. "She hates to lose an argument."

"Does she now? Well, I sure hope to see you two at the dance. Will you be there?" Nathaniel asked, looking at me.

"Yes!" answered Cora. She linked my arm with hers and pulled me back toward Nathaniel.

"Possibly," I replied.

"I hope so, Emmeline . . . either way . . . the choice is yours."

I glared at Nathaniel. He winked at me, pressed his hat over his hair, and walked away from the church.

* * *

The morning was fine as Cora and I walked along Downington Avenue toward Westminster College. During the past week, we had watched gardeners planting the tiny starts of trees around the grand building. Westminster would be opening at this new campus come fall, and I wanted in. Cora had agreed to join me for the orientation at noon.

The castle-like building stretched to the sky, with twin turrets of rich burgundy brick reaching almost as high as the spires of the Salt Lake Temple; however, it was more prominently placed on a hillside and less austere than the religious comparison. It looked like a fortress rising alone out of a sea of wild grasses and sagebrush, as the concrete sidewalks and formal gardens were yet to be complete.

Standing in front of the dark wooden doors, I gazed to the top of the cylindrical turrets and sighed. "It's a step up from Clear Creek School in Helper. Can I do this?"

Cora pushed me forward. "Oh, come on, Em, you had top marks your last year. You're brave enough to open that door!"

And I opened it, because I was eager to continue my schooling. I loved school, the smell of books, their titles seductively calling out to me, reminding me the world was infinite. I could seek it and it would be mine.

Cora and I entered the hall, a dark wooden cavern with soaring ceilings. Light entered through several narrow rectangular windows positioned high above our heads. The floor was stained hardwood and still smelled from a fresh coat of varnish. And it was wonderfully cool, even during the heat of July. The sweat evaporated around my neckline, giving me shivers. We took a seat.

Shortly, a woman with an authoritative step walked to the podium. She was wearing an official-looking nurse's uniform. Her hair, not pulled back in the customary knot at the nape of her neck, was cut short, hanging loose so it brushed her jawline. She seemed like a woman who made her own decisions. I liked her immediately.

"I'm cutting my hair like hers when we get home, watch if I don't," I whispered to Cora.

A redheaded girl sitting to Cora's left whispered back, "You should."

I startled at her voice. "It would look fantastic on you. You have a beautiful heart-shaped face." She held out her hand. "I'm Margaret Robinson, I saw you two at the fireside."

I shook her hand, recognition escaping me.

"Don't worry if you don't know who I am. With all of the attention Nathaniel was paying you, it's no wonder the rest of the room would be eclipsed."

"He does kind of command an audience," Cora agreed.

"Is he always like that? So combative?" I asked, as the woman with the modern hairstyle standing at the podium cleared her throat.

We stopped our conversation to listen.

The woman indicated she represented the field of nursing. She discussed the advances in medicine and how Westminster was working to establish itself in this new discipline, so there was money available for scholarships. I jiggled my foot with excitement. Cora squeezed my knee and we grinned at each other. Surely, my father couldn't object if he didn't have to pay for my education.

The orientation was dismissed and Margaret Robinson joined us in the application line. "Listen, he's been asking about you."

"Who has?"

"Nathaniel." Margaret and Cora said at the same time.

"Really, Emmeline, are you so thick?" Cora sighed. "It was clear he was interested in you."

"What did he want to know?" Cora asked Margaret for me. Her whole face shone with anticipation. My sister, the habitual matchmaker.

"How long you've lived here, if you have a suitor, how old you are. You know, the regular questions," Margaret answered.

"Well, tell him she doesn't have a beau. Yet. But he should call on her sooner rather than later, if he wants to catch her," Cora went on.

"Can't you let me talk for myself?" I put my hands on my hips. "Tell him if he comes to call, he should know I've fine-tuned my arguments about free agency. He should be prepared to discuss the topic with me." I smiled. I would be ready this time.

Margaret was silent for a few minutes as indecision swept across her face. Finally, she replied, "You might want to discuss polygamy with him."

"Why is that?" I asked.

"He's a Barlow, didn't you know?"

"A Barlow, what does that mean?"

"He's from one of the biggest polygamist families in the valley."

Cora inhaled sharply.

"Then why was he at our church?" I asked.

"Since the Manifesto, now polygamy is no longer allowed, the younger generation of Barlow children say they won't continue the practice and most of them go to church with us. But I wouldn't be so sure. . . ."

My excitement evaporated, leaving a void in my chest. "You should tell him, then, I'd rather he not call."

Margaret flushed and changed the subject. "Someone's been asking about you as well," she said to Cora. "I think I've heard about your dimples every day since he saw you."

Cora clapped her hands together. Moving to Salt Lake was exactly what she needed to get her mind off the incident in Helper. Every day that passed, Cora became more and more the lighthearted sister I grew up with. "Who, please tell me!" she squealed.

"My brother, Richard," Margaret groaned. "He won't let it alone."

"Which one was he? What does he look like?" Cora asked.

"He's got reddish hair, and he's pretty tall. . . ."

"Is he the one with the big smile?" Cora's words rose with anticipation.

"Some say he has a nice smile, yes," she said, and smiled widely.

"You do look like him. I can see it now!" Cora gushed.

We were finally at the front of the line. The woman from the college of nursing handed me an application. "Fill this out and have your records sent. Nearly half this starting class will receive financial aid, so don't hesitate to apply. Classes start in September."

Sitting at the dining room table, I filled out the application to attend Westminster. Distracted, I gazed out the window. The Wasatch Mountains rose up like a wave to the east, still a black silhouette; the morning sun defined the shape of crag and tree only in shadow. The prophet Brigham Young intended our valley be protected from the rest of the world by this formidable barrier of stone, safe from the gentiles. But I didn't feel safe, I felt vulnerable. My heart, unwilling to follow my command, was pushing me into unfamiliar wilderness. Why couldn't I stop thinking about Nathaniel Barlow? I felt betrayed by him, somehow. I had met him only once, and didn't particularly like him. So why was learning he came from a polygamist family so crushing?

I startled as my father cleared his throat. "You were daydreaming, Emmeline."

"I was thinking of an answer to essay question number three. 'Why do you want to attend Westminster College?'" I held up the paper.

He nodded. "So you're going to pursue this? Cora tells me you are likely to receive a scholarship, which is fortunate. The job at the prison doesn't pay quite like mining. But, Emmeline—"

"Yes?"

"I want you to know I consider this school thing a distraction, only to be entertained to pass the time. Don't make it your main priority. True happiness comes with starting a family."

I gritted my teeth, pressed the pencil to the application, and spoke as I wrote. "I want to go to Westminster because I think a woman can be more than a WIFE! There, I'm finished." I swung the application in front of my father.

"Well, whoever dares to take you as his bride will certainly have his hands full." There was the slightest hint of a smile on my father's face.

IVY BAYGREN

✣

Task completion: My greatest asset in college and currently, my life preserver. When all the other business majors were failing statistics, I read and reread the syllabus with the intent of simply making it through each assignment. The bigger picture? Who cares? Finish the list and pass when others failed.

Through the remainder of July and long days of August I was multitasking through grief and I was the star student. I had a plan and a deadline, which was Adam's birthday, August 24, a date in the future, but not so far in the future I could doddle. And it was working! I was the model of efficiency getting my house in order (#6) *and* finding a deeper meaning (#3), by taking advantage of the greatest invention since bacon—audiobooks. While painting, I meditated with Zen Master Thich Nhat Hanh, forcing a half smile on my face (a coping technique that actually seemed a little flimsy to me). I joined Cheryl Strayed and we strolled together along the Pacific Coast Trail in *Wild,* fancying myself a soul-searching survivor and a crack electrician. I mourned with C. S. Lewis the loss of his wife to cancer, while I applied varnish to the window seat, and insulated the attic.

Eventually my list of home renovations was full of bright red checks, it was Adam's fortieth birthday, and I couldn't get out of bed. What was the point? Nothing to do. List completed. No party to plan. I begged the flu, sent the kids off to get a supply of movies from Redbox and a dozen bagels to last the day. I al-

most didn't answer my cell when it rang. But whoever was calling wouldn't stop.

Pulling the phone under the covers, I pressed the icon to pick
up and held the phone to my ear, breathing lightly, not brave
enough to speak. "Ivy?" It was Stephen, his voice edged with
panic. "Say something right now that sounds rational, like 'I
was in the shower' or 'I was brushing my teeth, sorry for worrying you,' or I'm coming over."

"I finished getting my house in order and I've been searching
for a deeper meaning. I've surrounded myself with things I love.
I've done it all and it's his birthday and—"

"I'm getting in the car. You get out of bed and make some
coffee right now and I'll be there in ten."

Stephen and the kids arrived at the same time, and I won't lie,
Naomi and Porter were relieved to see him, dashing around the
kitchen to toast the bagels, sneaking side-long glances at my
face as I sat zombielike at the dining room table with my recovery plan in front of me, reading and rereading the steps. Had I
missed something critical? Stephen poured himself a cup of coffee, brought me a cup of Earl Grey, and settled himself across
from me.

"His birthday," he said.

"Yes. Not his happiest."

"That's probably true. Let me see your list." He slid the paper
in front of him.

"I was doing so well."

Stephen moved his finger down the column. "You've certainly kept yourself busy."

"I know. I rock at recovery."

Stephen was quiet as he sipped his coffee. Naomi walked into
the room and I gave her a weak smile.

"Why are you doing this again?" she asked sharply, her lower
lip quivering. "I thought you were taking me and Amber to the
mall." She had her hands on her waist, squaring her shoulders
like a matador braced for battle. Even in sorrow, disguised as
teen fury, she was lovely. A bundle of thin-hipped attitude, I saw
myself as I was decades ago in the long taper of her legs, smooth

and brown in her tiny shorts. Her hair was in a ponytail. The weight of her hair was mine; the rich auburn waves were Adam's.

Before I could respond, before I could apologize for my inability to pull myself together, Stephen said, "Olives."

We gaped at him like he'd turned into an alien before our eyes.

Naomi giggled, then glared at me again like she couldn't believe she'd let down her red cape. "Olives?" she asked, her shoulders less hunched.

"Ivy, what do you think of when I say 'olives'?"

"Vomit. I'm gagging right now." I wrinkled my nose. *Make me laugh,* I pleaded silently. If he could only make me laugh I could get out of this funk.

"Hear me out," Stephen said. His voice was so excited Naomi pulled up a chair, interested and no longer angry. "Did you always hate olives?" He directed the question to me.

"You know I used to love them," I replied. "Remember, I'd sneak into the kitchen on Thanksgiving and take enough to cap each finger. They'd make such a satisfying pop as they landed in my mouth," I said. "Mom was so mad when the bowl would be empty by the time she served the turkey." I could picture my mother in her burnt-orange apron, a plaid cornucopia appliquéd to the front. Missing her almost succeeded in distracting me.

"So what happened?" Stephen prompted, pulling me again through my ill-fated love affair with olives.

"Mom bought extra the year I was ten, remember? Three cans. She'd had it, so she challenged me to eat them all before dinner. God, I was thrilled."

"You ate three cans of olives?" Naomi said, grimacing.

I nodded. "Tough love, Grandma-style. Half an hour later I barfed a toilet bowl full of chopped olives and I haven't touched them since."

"So," Stephen said. "What if you binged and purged on memories of Adam?"

"Okay, you're completely messed up. I don't want to gag whenever I think of him."

"But maybe if you churn through all of the painful memories in an excessive and gratuitous fashion, they'll stop coldcocking you the minute you slow down," he explained. "What if you saturated yourself in grief, making it boring and commonplace, a little less nausea-inducing punch to the gut? And if you ceased to avoid your triggers, maybe they wouldn't trigger any response at all." Stephen was triumphant as he revealed another stage of his treatment plan. He shrugged. "I'm not certain it'll work, but think about it. Drew and I have Monday off. We could take the kids on an end-of-summer hike and you'd have the whole day to binge and blow."

"You're grossing me out. We're talking about my husband here."

"Let's put him on a pedestal and knock him off." Stephen beamed.

"Stephen, I can't think about this right now, but you did succeed in getting me out of bed." I smiled gratefully at him. "Naomi, Uncle Stephen has saved our day of back-to-school shopping. And even though I think you're a little warped, Stephen, I'll take you up on Monday."

Maybe he had a point with the olives. Or perhaps, I was willing to try anything. Plus, Monday was perfect, because it happened on a Monday.

Adam had hours, an entire day actually, to send me a sign, to do something. Anything. My red enameled pot was now cold to the touch, flaking oatmeal crusted the lip. The sticky note on the lid reading "oatmeal for you" was peeling at the corner. "Come on," I whispered. "If you're able to give me a sign, do it now. Make the phone ring, turn on the stove. I'll take anything."

Magical thinking was what I was engaged in, according to my book by Joan Didion. Soliciting a straitjacket was probably closer to reality. But no matter. This was my day to be as crazy or as magical as I wanted. I was eating the olives, so to speak.

The clock on the microwave told me Stephen would have the kids home within the hour. In the few minutes before Naomi and Porter walked through the door dragging with them the scent of mountain air and life, I would morbidly attempt to recall every detail of that day, one more time. My plan was to Never Forget

(#5), but also to remember in appropriate fashion without alarming my children, which would keep me out of the basket case category. However, if Adam wanted to shimmer faintly in the corner, I was ready for that too.

Adam died on a Monday.

At six-thirty that morning the radio alarm clicked on. I knew without opening my eyes his left hand was hooked over the top of my pillow, fingers twisted in my hair. Back then, I didn't find this sleep trait of his quite so endearing, especially when forced to pick at the snarls with a comb before getting into the shower. Oh, how I ached for it now.

He extricated his fingers from my thick strands, and like every day, spent several minutes lying flat on his back, his arms supporting his head on the pillow, listening to the news. That morning the broadcaster discussed rising tensions in the Middle East. I drifted in and out of sleep while he listened.

"Seems never-ending," he said after several minutes. "Turning it off now. Unless you want to keep listening."

I sleepily turned toward him and shook my head.

"Well, then. Good morning, sunshine," he said as I smiled at him. He shuffled toward the bathroom, absently rubbing his bare chest as he walked. He stopped at the dresser and pulled out his shorts and favorite running shirt, Big Red.

"One day you'll wake up and find that thing missing." I sat up in bed, pointing at the shirt, sheets around my legs. "Big Red is way past its expiration date."

"What are you implying?" Adam tried to look offended.

"I'm just saying I'll buy you five new running shirts, if you'll throw that tattered one in the trash," I teased, of course not meaning it.

"Not worth it," he said, flexing his biceps. "I'm like Sampson. You'll deprive me of the strength of my youth."

I giggled, picturing him in college, his scrawny, hairless chest in the same old T-shirt. Big Red, newly soaked in grief, had been tucked once again into the cardboard coffin and crammed under the bed, effectively concealing all of the clothing he wore that morning.

Chloe was whining softly as Adam hooked the leash to her collar. She knew what was coming and was anxious for her jog. "I'll probably be gone when you get home," I said to his back. "It's Field Day and Naomi needs to help set up. I'll leave the door unlocked."

He mumbled something ordinary, like, "Yep." And he was gone.

I made instant oatmeal for the kids in order to get them to the school by eight o'clock. We were almost out of brown sugar, so I added it to the grocery list taped to the refrigerator. I made extra for Adam, wrote on a sticky note "oatmeal for you," stuck it to the pot, and put on my clothes.

Porter emerged dressed in gym shoes with socks. I reminded him of the water activities planned for Field Day and made him change to sandals. Naomi had me braid her hair. We filled the back of the minivan with hula hoops, buckets, water balloons, and sponges, and drove to the school.

When we arrived, I begrudgingly realized I would have to help carry the Field Day gear onto the playground. I fretted I hadn't put on mascara. Dee Parker stopped me on the steps to discuss registration for junior high the next year. I was looking into the sun, wishing I had my sunglasses for most of the conversation. I drove home.

Down the hill a couple of streets from my house, blocking the entrance to Westminster College, a funky liberal arts school in our neighborhood, several police cars were turned at an angle, lights spinning, and I could see the tail end of an ambulance. I remember saying out loud, "I wonder what's up?"

Before entering the house, I spotted a clump of dandelions I could easily dig and retrieved a trowel from the shed. Tool in hand, one dandelion led to another. I could hear water was running in the house, so Adam must be home already, probably in the shower. When he came out, I figured I would ask him if he jogged by the police cars.

Since he was indulging in an unusually long scrub, I thought I might catch him in the shower and tease him about his pruned fingers and toes. Or maybe I'd join him. Walking toward the house, I swept my hand over the cascade of white petals on the Emmeline rose, releasing the fragrance into the morning air. It was then I noticed the driveway near the back door was soaked with water. Closing the faucet with an irritated grunt, I realized Naomi had left the hose running after she filled the water balloons for Field Day. I briefly considered Adam hadn't been in the shower this whole time, after all. The sound of running water had come from the hose.

In my memory of that day, this was where the unsettled feeling started. The pieces hadn't clicked into place, but I knew something was out of sorts.

I walked into the house and called, "Adam?"

Silence.

I said out loud, to reassure myself, "He must have been in a rush."

The pot of oatmeal had not been touched. My heart knocked in my chest.

"Chloe? Come here, girl!" I called.

I ran downstairs to Porter's room. Chloe liked to sleep under his bed when she was warm from her run. I reached into her hiding spot, patting desperately for her sleeping form. Empty.

I raced back upstairs holding my breath as I touched Adam's bath towel. Dry.

A sharp bark came from the backyard. A grumpy bark, the one Chloe used when she couldn't believe we had left her outside in the rain.

She was on the back porch, her black nose pressed to the screen door. Alone. I was immediately angry at Adam. And yet, I was also relieved. I figured he'd lost hold of Chloe and must be out looking for her.

I let her in and took off her leash. She began slurping water. I scratched her neck and asked, "Where's Daddy?"

Drawing the tip of my finger across my cheek I found it wet, my undeniable loss was drawing closer as I continued this path. But I must continue. I must Never Forget. I closed my eyes to see the scene unfold, letting the tears fall.

Adam never jogged without his cell phone, so I used our

home phone to call him, to let him know Chloe found her way back. There was a missed call from Adam's cell, but no message. I dialed his number. It rang once. Before he spoke I said, "Chloe's here. Where are you?"

A strange voice responded. "Hello? Am I speaking to a relation of Adam Baygren?"

My heart thumped so loud the rush of frantic pulse vibrated audibly against the earpiece. "He's my husband," I whispered, my voice shaking.

"I'm David Marks with the Salt Lake Police Department. There's been an accident."

I slumped against the wall as the officer spoke. Puddled in my kitchen, I learned the details of an event that would alter me forever: elderly woman appeared to black out behind the wheel, Adam died at the scene, entrance of Westminster College, detectives still present if I wanted to talk, no one else hurt, possible to retrieve personal items at the morgue in several hours. I pressed my cheek into the cool tile as the words washed over me, knowing my life had changed forever.

In one instant.

Their footsteps resonated on the front porch, drawing me to the here and now. Chloe barked as the doorbell rang, her nails clicking across the wood floor as she scrambled to greet the visitors. Through the opaque glass in the front door Naomi and Porter stood in silhouette with Stephen and Drew behind them.

"Walk around back," I called with as much strength as I could muster. Dwelling time was over and strangely, I didn't want to get caught. One more thing and I would be done. They couldn't know I'd made oatmeal again.

As I tipped the pot, glutinous mounds dropped into the sink, and I shoved them into the disposal with a spoon. I slipped the yellow Post-it reading "oatmeal for you" into my front pocket. I felt worn thin and a little disappointed. Did this day actually help? I wasn't sure. But time was up. The olives were gone. And Adam hadn't come home.

EMMELINE LANSING

Downington Avenue
1913

"Emmeline, what's taking you so long in there? We've had visitors come and go and you aren't out yet?" Cora knocked on the door of the washroom.

"I'm almost done. Who came by?" I wondered if Nathaniel would still call on me after Margaret told him I didn't want him to visit.

"Richard, Margaret's brother, and Levi Green, you know, the blond boy from the fireside. They want to escort us to the dance. Richard for me and Levi for you. Levi's really quite handsome, you know. And besides, you don't want to get involved with Nathaniel, do you, now you know he might want to carry on the polygamist traditions of his family?" My heart sank as she mentioned his name.

"I wasn't even thinking of Nathaniel," I retorted through the closed door, trying to hide the pout from my voice.

"So, we should walk with them, don't you think?" Cora said hopefully.

"If you want to, my lovesick sister, then let's."

Looking in the mirror, I shook my newly cropped cut, so my dark locks curled behind my ears and grazed my cheeks. Not bad.

Cora was leaning on the wall outside the washroom door as I

walked out. "Do you mind if I borrow your peacock feather for my hat. . . . Oh my goodness! Emmeline, what have you done?"

"Don't you think it looks dashing, like that nurse at the college?"

Cora tilted her head from side to side, assessing. "Try on my hat." She raced into the room we shared. "Here, if you press it down, I can hardly tell you cut it."

"Does it look so bad?" I groaned. "Here I had thought it was nice, but maybe it's too much. And now it's too late."

"Let me take another look. Take off the hat and spin around." She pulled a few stray hairs off the shoulders of my dress. "No, it looks nice, but it seems awfully modern."

"That's what I was going for."

"Hand me the scissors, I'll trim a couple strands you missed. And you'd better get ready for the dance. Richard and Levi will be here in an hour." She smoothed the bottom of my cut tresses and said, "It looks nice on you, Em. It really does."

"So can I cut yours?" I held up the open scissors.

"Oh no, I don't think so. . . ." Cora dashed into our room and slammed the door, giggling.

A fiddle was tuning up as we approached the church. Levi walked close by my side and graciously opened the door for me. He grasped my hand. "We should dance together first. They're tuning up for the Mormon Reel. It's usually the one we start with. Do you know the steps?"

"I've danced it several times back in Helper." I untied the silk ribbons from under my chin and removed my hat. "Where do you imagine the hat-and-cloak room is located?"

Levi took my hat and gasped. "You cut your hair!"

"I did." I shook my head to free the waves, though my face burned red. "What do you think?"

He gaped at me. Thankfully, Cora noticed my discomfort and grabbed my hand. "She looks wonderful and modern. Now let's go in."

All of the oak pews had been pushed to the edges of the meeting hall. At the far end of the room sat two men with fiddles. The rough-hewn floor was spread with sawdust and fresh-cut pine permeated the quivering air. As they pulled back on their bows, the room vibrated with anticipation. A line of young women stood side by side, backs to the wall, whispering and giggling, attention tight on the men who were elbowing each other and shuffling their feet.

Levi returned to my side as Richard whisked Cora into the dance line. "Your hair will certainly grow long again. You shouldn't worry," he said.

"I'm not worried," I growled. "I wanted it short. That's why I cut it!"

"It's just most men like a gal with long hair, that's all." Levi stuttered over his words, embarrassed.

"Well, I guess I'm not looking for most men," I said, and turned away.

I searched the line of dancers for Nathaniel's familiar face. I hoped he'd be here, since he'd made a special point of inviting me. Besides, things weren't going too smoothly with Levi. But he was nowhere to be found.

At the back of the hall was a table sagging with glass pitchers of lemonade and plates of cookies. I was heading toward a group of people standing next to it when I noticed him in the opposite corner surrounded by several boys. He wasn't talking to them. He was looking at me.

I raised my hand in greeting, as Levi linked his arm through mine. "Let's just dance," he said. I tried to straighten my arm to loosen his hold, but he clung like a barnacle. Nathaniel looked away.

The music picked up. The lines of young men and ladies moved together and apart, spinning round several times before linking elbows. The meeting hall, transformed by people and noise, was magical as we sashayed through the middle of the line, and turned in place. The line shifted and I was dancing opposite a boy I'd never seen. I was breathless as the room heaved and sighed to the music. My hair swirled about my neck and my skirts swished at my ankles. The movement was liberating.

Suddenly Nathaniel was across from me.

"There you are," he said, a crooked smile on his face. We moved together and back, not touching. As we slid together to link elbows, he put his hand on my cheek and we twirled. A current ran from his palm to my heart, my pulse resonating in his fingers. He appeared as startled as I. Finally, it was our turn to sashay through the line of the dancers. As we skipped past Levi, I felt his anger follow us. I didn't care.

We continued out of the dance line and Nathaniel led me, his arm still hooked through mine, out the back door of the church and onto the steps. The sky bloomed with sunset. The aspen near the creek were trimmed in gold. He tucked a curl behind my ear. "You cut your hair."

I pushed his hand away from my face. "Not you too."

"What?" he said, surprised.

"Are you going to tell me most men like a woman with long, flowing hair?" I grumbled.

"Quite the opposite, Miss Emmeline, I think you look *magnifique!*"

"Oh my, they didn't tell me you spoke French. Or do you flatter all of the girls this way?" I blushed. What was it about this boy?

"Okay, so I only know three words: *c'est, magnifique,* and *bonjour.* My grandmother was French and this is what I have to show for it." He grinned. "Really though, it suits you." He cradled the back of my head.

"But what I really love are these." He ran a finger along the bridge of my nose. "I have always been a sucker for a girl with freckles."

"Surely you tease." I laughed and wrinkled my nose.

"So, did you come to the dance with Levi Green?" he asked.

"Well, we walked here together, but . . ."

"Has he been singing my praises? Because he always misses the French and focuses on some of my other, less appealing traits," Nathaniel said.

Cora poked her head out the double doors. "Emmeline? Oh, there you are. Levi was looking for you. Hello, Nathaniel."

"I'll be right there," I called to Cora. I touched Nathaniel's arm. "What other less appealing traits?" Did he mean the polygamy? I needed to hear it from him.

"We should probably go back to the dance," he replied, holding the door open for me.

I grabbed his shoulder. "Tell me, what traits?"

"Later. Dance with me two more times and I promise I'll tell you more, at a later date. It will give you a reason to see me."

Levi was waiting by the door. He grabbed me by the waist and led me to the floor where the other couples were waltzing. Moments into our dance, Nathaniel glided past me holding fast to a girl I had seen him talking with earlier. They were perfectly synchronized and laughing with each other as they stepped in time.

At the end of the song Nathaniel tapped Levi on the shoulder. "May I cut in?"

"It looks like you already have your hands full," I retorted. "Plus, I promised another to Levi." Levi jutted his chin in victory and drew me back onto the crowded floor.

The fiddlers took a break after the song. Levi left to fetch us cookies and I sat on one of the pews to rotate my ankles. Nathaniel slid next to me and handed me a glass of lemonade. "Is this seat taken?"

"I'm not sure. Levi went to get cookies."

"You say he's not your date, huh?"

"Does it really matter to you? It looks like you came with someone as well. And it appears the two of you have shared many a dance." I would not let him get under my skin.

"We have." Nathaniel sounded like he was teasing me. He drained his glass. "But it's nice to see you're jealous."

"I'm not jealous. I noticed you danced very well together, that's all." Where was Cora? I needed a distraction.

"Emmeline." He took my hand. "She's my sister. We've been dancing together since we were children."

I exhaled loudly enough that he smiled. "So, how many sisters do you have?" I asked.

"Sixteen." His face was somber.

I gasped. "Brothers?"

"Twenty-two."

"Well, that's convenient. Are there any women in the valley you aren't related to?"

Nathaniel grinned. "Well, *you* aren't my sister. And now you know why I am so interested."

I stood up and put my hands on my hips. "Oh, thanks, you know how to flatter a girl. Now where's *my* sister?" I searched the crowd.

Nathaniel touched the back of my hand. His eyes were sincere. "Please, can we talk about this somewhere that isn't so crowded and noisy? I may be able to set your mind at ease."

"I am at ease, Nathaniel, but I'm ready to leave now."

Cora found me, and she had her hat on. "Levi's decided to stay at the dance, but Margaret and Richard are walking home now. Should we join them?" Her cheeks were flushed from dancing. She leaned into Richard as he guided her toward the door, his hand on her shoulder.

"Absolutely. I'm ready when you are," I replied, and turned away from Nathaniel.

"You haven't danced with me again," Nathaniel said, sounding deflated. "But I'll still call."

At the door I found Nathaniel in the crowd. He was still watching me. He kissed his finger and blew it in my direction. He was presumptuous and arrogant! Why couldn't I leave him be?

The sun warmed my back as I walked along Downington Avenue, grazing the tops of the shoulder-height trees outlining our sidewalk with the tips of my fingers. Ash trees, my father speculated as the city workers planted them. "Should canopy the street someday," he said. It seemed impossible since each twiggy start held only two dozen perfect leaves, golden with early autumn color, glowing like they were lit from within.

September had arrived and there were only two days until classes started at Westminster College. I was going—on scholarship! Father had asked me to go to the market in Sugar House for a few items, but the weather was so fine and my excitement so palpable, I couldn't help meandering, reveling in the anticipation.

Through the lazy silence I heard footsteps fast approaching. I swung around to see Nathaniel behind me. He tipped his hat. "Going my way, Miss Emmeline?" His jacket was over his elbow and I could see his muscled chest through his muslin shirt. Blushing, I gazed at his face. He smiled mischievously.

"Probably not. I'm taking my own sweet time to run to the market for my father." I couldn't let him know the second I heard the footsteps I hoped it was him.

"An amazing coincidence, because I too was going to the market for your father." He grinned, pushed his hair off his forehead, and set his hat back on his head.

"If that's the case, please hold these." I dropped the empty canvas market bags over his shoulder. "I'm not the sort to turn down an offer to carry my groceries."

Nathaniel walked by my side holding the bags. "Finally, a chance to get to know you outside of our usual confines. So, tell me about yourself. I know you're an independent sort; otherwise you wouldn't know about women's suffrage and you wouldn't have cut your hair. But what else makes you tick? What brought you to Salt Lake City?"

"It's a long story, but I'll simply say that my father got a job at the prison in Sugar House and we moved."

"From Helper, is that right?"

I nodded.

"And you plan to study nursing at Westminster?"

"How did you know that?" He'd been asking about me!

"Oh, you're the talk of the town." I rolled my eyes at him. "All right, I asked Margaret Robinson."

"It sounds like you already know all about me," I said. "I'm no big mystery. So tell me about you. I really shouldn't let you escort me to do my shopping, since you're practically a stranger."

"What do you want to know?" His words were guarded.

"To start, how old are you? Have you already served a mission?" I asked.

"You know how to get right to the brass tacks, don't you?" He shifted the bags to the other shoulder. "I'm nearly twenty-one. Yes, plenty old enough to go on a mission, and that's *really* what you're wondering, right?" he asked. "Why haven't I served?"

I was silent until he continued. "Well, my call has been somewhat delayed."

"Delayed?"

"Well, at first the church didn't want me. And now, it seems I *must* go to prove my faith." He sounded disgruntled.

"Why didn't they want you?"

"I know Margaret told you I'm part of the Barlow family. And you may know the Barlow family is on the outs with the church because we are . . . let me just put it straight, polygamists. My father won't abandon his wives, so my family is no longer considered members of the Mormon Church."

I worked my arm free of his elbow. "I don't want you to get any ideas about me. If that's how you are, we should end this outing right now!"

"*I'm* not like that, Emmeline! It's against church doctrine, and even if it wasn't, it's not for me! You see, in order to be called on a mission I needed to be a member of the church, in good standing, and it's taken some time to prove as much to my bishop. Now, at the advanced age of twenty-one, I finally got the call." He didn't seem too happy about this.

"Does that mean you're leaving? When?" I asked, my heart dropping.

"Does that upset you?" He stopped walking and rested his hand on my arm. I could feel the heat of it through my dress.

"It would be impossible for me to be *too* upset," I replied. "I mean, I've only just met you."

"Don't be so coy, Emmeline. I want you to care! But you'll probably be married with a babe in arms by the time I return. Anyhow, I leave in two months. I'm headed to jolly old England." He sighed. "It's a shame I have to fulfill my religious obligations just as things are finally getting interesting around here."

I was silent for several minutes as I contemplated telling Nathaniel the reason for our abrupt departure from Helper. I wanted him to understand my reaction to his polygamist past, but part of me didn't want to divulge Cora's secret.

"Why the silent treatment, Emmeline? Is there really no hope for us?" Nathaniel teased after a long pause in conversation.

"Against my better judgment, I'm going to tell you why my family moved from Helper," I blurted. "This isn't to be shared, though." Worry made my hands shake. I shouldn't trust him so soon with this secret, but I wanted him to know me.

He stood very still, his face etched with sincerity. "You can trust me, Emmeline. I'm a man who keeps his word." And somehow, I knew he was.

"I want to tell you about Cora and how it relates to your situation."

"Okay, go on. . . ." Nathaniel said, his face serious.

I took a deep breath. "Cora had a best friend in Helper, a girl named Millie Redding. They had been friends since Cora was five. And Millie was from a polygamist family."

"Oh, *that* situation," Nathaniel said.

"Anyhow, last year, Cora developed a crush on Millie's older brother and managed to spend extra time at their house. And, you know, Cora is a pretty girl—when she fixes herself up, boys notice."

Nathaniel nodded.

"Anyhow, one day Cora spent the afternoon at the Redding Ranch, presumably flirting with Millie's brother. I was watching for her return while I prepared supper. From the kitchen window I saw her arrival, but oddly Millie's father was walking with her. From the way Cora was shuffling, I could tell, even from a distance, something was wrong.

"Brother Redding asked after my father. While they spoke, I took Cora aside. Through sobs she told me Brother Redding had been paying particular attention to her for the past several weeks, but she thought nothing of it until earlier that day when he returned from Salt Lake on business. He dismissed his other children and asked Cora to play the piano for him. It made her nervous, but she didn't know what to say. After all, he was the father of her best friend and she had known him since she was a child. But when she finished playing he patted the couch and asked her to sit with him. And then"—I swallowed—"he asked her to marry him. He asked her to be his fifth wife! Cora was only sixteen and he was over fifty!"

I glanced at Nathaniel. His brow was furrowed. He didn't speak, so I continued.

"I decided to listen to what Millie's father was discussing with my father, so I crept to the window where they were talking. Brother Redding was preaching to my father the ban on plural marriage was only temporary. He said he had discussed it with the prophet Joseph F. Smith, who said criticism of the practice would decline as other problems took the focus of the federal government. Brother Redding reminded my father that the prophet had seven wives of his own. He told my father he'd received a directive to take another wife. He had prayed, and received word that Cora was the one!" I took a deep breath and continued. "It made me sick with fear my father would listen to him."

"But he didn't, right?" Nathaniel asked.

"No, my father doesn't believe in polygamy, but the following week there was a package addressed to Cora on the front porch containing several pamphlets discussing the benefits of plural marriage. Cora took one look at the bundle and walked outside with it. She dug a hole near the barn door and buried the whole thing."

"At least the girl knows what she wants," Nathaniel replied gently.

I nodded. "She's tough, but he wouldn't stop. He sought her out after school, even following her to her job picking apples from the local orchard. She hid in the limbs of an apple tree so he wouldn't see her."

I paused and glanced at Nathaniel.

He exhaled. "And he didn't stop pursuing her, so you were forced to move?"

"Yes, my father talked with him, but it didn't help. Cora got to the point she wouldn't leave the house. A month later my father announced he had a job in Salt Lake City. We moved the next week."

"That's awful, Emmeline. I ache for Cora," Nathaniel said. "But I've seen it before. In fact, a couple of years ago, my father took a wife twenty years his junior. I don't agree with his calling, or her decision to marry him, for that matter. That's why I don't want anything to do with the practice."

"So how can you stand to live in his house?"

"I love my family," he replied quickly. "And, if you can accept my word . . . I respect my father."

"Why?" I gasped.

"Because when he was faced with excommunication from the church, he stood by his wives. He won't cast them aside, not in title or in support. And I believe when he chooses a wife, they know what the life offers. They agree to the terms, so to speak. Cora clearly wasn't interested in Brother Redding, so he should have stopped pursuing her."

"You may think it's noble to stand by his wives," I shuddered. "But I can't understand why all of his wives would tolerate sharing him!"

Nathaniel shook his head slowly. "I don't understand either, Emmeline. I really don't."

By the time we finished the conversation, we'd arrived in Sugar House. The wide sidewalks were crowded with people running their Saturday errands. The streets were newly paved and a horse-drawn trolley line snaked up the center. I cast about, looking for a change of subject. Nathaniel must have felt the same.

"To your left," he said loudly, "is where I work—Sugar House Lumber Company. I cut power poles, cure them, and sometimes set them in new neighborhoods, like yours. You may have noticed my lumberman's chest." He flexed his arm. I blushed. I *had* noticed, and my pink face betrayed me.

"However, I'm not just brawn, I also exercise my brain." He smiled.

"Do you attend school?"

"I go to the University of Utah."

"Let me guess, you're studying something in the legal field, given your argumentative nature and quick tongue," I ribbed.

"You're such a sweet talker. No, I am studying to become an engineer, electrical, no less. Someone needs to light all of these new homes. I've a year until graduation."

I gazed down the street toward a series of new buildings. "I swear they build something new every time I come to town. Is that a firehouse next to the market?"

"Yes, and the next door down is Seagull Pharmacy, where a young couple in love could share an ice-cream float. What do you say, Emmeline? Do you have time before we do the shopping?" He pulled me down the sidewalk, a child begging for a treat.

"Who are the young couple you speak of?" I questioned.

"Us, of course." He laced his fingers through mine and we ran down the sidewalk, laughing.

After our float, on the way toward the market, we passed Granite Furniture, a big brick building with stenciling on the plate glass windows advertising "Furniture, Stoves, Ranges, and Rugs." Many families were standing outside, looking in and pointing. "Have you been in here?" he asked.

"I haven't much need for my own furniture."

"Do we have time to go in?" he asked. He was so distracting. I hoped my father wouldn't be angry at my delay.

We walked through the doors into a gigantic showroom. There were tables and chairs, buffets and beds. "Let's see. I think I'll buy you this table." Nathaniel ran his hand along an oval table made of dark stained oak. "Look, it says: fits up to eight chairs. It should work fine for our large family. It looks sturdy, too. You know, my brothers and I are rough on the furniture."

So he wanted to play.

"Well, if we must have a sturdy table for our large family, I'll need this finely crafted wardrobe for my many dresses." I pointed to a beautiful bird's-eye maple wardrobe. The door of the wardrobe held an oval mirror surrounded by carvings of fruit and vines.

"Anything for you, my darling!" he replied. "Dresses of silk and lace are all you'll wear."

"Fine. I'll also have this pouf to sit on. I will sit on this cushion in my fancy dress and watch my family of eight eat at their sturdy table," I said.

"And I'll buy this rocking chair. I'll rock and watch you as you select a silk dress from your wardrobe, and you'll sit on the pouf to pull on your stockings, one at a time . . . and you will . . ."

"Stop right there. I'm a lady and I'm not yet your wife," I teased.

He blushed. The thought of dressing in front of Nathaniel made me flush from my neck to my knees.

He stood from the rocking chair and put his arm around my waist, his hand pressed against my back. I leaned into him. "Maybe we should get to the market. Your father's probably wondering where you've gotten off to," he said in my ear.

We shopped in silence, the levity of the morning gone. Halfway home, Nathaniel stopped and set the bags on the ground. He grasped my hand. "Emmeline, I can't stand the thought of leaving you. It seems so silly. I mean, as you've pointed out, we've really just met. But there's something about you. Things are so easy when I'm with you. I don't know. I'm going to scare you away going on like this." He grazed my wrist with his thumb.

"Don't worry, I'm not scared." I brushed his hand against my lips.

"Between school and Nathaniel, I never see you." Cora was waiting for me at the doors of my math class at Westminster. "I had to wait for an hour outside this door just to catch you," she pouted.

It was true. Over the past month Nathaniel and I had spent every possible moment together. I was guilty of neglecting my sister and all of my other duties, for that matter. "I've missed you too, my darling sister, but he'll be gone soon enough." I sighed. "Then you'll have me all to yourself."

"Are you really so serious about him, Emmeline? He's leaving for two years. You're not going to wait for him to return and miss all the fun, are you?"

I linked her elbow with mine, avoiding her question. "Should we walk into Sugar House? I have money for a pastry. Dessert is fun, especially with my sister!"

"You didn't answer my question, Emmeline. How serious are you two?" she asked again as we walked toward town.

How did I feel about Nathaniel? I would marry him now, if he asked me. Thinking it, I could scarcely believe myself. Sure, I had always longed for a family, but somehow the husband in the equation seemed a mystery to me. I had been courted by many young men in Helper and none had caught my fancy. My father and bishop would remind me that my duty was to have children and love between a man and woman would grow over the years. It would be unbearable to me, living with a man I didn't love. But what were the options for a woman, really? There was school. So I'd thrown myself into Westminster College. And then Nathaniel came along.

"He hasn't asked me to wait for him," I said to Cora. "Oh, I wish he didn't have to go." My voice caught. I coughed like I had something in my throat, scolding myself for being weepy.

"It's just you've never had a boyfriend before," she said. "I mean, he's handsome and all, but what is it about Nathaniel that makes him so special?"

"I don't know . . . he makes me laugh. And he thinks I'm funny. He's proud of me for going to school. He likes that I'm smart. He encourages me to speak my mind." I shrugged, holding out my palms. "He argues with me and doesn't sulk when I win . . . though he always thinks he's the winner." I laughed.

Cora sighed. "I've had plenty of boyfriends, but I've never felt all that. Do you love him?"

My mouth fell open. "I've never said it to him. But I think I do, Cora. I think I must love him."

"Oh, Emmeline, what will you do when he leaves?" Cora sighed, heady with romance.

"Probably cry and beat my pillow," I said sarcastically. *In truth, I probably will,* I thought, and swallowed a lump in my throat.

"Two years is a long time to wait," Cora said.

"I can't imagine my life without him," I said softly, looking at my feet as I spoke. "It seems so dramatic. I feel silly, sometimes, with the emotion of it all."

"I know." Cora stopped walking as we arrived at the bakery. "The solution to your sorrow is as easy as pie." She laughed at her own joke as she pointed to the pies in the glass case. "Pie, see?"

"Great," I snorted. "I'll eat one piece every day while he's gone. He won't want me when he returns, I'll be so porky."

"Problem solved." She giggled. She pointed to a raspberry pie in the display case. "We'll have two pieces of that one, please."

As we sat at the little table inside the store, I thought waiting for him would not be as easy as pie. But forgetting him would be impossible.

I put my chin in my hand and sighed again. Cora wrinkled her nose at me. "Stop fretting and eat your dessert," she said.

"Easy for you to say," I grumbled.

"Easy as pie?" she replied. I slugged her in the arm and we laughed while we ate.

Our first autumn in the tidy redbrick bungalow meant it was time to plant some trees. The barren yard had provided no respite from the blistering heat of summer and we all missed the harvest of apples our property in Helper provided each season when the nights turned brisk.

Our father had purchased three tiny apple starts, and as a special treat, a cherry tree, no bigger than a walking stick. Cherries were Cora's favorite fruit.

Armed with a shovel each, Cora and I had set to work digging wide holes in the packed clay soil surrounding the house. Remembering the staggering heat of July, I longed for these trees to grow quickly. We were untidy twins, Cora and I, dirt staining our aprons. I was leaning against my shovel, back turned to the street, when two hands covered my eyes and strong arms pulled me against a familiar chest.

"Oh, let me guess. . . ."

The rumble of his laugh vibrated my spine. Nathaniel spun me around and kissed the tip of my nose. "You've got yourself a mess, Emmeline."

"Well, I'm no fragile flower. Cora and I've been hard at work."

"I would never call you fragile. But since you speak of flowers, I've brought you a gift of some."

"Flowers?"

"Well, someday," Nathaniel said, and retrieved a canvas bag he'd left on the sidewalk.

He reached into the depths and revealed an unimpressive, knotty stick with a few leaves clinging to it.

"Somehow less romantic than I expected." Cora poked at the stick with one finger.

"It's nothing much right now and it will require a little patience and tender care," he said. "But this is the start of a rosebush. Plant it with this side down." He pointed to the side without any leaves and handed it to me. "You'll need to water it every day until the ground freezes. Next spring you should see new leaves. It will grow big, so give it a home where it has plenty of room to spread out. It will bloom in June, each and every year, and will fill your yard with white snowball blossoms. The original start came with my grandmother across the plains in a handcart. She was with one of the first pioneer companies to make the trip from Nauvoo to Salt Lake City. Since she could only bring a few extra things to remind her of home in Illinois, she chose a small hand mirror and the start for this rose bush."

"Thank you. It's wonderful."

"It'll give you something to remember me by when I leave for my mission." He wrapped my hand in his, both our palms surrounding the twig. "Now, my love, we are bound together by this rose."

"It's not easy to wear a rosebush on a ring finger. . . ." said Cora, grinning.

"Hush, my sister. I think it's very romantic."

"She thinks it's romantic," he told Cora, who stuck out her tongue.

I caressed the rough surface with the tips of my fingers. I would plant this rose and tend it well. The rose and I would wait for Nathaniel together, taking strength from the rich soil of my new home on Downington Avenue.

IVY BAYGREN

⌒჻⌒

The garage door was gaping open, yawning like a dark mouth, as I pulled up the drive. I hadn't been able to park inside for well over a year, as it was a catchall for anything I didn't want to put away, and the staging area for all home repair projects. But this afternoon, through the open door, it was shockingly empty. Lawn chairs leaned neatly against the wall and the wheelbarrow was tucked into the proper corner.

Porter walked outside bouncing a basketball as I got out of the minivan. "Have you been out here already?" I said as I walked into the garage. "I think we've been robbed." I scanned the empty concrete floor. "Did you see anyone out here or hear anything?" I asked, my pulse shooting up. What could have been stolen to open up so much space?

Porter smirked. "Yeah, someone robbed the garage and swept up afterward."

"Okay, that does sound a little strange, but what's missing?"

"I don't think anything's missing. I was looking for the basketball pump when Drew and Uncle Stephen stopped by. They helped me find it, then Stephen made some comment about the state of disrepair and we all grabbed a broom. They were here all morning, plus they found two flat basketballs and pumped them for me." He stepped closer, assessing my mental well-being. "By the way, why were you gone so long? I thought you were just running to the hardware store."

"I did." I glanced at my watch. I'd been gone four hours. "But

I also got groceries," I said quickly. "Help me carry them in, would you?"

I pulled my phone out of my purse. "Why didn't you call?"

"We did."

I turned it on. Three missed calls.

"This thing's been on silent. Sorry." I pretended to turn the ringer back on. How could I have missed those calls? And how had I been gone for four hours?

I *did* meander at Home Depot, maybe a little bit, playing a game with myself as I walked the aisles. How many times had I searched for Adam in that store only to find him in a squat in front of the bolts or figuring out some solution in the plumbing section? So I'd let myself search for him, up and down the aisles, squinting in mock recognition at any man with dark hair and gym shorts. But four hours?

"They were waiting for you, but Drew had to go to work. Uncle Stephen said he'd be back later tonight."

Probably to check on me, I thought. I'd show him I was doing fine. "Great! I'll invite him for dinner," I said firmly.

As I called my brother, I wandered around the garage like it was a foreign land. Look at all this stuff I'd forgotten we owned. Rolls of wrapping paper protruding from a bucket, at least six pairs of ski boots, tin cans full of nails, folded drop cloths and, oh my gosh, the ice-cream maker our neighbor George Pearson had given us days before he died, nearly a decade earlier. I'd entirely forgotten we had it.

Stephen and I were finishing our phone conversation when I spotted it. "You'll never believe what I've found in the garage— an old-fashioned wood plank ice-cream churn from George."

"Good old George. God, I haven't thought about him in ages."

"George," I agreed, simply by murmuring his name. Our across-the-street neighbor had passed away over ten years ago, but I tried to conjure him sitting on a folding lawn chair in the center of his driveway, enjoying a morning cigarette, orange tip a hot beacon against the dawn sky. The neighbors on our close-knit street had dubbed him "The Mayor of Downington Avenue." An iconic resident for fifty years, he'd watched newly-weds move in, children grow up, and his aging neighborhood friends die.

"Yeah," Stephen continued. "Drew unearthed the dinosaur from under a mountain of drop cloths."

"I'm going to make ice cream tonight," I said with determination.

"Sounds ambitious. You might want to see if it works before you commit."

"Don't be such a wet blanket," I replied. "It *will* work. I'm looking up recipes right after I get off the phone."

I found Naomi in her room trying various hairstyles from a teen magazine and sent her and Porter up to Emigration Market for a bag of ice and heavy cream, two things I hadn't picked up at the store, and set to work cleaning the churn.

The day George brought it to us I noticed he was leaning heavily against the porch pillar, his face a pale mask. Tall and lanky, hands gnarled from manual labor with Union Pacific, he still had a ready grin, but something was different. It had been three months since his wife, Louise, had died, and he claimed he wouldn't be making ice cream again, at least not in this lifetime. In an effort to cheer him, I had promised a batch of homemade strawberry the very next weekend. But two days later we saw an ambulance in his drive. George was gone. After that, it was too sad to make ice cream, so the churn sat. And by the next summer, I'd forgotten all about it.

Stuck inside the metal canister I found a yellowed envelope inscribed with my name. From George? I ached knowing he had been gone so many years and I still hadn't used his final gift. Opening the flap, I pulled out several brittle index cards, each containing a recipe: Anne's Famous Lemon Ice, Delicious Summer Peach, and Mom's Strawberry. How lovely George had saved me the effort of looking up recipes. After reading them carefully and deciding what I had in my cupboard to craft one of these concoctions, I noticed a folded piece of newsprint at the bottom of the wood bucket.

Unfolding it, two photos fell onto my lap. I couldn't suppress my smile as I held them in front of me. I loved old photos, a window to a world I never knew.

The first was of George and his wife, Louise, standing in front of a house. My house! Between them was a woman, forty or so, dressed in one of those awful bell-bottom jumpsuits, her hair bad-perm kinky. Louise was on the woman's left, looking toward the camera with a tight smile—probably because the lawn was covered with tacky pink flamingos. Louise always liked a well-kept yard and I was certain she had a little something to say about the display of synthetic birds.

And my house! Aside from the flamingos, the porch was covered with scruffy green Astroturf, like when we bought it. The juniper trees we worked so hard to pull out were small in this photo. On the back, faded cursive read, "George, Louise, Lainey, and flamingos—September 1984."

I flipped to the next photo. This one was also of Lainey, much younger, though. Her hair was cut short in a pixie, her arms and legs were dangerously thin. She stared forward, gaze wide and startled, but despite that, she was stunning—incredibly beautiful. Standing in front of her was a young blond girl. Lainey was embracing the child, her thin fingers stretched over the girl's freckled shoulders. I smiled back at the child in the photo, whose eyes were half-moons of delight. Lainey and child were standing in front of our cherry tree; the green branches soared above the garage roof. On the back, the same handwriting read, "Lainey and Sylvie—Moving Day 1968."

I ran my thumb over Lainey's striking face in the photo. I met Lainey briefly while we were completing the loan paperwork. We didn't speak much, and I wasn't too interested in her. I mean, what did we have in common?

She was a frumpy woman, slightly overweight with glasses perched on her nose, dressed in an embroidered shirt tucked into her old-lady pants, with too many bangles and bracelets on her wrists. And I was overly critical of the art adorning her walls. Anything that wasn't a photograph was one of those dreadful 1970s black velvet paintings. Clearly, she had never caught up with the times. And who was I? A young professional woman with a baby on the way. I couldn't wait to change her house.

If I'd only known we would have *everything* in common. Each of us had lived in this house, a vessel that held our secrets and dreams. What joy and what sadness did Lainey experience as she stood in front of the same kitchen window, enjoying the same view? And what was Lainey's story? According to these photos, she wasn't always an old woman. How shortsighted to believe she was nothing more than she appeared on that day?

The metal chains of the swing set squealed, letting me know the kids had returned from the market. I longed for summer days when I could set a sprinkler under the swings and hours would be spent shivering in the sun. Minutes later, a car door closed and Stephen's voice mingled with those of my children. Tucking the photos into my back pocket, I knew it was time to make some ice cream.

Grilled chicken breasts, frozen broccoli, and instant rice (plus a bottle of wine), and we were ready for the lemon ice cream that had been rattling all through dinner. Naomi and Porter had been diligent about filling the wooden bucket with ice and rock salt and taking turns at the hand-crank until it became impossible to churn, indicating dessert was done.

We crowded around the canister and ate the creamy mixture without bowls, mingling our spoons. As we ate, I reached into my back pocket, took out the photos, and set them on the table. "Look what I found at the bottom of the ice-cream maker."

Naomi grabbed them, first looking at the younger photo of Lainey. "The woman is so pretty. Who is she?"

"Read the inscription on the back. Lainey is the woman who lived here before us."

"Really?" Stephen said, picking up the photo from 1984. "Oh, yeah, I think I remember her from the day you moved into the house. Didn't she leave a few things on the porch to pick up?" He gazed at the next photo. "Wow, time aged her. I can't believe this lovely girl is the old lady I met."

At Stephen's mention of Lainey, I recalled the day she'd returned to retrieve a box of books she'd left in the basement. I'd set it on the porch, like she'd asked me to do, and went about unpacking. Fatigued from a long day, and from the weight of Naomi pressing on my pelvis, I'd moved aside items we'd stacked on the couch and put my feet up. From there, I watched as Stephen encountered Lainey on the porch and exchanged stiff pleasantries. I didn't go out to greet her, actually ducking a bit so she couldn't see me as I sat silently by.

I continued to watch as she, and a woman not much older than I, walked across the street. A man I would grow to love myself, old George, met them on the porch. He affectionately patted the younger woman on the head, and he embraced Lainey. She clung to him, her desperate focus on my house, like he was the only thing keeping her from running back up my stairs and through my front door. The naked emotion made me feel like I'd accidently walked into a Victoria's Secret dressing room already occupied. You apologize and back out, but you know what you've seen and you can't forget.

I was sheepish for bearing witness, and I was jealous. And I was shocked by my jealousy. How could this woman hold the affection of my new neighbors? This was *my* house now, I reasoned with myself. It was fine to be protective of my place in it. I mean, how could a house hold two women in its heart?

I wouldn't tell Stephen my version of moving day. Even though he was my brother and had seen me at my worst, I was embarrassed to let him into the part of my world where I was an insecure little girl. Jealous of a woman who lived in my house? If only I could right my wrong and speak to her now. I'd invite her in and we'd share a pot of tea and revel in our connection, the mysterious nature of time and place.

"Everyone gets old," I said to Stephen, holding the two photos side by side. I would defend her now. "She lived in this house from the time she was a young mother until we met her, at least thirty years later. And she clearly knew George. What's her story, do you imagine? What might have happened in all those years?"

"Seems like your little unassuming home is yielding more than its fair share of stories these days," Stephen teased. "What about the embroidery you found?" he asked. "The one tucked away by ancient Emmeline of the overgrown rosebush?"

"My friend Emmeline." I sighed peacefully, because Emmeline's embroidery had offered respite from my continual search for Adam, rather than fueled it. Pondering her story gave me a needed breath from my incessant and fruitless search for a deeper meaning to his death.

"You know, Ivy, if you're actually interested, there are ways you could do a little research. I'm sure somewhere you could find maps, official documents, maybe a photo or two. Think about it, you could get some real facts about this old house."

"Sounds like chasing ghosts, and I don't even have time for my *living* friends these days," I replied, which was true and also not true. Adam and I had a decent group of friends—couples from his law firm, parents from the school; a few times a month we'd get together before a school carnival for appetizers or giggle together at a law-firm party. We'd even shared a couple of trips to Disneyland.

After Adam died, they didn't know what to do with me. How did I fit in? What could we talk about? Was it too soon to set me up? Once or twice I'd gone to a movie with the wives and inevitably the conversation turned to something about the husbands—discussion of family vacations or even a little bitch session about how they never picked up a dish. Then, as if realizing they had nothing to complain about, mouths would close with a snap. With a grimace disguised as a smile, they would turn the conversation to something benign, and we'd have a lengthy and forced discussion about current best-sellers.

The next time they thought about inviting the widow, it would be decided it was a little too painful, awkward, sad, embarrassing—or whatever. The calls dwindled soon after the funeral. I understood and I wasn't mad, because if the roles were reversed, I'd likely do the same thing. It was awfully hard to discuss death at a dinner party.

"If you have a free Saturday, think about it," Stephen continued. "A little project that doesn't require a hammer and nails might be a fun diversion."

ELAINE (LAINEY) HARPER

❧

Downington Avenue
1968

"So, tell me a little more about the photographs." The man leaned forward in his chair. I nodded at the psychiatrist . . . impossible to hold his gaze. I focused instead on his hands folded soothingly on his lap, their lack of jerky movement a brief respite. Individual black hairs pushed their way through the follicles on his fingers. I was certain crawling on his nails were untold amounts of germs, particles of food from his lunch, crumbs of excrement from his trip to the bathroom.

"Lainey. Eyes to me. Focus."

I took a deep breath and glanced at his muddy eyes. The skin surrounding the matching orbs was darker than his cheeks, like a fried egg in negative contrast. He studied me for several minutes, breaking his gaze only to write in a notebook balanced on his knee.

"What did you write?" I finally asked, my words louder than I intended.

"If you must know—eyes darting wildly." He held up his book.

I stood and lunged toward the door. I didn't need his diagnosis. I already knew everything he was telling me.

"Sit, Lainey. Tell me about the compilation of photographs you've brought. You must believe these are important." His voice was gratingly calm. Why was I here? He couldn't help me.

"I've already told you about the hole in my chest! I've told you all about the hole and I need someone to fix it."

My hand worked its way through the buttons of my blouse like a nervous spider, patting my middle, searching for the gaping fissure in my torso. The size of a salad plate, I could see it in my head. The wind blew right through it when I walked. My veins pulsed as they redirected the flow of blood around the abyss to my legs.

"So you believe the photographs will fix the hole?" He sounded sincere. It was his job to sound sincere.

I threw the stack of photos on the desk next to him and tried to become invisible in my chair.

He leafed slowly through the contents and finally he spoke. "How many weeks has it taken for you to shoot and develop these?"

"A couple of days."

"Seems impossible. There are hundreds of photographs here."

"I worked late."

He exhaled. "How long has it been since you slept?"

"I think I slept for a couple of hours Sunday night."

"Today is Friday," he said, and wrote something in his notebook.

"I know that." I tried to keep my attention on the doctor's face, but it kept slipping toward the photographs he had spread on his desk. The answer was in that stack, somewhere. If I could arrange it just right, the photographs would stop my heart from falling into the void.

He slid two of the black-and-white photos next to each other. "These are of children, am I right?"

"Girls."

"The same girl?"

"No."

"How do they relate to one another?"

"You mean you can't see it?" I could tell my voice was too loud, the tone too high.

He shook his head.

"It's her!" I picked up one of the photographs, a close-up of a nose and cheek. Tiny nostrils, turned up at the end, the cheek round to the side. I held it close to his face, the glossy surface grazing his nose. I pulled it back toward me and caressed the full bottom lip of the child in the photo with my fingertip.

"And this one is her hand. See how her little finger curves in, just so? And this one is her profile. Well, this eye wasn't blue like hers, so I had to develop all of the photographs in black and white, but see how her lashes nearly touch her eyebrow? She's got the most beautiful eyes. And this one is her left knee. It even has the tiny scar she got when she rolled down the grass hill in front of my parents' place and hit the sidewalk."

"When did you take all of these photographs?"

"I took them during the day, and developed them at night."

"Did the children know you were photographing them? This is serious, Lainey."

"I don't think so. Marcus showed me how to use the tele-photo lens."

"Marcus?"

"My ex-stylist. I slept with him so he would let me borrow his camera and darkroom."

The doctor coughed, and asked another of his questions. "When you say, *it's her,* to whom are you referring?"

"Sylvie," I said. "Sylvie, Sylvie, Sylvie! She's in these pictures. Put her together—fix the hole!" I was screaming now. There was a framed print on the wall behind the doctor, right next to his oversized diploma, a photograph of a crazy woman, short blond hair stuck out in clumps, eyes a bloodshot target surrounded by dark rings. Wild. Wild! Her mouth was moving.

I touched my hair. The woman in the print followed my movement. If that reflection was me, I was surely broken.

"Lainey, please sit down."

I slumped back into the cushioned chair.

"Is Sylvie related to you?"

I nodded.

"Where is she?"

"I've left her behind. Everything good and true about me is in her. The biggest and most important part of me is gone and it made this hole. Don't you see?" I patted my torso again, tracing my ribs with my fingers.

Suddenly exhausted, I rested my forehead in my hands and moaned, "Please."

"I'll try to help, but you'll need to answer a few more questions. Have you ever experienced this sleepless condition before?"

"A couple of times."

"When did these episodes start?"

"A year after I moved here, to Manhattan."

"How old were you?"

"I was eighteen."

"How old are you now?"

"Twenty-eight."

"So, how many times during the past ten or so years?"

"Too many to count."

"Is this time the worst?"

"You could say that," I said loudly, and jammed fingers in my ears. The Supremes were belting their latest hit on the office sound system and usually I loved the rich voice of Diana Ross. But today the guitar screeched and her velvet voice crashed against my own words, discordant and violent.

"Is something hurting your ears?" the doctor questioned.

"The music! Too loud!"

"Why, I can hardly hear it"—he leaned toward a radio on his desk—"but I'll turn it off. Sorry about that," he said, and wrote something in his notebook. "What's the primary sensation you're feeling right now?"

I shook my head, ears still plugged.

"Lainey, the music is off. Stay with me for a few more minutes."

I took a deep breath and spoke, my words slamming inside my skull. I wiped under my nose, certain it was bleeding. "I am right at the edge of figuring out how to create Sylvie with these images . . . the answer is right there in the stack of photos. I'm thinking in circles and I almost touch the answer and it slips past and I have to start again. And now I am frustrated with you because you keep distracting me . . . and I'm so close. And you're asking me these questions in this infuriatingly slow voice and I'm ready to leave now."

He nodded. "Is Sylvie your daughter?"

Tears sprung and I wiped them away roughly. I needed to keep my wits so I could get out. "Of course she is. She's six and she lives with my parents because I was too crazy to take care of her and now I've got this hole only she can fill."

I stood and with jittery hands stacked the precious photographs. Each one was a small piece of my baby. I could put them together if I could escape to someplace quiet. I needed to get out of here so I could concentrate.

"Just a few more questions. Have you tried to hurt yourself in any manner during the past two weeks? Or thought about hurting yourself?"

How did he know? I was silent.

"Well, have you?"

"I almost swallowed some of the chemicals while I was developing the photos. But it burned my mouth, so I spit it out," I said quickly.

"What were you thinking when you put the solution into your mouth?"

"That it might slow my thoughts, so I could figure out how to create Sylvie with the photographs."

The doctor nodded and wrote for several minutes in his notebook. I growled.

"Are you experiencing some anxiety, now?"

I pressed my palms into my sockets to stop my eyeballs from bouncing out of my head.

"Lainey, I am going to put you on some lithium to stabilize your moods and help you get some sleep. You'll be in the hospital for at least several days, and I will need to contact your parents. I assume they are your closest relatives?"

I nodded. Maybe I just needed some sleep. Maybe I wasn't entirely crazy.

"Am I actually sick?" I said through gritted teeth.

"I believe you have melancholia, or what many refer to as

manic-depressive disorder, which will need to be treated with medication. So, yes, you have a real illness. You'll need counseling.
And I think, for your sake, you need to visit Sylvie."

I shook my head. "She can't see me like this. Besides, my parents have told me I'm too unpredictable to be much of a
mother."

"You should get some relief from this medication. It will help
with the unpredictability. And let me talk to your parents. Do
they live with you here in the city?"

I crossed my arms in front of my chest, gripping the armrests
on either side of the chair to keep myself together. He needed to
know where to find Sylvie before the blackness smothered me.
"Not here. West. They live in Utah."

IVY BAYGREN

❧

"Mom, I'm going to ask you a question and you've got to promise you won't freak out," Naomi called to me from her room. I was changing after work and she and Porter had returned from their first day of the new school year. One nice thing about working at the bank part-time was I could be home after school for the inevitable rush of lessons and homework.

"Implying I freak out on a regular basis is doing nothing for your case," I said with artificial confidence. I was actually a little sensitive about my freak-outs, which were decreasing in frequency, but were by no means gone entirely.

"So you won't?"

"Naomi!"

"Fine." She took a deep breath. "You know how we talked about buying a new dresser when you painted my room. And you agreed that I'm running out of space for my clothes?"

"Yes."

"Well, I was wondering if I could, maybe, hang a few things in Dad's closet?" Her voice was timid, and I knew she'd asked the question from a distance so our individual tendrils of sadness wouldn't combine and multiply.

"Dad's closet," I said dully.

"You could use some of the space too," she said quickly. "You have all those new jackets and stuff for work."

"I'll clean it out soon," I dismissed her, with no intention of moving Adam's clothing. Of course, I knew our house had a

deficit of closet space. Apparently, when people had to hand
stitch every ensemble, they didn't collect things quite so rapidly.

"But what will I do with them? I can't just throw Dad's things
away," I said before she could ask again, wincing at the thought.
What will he wear when he comes home? I pondered reflexively,
and caught myself.

"Could you put it in storage?"

I groaned about the effort required, though we both knew the
work was not the problem. And after an hour, I acquiesced.

"Turns out we need your closet, Adam," I said the next day,
as I lugged several plastic boxes from Target out of the back of
the van. Once inside, I wrote with permanent ink on the lids,
Sentimental Clothing. As if I could catch the significance of Adam's
clothing with this simple name.

Standing in front of the closet I ran my hands across the rainbow of neatly hung dress shirts. I could imagine him standing in
front of the display each morning, choosing one and buttoning
it to the top. Still in his boxers, he'd select a tie and in seconds
he'd become a professional. Slacks felt less personal, though, so
I decided to start there. Removing the trousers from their hang-
ers and draping them across the bed, I thrust my hand into the
pockets of each pair before putting them in the discard pile,
searching for clues. Clues of what, I wasn't certain, but I couldn't
help myself.

His favorite gray pair, close to the top of the stack, contained
a crumpled receipt from Lamb's, the restaurant where his law
firm usually took clients. I smoothed the ball of fragile paper, a
knot in my throat. How pathetic this order of beef stroganoff
threatened to stop my heart. After a moment or two, I crumpled
it again and dropped it into the garbage. I would not wallow.
Near the bottom of the pile was a long-out-of-style pair of khaki
cords. Patting the pockets, I felt something bulky. With resolve,
I slid my hand into the slit and pulled out a blue pacifier, the
rubber tip cracked with age. Porter's. My throat closed with
tears. "Adam, I don't know if I can do this," I said out loud.

Setting the pacifier on the kitchen counter, I made myself a
cup of tea and went back to the bedroom. The warmth of the

mug comforted me as I sat on the bed amid the clothing Adam would never wear again. Socks, some worn out, some hardly worn. Work shirts, ripped and stained from fix-it-up adventures in the house. Dress pants with evidence of babies and lunches out. Some would go into the sentimental clothing box, some in the trash, and some to charity.

After filling two plastic boxes with all I couldn't part with, the closet was nearly empty. Picking up one container, I pushed through the back door, using my hip to hit the latch on the screen, and staggered toward the garage. The space under the workbench would house these remnants of sentimentality.

Though Stephen and Drew did a fair amount of cleaning, there was a bit more I'd need to throw away to make room for Adam's clothing, now that I'd grown accustomed to parking in the garage. Eyeing our bin warily, I continued to stuff items into its maw, the green lid propped open from the overflowing contents. In the far corner, where I intended to stash the sentimental clothing, was a clump of something the heavy push broom wouldn't pick up. I kicked at the unyielding clod with my toe, to no avail. Finally, work-worn and curious, I decided to play paleontologist, kneeling on the ground and picking at the impacted dirt with a screwdriver. It took nearly an hour, but I was on to something good. At the end of my dig, I revealed a hand print. The name scratched near it was shallow, the writing precise: *Hector.* Below it was the date: *1959.* An imprint of another life.

My little abode was about a century old, and apparently this garage was . . . I calculated using my fingers to tick off the decades . . . over fifty. The home was built in one of the original suburbs of Salt Lake City, the year, according to the deed of purchase, 1913. And over so many decades, we knew there were numerous mysteries hidden within the walls. Maybe even a body or two, Adam used to joke, shifting his eyes back and forth, suggesting perhaps he had hidden one himself during one of his remodeling projects.

And now, concealed in the garage, I'd found evidence of another man who changed the semblance of this house, leaving behind only the tiniest traces of himself. Did he reside here, like

Adam, unfolding his life day by day? I was suddenly drawn to discover the story of Hector. Not guessing, but with real facts like Stephen suggested. But how?

And would history remember the tale of my departed husband? I wondered, fitting my hand into the print. Could the story of his ordinary life transcend the bounds of his lifetime? Perhaps the changes Adam made to this little house would be his legacy. Perhaps . . .

Sliding the plastic storage container under the workbench, I obscured all traces of Hector, burying a relic of a past age with a relic from my own. My relic was the sentimental clothing of a man I loved.

The Utah State Historical Society was located in the old Rio Grande train depot, a couple blocks west of the city. And I was on a quest. The mystery of my hundred-year-old house had fully captivated my imagination. As I entered the depot, the *thwump* of my sandals echoed across the vast marble hall, which was entirely empty. A tiny gold placard on the heavy front door identified the significance of this lofty building, and below it was a sign directing me to the Historical Society on the second floor.

Standing in the middle of the expanse, I was lost under a domed desert sky. The periphery of the cavern was surrounded by closed ticket windows; their ornately decorated cages spoke to a time when rail travel was the elegant mode of transportation. Initially fighting the urge to test an echo, I realized the station was desolate, so I called, "Hello . . ."

A satisfying "Hello . . ." flew toward me from the far wall.

"Adam?" I hollered.

Jolting when my own voice returned the call—"Adam?"—I shook my head, shocked I actually thought he would respond the way he would when we lost sight of each other at the grocery store. "Ivy?"

Enough sentiment. There were the stairs. My progress toward them reverberated across the great depot, a location directing many a traveler toward their destination, for better or for worse.

Hours passed in the womb of documents, photos, census reports, and newspaper clippings. Some information was in paper form, some on microfiche, some digitized. I investigated until the words swam toward me, marred by my tired eyes. All my work directed me toward . . . nothing. Well, not nothing, but not much. Apparently my house was not registered, meaning it was nothing special, historically speaking. But for a girl who grew up in a subdivision of cul-de-sacs, new homes with attached garages, and double-sink bathrooms, *anything* a hundred years old seemed historically significant. I thought there would've been more.

Standing in line, I shuffled through the four sheets of paper I'd spent a full day researching. I just wanted to pay my hard-spent forty cents for the copies and go home, but the bifocaled clerk was taking her time with the man in front of me. Her cheeks were flushed as she calculated his total. As he reached in his pocket for a wallet, she giggled, and oh, dear God, did she actually fan her face and say, "Oh, Mr. Taylor . . ."?

Based on the fuss this grandmother was making over the man, I took some time to study his back. His wide shoulders didn't indicate he was the bookish sort, not the kind to spend hours in the hush of the Historical Society halls, but the sheaf of paper he was paying for told me he'd been successful in his search. He was either lucky or he knew what he was doing.

The apparent heartthrob, Mr. Taylor, was dressed casually, a stylish dress shirt tucked in to jeans, leather loafers, hair thick and brown, but well on its way to gray. I'd need to see his face to judge his age. I wanted him to finish with the clerk so I could ask him his research secret, because compared with his hefty stack, I'd bombed. Four pieces of information. That was it.

He took a step back, turned quickly, and bumped the hand that was gripping my treasure of information. My quartet of sheets fluttered to the floor.

"Oh, gosh. Sorry. I didn't know anyone was behind me," he said as he scooped the pages and returned them to my hand. His thumb grazed mine, and I jolted at the touch, feeling a bit like the loopy attendant. His mouth had the deep smile wrinkles and defined jaw that reminded me of a young Robert Redford.

"It's okay. It's not like I won't be able to put them back in the right order," I said, returning his smile. "By the way, how is it your research yielded a stack the size of a novel and I have a third-grade research paper?"

"I have a lot of practice, I guess." He shrugged. "And usually the property I'm researching has some historical significance."

"He's here every week," the attendant added, holding out her hand for my paltry purchase.

"Why?" I asked.

"Oh, a historic home bio is part of the package I provide to clients. It helps close the deal."

"The deal?"

"I remodel historic homes. Make them look like they did when they were first built. Some I flip, some are for owners. I replace hardwood built-ins, wood floors, and so on. If someone is interested in remodeling a home that way, they're usually interested in the history of the place."

I nodded. "The market's pretty weak right now. . . ." Why was I trying to engage in conversation with this stranger?

"It is, but I've had decent luck." He shrugged again.

"I've been trying to sell my house for months now. Do you have any tips?" I asked, my face flushing with the lie. Where was this coming from?

"An old home?"

"Yes. It was built in 1913."

"And you're putting together a bio?" He nodded at the papers in my hand. "A place on Downington Avenue? Nice street. Great trees."

"Oh, not a bio. I was just curious. I found a name etched on the floor of my garage and I . . ." Pausing, I considered telling him I'd been trying to find some meaning in my own life by looking for the ghosts that once inhabited my home. But it seemed a little weird and was maybe more than this hunky builder, this history aficionado, needed to hear.

He studied me as I worked to vocalize my plans. Distracted by his gaze, for the first time in maybe too long, I considered my appearance. My hair, too thick and straight to accept styling, hung in a heavy braid over my shoulder, a nondescript color— not quite blond, but not exactly red. When I was young, my mom always reassured me it was lovely and told me to keep it out of my face. This morning, however, I did manage a shower, so my hair was lovely *and* clean. Plus, I applied mascara, and my paisley sundress was one Adam liked. Suddenly self-conscious of my own analysis, I glanced at the floor.

After I failed to complete my sentence he said, "Well, it sounds like you've got a good start. And if you need any help remodeling or selling, you can call me. I'll see what I can do."

"What's the name of your company?"

"Taylor Historic Home Remodel."

I laughed. "That makes sense."

"I'm a sensible guy." He grinned. "My name is Theo Taylor." He finished his transaction as I fumbled through my coin purse for the dimes. Finally, he slid past me and out the door and I passed the money to the clerk. She was gazing at the spot he vacated seconds earlier, and though she struck me as a bit pathetic, I kind of got it.

Back at home I studied the paperwork. Hector's signature on the deed of sale was the same as the one in my garage. So he *was* an owner. In total I had:

1: A photo taken in 1972 when owner E. Harper (I assume Lainey) took out a second mortgage. The house was in a dilapidated state.

2: A deed of sale indicating owners Gianopolous purchased a foreclosed property in 1941. Signing parties: Hector and Eris Gianopolous.

3: A census list with the Gianopolous family: Hector (43), Eris (40), Adonis (18), and Calliope (15), dated 1944. So Hector would have been nearly sixty in 1959, the year the garage was built. His children would have been grown, probably moved out.

4: Another deed of sale dated 1913, the year the house was

built. The writing was so faded all I could read was the last name: Lansing.

5: I'd also found the closing documents from our purchase of the house buried in a box in the garage. Amazing what a good cleaning could yield. Aside from a multitude of hopeful signatures made by Adam and me, the paperwork contained a forwarding address for Elaine Harper. She'd moved to Colorado Springs in 1998.

These items were the skeleton framework for my research. My first step would be to send a letter to Lainey. She was likely still alive, and upon writing a quick note to let her know who I was and why I was researching our house on Downington, I felt a wave of absolution for ignoring her on moving day, like I was finally paying penance for pushing her out of the home so beloved by both of us. I wanted more photographs from Lainey, I wanted information; I wanted her to be my friend. At some core level, I thought we'd understand each other as well as family. We didn't share blood, but hadn't we shared something nearly as intimate? Before I could second-guess my enthusiasm, I slipped the letter in the outgoing mail slot and returned my attention to the other information I'd gathered.

Based on Hector's last name, Gianopolous, this was a Greek family. I'd have to look them up. Porter had joined me as I shifted through documents and was sitting across from me at the table, his face buried in a book, *Percy Jackson and the Olympians,* a cartoon representation of the Acropolis on the cover.

"Is that good?" I asked.

He didn't look up. "I'm at the best part. Wait one minute."

Finally he put his finger between the pages. "It's awesome! It reminds me of the Greek stuff I learned about in fifth grade, but brought to life." He ran his finger over the title, anxious to resume his read.

"Do you still have that book of myths you used for your project?" I asked, thinking the name Adonis was certainly myth-worthy. Wasn't he the one who fought the Argonauts?

"It's on the shelf in my room. I think," Porter said, opening *Percy Jackson* to his finger-marked page.

More hours into my research, I was hunched on Porter's bedroom floor, legs asleep. I'd discovered Adonis was a beautiful baby worshiped by his mother. I'd also found a mention of Eris, the mother listed on the Gianopolous census. She was apparently the goddess of chaos and discord. I bet she was one heck of a mother. Calliope was one of the nine muses, specifically song. And Hector was a Trojan prince, peace-loving and without darker motives. My hours tucked into *D'Aulaires Book of Greek Myths* was an interesting diversion, but not fact-filled. And the Greek myths were so convoluted, it was hard to see why we still studied them some two thousand years later.

I attempted to stand, my feet prickling as blood returned to my toes. I didn't have many solid facts yet, but I did know Hector Gianopolous lived in the house. His was a name to further research and another story to consider.

ERIS GIANOPOLOUS

Downington Avenue
1944

Adonis wanted to dig up the mutinous rosebush to make way for the Victory Garden. And I almost let him until I realized it would be yet another thing of beauty destroyed by the ugliness of war.

The lawn, however, the lawn I had nursed out of the clay soil, cracked like the desert after a storm, initially so reluctant to hold seed—my lovingly attended carpet of green had been demolished to support the war effort. I was desperate to convince my son, Adonis, we were doing our part, making sacrifices for our troops, and no further effort was required. If an animal sacrifice to the gods, appeasing them with blood on the altar, worked during ancient times, I was willing to sacrifice my lawn so my *most* precious thing wouldn't be snatched away. No meat. Fine. No coffee. Fine. No green grass. Please let the gods know we've done our part.

Calliope crawled along the newly furrowed dirt next to our house, dropping cubes of potato eyes into the trough. She was singing while she worked. She was always singing. The world could come to an end and her throat would be full of song.

Adonis followed his sister, covering the row with a shovel and tamping the dirt with his foot. The muscles in his back rippled as he moved and it was clear he was no longer my little boy. The girls at the high school had been sniffing around for a year, and though it rubbed against my very nature, I encouraged them. If Adonis happened to get one pregnant, his misguided dream of joining the Air Force would be thwarted. Thoughts of a dark-haired grandchild in my arms sustained me. Adonis would look lovingly over my shoulder as I held his child.

Unfortunately, Hector found the Sears catalog dog-eared to the bassinet section. He held it up, staring at my admittedly rotund belly, and asked me if I had anything I wanted to tell him. Three days I didn't speak to my husband for implying I might be pregnant. For Christ's sake, I'd already gone through the change. But Hector was no fool, and he made a point of throwing out the entire catalog, chastising me for attempting to twist the fates.

Calliope stood and rubbed the mud from her knees. I winced knowing she'd likely ruined Adonis's pants that she'd borrowed to work in the garden. Adonis took the empty bucket from her hands and, whistling, rinsed it out with the hose.

"The war will likely be over before we eat a single potato. This will have been an enormous waste of time," I said to them, crossing my fingers behind my back. Pray God the war would be over.

"We can still use the vegetables," Calliope said. She was excited about the tomatoes and eggplant. Things we loved to eat that had been hard to come by for a couple of years now.

"The war won't be over," Adonis said boastfully. "Unless Hitler's felt my bullet."

Calliope threw a wedge of potato at her brother.

"Unless you feel *his* first," I hissed.

"Mama." Adonis huffed, his whistle gone.

Calliope, trying to shift the mood, cleared her voice and put her hand to her mouth, mocking a microphone. "Through sheer will, Mrs. Eris Gianopolous has ended the war. Suddenly overnight, tanks are at rest, Germans and Americans are sharing breakfast of hardtack and a cigarette. How did she do it? Ladies and gentlemen, let's ask her."

Calliope approached me, holding her invisible microphone. I

smacked her hand and turned away, barely containing my tears. "Jesus, Mama, I was just joking around," she said, rubbing her forearm.

I didn't respond. How could I? It was exactly what I was trying to do—end the war. Bargaining with Victory Gardens and dreams of teen pregnancy. I was a tiny stone, helpless as the hours passed over me like waves against the shore, each bringing my son closer to the day he could join up. Two days now. Two days. Time was relentless and punishing. Tossed recklessly by time, most days I couldn't catch my breath.

If you leave, I'll kill you. Oh, God, that defeats the purpose. Hobble, maybe. A limp would keep you home, but not ruin your life. Death would ruin your life. Wait, trigger finger. I could cut off your trigger finger. Or even a toe would make a difference. But I remember when you sucked on that finger. Pointer and middle, soggy in your mouth, playing with blocks using your left hand.

The fingers on my son's right hand curved over his quilt and lay relaxed, thumb barely touching his mouth. His chest rose and fell with the slow, unhurried breathing of deep sleep.

Adonis opened his eyes the width of a thread and stretched his feet, arching them into the quilt. A quarter second later he was sitting upright, the whites of his eyes a bright circle around the dark caramel irises. "Jesus, Mama. I think I had a heart attack. Why are you hovering over me?"

"I was just coming to wake you for your birthday breakfast," I said quickly, startled by his abrupt movement. "Happy eighteenth birthday, Adonis."

"Couldn't you have called from the door, like every other morning? My heart, I swear to God, is hitting my ribs. Even on a birthday, it's not a very nice way to wake up."

He was being gentle with me, I could tell. If I'd done this any other morning he would have told me to get out of his room and slammed the door after me. But I was fragile. And he was preparing to shatter me.

"Eggs and feta?" he said, swinging his legs over the side of his bed.

"Yes."

"Mama?"

"Yes."

"It's a good thing. Most parents are pleased. And I'll be fine. Nothing can stop this mountain of muscle." He was out of bed now, clothed only in cotton pajama bottoms. He pounded twice on his chest.

"It's what every tough guy thinks. But if boys weren't fighting and dying, they wouldn't call it war," I said softly.

After the Japs bombed Pearl Harbor in 1941, I saw my boy had made his decision, from the square of his shoulders to the determination in his jaw. The very next day he was standing taller, trying to look like the man he would chisel out of the boy he was. Puffed up and fifteen years old, he was sure he could save the world, if only given a chance. So damn invincible. Where was the glory in death? I didn't see it. But I had time on my side, back then. Was I worried? Only in a fleeting way. By the time he was eighteen I figured, surely all the soldiers would've killed each other and the war would be over.

As I set the plate of eggs on the table, Adonis walked into the dining room dressed in a new blue button-down shirt tucked crisply into his khaki pants, his belt cinched tight around his waist, the polish of his freshly shined church shoes obscuring the fragrance of toasting bread.

"Thanks, Mama," he replied, his eyes darting from mine as he sat down.

I swallowed. "Dressed already? What are your plans?"

"I have a medical exam." He stared at me now, waiting for my response.

"Are you sick?" I touched his forehead, a weary smile on my face. Like I didn't know.

"No, Mama, I have an appointment at the doctor's office.

The medical exam is the last step," he said softly. "You know this already. We've talked about it a million times."

"Well, I hope the exam includes an IQ test."

The color rose in his cheeks. "Why can't you be proud of me? Bob's parents said they'll buy him a car when he comes home. They're going to reward him for serving his country."

"I guess I'll know who to talk to when I'm looking for a good deal on a new car."

"What? Who?" Adonis asked.

I sighed. "Bob's parents, of course. What's his last name again, so I can look them up after he comes home with the American flag draped across his casket? His parents won't really need his car then."

"You're acting crazy again, Mama. Please . . ." He searched my face, my throat constricting with his familiar gaze. But I couldn't stop.

"No, Adonis. Crazy is running toward a man carrying a gun and asking him to shoot at you."

"I'm leaving now." He walked out the front door and slammed it, as I reached for the knob.

Yanking open the door, a rush of spring air redolent with blossoming trees surrounded me, a cloying sweet scent of new life, just when I knew my son was headed toward a possible death. "Adonis, come back here. At least eat some breakfast! Dad and Calliope are already at the bakery and I made so much. . . ." I called to him through the empty street, desperation resonating in my words.

He turned to face me, contrasting emotions marching across his face. His gait was crisp as he made his way soldier-like across the lawn. Before he stepped onto the sidewalk, he raised his hand to his hairline and back down to his side, his fingers slicing through the morning air like a knife. He saluted me. And I was shattered.

Flipping through cookbooks was usually soothing, and though I had been at it for two hours, by the time he returned my grocery list was a paltry five items. Even my morning cigarette hadn't calmed my nerves. He was slipping through my fingers, intentionally putting himself in harm's way.

He walked through the back door an hour later, arms swinging freely at his sides, a smile on his face. "I'm hungry now, Mama. Are there any eggs left?"

He set a stack of papers on the table, sat next to me, and leaned back in his chair, supporting his head with his hands. Attempting to move them from my line of sight, I shoved the stack to the corner of the table. "Clean bill of health?" I asked, my voice shaking.

"Well, the nurse filled out the forms. Looks swell to me." He patted the paperwork.

"Glad to know we took such good care of your growing body so you can go destroy it." I wanted to wrap him in my arms. I'd stand in front of a damn tank if I had to. Why couldn't I hold him, shelter him?

"I'll miss you too. And now, I'll make my own eggs," he said, strutting into the kitchen.

I pulled the medical forms back toward me with the capped tip of my pen. The nurse had scrawled all of his stats on the official enlistment form—height, weight, vision, blood pressure—all the numbers physically defining my boy. All the numbers indicating he was fit to serve. DOA . . . MIA; those were the letters that would let me know he was no longer fit to serve. Or walk or breathe.

Hector had always had a little trouble with his blood pressure. I glanced at the forms, praying Adonis had inherited this condition. 119/82. Perfect. Damn it.

What to do? I resumed making my shopping list, using the recipes from *Betty Crocker* I had dog-eared. Potatoes, onion, beef. Maybe I could halve the beef and add some extra beans, to make up for the beef ration. I scrawled *canned beans* on the list using my black pen. My black pen.

The medical forms sitting next to my grocery list were meticulously completed with a black felt pen. Butterflies filled my chest. I could hear Adonis in the kitchen, the lard sizzling in the pan. He would crack the eggs any second now. My hand shook as I reached the tip toward the forms. All I needed was one little crooked line. One crooked line to save my boy. And it was worth it.

My pen touched down on the 119. In an instant the number read 149/82. I drew my hand back, viper-like, smacking my coffee cup with my elbow. The heavy mug careened backward and crashed into the window seat on the east wall of the dining room, the dark wood dented and splintered from the impact of the ceramic. The mug broke into several pieces and cold coffee splattered my skirt, drops of milky brew sprinkling the window-panes and pooling on the floor.

Adonis called from the kitchen, "What happened?"

"Jesus Christ. Adonis, will you grab a towel? I spilled my coffee!" I crawled on the wood floor, mopping the legs of the table. The butterflies flew from my chest and out of my fingers as I worked on the mess. Someday he would understand how goddamn lucky he was to have me as his mother. Someday when he was still alive and had a boy of his own. In the meantime, this was my little gift to him, and to me. My husband, Hector, was forever quoting the Greek ancients, and maybe there was a shred of truth to one of his favorites: "The ends justify the means."

LAINEY HARPER

Downington Avenue
1968

The sky in Utah was so blue I ached to float into it, to lose myself in an enormous quilt of oxygen. Gradients of powder at the horizon reached above the treetops into an endless azure so deep I was certain I could see the atmosphere cradle the earth in a gentle embrace. I had forgotten about the desert sky after so many years in New York City. In the city, the horizon ended with the skyscraper on the opposite side of the street. But here, I could see the miles stretch from one mountain range to another.

I had returned to the state of my youth to become Sylvie's mother in more than just title. I was aching to see her, but before I could assume the role I yearned for, there were a few hoops to jump through. And I would willingly jump through all of them in order to have her with me.

Finding my local psychiatrist was one of them. Dr. Yeager had scrawled driving instructions on how to get to his office from the airport on a sheet of yellow legal paper and mailed it to my doctor in Manhattan. I glanced at it lying on the passenger seat and turned the rental car right on 13th East. One of the requirements to receiving custody of Sylvie was to develop a close friendship, complete with weekly visits, with Dr. Yeager, who would monitor my sanity and report to the courts.

I had never been to this part of Salt Lake City, called Sugar

House. I grew up in northern Utah, near the Idaho border. There, the foothills rolled away from town, sun-bleached like gigantic dunes. Barren of green, they were a testament of the absence of rain. But here in the Salt Lake Valley, the granite tipped spires of the Wasatch Range loomed so high the peaks were obscured by distance, swaths of green split the granite, evidence of pine, pinion, altitude, and cold. Hovering tall and imposing, they were of comfort to me. They offered a boundary, something to stop the wind from blowing me away.

This little neighborhood I was driving through seemed long established, each street lined with trees stretching to the heavens, bark gnarled, canopying the asphalt roads with dappled, cool shade, offering relief from the overwhelming openness of the highway. Cozy places, under my bed or the floor of my closet, had always soothed me when the endless sights and sounds of the world were too much. The presence of these protective leafed giants did the same.

Gazing out the window, I wondered how I could capture this scene with paint and a brush. How could I hold this feeling of detached protection so I could gaze at it and find peace when the inevitable darkness crept into the corners of my mind?

It wasn't long before I meandered my way to Dr. Yeager's clinic on the grounds of a local college called Westminster, where he said he taught classes in psychiatry and maintained his practice as a doctor. Normal-looking, sane teenagers filled the sidewalks around the large brick buildings and I felt immense relief that it didn't look anything like the rundown Essex Sanatorium I spent several weeks in, recovering.

Dr. Yeager clasped his hands in his lap as I sat across from him, the gesture identical to every other doctor who had reviewed my case. I refrained from asking him if there was a course in medical school on the soothing hand fold. The lithium helped me to check my words. Not every thought had to be vocalized. It was the mark of a person in control.

He gazed at me over his glasses. He had the best hair a man his age could hope for, steel gray, thick, the slightest wave. His eyes were a piercing blue and as he assessed me, I figured he could probably see into my mind, a jangled mess of flashing lights, huge spots of the darkest black, all coated with a layer of Pepto-Bismol (my lithium, of course)—"coats, soothes, relieves." Thank goodness.

"How do you feel, Lainey? This is a big step for you." Blue lasers boring into my brain.

"I feel solid. Excited. Worried that even if I'm steady, Sylvie won't want me." I bit at my thumbnail. "I am afraid I don't know how to be a mother, not at all. What if I fail her? What if I start to spin and she's scared of me?"

Dr. Yeager nodded. "Seems like a bunch of natural emotions—and natural emotions are the goal here. Remember this advice when things seem difficult; mothers don't become mothers until they give birth. Mother and child learn together. You're stepping into this role a little later, but the rules still apply. Go with your natural instincts and take care of yourself at the same time."

He wrote in his notebook as he spoke. "Here's my recommendation for your treatment. I'm going to keep your lithium where it is, but if you start to feel overwhelmed, I want you to come see me as soon as possible. Some of my patients find it useful to develop an inner dialogue.

"Periodically through the day I want you to ask yourself: *How do you feel, Lainey?* If you feel sad, I want you to ask yourself the same question a couple of hours later, and if you feel worse, contact me. Now, if you ask yourself, *How do you feel, Lainey?* and you feel spectacular, able to conquer the world, and there is no external connection to this sensation . . . meaning you didn't get a promotion or win a race, I want you to monitor yourself. If it lasts, and this is the hard part, you'll also need to contact me."

"I hate never feeling spectacular."

"How long did the spectacular feeling continue during a typical manic episode?" Dr. Yeager used his fingers to frame the word *spectacular* as he spoke it. He readied his pencil over the page, waiting for my response.

"About a week." One spectacular week.

"Followed by?" The doctor didn't look up from his notebook.

"A month of frenzy."

"Did you sleep much during the period of frenzy?"

"No."

"Followed by?"

"A year when I wished I could die."

"Was the week worth it?" He searched my forehead again.

"No, but it makes me sad knowing I'll never have all the answers again. It felt like I could touch the stars."

"Steady wins the race, Lainey. Children need steady. Stay on your medication. Bring Sylvie to your next visit one week from now. Good luck." Dr. Yeager closed his notebook with a snap.

The next step in my treatment plan was to find a place to live near the good doctor, because our visits would be frequent and I wasn't sure I could afford a car. This meant I'd live somewhere in this neighborhood of old homes and tree-lined streets. All of the houses were smallish and many were rundown. Folks who'd lived here had already raised their children and had let their houses fall into disrepair as their age progressed and their health failed them.

I'd seen the same thing happen recently to my own parents. First they didn't fix the broken window on the garage, after that they waited too long to paint the trim around the windows. I knew leaving Sylvie with them took all of their time and energy. And I felt awful. But the last time I visited, the crazy crept in and I had to get away before there was blackness. I'd run back to New York. That was two years ago.

Cruising up one shady street and down another, I wished desperately for a "For Rent" sign. A couple of blocks in, I spotted a hand-painted sign reading, "For Sale—by Owner." I slowed to look at the house.

Red brick, tidy white trim, front porch spanning the width of the house offering cool respite from the glare of the day, cherry tree decorated with fruit, and in the side yard, the most fantastic swing set I'd ever seen. It had steel triangular supports as tall as the roof and three wooden swings with chains so long a little girl's toes could touch the clouds.

As I stopped the car, an old woman rose from a white-painted bench swing on the front porch. She had skin the color of cinnamon and a swirl of white hair piled on top of her head. Soft in the perfect places, I could imagine her embrace.

"Are you lost?" she hollered.

"Some might say that," I whispered to myself. To her I called, "Is this your house? Are you selling it?"

She absently caressed the bricks by the front door with the back of her hand. "It is. Would you like to take a look?" It was clear from her gesture she loved this house, and her affection made me love it too.

She led me through the front door. The inside of the house was dated; bright blue shag carpet, kidney-bean-shaped couch, and a television set in a wood cabinet larger than a refrigerator. "Are you from around here? I noticed the rental-car plates," she said, looking out the window.

"I grew up in northern Utah, but I moved for quite a while. I'll be settling in this neighborhood now. I *should* be looking for something to rent . . . but this place, that swing set. I don't know . . . it just called to me." I couldn't stop my grin. *How do you feel, Lainey?* Excited, but not disproportionately so.

"It's a nice place to raise a family." A smallish man joined us in the living room. "Our kids grew up and left us alone in this house. Grandkids are almost done growing too." He pointed to the wall above the couch. It was covered with framed photos of dark-haired children, pink round cheeks and olive skin, wedding photos and a large photo of a handsome young man in uniform. The photo display continued through the dining room and kitchen. The only variety in wall art were dozens of framed calendar type photos of Greece; white ruins, white houses, winding steps, blue painted doors, and blue sky.

"I'll be living with my daughter now," I said to the old woman as I imagined Sylvie's school photos on the walls of this house. Tears sprang to my eyes and I blinked hard so this nice couple wouldn't think I was nuts. Could Sylvie and I really be a family?

I cleared my throat. "What I really want to see is your swing set! Since my daughter is coming to live with me, I want things to be perfect, you know, really special for her in her new home. I want her to trust me, since this will be the first time . . ." I stopped. I was saying too much.

"Sorry, that was probably too much information. I probably sounded a little crazy." I giggled nervously. "Things have been rough. I'm kind of searching . . ." I studied the ocean blue shag as I spoke.

The man chuckled, a comforting, accepting noise. "We're used to crazy, aren't we, Eris?" He walked to his wife and slipped an arm around her ample waist.

She smiled and leaned into him. "Yes, this house has harbored its fair share and it's still standing. Surely it can handle you."

ERIS GIANOPOLOUS

Downington Avenue
1944

Ancient Greek philosophers weren't always right, it turns out. Two months after I'd scribbled one crooked line, on one little medical record, I was fully aware of *the ends*. Sometimes *the means*, means you get a big fat nothing.

See, through my somewhat devious actions, I hoped I would be spared the loss of my boy. And had I? No, Adonis was in the goddamn Air Force, and I hadn't been spared the loss of my son. Oh, he wasn't dead, not yet. But he shipped out the very day he graduated from high school, right as I had my hands in the dirt, ass in the air, weeding our Victory Garden. I was doing my part. Didn't he understand? Now he'd been gone a month. He was still alive, or so I believed, and on a tiny island somewhere in the Pacific Ocean, at war with the Japs. The Japs, for crying out loud. He wasn't even fighting Hitler.

At first, Adonis was denied enlistment, due to a medical condition. That condition being high blood pressure. I was thrilled, he was distraught. He went back to the quack doctor who reexamined him for free. Puzzled by the difference in the blood pressure readings, the nurse found a carbon of the form she had filled out on Adonis's eighteenth birthday. And Adonis figured out the rest. I denied it. Later, I thought I could reason with my son, appeal to his loyalty to his mother. But apparently, duty to country is stronger than the bond between mother and son. He moved out of the house that night and stayed with Uncle Nico until his papers were processed.

A long month ago, as he sailed out of my life, he hugged me, arms stiff across my shoulders, unmoved by my tears soaking his shoulder. My baby boy. My damn ungrateful son. Who could possibly keep him safe now he was so far from home?

Meanwhile, I remained tethered to this place, frozen by events as they swirled about me, stuck on the home front fighting a battle with my fear, which seemed to manifest itself in anger. As a result, I was seething as I stepped through my front door into my living room. I'd visited the open house of a new tract home built right across the street from my home. Go have a nice afternoon, Hector had told me. Go across the street and see where our new neighbors will live, he urged. So I did.

Apparently, even the president of the United States thought the war was nearly done, because there was a construction boom in our neighborhood. It seemed every empty lot was heaped with bricks and lumber, as here and there soldiers returned from the front, buying houses using GI money and scooping up little brides. And where was Adonis?

The two brand-new places right across from mine sparkled in modern freshness—kitchen counters made of gleaming yellow Formica, walls papered with rooster wallpaper. And each contained an electric refrigerator! Most importantly, each would have a service man moving in, just as I'd sent mine off. Gazing at all I didn't have, envy raised her head, a writhing serpent in my chest.

My house was a dismal old-fashioned mess. It had crouched on this street, doing nothing but rotting, for thirty years. The walls, and even the ceilings, were blanketed with floral wallpaper in tones of taupe and blue. We'd hung the wallpaper when we moved in, but now it seemed unbearably fussy. The living room and dining room floors were wood, dark-stained and cracked, the window seat was oak, cushion still stained from the coffee I had let fly months earlier—a testament to the mess I had made with Adonis and all of that blood pressure foolishness. I could scarcely bear to look at the pockmarks peppering the front of it.

There was a coiling in my gut. If only I could fix something, set order to this mixed-up world. There were so many things I couldn't change. I had a list, as long as my arm, of things I couldn't mend: Of course, Adonis. There was also the size of my ass. Plus, we only had meat once a week, which I suspected was horse or dog. Finally, I didn't have a single modern appliance, save the radio. Even my Uncle Nico bought his wife a new refrigerator last year.

Perhaps a little overhaul was in order. A little project to soothe the serpent. My fingers twitched with anticipation as I dashed outside to retrieve the sledgehammer. Back inside, I weighed the metal in my hand, warming it with my nervous fingers, looking around for something to destroy. Finally, I lifted the iron mallet over my head, *goddamn war,* and brought it down on the window seat. The hardwood splintered and popped, destroying evidence of the rift between me and Adonis.

Change was coming.

Frank Sinatra's voice filled the dining room as I worked. Oh, God, that man could sing. I hoped there wouldn't be another war update to smother my reverie. The less I thought about it, the better I felt, and it wasn't long before the window seat was a pile of debris.

Though unwanted, my thoughts inevitably drifted to Adonis. More houses than I could count had gold stars in their windows. Gold stars numbering in the thousands across the country, signifying all of the fallen sons. Boys were dying and their weeping mothers changed their proud navy stars to gold. The misguided patriotic pride smacked me the wrong way. I refused to hang a star. I didn't want Adonis over there in the first place. I wasn't proud or patriotic. Why couldn't Ares, that angry god of war, simply look past my child?

Work once again made the hours fly. School was out before I knew it, and Calliope wandered into the kitchen with her friend Janet, a blond girl with hips as wide as my palm. "I love Frank Sinatra too," Calliope yelled. "But how can you think with the music so loud?" Janet giggled and Calliope harmonized with Sinatra while she sliced apples for a snack.

Calliope wandered into the dining room, an apple in her hand. She gasped as she discovered the mounds of debris. "Mama, what in God's name?"

"I'm modernizing this old place," I said quickly.

"Dad's going to know you're *modernizing* because you're worried about Adonis," she said, using her fingers to circle the word. "You always tear something down when you're distraught."

"That's not true. I'm simply making things nice for this family." I turned away from her as I spoke, so she couldn't see the truth. "First I'm going to get rid of the window seat."

"Yes, I can see."

"Then I'm going to paint right over the old wallpaper, no matter how many coats it takes. That will brighten up the place! There won't be a lick of stained wood in the whole house, because after I paint, I'm looking into new carpeting and maybe a refrigerator."

"You sound like an advertisement on the radio," Calliope said, her mouth curling into a fatigued smile.

I slumped onto a dining room chair, suddenly exhausted by my angst-filled burst of home improvement. "Hector's going to throw a fit, isn't he?"

Calliope stood beside me and put her hand on my shoulder. She shooed Janet, who quickly left the room. "Dad usually comes around. But Jesus, Mama, you've really made a mess this time."

"It's just—"

"Adonis, right?" Her voice was flat.

"Without him this home is nothing. This family is absolutely nothing."

Calliope stopped touching me. I heard her swallow a sob as she walked out of the room. "I'm still here. And so is Dad," she said from the doorway to the kitchen. "Are you really saying we're . . . nothing?"

As the rumbling Granite Furniture delivery truck pulled in front of the house I felt a little prick of delight. I clapped my hands together a couple of times and, realizing what I had done, let my hands fall to my sides and frowned. This was simply the final step in my not-so-little modernizing project, no need to do a backflip, for Christ's sake.

"Are you excited, Eris?" Hector smiled knowingly. Oh, he had come around. In the past two months while I destroyed, and gradually rebuilt the inside of our home, he'd borrowed money from Uncle Nico to purchase wool carpeting for the whole house and a new refrigerator, knowing this project to soothe my beast would help him too. The busier I was, the less I fretted about our son. Two weeks of quiet contemplation while painting gave me a moment to realize exactly what Hector was doing. I loved him for it. And I hated him for it too.

"It's about damn time they got here." I didn't want to appear giddy. "We'd better check the carpet before they haul it in. I told you the girl placing my order was an idiot."

Hector kept smiling. He acted like he was giving me a gift. But I had earned it. I had earned every square inch of it by scraping and sanding and painting. Every day I worked my fingers into blisters, while Hector escaped to the bakery to cook up sweet pastries for the fat ladies in town.

Two burly boys dragged a roll of carpet out of the back of the truck, and, holding the ends, made their way onto the porch. I stopped them at the door. "Hold it!" I said, maybe a little too loudly. "I need to see if you have the order right."

"It would be easier if we could set it down inside. We'll need to cut the strap so you can see the color," one boy said, shifting his load so it rested against his hip.

"No. Cut it right there on the porch. I won't take possession until I inspect the product."

The men groaned and shifted the heavy roll between them. "Just let them in, Eris," Hector said.

I scowled at Hector and backed away from the door. "Fine. If things are shipshape, there'll be no trouble." Hector put a comforting hand on my arm and I flicked him away. This purchase was a lot of money. I needed my wits about me.

The men set the heavy roll in the living room and cut the strap. The edge of the carpet flopped open and there it was. Blue the color of the Aegean Sea, and it was soft too. I ran my hand over the shag. The thought of it under my bare toes thrilled me.

"Looks fine, boys," I said. "Go ahead and get it laid. But I have a question before you start."

"Yes, ma'am?"

"You two look like strong boys. Aren't you fighting age?"

I thought of Adonis, throwing himself in harm's way, and my throat tightened. Yet these able-bodied boys were standing in my living room, safe in the United States, honoring their country by earning a decent wage laying carpet. I pictured Adonis in an ill-fitting tool belt. Not so dashing as his Air Force cap, but if he was standing here in my living room, I'd know he was alive.

The blond boy straightened up, looking proud. "Just enlisted, ma'am. I graduated early, been waiting to turn eighteen. I can hardly wait to get over there and have my shot at Hitler!"

"Medical deferment." The second boy hung his head.

"What's wrong? Blood pressure?" I pressed my index finger to the bridge of my nose to stop the pounding.

"I'm diabetic." The boy looked ashamed, knowing his body had betrayed him.

"So only the strong, healthy boys are sent over to be killed? The rest of the weak, sick and injured are left here to do the work on the home front?"

The diabetic's jaw dropped.

"Eris. Enough," Hector hissed. I *had* probably gone too far.

Hector quieted me by talking loudly. "Sorry, boys, we have a son in the Pacific, my wife here is still trying to accept it. War's pretty hard on a mother, you see."

Both the boys nodded, but the diabetic boy didn't raise his eyes from the carpet he'd been carrying. Hector dragged me into the kitchen. "Jesus Christ, Eris. You need to relax."

"I was simply asking a question. I wondered how two able-bodied men managed to avoid this damn war. And you know I get nervous when we spend a lot of money."

"This carpet was your idea, remember." Hector was losing his patience.

"I earned it." I was pleading for absolution now.

Hector made for the back door. He was going back to manage our place, Hellas Bakery and Market, and I was to supervise the carpet installation by myself. I wished he would stay. "Remember, Eris, before you talk with those boys again, 'Wise men speak because they have something to say, fools because they have to say something.' "

Knowing I shouldn't open my mouth again, I glared silently. I hated his never-ending supply of quotes, and he knew it. Stupid canned wisdom.

"So, uh, I guess we'll get going, Mrs. Gianopolous." I jumped at the boy's voice, embarrassed at my outburst.

"Fine. I'll be in the yard," I called as Hector returned my glare and made his way to the car.

The October air was like ice. It had been an especially cold autumn. I inhaled deeply to clear my head. The cherry had already dropped its leaves, barren branches clawing the blue sky. The Victory Garden was mounded with decaying, frozen lumps of leaf rot, and the whole yard could use a good raking. Even the big old rosebush was barren and twiggy. Just the drab muddiness I had been trying to empty from my life. I wanted to go back inside and rub my feet on the soft ocean blue shag, but I'd probably say something offensive to those boys.

I dragged the rake repeatedly across the frozen ground until my back ached from the effort. The unruly wind was picking up and defying me, leaves twirling from the numerous piles I'd gathered.

The diabetic boy stuck his head out the back door. "Ma'am? We're going to take a lunch break. Then we'll finish up. If you could come in and sign for the carpet now, we won't have to worry about it later." I figured they wanted me to run errands so I'd leave them alone, the grumpy Greek lady on Downington Avenue.

Inside, the blond boy was writing the receipt. I wandered into the dining room, poking at the finish around the baseboards with my toe. I peeked at the receipt, making sure he had the price right. He did, but the dolt was spelling my name wrong.

"It's spelled G-I-A-N-O-P-O-L-O-U-S," I said, pointing at the receipt. "It's a Greek name, with much history."

The boy nodded and ripped the page to start fresh. He let the old receipt drift to the floor. "Okay, Mrs. Gianopolous," he said with forced kindness. "Take a look and see if everything looks swell. Sign while we're gone and we'll finish the install."

Locking the front door after the boys, I took off my shoes. The fibers of the carpet tickled the arches of my feet. I tiptoed the length of the living room and skipped a full circle around the dining room. Finally, dropping to my knees, I inspected their handiwork.

There was a timid knock. A lanky silhouette was visible through the etched glass in the door. I growled softly to myself, "Go away." But whoever was there didn't budge. Reluctantly, I stood, slipped my shoes back on my feet, and unlatched the door. The man standing on my porch was skinny, knobby elbows and knees. He also looked to be fighting age.

"Can I help you?"

"Well, I'm your new neighbor. From across the street." He waited for my acknowledgment and, receiving none, he continued. "I saw you were getting some carpet installed. Thought I'd check on the progress."

"You're from across the street?" I'd seen a moving truck earlier in the week. I tried to forget the gleaming yellow countertops that now belonged to this gangly young man.

"Yes, ma'am. Name's George Pearson. My wife, Louise, is home now. We have a newborn that's keeping her up most hours, so she's napping." He smiled. "Say, that's sure pretty carpet."

I smiled, unable to help myself. "It is, isn't it?" I touched an edge with my toe, eager to get back to my inspection. I didn't want to encourage a lengthy conversation.

Without my words to further him, George said, "So, I guess I'll run. I'm on the train to north Pocatello tonight. If you need anything, you tell me or Louise. Nice to meet you, neighbor."

George lit a cigarette as he walked from my porch. He was a nice guy *and* he was a smoker. A guy like George might be a decent addition to the neighborhood. My bare feet on the new carpet felt like taking the first step into a cool pool on a summer afternoon. I smiled to myself. Turns out it *was* a good day.

LAINEY HARPER

❧

Downington Avenue
1968

"Elaine, are you having another episode? Your voice has that high-pitched twang it gets when you start to lose it." My mother sounded worried on the other end of the phone.

"Could the two of you meet me at the house? It's only blocks from the doctor's office. It has this fantastic swing set and a huge front porch," I was pleading, but I wasn't crazed. The house felt right.

"How will you afford it?"

"I sent money for Sylvie while I was working. Didn't you say you had put some of it aside? Maybe enough for a down payment? And I'll get a job here."

"We were saving the money as a nest egg. Something for a fresh start," my mom replied.

"That's what this is, Mom, my fresh start, don't you see? A house will anchor me. It will be something solid for Sylvie."

"It sounds like a lot of work and you're still fragile. Don't bite off more than you can chew. You know you don't have many more chances. Not with Sylvie, not with the courts, not with us. It's not healthy for her to live with uncertainty."

I nodded into the phone. If I was going to do this, I needed to get it right.

*   *   *

Sylvie clung to my waist, looking longingly at the swing set as I talked to my parents. We'd gathered in the backyard, seeking shade under the large cherry tree while we debated the merits of house ownership given my tenuous mental state.

"Do you want to swing?" I asked Sylvie, smoothing my hand down her blond braid.

She nodded.

"You should go! I'll stay here with Grandma and Grandpa," I said, and gave her a kiss on her head.

She threw herself on one of the wooden seats, pushed off from the ground and pumped her skinny legs with all her might. My parents and I watched her wordlessly. The hole punched in my chest was closing with every arc.

I kept expecting the old couple who owned the house to join us in the yard, but there was no movement from indoors. Minutes later, a lanky middle-aged man sauntered across the street. He dangled a key in his hand. "Eris said to let you in. One of their grandkids had a birthday party. I'm George Pearson, I live across the street, 'long with the wife and a couple of kids."

A short woman with a dandelion puff of hair walked over and stood next to George. She put her hands on her hips and smiled. "I'm Louise, the wife."

Louise inspected me from head to toe. I was used to people scrutinizing my looks, but I felt my face flush under her gaze. "Eris said you were one of those modeling types, thin-limbed. All elbows, knees, and lashes," Louise said.

I swallowed. "I did some modeling up until a couple of years ago. It's why I moved from Utah," I mumbled. I hated talking about my time in front of the cameras.

"My daughter, Patsy, will die when she hears you were a model! She can't keep her nose out of those fashion magazines. She'd love to be a model herself, but she was blessed with her mother's height." At her comment, though she spoke her mind, I knew Louise was on my side.

"It's not really a healthy career anyhow. It breaks anyone who is fragile," I replied.

"All the same, she'd kill to have legs as long as yours." Louise pointed toward Sylvie, who was swinging so high the chains popped at the top of each arc. "Your daughter got your legs. She can really put that swing through its paces."

"She likes it, don't you think, Mom?" I said, and smiled widely at my mother.

She groaned. "Elaine, it's a lovely house, but I think the obligation is too much for you right now. . . ."

"I disagree," my dad said, joining the conversation. "I think this might be the right move for Elaine. The house will keep her here, it will require hard work, and if she leaves again, we can sell it and keep the money for Sylvie." His voice was light, but I knew he was serious. I had this one chance to prove my stability to myself, to my parents, and to Sylvie.

"If it means anything, we'll be staying put for a while," George said. "We've got a nice little neighborhood here. We look out for each other." Louise nodded in agreement.

Sylvie got off the swing. She stood on her toes and wrapped her arms around my waist again. As I put my hands on her shoulders I sensed her tender bones under her skin, fragile. My baby, my daughter, my responsibility. *How do you feel, Lainey?* I asked myself. I took a deep breath. I felt a whisper of hope.

The hours of mid-morning had been spent in the backyard watching Sylvie race through the sprinklers. Relaxed, I slipped my sunglasses on and raised my face to the sun, hoping for a coveted sea-and-ski tan. I must have slept, because when the phone rang, I saw Sylvie was now playing on the swing set, a red blush on her shoulders.

"Put your jumpsuit on if you're done in the water," I called. "It looks like you're starting to burn."

Sylvie leaped off the swing and ran toward her towel and discarded clothing as I dashed into the house.

The next thing I heard was screaming.

The phone clattered to the floor as I ran into the yard. Sylvie had collapsed and was writhing and clawing at her chest. I picked her up and she continued to scream, tears blurring her cheeks, her face purple with exertion.

"Sylvie! What happened? Oh, God." I tried to get her to look at me, but her eyes were slits. "Please, Sylvie!" Her back arched in my arms as she slapped at her own body.

"What? What is it? I don't know how to help you!" I called, my tears joining hers.

Finally she drew in a long shuddering breath, grabbing for the zipper on her jumper, and yelled, "BEE!"

"Bee? Did you say *bee?*"

She nodded and grasped the zipper. I yanked it down and a wasp the size of my small finger flew from the opening. I knocked it to the ground with the back of my hand and stepped on it with my bare heel. Sylvie was covered with a dozen anthills of swollen skin.

I picked her up and ran into the house. "What do I do? Oh, God. Are you allergic to bees?" I asked her. Like she would know. I should know! I was her mother!

Her cries slowed, and I checked her breathing. She seemed to be drawing breath, but she was still moaning. The disconnected phone was buzzing from disuse. Still holding her, I ran to it, clicked several times to hang up and dialed my mom.

By the time she answered I was nearly as hysterical as Sylvie had been minutes earlier. "Mom, Sylvie's been stung!"

"Elaine! I can't understand you. Are you spinning?"

"Not me. Sylvie! She's been stung by something and I don't know what to do!" I cried into the phone.

"Deep breath, Elaine. You can do this. Does it seem like her breathing is labored? Are her lips bluish?"

I put my hand on her narrow chest and rested my fingertips against her steady heartbeat. She was breathing deeply, drawing extra breath for each cry. Her skin was ruddy.

"No. I think she can breathe. Can you breathe, Sylvie?"

Sylvie didn't respond.

"Do I take her to the hospital? Do I call an ambulance? I don't know what I'm doing!"

"I don't think so, if she seems to be breathing. You can soothe her and monitor her recovery, because you are the only one with her right now. Focus so you can help her."

"Okay. Okay."

"What did you do when your pup, Molly, ran into the electric fence?"

"What does that have to do with . . . ?"

My mother responded calmly. "Everything. What did you do?"

"I held her."

"Hold Sylvie. Watch her breathing. Put a cold cloth on her bites and hold her."

I hung up and shifted Sylvie so her head lay across my lap, her legs stretched across the sofa. I smoothed her hair away from her forehead and caressed her cheeks, drying her tears.

"You're going to be fine, honey," I said. "But that wasp got you good."

Tears started fresh. "It was so mean. It wouldn't stop stinging," she sniffed.

"Yes, it was."

"You got it though, didn't you? You killed it so it couldn't sting me again."

I blinked, trying to remember what I had done to the wasp. I was acting on instinct, I hardly remembered crushing it. "I guess I did."

"Thank you," she said, curling up in my lap. I stroked her hair until she fell asleep. I held her while she slept, monitoring her breathing. I was holding my daughter. I had managed to soothe her pain. Maybe, just maybe, I could do this.

One month after we moved in, the bell rang at Garfield Elementary and Sylvie started first grade. Without her omnipresent chatter, the house was eerie in its silence. Adrift, I walked from room to room, unsure of my new spot in this old house.

Yet, there was the porch swing, so hopeful someone would sit to enjoy the evening breeze, and there was the swing set already proven its weight in gold, and finally the cherry tree that fed us during the long days of July while I moved my meager belongings into our new quarters. The house felt like a favorite shirt, worn, out of style, and beloved. Maybe it was Sylvie, but more than any other place I had lived, it felt like my home.

Now I must pay for it. I needed an income.

As I pondered my plight, I grabbed my kitchen scissors and tried to snip the random stains from the worn aquamarine carpeting that rolled like a littered ocean over my living room and dining room. After trimming a radius of about four feet, I gasped. What had I done? The carpet was now a mangy blue, the various lengths of fibers making it look worse than before.

Taking a deep breath, I closed the scissors, stabbed the sharp end into the carpet pad, and yanked. A couple more stabs and a couple more tugs and the ugly sea of carpeting lost its grip on the tack strip at the edge of the dining room. *How do you feel, Lainey?* Determined. And that was a good thing, right? Before long, I had moved my Formica dining table onto the front porch and had pulled the rug from the entire dining room.

As I worked, one thought kept repeating itself in my head: "The path will be revealed." I chanted the mantra out loud, mostly to keep the silence of the house from invading my sense of purpose. "Goddess of Shag, hear my plea. Reveal my path. How will I make the payments on this house?"

As I yanked at the carpeting, I was thrilled to find the wood floors under the rug were in good condition. The old Greek lady must have waxed and buffed them weekly until she finally covered them. But the best discovery, by far, was a sales receipt for the original carpet installation, lost for decades between the oak floor and the disintegrating carpet pad. It was handwritten on Granite Furniture letterhead, dated October 12, 1944. The receipt was made out to Eris Geeannopolis, the last name crossed out and the receipt never completed. Let's see, right now it was 1968. So the rug was nearly twenty-five years old! No wonder it was in such bad shape.

Back aching, I dragged the first roll of spent carpeting out the front door. George Pearson was sitting on my porch swing. "You looking for something special under that old carpet?" I jumped at his voice. Maybe George heard me chanting to the Goddess of Shag.

"It's funny you should ask. You see, I was hoping I would

find some buried treasure to help me pay the mortgage. But all I found was an old receipt. Wanna see it?"

I rushed into the living room and snatched the carpet installation receipt from the dusty floor. He took it in his hand and gently rubbed his finger over the date. "Oh my, I remember the day Eris had this carpet installed. It was right about the time Louise and I moved in 'cross the street. I was, let's see, twenty-four years old. Bradley was only 'bout six months or so. Oh Eris, she was really something! She'd scarcely finish one project when she'd be off on another. Nervous energy, Louise always said. But I think Louise was just jealous. Eris could outwork the whole street." He chuckled. "'Course she kept her family plenty busy. We'd hear her hollering all day long."

I pictured the soft Greek lady with the warm smile. I couldn't believe the woman with the brown-eyed grandchildren would yell at anyone.

"I do have an idea that might help you earn a little money," George said. Then, as if blindsided by a memory, he stopped talking. His eyes were fixed on his own home across the street, almost like he was trying to recapture the year he moved in. He was picturing his home freshly built, his wife a young woman with a baby on her hip. He was pondering 1944.

IVY BAYGREN

Naomi had filled Adam's closet the day I'd moved his sentimental clothing to the garage. Clothing for a teenage girl isn't so
much about sentiment as abundance. She still needed a new
dresser, or so she claimed, so we made another trip to Target in
search of a chest of drawers that would fit into the cramped corner of her room, one within our budget, and had come up
empty-handed. However, I'd bought her a sweater and a pair of
boots that made her look like a cute construction foreman, further compounding the space issue.

We were driving in the minivan. Naomi was messing with the
radio, and I was reveling in being next to her, snug in our co-
cooned companionship, pillowed by the soft rumble of street
noise. It was perfect for a relationship that seemed to slip like
water through a clenched fist if I held too tightly. It was as it
should be as she became more independent. But for this moment
I was pleased to have her belted next to me, mine alone.

She squealed, breaking my reverie. "Look over there!" Naomi
was pointing out the window, her gestures more dramatic than
would warrant in this situation.

"Let me pull myself from the roof," I said, squinting out the
window in the direction she indicated. It appeared she was ges-
turing toward a handwritten poster board nailed to a telephone
pole. It read "Estate Sale—Friday, Saturday, and Sunday." Beyond the sign was a small white-shingled house. Long tables ran
the length of the patchy lawn, like rows in a plastic garden, cov-

ered in colorful mounds of bric-a-brac. Scattered among the tables were a couple of dated armchairs, several large lamps, and a dresser. "Is that what you're pointing at? The dresser?"

She nodded. "Just pull over and we can take a look."

I pulled into the parking lot of a Kentucky Fried Chicken and flipped around—anything to continue our afternoon together. If Naomi wanted to go to a garage sale, I wanted to as well.

In front of the house, Naomi pulled the visor down and tugged her lip gloss out of her pocket. She smacked her freshly coated lips in the mirror, hopped out of the van, and walked eagerly toward a table laden with old vases. I wandered behind her, befuddled. And then I saw him.

He had his back turned to us, writing prices on a roll of stickers and sloppily attaching them to items on a table stacked with Christmas ornaments. He had long, dark hair, messy in a badboy way Naomi and her friends seemed to appreciate. A sleeve tattoo adorned his right arm. He could be no more than eighteen. At our approach he turned around. "Hey, let me know if you need prices on anything." I pursed my lips as he scanned Naomi, her legs long in her jeans, her print T-shirt tighter than I approved of.

But before Naomi could speak, his phone rang. He slipped his hand into his front pocket, and mouthed, "One second."

I hung close to Naomi, who was absently picking up vases, plastic flowers, and ceramic salt and pepper shakers. Clearly she was eavesdropping on his telephone conversation, so I did the same. I silently held a pearl necklace to my throat and Naomi gave me a thumbs-up, her eyes lingering on the boy.

I wandered to another table stacked with books—a set of encyclopedias from 1974, a collection of *National Geographic* magazines from 1960 to the mid-1990s, and perhaps twenty old phone books—inches thick with wrinkled yellow pages. I glanced at my tiny iPhone in relation to this mass of printed information. The irrelevance of the telephone book was certainly a testament to changing times.

When I was a child, my mom made the latest version of the yellow pages my booster seat at the dining table until I was able to properly reach my plate—practical and functional. I wondered if these relics had been used in similar fashion, boosting a generation of bottoms.

Stacked between dozens of somewhat empty three-ring binders was a black plastic photo album, one of those with gold embossing and thick plastic slots for square photos. I pulled it out and opened it. Who would sell a photo album? Perhaps the boy with the tattoo had no sentimentality. I glared at his back.

"Cremated," I heard him say into his phone. "Around their house and yard, but I don't know why. My grandparents' place is wedged between a KFC and a gas station, though it used to be surrounded by fields, my grandma used to say. It's surrounded by strip malls now. It'll be torn down within the month." He paused and put a price sticker on a ceramic angel. "Sounds cool . . . but later tonight. I have to put all this shit back in the house before I can leave."

I intentionally tuned him out. "All this shit" meant something to his grandparents, a treasure of things collected lovingly and fruitlessly through a lifetime. What endures if not the physical manifestations of a life? I thought, melancholy washing over me at his shallow words. The things we buy? The things we build? I couldn't think about it. I wouldn't think about Adam.

The first page of the album contained images of an outdoor wedding, black-and-white photos of a fuzzy bride and groom standing in front of an unattached brick garage that looked much like ours. I flipped to the next page, the groom dipping his rather large bride in front of a rosebush climbing up the back corner of a brick house, which—

"Naomi, come here!"

Naomi blushed, embarrassed her mother was beckoning her, and walked begrudgingly over. "What?"

"Look at this house, count the windows, see the tiny panes at the top? And what about this rosebush?"

Naomi squinted and turned the page, revealing more photographs of the home displayed as a backdrop to the celebration. "It looks like ours, but where's the swing set?"

"I don't know, but oh my God, I'm buying this. What if this

is really our house?" My hands were shaking as I quickly turned the pages.

The boy hung up and sauntered over. "How much is this?" I asked with forced casualness.

"I don't—" He took the album out of my hands and opened it. "How did this get here?" He turned a page or two and I wanted to snatch the book from his hands and run to the car. "These photos don't even belong to these grandparents, this house belonged to my mom's parents, and"—he turned a few more pages— "I think this belongs to my *dad's* mom. Oh my God, I think this is my grandmother's wedding. I can't sell this. Sorry." With a sidelong glance he walked toward the front porch to put the album with his own things.

"Wait," I said. "I think the house in that book is where I live now. Do you know the address of the home?"

"Nah, it belonged to my great-grandparents, they died before I was born. Even still, I'm sure my dad still won't want me to sell the album."

"What if I take it for a couple of minutes and make copies of the photos? I'll bring it right back."

"Mom," Naomi gasped. She was turning the hot red of a mortified teenager. "You're being super creepy. It's a *family* album."

The boy continued his retreat.

"What if we stand here and look through it really quickly?"

Another browser wandered over with an item in his hands, looking for a price. "Sure, I guess," the boy said. "You can sit on the porch while I help this customer." He was definitely wary. We'd have to be fast.

"Naomi," I hissed as he turned away from us. "Take out your phone. We're going to take as many photos of this album as we can before he notices."

Her jaw dropped, even as she did as I said. "I can't believe I'm helping you. You're crazy."

"This is research. It's about our house. This is the gold mine I couldn't find at the Historical Society," I opened to the first page, and she took an individual photo of each image.

"It's probably not even our place. I don't know if you've noticed, but every street has half a dozen houses that look just like ours."

"I'll fully inspect the photos later." I flipped to the next page. "Keep snapping."

We made it through five plastic sheets, or about twenty photos, before the boy made his way back to us. Naomi quickly slid her phone in her pocket. "Was there anything else you were interested in?" he asked, letting us know our time with the album was complete.

I pulled a scrap of paper from my purse and wrote all of my contact information on it. "I'm Ivy Baygren and if you'd give this to your dad, I'd love to talk to him. I've been doing some research on my house and any information—"

He tucked it into the pages of the album. "Sure."

"One more thing, if you don't mind?"

The boy stepped away from me. I was pushing my luck. "What's your last name? It was your dad's mom, right? Let me think, she would be your—"

"My last name is Cresconi, but my grandma was proud of her Greek heritage. Her maiden name was Gianopolous."

I flicked my eyes to Naomi, who at some point must have listened to my musings about the shreds of information I'd found at the Historical Society. Gianopolous. She grinned, knowing what I knew.

"Could I call your dad?" I hollered over my shoulder as Naomi guided me toward the car. "Would you give me his number?"

His lip curled in a snicker. "Don't worry, ma'am. I'll be sure to let him know he should give you a call."

The neighbors were likely annoyed I'd let mounds of golden leaves from the ash trees at the front of the house swirl from my unkempt yard into their neatly raked ones. They were probably keen to my secret; let the leaves rake themselves using the power of the wind. The air whipped through my hair, twisting my ponytail in knots. I faced the gust, letting it steal my breath for a moment or two before I began. Unceasingly tenacious, these trees produced pounds of leaves every year. And every year we cleaned them up. This was life, I supposed. Rake and repeat. However, this year I was the only one holding a rake.

When the kids were younger, Adam and I would heap the colorful piles near the swing set, all raking done on a brisk weekend afternoon, so Porter and Naomi could launch themselves into a golden autumn cushion. But today the creation of a chlorophyll summer would be tucked industriously and unceremoniously into dozens of black plastic bags, because the kids were too old to catapult into a pile of semi-crunchy leaves.

As I worked in the front yard, a long russet-colored Buick glided by the front of our house. The car was identical to the one our neighbor George Pearson used to drive. I waved out of habit, dropping my hand quickly as I remembered George had been dead for years. It certainly wasn't him. I kept stuffing the leaves, ignoring the car because I would not engage another stranger. Just the other day at Emigration Market I waved and called out to a woman I thought was the mother of Naomi's friend, Amber. Naomi was shopping with me and was so mortified she sat in the car while I finished up. Even worse, I landed in line behind the familiar-looking stranger, who didn't seem to think my mistake was very funny. Not making the same mistake again.

However, seconds later the Buick coasted by again, going the opposite direction. Looking up from the bag I was stuffing, I tugged my baseball hat farther over my head, wishing I had washed my hair. Maybe it *was* someone I knew. I smiled absently over my shoulder, not making direct eye contact, but letting them know I was aware they were trolling my neighborhood.

As if encouraged by my grin, the car came to a jerky stop. Nowhere near the curb, the back end of the Buick angled into the middle of the street, but undaunted, the driver turned off the car and opened the door. The woman who emerged looked like one of those old folks on the *Today* show who had amazingly made it to one hundred years. Willard Scott always announced how they still attended church every week and how they loved to spend time with their seventy-five great grandchildren. She was one of those.

I took off my work gloves and dropped them onto the pile of leaves. Resting my hands on my hips, I anticipated our encounter. The driver was so tiny it seemed a child might have stolen the car for a joy ride. But as she rounded the hood, holding on to the ornament with one hand for support, it was clear this was no child. And she was no one I knew, either.

Now resting her hand on the ash tree, her emerald green sweater hung so loosely about her bony shoulders it appeared she'd tucked a hanger under the cable-knit. Her white hair was pulled up in a bun, several strands escaping to frame her creased face. I couldn't believe they actually let this woman drive a car. I glanced at the Buick, intent on memorizing the license plate so I could call Driver Services or someone who could confiscate her keys.

I smiled warily. "Hi there. Are you looking for someone?"

"Oh, I'm on a drive down memory lane." Her voice was clear, not like the tremulous tones of the aged.

"Well, this is Downington Avenue." I spoke loudly, letting her know she was probably lost.

"I know, dear." She gazed at the house. "I only stopped because you seem like you could use a break from the raking."

"It *is* a lot of work. . . ." I let my words trail off and reached toward the rake lying abandoned on the ground, hopeful she'd understand I should probably get back to it.

"I've seen you in the yard, always busy with something, shoveling, mowing, or raking." She smiled in a nonthreatening way. "You or that husband of yours."

I gasped. "Do I know you?" Silently I reminded myself there was nothing to be nervous about. I could bench-press this old lady. Physically, she was no threat to me, but she was creeping me out.

"No, no. I like to drive by the house from time to time . . . used to drive by every time I came back to Utah to visit family. Now my husband's passed, I live here with my oldest daughter. These days I swing by when it's on my way."

"You drive by *my* house?" I glanced over my shoulder, gazing at the front porch and swing.

"Well, she's mine too." The lady smiled, like she was teasing me.

My mouth dropped open. "Did you live here? In this house? How long ago?" I barely resisted the urge to tell her I'd been looking for evidence of her in the walls of my home.

"I was just a girl, maybe ten years old when I moved away, but it took years before I lived in another place I could call *my* home. Not until I met my husband. So this old place holds a special place in my heart." She took her hand from the trunk of the ash tree and placed it on her chest. Without the support of the tree she swayed alarmingly, and I grabbed her elbow to steady her.

"Would you like to come in? I could show you around."

"I thought you'd never ask." Without pause, she linked my elbow with her own.

Her arm felt brittle through her sweater, but her stride was strong as we made our way up the steps onto the porch and through the front door of my home. Our home?

"Tell me what you remember, tell me what's different. I always wondered about who must have lived here—what the house might have looked like before. I've been remodeling a little, and investigating," I said in a rush.

She nodded. "Well, for one thing these ash trees by the sidewalk are bigger." She glanced to the right. "And by the looks of it, you have the same porch swing we had when I was a girl."

"The same swing . . ." I said reverently. I'd always loved that swing.

Once inside, her gait became almost girlish. She walked directly to Naomi's room. At the door, she hesitated. "I wonder if it's still there? If you don't mind?" she asked.

I nodded. I wasn't sure what she was up to, what secret about the house she might possibly reveal. She opened the closet door and grazed her fingertips over the painted surface. What in the world?

"There it is, or at least I think that's it. Touch your finger right there. See if you can feel an indentation."

I pressed my fingers against the wood lightly. There was something there, but it wasn't remarkable. Every door in the house had layers and layers of finish and varnish that had chipped through the years and been touched up. The inset panel I was touching was covered so thickly with white paint the beveled trim was barely discernible.

"There are some odd bumps, I think. Adam always talked about stripping these doors, to get down to the oak, but remodeling isn't as much fun without him," I mumbled.

"Is Adam your husband?" she asked.

"Was," I said, looking away. "Never mind. What should I find here?" I asked quickly. I didn't want to talk about Adam with a stranger, even if she had lived in my home.

She smiled so widely, individual facial features were lost in the wrinkles surrounding them. "I did that," she said. "My initials—EDR. I carved them the day I moved. This is, or was, my room."

I was picking at the paint surrounding the old woman's carved initials while she sat precariously on the edge of Naomi's bed. We were set for a revealing historical chat when Porter burst into the house followed by five other boys, reminding me that it was my turn to drive them to lacrosse practice. The old woman told me her name was Bitsy and she would visit again soon. I helped her to her car and waved at her as I backed down the driveway with a van full of boys dressed in blue jerseys. I hadn't managed to get her telephone number, or even her last name, as I instructed Porter to remember his stick and water bottle.

And two weeks later she hadn't returned. I knocked superstitiously on my wood table, considering Bitsy could have died between the date of our visit and today. Impossible, I attempted to reassure myself, not when she was so close to revealing a chapter in the secret life of this house.

Chloe suddenly barked and dashed to the door. Startled, I glanced up in time to see the retreating back of the mail carrier. Expecting a package from Zappos, I opened the door as soon as he left the porch. No package, but the mail was piled in the box. I flipped through it as I wandered into the dining room. In the middle of the stack was an envelope bearing only my first name and address written in a shaky hand. I held my breath as I opened the envelope.

Dear Ivy,

I have taken a spill and broken my pelvis. And my daughter has taken away my keys, so sadly my next visit will be delayed. The good news is, I'm not dead yet. The day you and I talked, I had wanted to share a secret with you. It seems you are spending much time with your own memories, so I thought you might enjoy reading a few of mine. I have hidden a memory book from my childhood in the door panel behind my carved initials. With any luck it is still there. Look for it if you wish.

However, I have been worrying myself silly about finding this book, not because I want to see it, but because I don't. I realize these are memories captured decades ago, some written by a sad and broken ten-year-old girl, some written by my mama. The best of these memories are like polished stones, beautiful because I have retrieved them so often, touched them, soothed myself with them. I am not sure I wish to see these precious stones in their rough state.

Therefore, I hope you find the book, for your research. Read it and imagine me at age ten, but don't return the memory book. It is yours to keep. You see, I have my best memories right where I want them. It turns out, I took them with me. I will have my daughter drive me for a visit as soon as I am able, because even if you don't find the memory book, I have more stories I can tell you about your home, if you are interested.

Until we meet again,
Bitsy

ELSBETH (BITSY) ROBINSON

Downington Avenue
1933

A cloud of steam from my own breath greeted me as I woke. It seemed impossible that the house could get any colder than it had been the night before, but it was. Shadows loomed monstrously on the wall of my bedroom, menacing in the dark of winter dawn. Something had awakened me, though all was silent now. I listened intently until I heard it again. There it was . . . a choking noise. I crept from my room to see Papa hunched in the walnut rocking chair Mama had rocked me in as recently as my tenth birthday, though the last time she held me my legs nearly dragged on the ground as she sang a familiar lullaby.

Papa was staring into the empty fireplace. I intended to ask if I should start some hot water, but before I could speak he repeated the choking noise and rubbed his face with his hands. He didn't see me. He whispered my mama's name. I crept away, because I didn't want him to think I was spying on him. And I didn't want him to know I'd seen him cry.

I crawled back into bed and pulled my quilt over my head. I would go back to sleep. It's just what I would do. But I couldn't stop listening. I heard the creak of the front door and a scraping noise. The door shut and after several minutes I crept from bed again. What was my father doing, going outside on a morning as cold as this one?

I pulled back the curtains an inch or two and gasped. Papa held the rocking chair by one wooden armrest high over his head. His mouth was open in a silent scream. As I watched, he smashed the chair down hard onto our front walk. He raised his arms again, still holding the chair. The tapestry cushion came loose and fell to the ground. One of the curved runners snapped in half. He slammed it again into the unrelenting concrete.

I flung open the door.

"Papa!"

His face was ashy and he was wearing the same clothing he'd worn the night before. "There's nothing else to be done," he said softly, and he dropped the chair to the ground. Shards of polished wood flew into the snow.

"What are you doing?" I whispered.

"Go inside, Bitsy." His voice held no anger. Only sadness.

I slipped into bed and tucked myself into the smallest ball I could. I wished I could hibernate the rest of the winter, just like a brown bear. I pulled the blankets over my head and tucked the edges under my toes. I put a corner of my quilt into my mouth, like I had when I was three. It felt dry and scratchy on my tongue, but I didn't care.

I heard the snapping and popping of fire, and warmth, like gentle fingers, found me inside my cave of quilts. We didn't have any wood or coal, so what was Papa burning? A thought turned in my head. Papa was burning the rocking chair. Papa was burning the rocking chair! We'd run out of coal two days earlier, that's why the house was so cold. But Mama's rocking chair? I swiped a hot tear that rolled across my cheek as I hurried once again from my room.

"Papa!" I raced toward him. He didn't look in my direction.

He was sitting on the tile hearth, absently tossing splinters of the chair into the blazing fire. Fingers of flame were leaping from the burning cushion onto the hearth and reaching brightly toward the wood mantle.

He was mumbling, "What else can I do . . ." Couldn't he feel the heat?

That's when I noticed the red leather memory book resting in his hands. The book Mama wrote in. The one all about me. He was smoothing his fingers over her written words and whispering, "I can't do this without you."

His words made my teeth chatter. I leaned against the wall.

He opened the book wide, and with shaking hands he ripped the front cover clean off. The book dropped to the hearth, too close to the flames that were lapping against the chair cushion.

"No," he gasped and bent to retrieve it, but I was much faster. I dashed to him and grabbed the remaining pages out of his hand. I raced back to my room and slammed the door. I hid the book under the mattress and covered myself once again with the familiar comfort of my quilt.

I would lose Mama entirely if he burned her words, and I would never let that happen.

I hid in my room the whole day; the fear Papa would burn the memory book kept me as quiet as a mouse. But he didn't come for me. After the house was silent, I retrieved the book from under the mattress and opened it to the first page. I touched Mama's familiar cursive. A tear slid off the tip of my nose and her words disappeared where it fell, melting into the paper.

"No!" I blotted the moisture with my little finger and blew on the page until it was dry, then I started to read.

October 1922

Elsbeth Dorthea Robinson was born October 12, 1922. Her father (my husband), Richard, gave me this wonderful memory book to record the significant events of her life. Elsbeth was delivered by my own sister, Emmeline, a practicing nurse at Holy Cross hospital. The labor lasted nearly nine hours. Richard boasted he now has two girls to love! The birth of our precious child has been long awaited and we are blessed to have her here. I am affixing an ink print of her tiny perfect foot I received in the hospital.

These words were written by my mama, but not the Mama I knew. I wanted to touch her words during a time I would remember. I turned several pages.

December 1922

My darling baby girl has celebrated her first Christmas. For the holidays, I sewed for her a red-and-white striped creeper and a matching bonnet. She looks like an itsy-bitsy candy cane and sweet enough to eat. Today we will go calling. My father will take the whole family in the carriage to visit my beloved sister Emmeline and her boys. Bitsy will meet her cousins for the very first time! Emmeline doesn't bring her children to visit very often, and I miss her so.

As I reread this entry, I realize I have called Elsbeth by her nickname, Bitsy, for that is what we usually call her.

Still too early. I wanted *my* mama. I turned to the middle of the book and smoothed the ivory pages.

June 1928

Another milestone for Bitsy today, and not a pleasant one. She received her first (and hopefully last) whipping. I am writing this as I watch my little girl sleep. Her mouth is red-stained from eating cherries and spitting the pits into her father's new car. Her eyes are swollen from crying. She looks so peaceful in slumber, but sometimes I think the devil gets a hold of this little one. . . .

Oh, boy did I remember that day.

Mama said I had to keep the name Bitsy until someone more *bitsy* than me came along. Someone more bitsy for Mama to hold in her arms. So last night I prayed for Mama to get herself another baby, so I could become Elsbeth Dorthea Robinson, a much more respectable name for a girl of five years with my amount of smarts.

This morning when I mentioned my plans to Mama, she told me, "Bitsy, if prayers were really answered in that manner, I'd be calling you Elsbeth, because you'd already have a little brother or sister."

I pondered for a moment.

"But Grandmother Robinson said I should always say my prayers. So God will know where I am and what I need," I protested.

"So, Bitsy, do you imagine Grandmother Robinson told God she needed to suffer like she did?" Mama asked softly.

My mouth dropped open. I thought of my Papa's mama, her shrunken, gray body lying so still on her bed. I remembered her moaning in the darkest days of her sickness and a shudder ran up my spine. When Grandmother was near death, my mama nursed her, sitting with her every day, holding her hand and giving her sips of water, but she couldn't stop the noise. We would bury my grandmother tomorrow. Mama said we would cover her grave with the white flowers from Aunt Emmeline's rosebush.

"Cora, that's enough," Papa called from the dining room. "Bitsy, you keep praying. Keep your own faith. Your grandmother probably *was* praying to die at the end. Sometimes bad things happen. It's God's will."

Mama sighed. I guessed she wasn't so friendly with God at the moment. She picked me up and held me tight on her lap. I squirmed a little. I wasn't a baby anymore, and I didn't need to be held like one. I was five years old, nearly old enough for school.

"Even if we *do* get another baby, I believe I will always call you my Itsy Bitsy," she whispered into my ear. She gave me one last squeeze and I wiggled off her lap.

I stuck my tongue out at her. She giggled softly and patted me on the bottom.

"Now go outside and play, my little Bit."

I ran past Papa and his father. The two men were sitting at the dining room table looking over several stacks of papers, which Papa called his ledgers. Grandpapa slumped his chin against his palm as he spoke. He was exhausted from Grandmother's sickness, my mama had told me. As I zipped past, I upset several of the sheets, which flew off the table and landed on the wood floor.

"Bitsy. Go," Papa called toward my retreating back.

I galloped into the backyard. Papa's new car was parked toward the back of the house in the sparse shade of our little cherry tree. It was the newest car in the neighborhood and the first car Papa had ever owned. He was very proud of it. He had an old truck he drove on the farm, but it was used for hauling feed or moving cattle. Now we had a car to drive around town. I slid into the front seat. I cranked the steering wheel from side to side and pretended to drive myself to call on my best friend, Polly. We would pack up a fine picnic of strawberries and ham and take it to Liberty Park, where we would play in the water until it was time to eat. My stomach growled.

That's when I noticed the cherries were ripe.

I got out of the car and shimmied up the trunk of the cherry. I wasn't very tall, but neither was the tree. I could reach most of the ripe cherries from my low perch on the sturdy part of the trunk. I plucked two bloodred morsels and popped them in my mouth. The sweet juice kissed my tongue. I swallowed the fruit and spit the pits to the ground. One pit bounced from the dirt below the tree and landed on the running board of the car.

I tried to repeat the trick several times, but was unsuccessful. Pits flew out of my mouth every which way, never landing where I intended. However, one misfire sailed through the open window nearest the driver's seat and landed *plop* on the creamy leather interior. Now that was something! The window was a much more accessible target, so I refocused my efforts and aimed for the inside of the car.

I ate so many cherries, and spat so many pits I felt a roiling heaviness in my stomach. Without another thought, I shimmied down the tree and ran into the house to find Mama. She was asleep. I didn't want to disturb her, so I crawled quietly to her side. She roused briefly and laid one arm over my back. I rubbed my swollen belly until I joined her in slumber.

"Elsbeth Dorthea, you get out here this instant!" My father's voice cut through my sleep. He sounded angry, and as I struggled to wake I wondered why.

Mama stirred. "What did you do, Bits?" Mama sounded worried. She stood up and we walked apprehensively toward Papa's voice, which called again from the backyard. This time more insistently.

Mama and I hurried outside. Papa was waiting there, holding his leather belt. His face was a mask of fury. He was standing next to his car. The driver-side door was open.

I gasped. The cherry pits!

"Richard, what in heaven's name are you doing?" Mama sounded angry.

"The girl needs to learn some respect." He turned toward me. "Bitsy, I have worked hard to provide for you. You want for nothing. You have the dolls you want, don't you?"

I nodded.

"You have all the food you can eat, don't you?" He continued without pause. "I've worked to buy a farm to support this family. I buy one nice thing for myself. One reward for a job well done and you think nothing of spitting on it?"

He walked tightly toward me and yanked my hand. "Now come over here and look at the mess in the car. I'll be lucky to get the stains out of the leather." He shoved the back of my head toward the open door.

I was surprised at the cherry pits blanketing the bench seat. Red smears polka-dotted the tan leather. Did I do that?

"Lift your dress, Elsbeth." Papa's voice was steely. My legs shook as I complied.

"Richard, this isn't necessary. You're upset from your mother's death. Don't take it out on Bits . . . just have her clean the mess." Mama called from the doorway.

"It *is* necessary. The girl needs to learn the value in hard work. I worked hard for this car, Cora."

Tears started as I lifted my skirts. Papa ran the belt across my thighs five times. After the fifth swipe Papa put his belt back in his pants and I felt the comforting hand of Mama as she led me, teary-faced, back into the house.

She took me into the little bedroom located next to the kitchen. She laid me on the bed and took down my britches. Her hand was cool across my burning legs.

"Now, now, it's not so bad, Bitsy. Whatever made you spit those pits into your papa's new car?" Mama pulled my pants back up and smoothed my skirts.

"I don't know." I sniffed. And I really didn't. In fact, until I saw Papa near the car, I had forgotten I had spit the pits in the automobile at all.

"Neither Papa, nor I, nor God, looks kindly on a child who isn't grateful for the gifts they receive."

I nodded solemnly, wondering if God already knew about the cherries. Or if I cleaned them quickly, he possibly wouldn't find out.

"Your father works hard to provide for our family and we should be grateful to him. I'm going to have you help him clean his car, but first I have some good news during this sad time," she said, forcing a smile.

"What good news?" I said quietly.

"Well, Bitsy, you saw Papa and your grandfather working when you went outside to play?" she questioned.

I nodded.

"We're going to use the money left us after Grandmother Robinson died to buy this house from my father, Grandpa Lansing. He'd like to move back to Helper, to be near the grave of my dear mama. With that money we can afford to buy this house from him, at a good price. Your papa thinks we can buy this house and still afford the farm. And this room will be your very own bedroom. Eventually, we'll sell this house and build a new one on the farm, but until that time . . ."

"But I've slept in this room with you and Papa my whole life."

"You're old enough to sleep alone, and it's probably for the best. Papa and I will move into Grandpa's room. We can put some new paper on your walls and you'll have a place to display all of your dolls. This little room hasn't seen new paper since I slept in it with your aunt Emmeline," she mused to herself. "We'll start moving things after the funeral. Now go outside and help your father clean his car. Work extra hard and he'll forgive you."

"I will, Mama," I gulped.

IVY BAYGREN

❧

"Keep your fingers clear of the blade," I said as I wiggled the bow saw sunk deep in the trunk of our cherry tree. It pinged like a banjo with the movement. If we stopped now, I could imagine the saw becoming a permanent fixture, like so many other things we'd hung from the branches.

"This is really hard," Porter groaned. "Naomi, you take a turn," he said, and stepped back. Naomi yanked on the saw, lost her grip, and fell hard to the ground, exhaling sharply.

"Can't we just call a professional to cut it down? This is so stupid," she said, looking up at me, her eyes narrowed.

"The arborist costs three hundred dollars. We need to get the saw unstuck, take a few more passes at the cut, then TIMBER!" I smiled at my two kids, who scowled back. Removing the cherry tree was breaking my heart, but I had determined I would keep my spirits high enough to complete the job.

"I get to yell TIMBER when it finally falls!" Porter exclaimed, his face relaxing.

"That could be next week," Naomi grumbled.

"Don't be such an optimist, honey," I said, and she reluctantly grinned.

"I can't believe we have to cut it down." Porter gazed up into the leafless branches. Our once glorious cherry tree was dead, a victim of the bore.

"Remember the year when all of our meals contained cherries?" Naomi asked, standing and dusting her bottom with a gloved hand.

"Dad hated a single cherry to go to waste," I replied. "My fingers were stained pink that whole summer."

"Cherry pie . . ." Porter sighed.

"Cherry pancakes, cherry chutney, cherries over pork, cherries jubilee, cherry syrup . . . what else did we have?" I said.

"Cherry poop," Naomi giggled.

"Oh, boy, you ain't lying." I laughed.

In truth, I hated the cherries that year, the never-ending abundance. It was the swan song of the tree. The next season we had half the cherries we had the year before, and Adam was worried. Several of the highest branches had lost their leaves.

But even as I listened to him lament the possibility of the bore, I was silently rejoicing. Adam's compulsion to let nothing go to waste had made me significantly less enamored with cherries. It also made me wary of planting another fruit tree to replace the cherry when our tree was deemed terminal. I didn't want never-ending cherry production replaced with an inexhaustible apple tree.

The next year, though, I had joined the band of cherry tree mourners, which already included Adam, Naomi, and Porter. Especially Porter. He loved that tree. And because he loved it so deeply, its slow decline made me ache.

Looking up, my hands still wrapped around the saw, I could see hanging from the barren branches ropes for dangling flashlights and swords, two hand-painted birdhouses, and a hula hoop. The hoop had been stuck in the highest branch for years, thrown high in a game, irretrievable forevermore. All items, once obscured from view by leaves during the summer, were now painfully visible.

Like so many other projects around the house, I had procrastinated on cutting down the tree. I rationalized I wasn't strong enough to cut it down myself once Adam was gone. My next excuse—the money. Recently, though, I realized that refusing to take down the cherry was related to my tendency to hold on to dead things. If the trunk was still firmly rooted in the ground, couldn't it, if given enough time and water, simply start to grow again, brittle branches resurrected, sprouting buds of green?

It would be a miracle, the arborist told me. But if the miracle of cherry could occur, might not another miracle, another resurrection be possible? And so the dead tree stood in our yard until today.

The nail in the coffin for the cherry tree, so to speak, was the demise of the beloved hammock and a broken wrist. It happened yesterday, and even as we worked this afternoon, Naomi's friend Amber was home icing her compound fracture before a cast could be wrapped around her arm.

Any good hammock, given the rhythmic movement of two thirteen-year-old girls, deep in a conversation of pure gossip, would trace quite an arc. The hammock was whizzing through the air when the bolt Adam had driven into the trunk pulled out of the decayed wood. Amber hit the ground first and held out her hands to shield herself as Naomi catapulted toward her. Bottom line, we were entirely responsible for the break. The combination of the faulty bolt, the rotten tree, and Naomi's shoulder worked together to crush Amber's wrist.

In penance for neglecting to cut down the deceased tree, its removal was first on my list of things to do today (#6—Get your house in order), and I'd asked my kids to help.

"Remember when we'd pretend each branch was a bedroom?" Naomi said to Porter as they tugged at their end of the saw. "And we'd pass bags of Goldfish crackers using a pulley we made with the jump rope?" Naomi pointed to the faded jump rope still hanging from a high branch.

Porter nodded. "Remember when I pretended I was Tarzan and I tried to use the rope to swing to another branch?"

"Huge fail!" Naomi laughed. "And he has the scar to prove it," she said to me.

"I don't remember that," I replied.

"It's because we hid Porter's injuries from you. We didn't want you to make us take all of the ropes down," Naomi said.

"What were your injuries?" I asked Porter, trying not to be offended.

"Twelve stitches," Porter said. "Dad took me to get them."

"Stitches! How could I miss stitches?" I exclaimed. "Do you really have a scar?"

"Yes." He grinned.

"Where?"

"On my butt! Wanna see?"

"Yes, because I can't believe I didn't know about this!"

"He snagged his butt on a branch. You should've seen the blood." Naomi giggled.

"Where was I?"

"I think you were at work. Dad told you we had gone to the hardware store when we got back from the Insta-Care. And for a week he told me to fake going to swim lessons."

"What?"

"Yeah, you would take me to the pool and I'd stand there for an hour. It was nearly impossible to sit. Right before you picked me up, I'd wet my hair."

I dropped my end of the saw. "Show me the scar. I can't believe you could hide this from me."

He turned around, dropped his pants, and sure enough, a scar the length of my pinky zigzagged across his butt cheek.

"Porter, jeez, I'm right here in front of you," Naomi squealed. "I don't need the full frontal, gross!"

Porter yanked his pants, covering the scar.

"When did this happen?" I was annoyed.

"The summer before Dad, well . . . you know." Porter's voice drifted. "Anyway, what would you've done if you found out?" he asked, changing the subject.

"I probably would've made you stop playing so high in the cherry tree," I conceded.

"That's what Dad and I thought. He told me some rewards are worth the risk."

As Porter fastened the button on his shorts, the phone rang. Typically, I wouldn't drop everything and run, especially because there was more to be said on this subject, but I was conflicted about the stitches. Did Adam really hide an injury from me? I imagined it was him calling as the phone continued to chime, and as I walked through the back door I was mentally preparing myself for an argument with my husband.

It obviously wasn't him. The woman's voice on the other end sounded hesitant and a little sad. "Is this Ivy?"

"Yes?" I matched her tone.

"This is Sylvie Crossland. You sent a letter to my mother, Lainey Harper. I think you live in our old house."

"Lainey!" I squealed. "I did send a letter!"

"I'm not Lainey, I'm her daughter. My mom passed away only a couple of months ago, which breaks my heart because she would've loved to hear from you."

"Oh, I'm sorry." How many times had I been on the other side of this type of conversation and no one had ever said anything more profound than *sorry?* Now I knew how they felt. Sorry wasn't enough, but it was the truest of sentiments. I would never know what Lainey meant to her daughter, but I was sorry she'd lost someone she loved.

"Thank you," she said. After a brief pause Sylvie asked, "So, how is the place? I think my mom spent the best years of her life there. It certainly seemed to haunt her this last little while."

"Haunt?"

"She thought a lot about it. She was an artist and our house—your house—was her most recent subject. I think she painted it from every angle, using every color." Sylvie laughed now. "If you wanted an artist's rendering of a place in all of its Van Gogh glory, you should see her work."

"I'd love to—"

"Better yet, let me send you a couple of the paintings I have here. Though I hate to separate from any of her pieces, there are plenty to go around. You have no idea."

"I'd love one."

"I'll do it," Sylvie said. "I have your address, of course. Maybe a couple of her paintings will satiate your curiosity about the place when we lived there. I have to tell you, though, it wasn't anything spectacular back then. My mom wasn't much of a housekeeper. Well, you saw the house when you bought it, but it was our home. She was sad to leave."

After we hung up, I raced back outside to my children, who seemed worried. They likely suspected I was inside the house fuming about stitches (and Adam) and I would have been, had I not been so excited. I told them about Sylvie and the paintings of our house. They were strangely quiet.

"So you're not mad about the stitches?" Porter finally asked.

I swallowed, fighting the overwhelming urge to protect my children at any cost. "I'm not going to be mad, because Dad was right."

Both kids stared at me.

"Some things are worth a little risk. If you had stopped playing in the cherry tree, look at all of the fun you would've missed through the years."

"I miss him," Naomi said, looking down. She covered her face with her gloved hands, her shoulders jerking with silent sobs.

"Me too." I dropped my end of the saw and went to her.

I held Naomi even as she tried to pull away. "I hate this," she said. "If I start crying, sometimes I feel like I can't stop."

"I know," I told her. Porter's thin arms reached around the two of us, holding us while we embraced. We stood silently until Naomi sniffed and shook her head, strong once again.

Wordlessly, we resumed our spots at opposite ends of the saw. I gazed into the bare branches of the once grand tree, remembering it the way it appeared in the photo of Lainey on the day she moved into the house, vibrant green branches reaching into the sky. The very same tree provided dappled shade at an evening wedding for a young Greek woman. I figured she must be Calliope, the daughter from the census, and the grandmother of tattoo-boy. The tree had stood strong and healthy for decades, and today we'd be cutting it down.

"Boy, I wish he was here," I said, pulling at the saw, releasing it from captivity in one loud snap. We moved the blade back and forth, filling the air with sawdust. "The three of us together aren't as strong as Dad was alone." But the three of us together are stronger than only *me*. I must remember that.

*   *   *

Adam's familiar palm rested heavy on my shoulder. His finger slipped under the collar of my T-shirt, beneath the strap of my bra, and pressed into the soft flesh beneath my collarbone. Angrily, I shifted away from him, wringing soapy water from the dishcloth into the full sink. His hand returned, hot on the small of my back. Again I moved away, but this time my abrupt movement was an effort to avoid looking at his face. Though asleep, I was conscious this was a dream. If I didn't search for his eyes, he would linger.

Between memory and dream Adam always found me. "We ate without you," I whispered to him. "We couldn't wait any longer." I didn't seek a reply as I attempted to hold on to the pressing sensation that he *actually* stood behind me. If he responded, I'd lose him. His voice, if audible, slipped from wavering presence to memory.

He pulled me to his chest, wrapping his arms around my waist. I leaned my head back into his shoulder, the stubble on his chin rough against my cheek. Resting my hand across his, the band of his wedding ring was smooth under my fingers.

Stop.

Too close. Too many pieces in this dream were real. Aware I was in my midnight bedroom, when he responded, his voice was a memory. The weight of his arms, the heat of his chest, drifted away as I recalled his voice.

"Mumford, again. That windbag can take twenty minutes and turn it into two hours of wasted breath. I'm sorry I was late."

I searched the memory for fine detail I may have missed in a past recollection. "I've saved you some salmon," I said as I opened the fridge.

"Where are the kids?" he asked. He was wearing a white-and-lavender striped dress shirt, the top button undone, his navy tie loose. His green eyes sparkled. The question was loaded.

"Porter's already in bed, Naomi's sleeping at Amber's." I had the cold plate in my hands, reaching toward the microwave. I was still angry he'd missed eating with the family. Late nights

when the sun left the sky well before the dinner hour were torture for me. This time of year, I needed him home after work.

"Don't look at me that way, Ivy. You've missed me, I can tell."

He'd taken the plate from my hands and set it on the counter.
He pressed me against the stainless steel refrigerator, one hand
on my right shoulder, his other grasping my wrists as he pinned
them above my head. He touched the tip of his tongue against
my lips and I groaned. "See?" he laughed.

"You're not fighting fair," I squealed, and wiggled from his
grip. I ran into the bedroom and slammed the door.

"You're teasing me now, aren't you?" He whispered against
the crack.

"No! I'm really mad," I said as I slipped out of my sweater.
It's not like our sex was always spontaneous, but I wanted him
on me. The pressure of him, his physical weight as our bodies
met. I yanked at the waistband of my black knit skirt. It fell to
the ground, my hand fighting his twist on the door knob. Porter
was in his crib; even if he woke, he wouldn't see us. I could be
reckless.

A timid knock on the bedroom door, and I was ready for him.
"Who is it?" I answered coyly.

Adam pushed hard against the door, wearing now only his
tie. "So beautiful," he whispered, pressing his hand against my
cheek. We fell together onto the bed. Sheets surrounded us as we
twined our bare limbs around one another. . . .

The memory complete, I returned to the lonely dark, the
evening of my reality. A tear left my pressed lids and slid toward
the pillow, a dense fatigue pinning me to the mattress. I touched
his side of the bed, empty and cold, and Chloe licked my hand.
I was usually happy for the company, but tonight I resented her
foreign presence. I tucked my hand under my chin, urging him
to find me again as I drifted into slumber. . . .

Rushing out the door, I had a glass casserole dish in my hands.
I'd made cherry cobbler, Adam's favorite dessert. For some reason I was dressed like an actress in a costume film, the rustle of
my full calico skirt brushing my ankles. The passenger door of
the minivan, a vehicle incongruous to the old-fashioned dress,

was open, waiting for me to get in. My hands full, I tapped it with my toe and the sight of my shoe surprised me, a leather boot with tiny buttons on the side. Swinging the door closed, I asked Adam, "Where did you say we're going?"

The interior light of the minivan flashed, inflaming the night. "Where do you want to go, Ivy?" The voice was not Adam's and was only vaguely familiar.

Startled, I glanced over to see Theo Taylor, the man from the Historical Society. His hand gripped the key in the ignition, a broad palm pressed against the steering wheel. He grinned at me, the lines around his mouth carved into a smile that made my heart flutter.

A shard of sunrise cut across my face, not the interior light of the minivan after all. Just a dream. Chloe licked my hand and jumped from Adam's side of the bed. It was morning.

LAINEY HARPER

Downington Avenue
1969

"Couldn't we use a little summer?" I said to Sylvie as we cuddled in her twin bed, the down comforter holding the cold of January at bay. She leaned her head into my shoulder and I felt the moisture of her breath on my neck.

"Uh-huh," she said, and started humming quietly. The hour was early and we were both unwilling to face the cold house. Like the doctor had promised, gradually, over the past six months, I had grown into being Sylvie's mommy. I still wondered if I was doing the things a good mother would do, but the hole in my chest was gone.

I pondered my new role as I drifted in and out of slumber. Being half asleep was like hovering on the edge of a delicious dream. Sylvie was such a calm child, which was fortunate, because I was often tired. While on the lithium I felt like cellophane, floating in my own calm sea. I was so flat, so empty of the intense passions that had occupied my brain since I was young. Was I even the same Lainey? Or an imposter cloaked in a familiar body? Along with my emotions, Sylvie's laughter was heartbreakingly muted. Every time I swallowed the pills, I mourned the good parts of the person I had been. Did Sylvie deserve a mother with more energy? A mother who was more fun?

Sylvie rolled from my shoulder. "Remember the day last sum-

mer when we both ran through the sprinklers because it was too
hot in the house?"

"Yes. And we lay flat on the cement to dry." I imagined the
sun as it warmed the chill off my body. A delicious heat, not
warmth from exertion, but the shiver of evaporation. I was so
sick of winter. "I also remember you tried to eat the driveway,"
I continued.

"I wasn't eating it," Sylvie protested. "I was licking it because
the wet cement smelled good. But you thought I was hungry, so
you said we could get ice cream. And you let me get a triple
scoop, remember?"

I smiled. "I remember. You weren't hungry until the next
morning. What flavors did you choose?"

"Chocolate, strawberry, and chocolate chip," Sylvie sighed.
"That was a great day."

I sat up quickly, a spectacular connection buzzing in my
brain. It was a moment when I felt like the old Lainey. Or the
old Lainey when things were going well.

"Let's do it again!" I slid my legs over the edge of her bed and
made my way to the thermostat, turning the dial to eighty. "Let's
make it summer in the house and eat nothing but ice cream!"

Sylvie got out of bed and followed me, going into the kitchen
and opening the freezer. "We don't have any ice cream in here."

"Put on your parka," I said. "Let's go shopping!"

Sylvie slipped her coat over her nightgown, her grin as wide
as her face. I returned her smile. Suddenly, I felt perfect, border-
ing on spectacular.

We rolled the cart through the empty aisles of Emigration
Market, the only two people stupid enough to go shopping on a
frigid morning before eight o'clock. The store displayed a rainbow of ice-cream bricks stacked higher than my head. Sylvie
clapped her hands, joy leaping from her fingertips.

"Let's see, how many days until Christmas break is over?" I
counted on my fingers. "Today is Wednesday . . . Thursday, Friday, Saturday, and Sunday. We'll need enough ice cream to last
us five days."

Sylvie gasped. "Is that *all* we'll eat?"

"We'll also need cones, hot fudge, and cherries."

"Won't we get sick?" Sylvie fretted.

"We might get sick of ice cream, but we won't die or anything. So start choosing."

Reassured, Sylvie opened the glass door of the upright freezer.

"You two having a party?" The checker looked at us warily as he typed the cost of our items into the cash register.

"We're pretending it's July!" Sylvie squealed.

"It *is* July!" I agreed, and pointed out the plate-glass window at the front of the store.

The snow was swirling, distorting the view of the icy street. "If you say so," he said with a shrug.

By the time we got home, the house was practically hot. I took off my coat and put on a sundress. Sylvie slid into her shorts. We filled two of the cones with triple scoops and sat on Sylvie's quilt, which she had spread on the floor, picnic style.

"You're not like any other mommy I know," Sylvie said as she licked the top scoop.

"Is that a good thing or a bad thing?" I held my breath.

"Good!" Sylvie responded.

I relaxed somewhat. "Good in what way?"

"Ice cream for a week, of course! Grandma would only let me have ice cream on special occasions." She took another lick. "And you're more beautiful than the other moms. My new friend Karen said you're the prettiest mother in the whole school. She said her dad thinks so, too. And when Karen's mom heard that, she got mad."

"I don't know if that's a great thing," I said, but I smiled. I couldn't help myself. I had spent years hearing about my blossoming, fragile beauty, and even more years hearing about my broken, fading beauty. Any compliment these days was welcome.

After the ice cream, I fetched the nail polish. As I spread Peach Dream on Sylvie's toes she said, "Tell me about my daddy. Grandma always said *you* would tell me, because she didn't know him."

I inhaled deeply. "What would you like to know?"

"What was his name?" she said. I could tell she was looking at me, but I concentrated fully on her toes. I could be much more convincing if her innocent blues weren't searching my face for the truth.

"His name was Roger." I think. Or maybe Stan. It couldn't have been Fabian, or Sylvie's eyes would have been brown.

My thoughts stretched back seven years, to the holiday shoot for *Vogue,* taken in London. It was my first time out of the country and I felt like I could fly. I was daring and seductive. My portfolio bio advertised that my golden eyes were wide and haunted. The tilt of my head showcased my fragile neck. The pout of my full lips implied I was vulnerable. I believed it. I showed it to the camera.

Turns out fragile, vulnerable, and haunted are much more appealing than *broken.* That shoot was the pinnacle of my modeling career. In the photos, I was all of those things, fragile, vulnerable, haunted, and *especially* broken. All poignantly captured in the *Vogue* 1961 Holiday spread.

I was also pregnant.

When we wrapped the shoot, my weeks of *daring* and *seductive* slid into a cascade of obsessive thoughts. I had betrayed every truth I had grown up with. I was easy. I was a slut. I was going to be the worst kind of mother. I could hardly keep my focus on the camera. My eyes darted wildly, looking for the answers, the divine connections I'd made only days earlier.

I had begun my first spectacular slide into madness. The men I believed were soul mates, the men I easily seduced, quickly went their own directions. Roger discovered I'd been with other men; Fabian returned to Italy, claiming he was already married. Stan tried to stick around for longer, but by that time I was paranoid, continually asking him where he had been and who he had been with. He gave up.

Several weeks later, my mom flew to Manhattan and found me alone in my apartment. I had locked myself in because I knew something was terribly wrong with my brain. I hadn't bathed for two weeks. I didn't have the energy to answer the telephone. She accused me of taking drugs, but I hadn't. Finally convinced, she took me home, nursed me back to health, and there I had Sylvie.

Lovely Sylvie, ears as fragile as a seashell. I would certainly break her. So I left, whispering onto the top of her perfect fuzzy head that I would figure things out and come back to her. It took me six years on a roller coaster of steep emotions before I finally sought help and came home to be the mother of my little girl.

"Did he ever meet me?" Sylvie asked, snapping me back to reality.

"He died before you were born, but he would've loved you, if he had." I had created this story, knowing the questions would eventually come, but it was much easier to rehearse without Sylvie searching my face.

"What happened?" There was genuine sadness in her voice. I reassured myself it would be worse if I told her I had no idea who her daddy was. This was better.

"I worked with your daddy and we were married in New York City. Remember how I used to live there?"

Sylvie nodded.

"One day on his way to work he was in an accident. He drove a moped, like a little motorcycle, and he was hit by a car. It was so sad. I left New York and came back to Grandma and Grandpa to have you. They wanted to keep you until I grew up a little bit."

I finally returned her gaze. "But now we're together." I hugged her. "Being with you makes me happier than I've ever been!"

"I'm happy too, Mommy." Sylvie smiled and lifted her foot to blow on her completed toenails. "Do you want me to paint yours?" she asked.

Oh, I envied her innocence. "Yes, please. I'd like Bubble Gum Pink," I said, and angled my foot toward her hands.

In the days that followed, we watched every possible episode of *The Yogi Bear Show* and *I Love Lucy*. We pretended to be models and I took photographs of Sylvie in her summer outfits. Sylvie got out her set of watercolor paints and we painted sunsets, oceans, and umbrellas. It had been years since I'd spent much time with a paintbrush in hand, and I'd missed it. Often I'd thought how to capture a scene, hold it still and quiet so I could enjoy the placid paper, but when forced to sit, I was quickly discouraged by my lack of talent. Impatient with my results, I would move on to the next obsession.

The following Monday, Sylvie went back to school and I had to turn the thermostat back to a winter temperature. The two Westminster students who'd rented a makeshift room in our basement had returned from their Christmas break and complained their apartment was sweltering. Turns out my neighbor George had heard my Goddess of Shag plea. The day I ripped out the carpet he suggested I fix up and rent the room downstairs. He knew Eris and Hector Gianopolous had the basement plumbed and my parents had provided a little money for renovation, so I'd added a toilet, a sink, and a kitchenette. There was demand because of the proximity to the college, and the students paid much of the mortgage. Thank you, Goddess. Thank you, George. So far the renters hadn't questioned my sanity, and I couldn't afford to have them leave.

My sundress was crumpled in a heap in the corner of the bedroom. I shrugged off my pajama bottoms and slipped it on, though this time I covered the spaghetti straps with my parka. I wasn't quite ready to let go of summer. Sylvie's paint sets from Christmas were still strewn across the table. I trailed my fingers over the colors. So beautiful. I decided to paint a little more before I put everything away.

As I dipped the brush in the pots, my thoughts blurred. I filled every blank space on the porous paper with a swirl of greens and blues. I dropped the completed painting to the floor and began another. Shadows and shapes shifted under my powerful brush. I was good. I was spectacular.

I didn't look up until I heard a sharp knock on the door. Louise was standing on my porch holding Sylvie's hand. Sylvie's face was smeary with tears.

"She's been knocking on the door for twenty minutes. Couldn't you hear her?" Louise shifted her attention to my paint-splattered hands and rumpled summer dress. "It's January, Lainey. What are you up to?"

Glancing down, I was as surprised as she was. I grabbed Sylvie's hands in mine. "Oh, baby, I'm so sorry! Mommy is sorry. I couldn't get my mind off this little project and I didn't notice school was out."

She let me pick her up and settled her sweaty head into my shoulder. My whole body sagged with guilt.

"Thank you so much, Louise. I don't know where my brain is sometimes."

Louise still looked a little put out, but her face softened. "Keep your wits about you, Lainey. Can we help you with anything?"

"No, no. I was excited about a project. It's not a problem." I closed the door and sat on the couch next to Sylvie, smoothing her damp hair off her brow. "I am *so* sorry, sweetheart. I picked up the paintbrush . . . I don't know. I didn't look at the clock. I shouldn't have forgotten you. It won't happen again, not ever," I pleaded.

"Ask yourself." I could hear Dr. Yeager's voice in my head. Okay, I would ask: *How do you feel, Lainey?* Guilty. But fine. I was pretty sure I was fine.

"Can you watch a show with me?" Sylvie asked as she stood in front of the television.

"How about I clean up and make dinner while you watch?" I replied.

She nodded. I turned on the set, but as I cleaned, I realized I had a few things to finish on my most recent painting. Hours later Sylvie told me she was hungry.

Swallowing my shame, we drove to the Hunan Garden where I let Sylvie order anything she wanted. She left the restaurant with bags of leftover Chinese, and I left with newfound inspiration. I painted Chinese words through the night, the meaning of the symbols clear to me as my brush moved across the paper. Chinese society had advanced thousands of years before the Americas. They had created paper and gunpowder. They understood the universe, and through the characters I was painting, their ancient mysteries were revealed to me.

Sylvie wanted to call my mother in the morning as she dressed herself for school. She asked if I'd painted all night when she saw the stacks of paper surrounding the table. I served her some leftover Chinese food and promised I would be done painting right after school.

Around noon, I filled the very last piece of paper in the house and knew with absolute certainty some of my work was worthy of display. I put on my most flattering shirt, an off-the-shoulder peasant blouse. I stacked my wrists with bracelets, hoping to look worldly and exotic. In my mind I could read the newspaper headline, "Former Model Turned Successful Painter."

A stack of my art, some still damp, filled the front seat of the car. I drove the streets of downtown Salt Lake City looking for a gallery. I left several of my paintings at every gallery I could find. Standing poised at the reception desks, I intended for my audience of curators to notice the pout of my lip and the graceful curve of my shoulder, highlighted by the peasant blouse. I ended my tour at the Museum of Fine Arts at the University of Utah. I apologized the work wasn't framed, but said that the gallery could choose however they wished to display the pieces. The receptionist took a small stack, hiding her mouth with her hand. She was giggling.

"What?" I said to the girl.

"Nothing . . ." she said, frightened now.

"I'm not crazy, you know?"

She stared.

"I'm an artist!" I yelled at her, and ran from the lobby.

I may have wandered for a while, because it was dark by the time I returned to my car and my temples were pulsing. I wasn't feeling so spectacular and I knew there was something I had forgotten. I slammed the car into reverse. Sylvie!

Turning onto Downington Avenue, all of the lights were on in George and Louise's house. Their curtains were open, Sylvie's face was pressed against the glass, her mouth was open with fear. I flung open the car door.

George met me on the front porch. "No excuses, Lainey. I've called your parents, who gave me the name of your doctor. Your mother will be here for your appointment tomorrow morning. Tonight Sylvie will sleep at our house." He put a comforting hand on my shoulder to soften his stern tone. "Take a couple of minutes to say good night to your daughter and go get some sleep."

Sylvie pushed past George's long legs and fell into me. My knees hit the porch as I folded her into my arms, soaking her hair with my tears.

Dr. Yeager folded his hands over the notebook lying across his knee. "You need to answer me honestly, Lainey. Have you been taking your medicine?"

The ringing in my head was rhythmic, a tambourine attached to a lawnmower. I could scarcely hear him. My mother squeezed my leg a little too hard. "Have you?" she asked, the cords in her neck tight with worry and anger.

"I have," I stuttered. "Well, mostly."

The doctor sighed and opened his notebook. "You are supposed to be taking, let's see, three hundred milligrams, three times a day. What are you taking?"

I couldn't stop staring at the fish tank on the far side of Dr. Yeager's office. A paperweight in the shape of a beehive sat on the corner of his desk. I knew I could kill every fish in the tank if I threw the heavy object at the glass. And I was terrified I would do it. I sat on my hands, my fingers twitching as I tried to control my thoughts. I couldn't shake the image of the orange creatures flopping on the sculpted shag, eyes bugging, mouths moving silently, begging to breathe. I made an O with my lips, imitating the fish, desperate for air.

"I can't treat you effectively if you don't take your medication as prescribed," the doctor said, more loudly this time.

I covered my ears, trying to block the jangling in my head. "I can't hear you! It is too loud in here!"

I read Dr. Yeager's lips as he spoke to my mother. "We need the sedative to work before we can talk to her."

My mother nodded, her lips clamped tight.

Fingers jammed in my ears, I watched the minute hand of the desk clock creep forward. After ten minutes of my skin crawling, I smiled weakly at my mother, the effects of the sedative seeping into my hysteria, quieting the tambourine.

"Lainey, how much medicine are you taking daily?" The doctor repeated his question.

My sandaled feet were embarrassing, toes purple from cold, nails still painted pink. It seemed so long ago that Sylvie had painted them. I shuddered, ashamed I had failed. I thought I was strong enough to handle things by myself. "I take one dose, in the morning."

My mother huffed. "Lainey, you can't do this to Sylvie. You promised!"

"I know I did." I started to cry. "But last summer my levels were nearing toxic. Toxic, Mom. Every day I felt like I was taking poison. When the doctor reduced my dosage, I felt like the person I used to be. The person I could be if I wasn't taking the lithium."

My mother accusingly swung her head toward the doctor. "Toxic?"

"It happens. It's why we monitor patients so closely," Dr. Yeager explained. He searched my face. "Please tell me what happened."

"When you reduced the dosage, I felt alive. The tremors in my hands stopped and I wasn't so flat. This medicine keeps me steady, but it robs me of everything else." I took a deep breath, trying to control my tears. "So I took a little less."

"If you can't take your medication as prescribed, Lainey, you will rob *yourself* of your *daughter*," said the doctor, in his matter-of-fact tone. "If you don't cooperate, I'll be forced to call the Children's Bureau, and you will likely lose custody of Sylvie. Is that what you want?"

"No, oh please, no," I pleaded, tears starting again.

"I really want this to work for you," Dr. Yeager continued. "I've seen genuine fondness between you and Sylvie. It would be heartbreaking for her to be taken away. I've decided to give you another chance. The girl who answers phones in the counseling center next door quit this morning. You can have her job. It's part-time and you'll sit right outside my office. I'll monitor you daily. You're going to be on an increased dosage of lithium, to see if I can avoid the crash after this episode, but I guarantee you are going to feel flat. And you are going to have to deal with it."

"Can Sylvie stay with me?" I choked on the words.

Dr. Yeager nodded. "For now and closely supervised. You're lucky to have such good neighbors"—he referred to his note-book—"the Pearsons, who've agreed to keep an eye on things."

My mom leaned forward in her chair, her chin resting on her fingertips. It was the position she would take when I was a child and would dissolve into tears at the slightest thing, or when I ran headlong into an obsession she couldn't quite understand. I called it her *Thinker* pose.

"This thing Lainey has," she asked. "What did you call it?"

"Manic-depressive disorder."

"So it's a *real* condition that can be treated successfully with medication?" She seemed somewhat relieved it was an actual disease. It was validation she hadn't failed in parenting me in some integral, deep-seated way.

The doctor nodded. "It is a chronic condition. She'll have the illness her whole life, though on average most people with the illness don't live quite as long as the general population."

"What would cause a shortened life span?" My mom put a protective hand on my knee.

"Patients often take their own lives if they don't stay on their medication. Their manic behavior sinks into a depression so deep, they can't fathom living another day." The doctor stared hard at me, igniting my skull.

My mother gasped, the doctor's stern warning hitting a nerve. "Lainey, you have to cooperate. For yourself and for Sylvie."

I nodded. I wanted to live for Sylvie. I wanted to live for me. "I'll take my medicine. I promise. . . ."

"After you stabilize, we'll work on some therapy to help you tolerate the side effects of the medicine. Some patients take up a new form of rigorous exercise, which they find helps fire the natural endorphins. Some play an instrument. Anything that stirs a passion will help. I recommend to my patients that they do at least one thing that they love, just for themselves, every day." He paused and opened his notebook. "Do you like coffee or ice cream? What's your favorite indulgence?"

I blinked, confused. "I like both. Why?"

"As part of your therapy, at least in the beginning, I'll insist you walk to the campus cafeteria after your shift and get an ice-cream cone to eat on your walk home—or coffee, if it is too cold for ice cream. And you'll *walk* to and from work, which will also help to elevate your mood." He finished writing and closed his notebook. "Finally, you will take your medication as directed. You need to be in my office by nine o'clock tomorrow morning. Dorothy will train you."

On the way out of the office, the receptionist, Dorothy, smiled at me. "See you tomorrow," she said as I walked my sandaled feet out the door and into the snow.

Six months, it took for me to level out. Some days I would sob, some days I would sleep, but every single weekday I walked to work. I answered phones and visited with the doctor. When Sylvie came home from school we would watch *The Brady Bunch* and she would tell me about her day. The evenings when I could barely get off the couch to fix TV dinners, I tried to reassure myself it gave us more time to cuddle.

Now in July, I had finally found my rhythm. And there was plenty to catch up on. However, the withering midday heat had inspired me to remain in the swamp-cooled interior of my house until dusk. Night was my favorite time for yard work, the moon frosting the yard in tendrils of silver, the wrenching glare of day gone to bed for the night. And staying up late was okay, as long as I slept eventually, I reassured Sylvie as I headed outside. She watched me silently. My mother had lectured her about the signs of a spin. At her tender age, she was vigilant. And to stay in our own house, just the two of us, my mom required Sylvie and I check in with her daily via telephone. Sadly my disease had created a caretaker of my seven-year-old and continued my mother's caretaking into her golden years.

As I walked outside, tumultuous music made by the legs of crickets filled my ears. Based on the volume, I imagined a band of invertebrates lined up around my house, their hard-shelled bodies strapped with miniature drums and violins. I was eager for some time under the stars. The increased dose in my lithium had made me a stable parent, but I mourned my lost connection with the universe. At times I even felt detached from my own voice, my own hands. But Sylvie was worth it.

I began my evening of yard work by trimming the colossal Emmeline rosebush. It had long since dropped its snowy petals from the June bloom, and the branches were taking advantage of my neglect to stretch their barbed fingers into the driveway. Every time I backed the car my parents let me use out of the garage, the thorns hit the paint like fingernails on a chalkboard.

Last summer, just after we moved into the house, I asked George about poisoning the bush. I'd already worked to dig it out, but it was so firmly entrenched I actually broke the shovel trying to pry the root ball out of the ground. All of my effort resulted in only a couple of snapped branches here and there.

"Lainey, you can't kill the Emmeline rosebush," George said as he wandered into the backyard, pondering my question about poisons. "Those old-fashioned roses have as many lives as a cat. Besides, the bush has been here as long as the house. The roots probably stretch the size of the yard."

"What did you call it?" I asked. "Does it have a name?" I tried to hide my frustration. His sentimentality was not helping me to clear the path to my garage.

"Emmeline. It's the Emmeline rosebush according to old Mrs. McConnely," George replied.

"Who?"

"Mrs. McConnely." He gestured at the bungalow on the opposite side of the street, two doors down from his own house.

"Oh, I thought the Wrights lived there." I squinted at the house, as if seeing it for the first time.

"No, no. You never met old Mrs. McConnely. Lived there when I first moved in, one of the first residents of Downington Avenue. By the time we arrived she was a few cards shy of a full deck." He knocked on his skull. "Lived most of her life in that house. She could only talk about the good old days by the time we moved in. She told me about a young lady who had lived in your house, way back when. Emmeline was her name and she planted the rosebush when the house was new."

As he spoke, I gazed at the Wrights' house. Their teenage son was sitting on the porch. It was hard for me to imagine another family living across the street, but in a house as old as the Wrights' house, and I supposed my own, there must have been many who shared the walls.

I worked quickly, mounds of trimmed rose branches surrounding my feet, the moon bright overhead. In less than a week astronauts would be walking on the moon. Last night, Sylvie and I had watched hours of television, witnessing the liftoff of *Apollo 11* from the Kennedy Space Center. Tonight the moon was so near, I was certain if I squinted, I could see *Apollo 11* as it rocketed toward the lunar surface. I sighed. To see the earth from space and float freely among the stars would be spectacular.

Spectacular. That word. I dropped my clippers and walked back into the house for my pills. I had forgotten them after dinner. Sylvie was still up. I glanced at the clock. "Honey, it's after ten. We need to get you to bed." I swallowed the pills I held in my hand.

She yawned and turned off the television. "Okay, *Hollywood Palace* ended anyway. How's the yard?"

"You should come out for a few minutes. I didn't even use my flashlight. The moonlight is as bright as day."

We walked outside together. Moonbeams crested the tips of the lawn. The warmth of the night kissed my arms. I shivered and pulled Sylvie to my side as we explored the corners of the yard, brand new in the ethereal light.

"I'm going to swing!" Sylvie cried when we neared the set.

"Me too. Let's see if we can touch the moon with our toes."

We stretched our legs, toes pointed as we pumped. At the top of the arc my toes shadowed the distant rock. Sylvie's laughter sparkled in the night air. "Wouldn't it be funny if Neil Armstrong steps off his rocket and sees our footprints on the surface of the moon?" she said, her words alternating between loud and soft as the swing flew through the inky sky. We decided to lay blankets and pillows on the grass and sleep every night under the bright moon and stars, until *Apollo 11* touched down.

My parents came to celebrate with us on the night of the moon landing. Sylvie and I prepared a celebration dinner of Swiss cheese sandwiches. Specifically Swiss cheese, because after nearly a week of staring at the moon every night, Sylvie insisted the astronauts would discover the moon was *actually* made of cheese. We gathered around the television set to see Neil Armstrong step onto the lunar surface. He would be walking on the Sea of Tranquility. What a perfect place to land.

"Listen now." My father hushed everyone as Neil Armstrong prepared to speak. "These words will be momentous. What do you think he'll say?"

"Who left these giant toe prints?" Sylvie whispered.

I held my finger to my lips, my body shaking with silent laughter. Sylvie put her lips to my ear. "There's a giant one-toed alien living on the moon! Please help!" Sylvie and I laughed so hard my father made us go into the other room.

He pumped up the volume. "Seriously, you two," he grumbled. "You have no appreciation for history in the making."

My mother's eyes were misty as she watched me giggle with my daughter. *How do you feel, Lainey?* So happy, I could touch the stars.

It was a slow day at work and I was looking forward to my ice-cream cone on the walk home. I did love my prescribed ice-cream therapy, but it was making me fat. I no longer had the sharp angular jaw and flat stomach I had when I was modeling. Anything for a clear head, I shrugged to myself.

I pressed my cheek into my hand, bored. I hoped Dr. Yeager would step out and notice the lack of traffic in the office and offer to let me go home early.

Dorothy, the other receptionist, was a student at Westminster, and often she would study when things were slow. Now I was feeling better, I vowed to bring a book or crossword puzzle, something to occupy my mind. Today, however, I had nothing. Dorothy had left her books and notes from Drawing 101 stacked on the corner of the desk we shared. I leafed through her notes, hoping to kill an hour.

The lesson on the top of the stack was a discussion on contrast, a study of light and dark. Reading her fastidious notes, it appeared she had written about her observations of an artist at work, probably an example sketched by a professor. She was a keen observer, and had meticulously detailed the technique in written form. She had noted supplies used, hand position, and pressure on the pencil. Even if I had been sitting in the studio, I wouldn't have noticed the particulars she had. I wondered if I could learn the technique secondhand.

Below the notes and textbook was a half-empty sketch pad and three charcoal pencils. "I'll use just one," I apologized to the emptiness as I tore a page of creamy paper. I would give it a go. Pencil in hand, I reread in her notes about drawing an object with an undefined light source. Casting about the office, I realized this was the perfect place to try. The large room was lit by several overhead lights and a couple of wall sconces. My mind was filled with wonderful words like *achromatic* (no color) and *chiaroscuro* (literally, light and dark in Italian). I picked my subject. On the entry table was a ceramic bowl full of apples. I put my hand to paper and drew quickly for several minutes.

Terrible! What was I thinking? I erased and tried again. Even worse! The apples were flat, and the bowl even flatter. The charcoal didn't add dimension to my picture, it added smudge.

How to create contrast without a certain light source? I had always been drawn to photos and paintings with an abundance of chiaroscuro, contrasting light and dark. I said it out loud, relishing the sound of the word on my tongue.

Draw something you love, Lainey. Draw chiaroscuro.

I thought for a minute. Color was critical. I couldn't even imagine creating something without at least a little color. Sheepishly, I fished around in the drawer where Dorothy stored her purse during work hours, looking for colored pencils or crayons or something. At the bottom, under a spare pair of pantyhose, I found a small box of color pastels.

Now, what subject had chiaroscuro? Glancing out the window, I noticed the leaves on the maple were bright red. The ash trees on Downington had also turned, and last night the sky had been filled with swirls of navy from an approaching autumn storm, contrasting sharply against the gold ash leaves lit by an unobscured sunset. The street scene would be my subject.

My hand moved in rapid bursts as soon as the pastel touched the paper. I knew vaguely what I wished it to do, but if I consciously had to tell the limb to perform, it would have flipped over like a dead fish. My vision was unfocused, creating an unsettling shift in perspective. The sensation was not at all unpleasant, though. I enjoyed the cool detachment resting somewhere behind my temples.

As I put the pastel down, my focus resumed its normal state. I held the paper at arm's length. The leaves were blocks of color, but they seemed to shift and sway. The sky was oppressive, but it contrasted brilliantly with the leaves. It appeared I had placed a light under the paper, so vivid was the illustration.

I stared at it for a long while. My heart thrummed inside my chest, threatening to burst through my fragile ribs. It wasn't spectacular, but it was pretty good.

Unbeknownst to Dorothy, I made copies of her notes. Now, I had an imposing stack of materials sitting on the dining room table. Each time I glimpsed it, a thrill coursed through my body, pinging off my stomach, knees, and fingers. "Do at least one thing that you love each day," the doctor had said. So I would.

Sylvie was at the table using her crayons, creating a masterpiece of her own.

"Care if I join you?" I asked.

Sylvie handed me a piece of paper. "Come draw with me," she said.

I picked up a crayon and sketched an apple, lethargically coloring it in. "Hey, didn't you get a box of oil pastels from

Grandma and Grandpa for Christmas?" I asked, suddenly remembering the box of bold colors she kept in her room.

Sylvie nodded and retrieved the unopened package. Wordlessly she got a fresh page of paper, opened the box, and selected the red pastel. She drew a cherry red arch stretching from one side of the paper to the other. Pressing hard on the pastel, she layered on the color. She blew off the stray chunks, put away the red, and picked up the orange. Clutching the stick and humming to herself, she created the world's brightest rainbow.

I watched her as she worked. Her face was smooth and content in concentration. I had much to learn from my daughter. As a child, I never worked carefully through a project. Most of my attempts at art took on a sort of frenzy, page after page of the same thing in varying degrees of quality. It absorbed me, rendering the rest of the world invisible, but that couldn't happen now. In order to use drawing as a form of therapy, I needed to slow down. Calm would replace mania.

"Do you mind if I use the pastels, too?" I asked Sylvie.

She slid them toward me. "What are you going to draw?" she asked.

"I don't know. Do you have any suggestions?"

"Hmm . . ." She put the tip of her green pastel against her chin, leaving an emerald freckle on her face. "How about a clown? You know, one with a big red nose and blue makeup on his eyes. Give him a striped floppy hat with a flower that squirts."

"Hmm . . . a tall order," I said as I glanced at Dorothy's notes.

I would try to incorporate some of the lesson into this clown picture for Sylvie. I started with the sky blue triangles above the clown's brows, moved on to create his eyes creased with laughter, his mouth lined in red. The striped hat flopped toward his rosy cheek. As I worked on shadowing the folds in the hat to give it dimension, a contented humming filled my head.

Sylvie was hard at work on a smiling sun peeking from behind her rainbow. The humming wasn't coming from her. I held my breath and the humming stopped. I checked myself. Frenzy? Spinning? No. *How do you feel, Lainey?* Calm. I smudged some of the lines, rounding the cheeks on the clown and adding a white dot of sparkle to his eyes.

I intended to clear the dinner dishes, but instead I wandered around the dining room studying the sheets of completed drawings taped to each wall. Here and there I had nailed a painted canvas. The dining room was literally "papered" with my work. There were times I wanted to rip down the sorriest of my endeavors, but I could tell I was getting better. So I kept at it. Sylvie had hung little bits of blue ribbon on the art she liked the best. Regardless of the quality, her favorites were clowns, puppies, and rainbows. Dorothy agreed to let me use her notes from class, so I didn't have to sneak them, and I tried to incorporate some of each lesson into a picture either requested by Sylvie, or a subject I loved. I'd recently attempted acrylics, which dried more quickly than oils, but still had a pizazz that appealed to me.

However, something was missing from my artistic attempts, some depth or understanding or wholeness I continually tried to capture. My pictures were missing *life,* and I wasn't sure how to illustrate it. I yearned for the cosmic connection I felt when I was off the lithium. Longing for emotions as vivid as my drawings, I stopped and checked myself. Steady was better. Connected would last only a week. Depressed would last months. And I had Sylvie. Staying steady for her was worth being flat.

After filling the sink with soapy water, I opened the window to catch a breeze. The draft from the swamp cooler never quite reached the kitchen, and I still had a sink full of dishes to do. Willing the evening air to find the back of my neck, I scooped my hair high under my bandanna.

A scent floated through the open window, a combination of baking bread, fresh-cut grass, and rain. Sylvie walked into the kitchen. "We should play Clue when you finish the dishes," she said, sniffing the air. "Are you baking something?"

"No, I think it's coming from the window." I took off my dish gloves. "I know," I said, touching my finger to my temple, "let's go investigate, like in Clue. This is a real-life mystery."

Sylvie giggled. "I want to make a guess. I think the smell is coming from George, in the kitchen, with a cookie sheet," she said.

"Good guess, let's see if you're right," I said, and caressed the back of her hair as we walked out the door.

Outside, the fragrance changed somewhat. "My turn to guess," I said. "I think it is Mr. Wright, in the front yard, with the lawn mower."

Like bloodhounds we circled the yard, noses in the air. We centered our quest at the kitchen window and slowly worked our way around the yard, calling "hotter" and "colder" to each other as a breeze would float the scent toward us.

Finally Sylvie called, "I found it! It's the Emmeline rosebush!" She buried her face in the mounds of white petals. "It's like cotton candy. Smell."

She tugged it toward me and I grasped the blossom. "Ouch!" I touched the tip of my finger to my tongue, the rusty taste of blood in my mouth, yet the fragrance rose toward me, sweet but not cloying. Such untamed beauty, and I'd wanted to kill it. Thank the heavens I failed.

Sounds of a backyard party filled the night sky. The street in front of the Pearsons' house was filled with cars. Someone was playing the guitar. Sylvie and I wandered into our front yard at the same time George opened the front door of his house. Standing on the porch, he struck a match and brought a cigarette to his lips.

"Lainey, is that you in the dark?" he called.

"Yes, looks like you're having a party!" I yelled back.

George walked across the street. "Yep, that's why I'm out here in front smoking. It's Patsy's sixteenth birthday. She has about twenty girlfriends in back. And now the boys are starting to show up. It's best if I stay away."

I laughed.

"Say, we've churned some strawberry ice cream," he said. "Would you two like a little?"

I was never one to pass up ice cream. "What do you think, Sylvie, ice cream?" I squeezed her hand.

"Yes, please," she squealed.

I brought the tips of her fingers to my lips. They smelled like sunshine, roses, and love.

After ice cream, I tucked Sylvie in bed and wandered back outside, studying the endless sky. No moon out tonight, not like the week we slept outside waiting for the astronauts to land.

The Milky Way twisted through the blackness. So cosmic, so connected. So distant, yet so permanent. These same stars had been shining long before me, long before dinosaurs roamed the earth, long before anything and everything, and yet, they were still shining for me. It reinforced my insignificance, and at the same time, told me I was a necessary part of everything that simply *is*.

How could I capture that feeling in the rest of my life? Could I capture it in my art so I could hold it with me through the days when sadness stood at the door, knocking? Though melancholy hadn't reached for me lately, I knew it would return.

What if I could paint the blackness, pricks of light shining and swirling in the sky? As I drifted to sleep, the night sky was ablaze from the strokes of my dream brush, my body awash in the humid smell of earth and rose. Soaring and grounded all at once.

The next day was wash day. Hanging a freshly pressed blouse in my closet, I knocked loose a dress I had worn in a photo shoot. A long, black velvet number from another life. The photos had been taken at the tail end of my modeling career, and had appeared only in local newspapers. I was advertising jewelry for Mother's Day. I had to buy my own dress for the gig, which is why I owned it. I wondered if it still fit.

After slipping out of my robe, I eased into the black velvet. Sylvie spotted me in front of the mirror. "Oh, Mommy, it's beautiful," she sighed, and ran her hand along the rich fabric.

"Can you reach the zipper and pull it up? I'm not sure if this thing will fit," I said.

And it didn't.

Sylvie tried it on next and paraded back and forth in front of the mirror, admiring her eight-year-old body from all angles, holding up her hair and making kissy lips. The plunging neck hung to the bottom hem of the T-shirt she had worn to sleep.

I touched the plush nap of the fabric as I returned the dress to the closet, as black and soft as the night sky. I had an idea. The dress was never going to fit me again, anyhow. And if it did, where would I possibly wear it? I measured a portion of the skirt against one of my empty canvases, and cut a square of velvet. I stapled the edges around the canvas. There was the black of my night sky. Now I would paint the universe.

I found my book of constellations from an astronomy class I had in high school. I painted them. It included photographs of the aurora borealis, so I painted it, colors swirling in the night sky. I painted until I ran out of velvet. *How do you feel, Lainey?* Spectacular.

I checked that I had taken my pills and I vowed to take my paintings to work the next day to show Dr. Yeager what I had been up to. Spectacular or not, I needed the doctor to tell me I was not starting to spin.

Sylvie watched me paint throughout the evening, worry etched across her features, nibbling her nails. At bedtime she curled up next to me to be certain I didn't stay up. Comforted by her warm presence, I slept soundly—good news. I woke easily. I dropped Sylvie off at the sitter and walked to work, several of the cosmic paintings tucked under my arm.

"Your blood work indicates the lithium is at proper levels. It should be doing its job." Dr. Yeager stared at me, assessing my sanity. "How do you feel, Lainey?"

I'd heard the question before. "While I was painting, I felt remarkable, linked to the universe and proud because I thought the paintings were decent. But not frenzied. I could work methodically, but I didn't want to stop painting." It was easy to return his gaze. I wasn't twitching.

"Patients with your condition tend to latch on to various things throughout their whole lives. Call it an obsession. Some people count, some people exercise. Your obsession seems to lean toward the artistic. Remember the photographs of Sylvie, and the Chinese art?"

I nodded and groaned. Did I remember?

"I think painting is a good form of therapy, but again, you need to monitor your emotions. Not sleeping? You should worry. Can't get out of bed? Worry. If you have anxious or repetitive thoughts? Worry." He wrote in his notebook and continued speaking.

"I think you're fine right now. And"—he smiled—"the paintings on black velvet are dramatic and beautiful. Would you mind if I keep a couple to hang here in the office? A lot of people pass through here. Maybe you'll even sell one or two."

That afternoon, I drove to the fabric store and bought a bolt of black velvet, similar to that of my gown, except the nap was shorter. I figured it would hold the paint without crushing, and I set to work building canvases. The fabric was soft, alive. I could hardly wait to create something vivid and full of chiaroscuro in the midnight sky.

"To me, they're fantastic. Real groovy! Do you have anything else you're working on?" Dorothy's uncle was leaning against my desk. He had on a blue suit with huge lapels. I couldn't help but stare at the gold rings encircling each finger.

Dorothy had called in sick that day. Her uncle from Las Vegas had dropped in to surprise her. However, the surprise was his when he saw I was sitting in her spot at the reception desk. After we figured out he was in the right place, and that Dorothy was the one missing, he noticed my paintings.

He was speaking of my representation of the rising moon, low and orange, pocked with craters, vivid against the velvet background. On the opposite wall hung a series of five clowns, each with a different expression. These were the ones Dr. Yeager had chosen to display. He said they were a spectrum of human emotion, in clown form; humorous and tragic at the same time.

I pointed to the clowns. "I painted those too. And really, it's funny you should ask if I have more. It seems whenever I start something like this, I don't know when to stop." I blushed at my admission. "I have at least twenty-five complete at my home."

"Are they for sale?" he asked, stepping behind my desk to get a closer look at the clowns.

"Sure. I guess," I said.

"I own a couple of motels in Vegas and we're updating the rooms, new bedspreads and the like. I need some new art, something edgy and modern."

My heart danced in my chest.

"I'd need about a hundred," he continued. "Maybe more if guests buy them. It happens sometimes. Can you paint western scenes, you know, cowboys and horses? Or the Vegas lights? Maybe a gambling table or two. What do you think?"

I nodded. "Yes, I'll try." I tried to remain stoic, businesslike, but I couldn't stop my grin, so wide it made my cheeks ache.

Money from painting. From doing something I loved! Plus rent. Plus my wage from working at the Counseling Center. I was going to make it! *How do you feel, Lainey?* Spectacular, I thought. Well, almost. And for me, that was perfect.

IVY BAYGREN

❧

"What's this?" Porter called from his basement bedroom.

"Keep looking," I hollered from the kitchen. "You've got to find those instructions if the Science Fair board is due tomorrow." How could I forget? Science Fair due the day after Thanksgiving break was our punishment for a long weekend of gratuitous eating. Attitude adjustment; be *thankful* we had the long weekend to wrap up Science Fair loose ends.

More than a few loose ends to wrap up here. Was this little slip in scheduling Porter's fault, or mine? I probably should have kept better track of due dates, because it was Sunday (the day before deadline) and Porter didn't even have a hypothesis. A little voice in my head told me the *with-it* parents had likely pulled together an award-winning board weeks ago. I took a sip of wine and continued chopping carrots, ignoring the voice.

"It's an old newspaper article," Porter continued, undaunted. I heard him wander up the stairs, his feet shuffling as he read. "It's about Lainey, that woman whose photos you found in the ice-cream churn. The one whose daughter called."

"Really?" I said, reaching out my hand, recalling the photos *were* wrapped in a piece of newsprint. "Where did you find it?"

"On my dresser under a bunch of stuff."

I'd probably left it down there when I was reading about the Greek myths. Oh, Lord, had his room not been cleaned since that day? He handed me the paper, which was a listing of what appeared to be current events. Or current events in 1973. One was circled in red ink, reading:

> Gallery Showing: Spectacular Stars on Black Velvet. Local artist Lainey Harper paints for therapy, but her art inspires us all. October thru December 1973 at the Salt Lake City Public Library, 500 South 200 East. Free to public.

Black Velvet! Was this the type of art Sylvie was talking about in her note? I recalled Lainey's walls when we previewed the home, a gallery of black velvet paintings ceiling to baseboard. I judged her for her abundance of tacky hangings, but now I realized it was *her* art. It meant something to her. And therapy? Why therapy? I'd have to ask Sylvie after I received the painting she was sending.

Perhaps like me, Lainey had suffered some kind of loss or bore an unbearable sadness and her art was part of her personal recovery plan. I ducked into my bedroom, found my list of carefully written steps tucked into the bedside drawer, and read them again.

1: If one glass of wine isn't enough, pour another (I won't erase this—wine does help)

2: Surround yourself with things you love (I'm thinking my family and my home)

3: Find a deeper meaning (not sure about this one, but it sounds good)

4: Get the dog to sleep on his side of the bed (Chloe started sleeping on his side after the funeral, which means I can immediately check something off)

5: Never forget (not sure if this is a step to recovery, but I must never forget Adam)

6: Get your house in order

In researching the history of my home, what was I attempting to accomplish? Somehow it did seem therapeutic—a part of my recovery plan. Perhaps in pondering these women and their stories, using the clues I'd found within the walls of my home, the Easter eggs, and any other information I could dig up, I'd found the bones of their past, the only things remaining after the actual person was gone. Any story was possible beyond that. The way these women may have struggled with love and loss, their lives infused into the brick itself, they had been helping me create a guidebook for my own life.

That was it! I would add another step to the list to formalize it.

Determined, I found the pen Stephen and I had used to craft the original list and added one more step. Number 7—*Understand there is a little sad in every story.*

Clearing the dinner dishes, I listened to Naomi and three of her friends in the dining room huddled around the Scrabble board. The girls gossiped as they lackadaisically played the game. Every couple of minutes they'd burst into bawdy laughter. I leaned into the dining room simply to gaze at the back of Naomi's head; her chestnut curls cascading down her back, her effortless beauty. Most days I felt haggard, worn thin from grief and worry. My old beauty regimen of soap, water, and mascara didn't seem to cut it these days. If my cheeks ever sported a youthful blossom, these days it was entirely Maybelline.

I sighed and took another sip of wine. I was nearly done with my first glass, which meant I was feeling pretty good. "Step #1— If one glass of wine isn't enough, pour another," was my favorite step of all, simply because it required very little from me. And I loved wine. Okay, I'd said it: I loved wine. Besides, it was Science Fair night; I wasn't driving anywhere.

However, I was cognizant of the addictive qualities of alcohol. I tried not to drink on the days when Adam's absence felt like a hollow in my chest and thoughts of him made me hyperventilate, the mornings I emerged from a dream and he had been real. Those days I knew if I drank to dull the pain, I would never put the bottle down.

I slipped on my dish gloves and filled the sink. As I scrubbed the red soup pot, the tomato-stained broth mixed with the spent bubbles, painting the sink a pinkish color. After the last dish, I splashed the porcelain with the hot water and watched as the last of the rosy bubbles slid down the drain.

Musing that I'd probably spent more hours of my life standing at this sink watching bubbles swirl down the drain than I had on *all* of the vacations I'd ever taken, I rested my elbows on the counter and whispered calculations to myself. "Let's see . . . three meals a day. No, dishes for two. Okay, two meals a day. Thirty minutes a meal for dishes. We moved to this house in 1998, that's—"

Naomi walked into the kitchen as I leaned on the counter, using my yellow gloved fingers to tick off the hours.

"Mom, can we have something to drink? And what are you doing?"

"I'm discovering the meaning of life," I said, not taking my gaze from my hands.

"No, really?"

"Really."

"So, before I grab the root beer, tell me: What is the meaning of life?"

"Okay, here it is." I paused dramatically. "If I don't enjoy doing the dishes, I miss out on two weeks of fun every year."

"Huh?" she said as she selected four glasses from the cupboard, barely looking at me. "Doing dishes is the meaning of life? That's just sad."

"Well, think about how many minutes I spend each day doing dishes: At least an hour every day, usually more. That's three hundred sixty-five hours in a year, which might not seem like much. But I've done the math. It's fifteen whole days, and—"

"Naomi, it's your turn!" Amber hollered from the dining room.

Naomi grabbed the root beer from the fridge. "Coming!" She turned to me. "Scrabble. Way more fun than dishes," she said, and returned to the table.

"Maybe if you did the dishes more often, you'd know what I am talking about," I teased loudly, taking off my gloves.

"Didn't you say you enjoyed it?" She laughed, and I heard her take a gulp of root beer.

Seconds later, Amber let loose a gigantic burp and croaked, "Na-o-mi" in the middle of her belch. All of the girls erupted into laughter. I giggled, because, let's face it, it was pretty funny. The sheer joy of my youth had morphed into something more like quiet contentment now that I was grown, but I got it.

However, there was more to think about, regarding the meaning of life. And dishes. How many women, over how many years, had leaned over this very sink? Eris, for one, Emmeline, and Lainey. Even if Bitsy hadn't been old enough to wash dishes, there was still her mother, Cora. Had any of those women, other than me, pondered the hours spent on this mundane task? I swirled the last drops of wine in my glass. Maybe it was the wine that made this line of thought extraordinary.

"Mom." Porter wandered back into the kitchen. "If you're almost done, Nathan is coming over to work on our project." He had the phone pressed into his thigh.

I reactively groaned because I knew their project involved making several batches of cookies using different types of flour. Along with supervising the baking, I'd be washing cookie sheets until midnight (more dishes), not to mention sweeping up copious amounts of spilled flour.

I stifled my grumbling, knowing one day I would be sad the days of Science Fair experimentation in the kitchen would be over. I should appreciate the mundane. Maybe I should add this step to my list too. I wondered what Stephen would think of the addition of two steps in one night and decided against it. Besides, Porter was waiting for my answer.

"Sounds good," I said energetically. "I can hardly wait to taste test the cookies." I ruffled his dark waves with my hand. It did sound good. And I meant it.

When I returned from work the next day there was a package on the front porch—and not an ordinary shoebox-sized package. I'd been waiting for something from Sylvie for a couple of weeks, and I didn't want to call and bother her, but every time a

UPS truck rumbled down our street, I'd race to the door and wait. Then excitement fizzled as the brown vehicle would stop in front of the neighbors to deliver yet another package from Amazon. But today, in the manner of a watched pot, it had arrived.

It was about the size and shape of a windshield, and I had to angle it lengthwise to get it through the door. I'd determined sight unseen that even if the painting was on black velvet, I'd hang it in the house as a tribute to Lainey, but looking at the size, I was beginning to have doubts. Pulling back the layers of packing paper was like pulling back the sepals on a rose, each layer revealing yet another petal inside.

Mostly unwrapped, but still in the box, vivid hues reflected onto the paper surrounding it, as if it had an aura. Setting aside two smaller painted pieces and a sheaf of paper enclosed in the package, I removed the large painting from its wrapper and awkwardly placed it against the back of the couch. I stood back to admire the work.

Spectacular could not begin to describe it. It was a painting of my house, as if a camera tripod stood in the middle of Downington Avenue. However, the perspective was distorted, like looking at my home reflected in a rounded doorknob. The front door was dead center of the convex angle and the windows and porch curved away from the focal point, creating fluidity to the solid structure. Not composed of natural hues, the full color wheel was represented; shades from the lightest orange to a purple so vivid it hurt to stare at formed each brick and dormer.

The front door was cerulean, the porch swing fuchsia, and dramatic curling clouds filled the sky, looking like the aurora borealis had blossomed behind the golden ash trees. Though not on velvet, the entire canvas had been painted black, and light and shadow had been superimposed upon the night. Despite the mismatched palate, it was clear this was my home. It was stunning. It was shocking. It was shockingly stunning. It would never match my Pottery Barn décor. And that's why it was perfect. Sylvie had taped a handwritten note to the back of the canvas.

Dear Ivy,

In sending this particular painting, I may have given you the handmade sweater from hell, if you know what I mean. Am I glad to get rid of a painting this large? Well, yes. But I think more than any of my mother's other paintings, this one captures the essence of the house. If joy and tragedy could be assigned a color, this painting would be an illustration of all she experienced in our (your) home. Life wasn't easy for my mom, but she managed to earn enough from her painting to support the two of us through my childhood. Even now, I receive royalty checks from pieces being sold at galleries across the country. Nothing she sold is of the home on Downington, however. These were painted during one of her obsessive phases near the end of her life. She always said painting in a rainbow of vivid colors helped her erase the blackness in her mind.

However, if you want to burn the painting, you may. There is no obligation to love and display this unusually large piece. Sometimes it's a nice ritual to rid yourself of excessive emotion (and the two smaller paintings might be easier to hang on your wall). I've also taken digital images of my mother's other representations of the house. You'll see none are quite so all-encompassing—instead focusing on tiny details. There's a study of the tile we had on the bathroom floor, one composed entirely of doorknobs, the view from the kitchen window, and several of the rosebush. Enjoy, and if you want to chat, give me a call.

Yours,
Sylvie (and Lainey)

After dinner we spread the paper copies of Lainey's paintings on the dining room floor, and Porter, Naomi, and I tried to match each picture with its location in the house. It was tricky, given Lainey's abstract representation, and the changes Adam and I had made in the fifteen, or so, years we occupied the dwelling, not to mention the sheer volume of work she'd completed. It was like solving a life-sized jigsaw puzzle, as the eight-by-eleven sheets when placed end to end filled the entire dining room (we'd even scooted the table into another room to uncover extra square footage on the wood floor).

"She's rather industrious, don't you think?" I asked the kids around bedtime, when we still had nearly a dozen images left to place.

"Or manic," Naomi said.

"Do you even know what *manic* means?" I asked.

"Yes, Mom, we had a unit on mental illness in health class."

"And you're an expert?" Though before I spoke, I imagined she might be spot-on, since the newspaper article reported that Lainey painted for therapy, and Sylvie's note mentioned blackness in Lainey's mind. Was this the sad part of her story? I wondered if Sylvie would tell me more details about their time in the home. I wondered if it would be too personal to ask.

After the kids were in bed, I tucked myself under the down comforter and supported my back with pillows, cradling Bitsy's memory book on my lap. I'd stacked Lainey's paintings next to Emmeline's unfinished embroidery, and the printouts of the photos we'd snuck from the Gianopolous album on my left. I was in the center of a patchwork quilt of lives, each having been lived under the same roof. I was a small part of a much larger story, connected through these women to something timeless and powerful. Surrounded by Lainey, Emmeline, and Eris, tonight my nighttime reading would be about Bitsy. It seemed only fitting.

I opened the wide manila pages to the pressed-flower bookmark tucked into Bitsy's memory book and touched the words where I had left off. Savoring these memories was only half of my reading process. With every entry I had woven a scene full of rich detail that the faded words lacked. I knew her. In my mind she was not the brittle woman in the green sweater, but a tiny redhead with a penchant for mischief. I wanted her to answer my every question, to relive her life with me by her side, but from her letter I knew this was not what she desired, so I would settle for imagining.

Like with Eris, I'd used the facts found within the pages to fill in the framework of Bitsy's years in the home. Tomorrow, on my day off, I planned to revisit the Historical Society to look up Richard Robinson, Bitsy's father. I pressed the bound book to my chest. Last time I read, I learned Emmeline (of the rose and embroidery) may very well have been her aunt—so many pieces to this puzzle. I longed for Bitsy's return visit, but in the meantime I didn't know how to contact her. So I'd research.

I wondered if I might see Theo Taylor again. Could we encounter one another at the Utah State Historical Society? Now that I'd met him, I noticed his signs hung frequently around my neighborhood—TAYLOR HISTORIC HOME REMODEL—and each time I passed one, I felt a nervous thrill. Edged with nausea. The fact that my body responded in this visceral manner seemed a betrayal to Adam. How dare I? It hadn't even been a year since Adam died, so why did I want to talk with him? Surely he wasn't the only person who would understand my quest to discover the stories in my home. And yet I continually searched for the signs with brown-and-white craftsman lettering. I'd memorized the telephone number. I'd dialed him, a question about the neighborhood practiced on my tongue. I'd let it ring, hearing his voice on the machine, and hung up, the nausea returning as I ended the call.

I took a deep breath, ridding myself of these traitorous questions. I opened the memory book and returned to Bitsy's world.

BITSY ROBINSON

Downington Avenue
1930

June 1930

It looks that we will be staying put in this home on Downington Avenue for a while longer. But someday I would love a new home to call my very own, as I have lived here since I was a girl. In a fit of optimism, and because I thought I might soon have another baby, Bitsy and I selected a kit home from Aladdin House catalog, a grand four-bedroom (The Strathmore) to be situated on our farm property, but things are worrisome around the country. Richard speaks frequently about the stock market crash. He's not certain if it will affect us here, but he believes we should wait. It also appears, yet again, a new baby is not meant to be. This is the third time I've tried to bring Bitsy a sibling, and have failed. As I write this, Bitsy is preparing a "staying put" party. Such a sweet girl. I believe she intends to cheer me. Her friends arrive shortly to celebrate. . . .

I pulled my finger out of my mouth with a loud pop. Looking to assure myself no one was watching, I stuck it back into the bowl of cake batter and scooped up another mouthful. Delicious. Mama was in the next room working on correspondence. She allowed me to bake this cake by myself to celebrate "staying put" in our house. But she didn't know!

Like bubbles, my excitement rose to the surface and jumped out of my mouth in a giggle.

"What are you laughing about in there?" Mama called from the dining room.

"Nothing," I called back, and put my hand to my mouth to stop another bubble from bursting. I was baking a cake for a surprise party for Mama! She had been so sad lately. Papa said he wanted to give her something special since we won't be building her dream house. Not right away, at least.

As I baked, he said he was going to the farm, but he actually went to fetch a new dress my aunt Emmeline had ordered from the Sears catalog. A month ago, Mama had dog-eared the page I showed Papa, and he had it shipped to aunt Em's house. Papa was also bringing my aunt home with him, and then we would go to the movies at the Marlow. He had promised we could see *The Karnival Kid,* starring Mickey Mouse and Clarabelle Cow. Polly had told me all about it at school. She was always the first to see the movies, but this time I would be behind by only a couple of days.

Mama helped me take the cake out of the oven and returned to the living room to finish the mending. I was watching over it as it cooled, picking at the baked-on drips from the edges of the cake pan when I heard the car roll up the drive.

"Bitsy, open the back door, would you," Mama called. "It looks like your father came home early from the farm."

I squealed, just a tiny bit. I couldn't help it.

"You sound like a goose," she called. "What are you up to in there?"

"I touched the cake pan. But I'm fine!" I fibbed, and ran to open the back door.

Aunt Emmeline held a stack of three dress boxes. She put her finger to her lips. Papa carried a bouquet of white roses cut fresh from our yard. They rested elegantly in a new pink cut-glass vase I also recognized from the Sears catalog. He slipped past Emmeline holding the roses and walked into the living room to distract Mama.

"Why are there three dress boxes?" I whispered to my aunt.

Aunt Em handed me one box, and motioned for me to follow her. She picked up the other two boxes and we tiptoed into my bedroom. She opened the smallest box and pulled out the loveliest buttercup yellow dress I'd ever seen. It had a white boat collar and two tiers of ruffle on the skirt. She held it to my shoulders. "Perfect," she said. "Let's get this on you."

"I thought the dress was for Mama," I whispered, shrugging out of my navy jumper.

"There's one for her. Your papa thought you should have something nice to wear for the celebration too," she said, and opened the next box. Inside was the dress for Mama, also yellow for spring. It was the one she had chosen, with cap sleeves and a drop waist. The gossamer fabric seemed alive and I sighed as I touched it. Aunt Em tucked it back into the box and closed the gift.

Finally, my aunt opened the last container. Inside was a dress for her. It matched Mama's, except it was soft green. She dropped her cloak to the ground and quickly changed into it. "Hurry now, Bitsy, I don't think Richard will be able to occupy her much longer." She smoothed her hands along the skirt. "Your mama and I used to make matching dresses for each other every spring when we were young. So when I saw Richard was buying her a dress, I bought one for myself, for old time's sake."

She spun in place and she was beautiful, but nowhere near as beautiful as my mama. Fidgeting while she straightened my collar, a bubble of excitement popped and I giggled. I slapped a hand over my mouth. I turned around three times to see how far the skirt would swirl from my knees, hand still over my mouth, just in case.

Aunt Emmeline grasped my hand and said, "Let's sing 'Pop Goes the Weasel' as we walk into the living room! She's going to be so surprised!"

I saw Papa's silhouette through the glass in our front door and moments later heard his key in the lock. It was dark outside, though we hadn't eaten dinner yet. January was a black, cold month. I was now in the third grade and therefore practicing my cursive as I sat at the dining room table, but it was hard to concentrate tonight. Mama was nervous and pacing around the kitchen. She kept walking to the front door and standing silently, waiting. After a moment, she would drift back to the kitchen, stir the pot, and return to her post in the living room.

I looked toward the door anxiously, swallowing the butterflies that threatened to fly into my throat. Mama was in the kitchen, and heard the click of the lock when I did. She rushed in, holding a dishcloth in her hands, wringing it as she walked.

"Well, how many head did you sell?" she asked quietly, as Papa shuffled in, stamping his boots from the snow.

"It wasn't good, Cora."

"Tell me." She put a hand on his shoulder and gently helped him out of his heavy winter coat.

"I didn't sell a one of them," he said, his voice taking on an edge of anger.

Mama gasped. "Not one?"

He shook his head.

"What will happen, then?" she asked.

I sat frozen at the table, waiting for his answer. I knew we needed to sell the cattle to pay for the farm.

Papa put a reassuring hand on Mama's cheek. "You can save your worry for a while. I sold the automobile—the LaSalle." He swallowed. "I managed to fetch a decent price for it, since it's still in good shape."

"Oh, Richard, I'm sorry," Mama said, but I could see her relief as her shoulders relaxed.

"I took the streetcar home, but I have cash in my pocket."

Papa's smile didn't touch the rest of his face. He reached into his front pants pocket and pulled out a stack of dollar bills.

Mama touched the money and exhaled. "How long will this take us, do you think?"

"Only a couple of months . . . into early spring and the next auction. I'll keep the cattle fat and hope they sell."

Papa pulled up a chair next to me. "What are you working on, Bitsy?"

"Cursive." I held up my page proudly. There were two things I could do well in school. One was reading and the other was cursive. Mama also said I did an extra fine job at talking out of turn.

Papa gazed absently at my paper for a moment, his eyes drifting to a rough patch on the table. He rubbed it with his finger.

"Papa?"

He startled. "Yes, Bitsy?"

"So did anyone sell any cows? I mean, what will people eat, if you can't sell the cattle?"

"That's a good question, Bits. The government bought all the cattle off the Trimble farm, as the property went on the auction block."

Mama peered around from the kitchen. Her voice shook as she spoke. "The Trimbles lost their farm?"

"That they did," Papa said.

The Trimbles worked the property next to ours, and lived there too. I had spent many an afternoon on their tire swing with the three Trimble children as my parents worked on our property.

"Where will they live now?" I said, as I thought about their cheerful white house.

"I guess they'll try to find a place. They got a bit of money from the cattle." He patted my hand.

"How much did they get, Richard?" Mama hovered above Papa and me.

"Two dollars a head." His eyes stayed glued to the spot on the table.

"Two dollars? We pay more than that per head to feed them. Every month!" Mama sounded desperate.

"I didn't sell. Prices will rise come spring, I imagine. In the meantime . . ." Papa showed her the money from selling the car again. "And I had one butchered. We won't go hungry." As they counted the money together, considering how long it would last, I worried about the Trimble children and everyone else in the world who wouldn't have meat to eat, since no one could afford to buy a cow.

Mama held my hand tighter and we stepped off the curb into the street. Cars were parked at an angle along the main street in Sugar House. The sidewalk in front of the firehouse was crowded. Folks were standing in line, silently staring straight at the backs of the people in front of them, angry.

"Will there be a party or a picnic there?" I asked doubtfully, since those people didn't look like they were much in the mood to celebrate.

"No, no. They're waiting for the breadline to open," said Mama.

At the mention of bread my stomach grumbled. It was nearly lunchtime. "Can we get some bread, too?"

"We have food at home, but maybe we can get a little something at the market. I need to pick up some thread and a couple of other things. Let's cross."

She tugged me into the street when it was empty of automobiles. Halfway across, I dropped her hand. "Watch me, I can jump clear over the streetcar rails!" I teetered on the closest of the iron beams that crisscrossed the middle of the wide street.

Mama checked both ways up the line as I balanced precariously. "Okay, Bits, jump, but be quick about it."

She stepped back to watch me. I leaped and landed. She followed behind me, clapping her praise. Together we hurried to the other side of the street and into the market. I immediately headed for the aisle that held the toys. I used to get one new thing every time we shopped, but it seemed ages since I was able to bring home a new toy. "Can I stay here?" I begged. "Please?"

"I guess so, but we can't buy anything today except a treat to last us until we get home for lunch," Mama replied as she strolled away.

I hurried to the paper dolls. There was a fresh new copy of the same Sunshine Cut-Outs I'd been playing with since Christmas. The book of paper dolls had been my gift from Santa. My set was the sports series, and my favorite outfit was the yellow dress for spring since it was the same style as mine. Unfortunately, my Sunshine Jane's yellow paper dress had only one tab that still stayed folded, and the tabs on her winter coat had ripped right off. I closed the book of Sunshine Cut-Outs carefully and put it back on the display. Next to it was a mother-and-daughter cutout book. The mother had a short, bobbed haircut like my aunt Emmeline. Her dresses didn't hang to her ankles like many of Mama's, but had short sleeves, and the skirt hung only past her knees. She was very stylish. I ran my thumb over the thick, glossy paper. Oh, I wanted these dolls. I hooked the folded booklet of paper dolls under my arm and ran to find Mama.

She was two aisles over. I held it up for her to see. "Oh, Bitsy, they're darling." She pondered the items she held in her basket, two spools of thread, some safety pins, three bars of soap, and some Clorox bleach. She opened her coin purse. "I don't think we're going to have enough money today, and I need these other things." She bit her lip, considering each item.

"It's all right, Mama." I turned away before she saw I might cry.

"But, Bitsy, I have an idea. Bring the paper dolls back over here. I want to look at something."

She touched me gently under my chin as I held the book out to her. "Don't be sad, Bits. This is going to be good. Let's see, each outfit has four or five tabs, but the paper is thicker. We could use some glue to paste a couple of pages together and it would work fine."

"What are you going to do, Mama?"

"Run, go get me some paper glue. We have enough for that. We're going to make our own paper dolls from the Sears catalog! I've saved two catalogs. Your dolls will have more clothes than they can wear in a year!"

I fetched the glue and returned the cutouts to the shelf. I could barely contain myself as we waited to pay. "There are even bicycles in the catalog, Bitsy. Your dolls can have furniture and bicycles." Mama squeezed my hand. "Now stop bouncing and save your energy for the walk home. We'll get to making the dolls right after lunch." It seemed ages since I had seen her smile so wide and happy.

Outside the store a man stood with a box of the reddest apples I had ever seen. My stomach growled as we walked by. "Oh, Bitsy, I forgot to get you a treat. Do you want an apple?" We turned back toward the apple seller. He lifted his face toward us and I recognized him in the shadow of his hat.

His eyes widened and he flushed as red as his tower of fruit. Finally he stood and took her hand. "Sister Robinson."

"Brother Gibb?" Mama stuttered as she said his name, surprised. "I thought you worked at the . . ." her words trailed off.

"This is my first week in the apple business." He smiled weakly. "The bank I worked at shut down a couple months ago."

"Oh, I'm sorry."

"I thought it would be easy to get another job, but . . ." He shrugged. "So, would you like an apple, little miss?" He stared at his feet as he spoke.

"How much?" asked Mama as she patted her flat purse with worried fingers.

"A dime. But since I know you two ladies, free for you," he said.

"Oh, no. We can't take one for free, but I only have"—she dug through her coin pocket—"a nickel and a couple of pennies." She held them out to him.

He shook his head and handed me the apple.

"Please," she said.

He nodded slowly and opened his empty palm. He cast his eyes down as he accepted the change. "I'll see you at service on Sunday," he said softly.

I bit into my apple as we walked. Sweet juice filled my mouth. "Brother Gibb is lucky to have such a lovely job, Mama. If I were an apple seller, I'd eat apples all day long."

Mama gasped and yanked up on my arm. "Hush now, Elsbeth," she hissed.

I wrinkled my nose at the scolding, but the next bite I took was tiny and I chewed as quietly as I could. I didn't know why she was so angry, but I did try to hold my tongue for the rest of our walk back home.

"It's really a shame we couldn't get you a new coat for your birthday, Bitsy. This one's tattered all about the sleeves. I don't think even the finest seamstress could take the wear out of it." Mama spoke without looking up from her sewing.

I nodded absently. Mama had taught me to knit and had given me a skein of mustard yellow yarn for my ninth birthday. I was trying to knit a scarf for myself. It wasn't as easy as I thought it would be. My stitches were uneven, so the scarf was easily a couple of inches wider on one end than the other. I held it up to assess the quality when Mama glanced over.

"Oh, Bitsy, you should probably pull out the last couple of rows. Remember, if you give a little tug on the trailing yarn you can tighten your stitches up."

"It's just fine, I think," I said through clenched teeth. There was no way I was going to unravel this stupid scarf. Knitting was no fun and I was aching to get outside where the leaves were swirling in the street. "I'll finish it later," I said as I gazed longingly out the window. I put my knitting on the floor and stood up.

"Stay seated, Bits. We're working on winter clothing this afternoon. Do you think it is fun for me to reline this old coat of yours? I'd rather buy you a new coat and make something pretty for the house. We've got to do what needs to be done." There was firmness in Mama's voice that made me sit down and resume plucking at my scarf.

Mama got up, knelt by my chair, and draped the golden yarn

over my fingers. "See, wrap it like this and give it a little tug at the end after each stitch." I pulled a couple successfully. She stood and patted me on the head. "The yellow will look so lovely with your auburn hair. And I thought I would fix up your old blue scarf for myself." She pulled it from the yarn basket. "I'll add a loop here and pull these ends that've worked loose. The color is quite lovely."

"I thought you said you wanted something new this winter, to go with the coat Papa bought you two seasons ago."

"Well, that was before, Bitsy. Things aren't quite as rosy this autumn. Your papa will be happy if we don't spend too much on new clothing. It will be all we can do to make the payments on the farm and this house," she mused.

"I know, Mama. Sister Boyden taught us a saying at church to help us through the lean times. She made us memorize it along with a passage from Nephi. Do you want to hear it?" I asked eagerly.

"Of course. I'm listening." Mama resumed stitching the blanket into the lining of my coat.

"Use it up, wear it out, make it do, or do without," I said, proud I'd remembered all of the parts.

"I like that. I really do. What would we be doing today, do you think?" Mama asked.

I tilted my head, thinking, "Make it do! You're making do with my old coat and the blankets, aren't you?"

"What a smart girl. What else?" she asked.

"I don't know. I'm *making* something?" I responded hopefully.

"Not quite. I'm *not* getting a new scarf for myself, so what am I doing?" Mama asked playfully.

"Doing without!" I yelled. I was good at this game.

"Right again, my little Bitsy girl. Right again." Mama sighed and passed her hand over her swollen belly. The baby inside was getting big. I could hardly wait to have a sister. Mama grimaced as she rubbed. I guessed she wasn't very happy about doing without.

I wished I had curled up right there on Mama's lap and held

her close. I wish I had told her I loved her. Because that day was the last day my mama had on this earth. And when she died, she took the baby with her.

The first Christmas without Mama had come and gone. Aunt Emmeline had invited us to her home to celebrate, but Papa hadn't been much in the mood, so there had been no celebration in our house, not even a Christmas tree. Now we were at the beginning of a brand-new year, and I was sitting at the table angry at Papa, and sorry for myself.

It was warm in the house, finally. Papa mentioned he'd bought a little coal on credit and things were looking up. And that was something to be cheerful for, I told myself. Of course I didn't say anything to Papa when he told me, since we hadn't spoken for a whole week. Not since he had burned Mama's rocker and tried to set flame to the memory book. Maybe his memories of Mama were too painful, but I couldn't forgive him for trying to burn mine.

There was an insistent knocking on the front door, which caused me to startle. Through the opaque glass I could see the silhouette of a woman, the roundest woman I'd ever seen.

Papa called from the kitchen, "Answer it, please. I'm expecting someone." His voice was strained. He had been wearing his fake cheer like a mask all morning long. I stuck my tongue out at him, though he couldn't see it from the kitchen, and made my way to the door.

I opened the wooden door two inches and the woman pushed it the rest of the way. "Mind if we step inside? Mighty cold out today." She shoved a tiny boy in front of her through the open door. I could hardly see him through the folds in her long skirt. Slamming the door against the wind, she rubbed her arms, shivering. Her eyes surveyed our bare living room, before landing back on my face.

"What's your name, darlin'?" She touched me lightly on the head. "My, you have pretty hair."

Who was this woman? Where was my father?

Suddenly he appeared from the kitchen. "You must be Mrs. Brimley."

She smiled. Her face was wrinkled, but warm. "I am. And this is my grandson, Redmond." When she said his name, he stepped back into the security of her voluminous skirts. "He's a little shy. Met *me* for the first time two weeks ago, and here he is just five years old. His parents are both in California, trying to earn a living. Times are tough. . . ." She shook her head and patted Redmond on his.

"Times are tough," my father agreed. "I propose we have you sleep in the living room here. We'll move Bitsy's mattress in for you. You can close the pocket doors for privacy and the fire will keep you warm." Papa was speaking of *our* living room! Once it held our entry table, a couch, and Mama's rocking chair. Now it was nearly empty. We had sold the couch and the table, and of course the rocking chair had burned.

I put my hand to my mouth. Were they really going to sleep in our house?

"Looks fine. Redmond can sleep on the floor. I'll watch them both while you look for work, like the advertisement said." As she spoke she reached out through the front door and pulled in two suitcases and a roll of blankets.

"But my papa works on our farm," I protested. "I can go with him when I'm not in school."

Papa put a hand on my head. "Not anymore, little Bit," he said.

"You lost the farm, didn't you?" I hissed.

Papa's eyes were red-rimmed, but he didn't blink as he nodded. I didn't even know what "losing the farm" meant, but he and Mama had said those words so often in hushed voices, I knew it must be bad.

It was too much. First Mama, and now these people sleeping in our house! I ran from the room and I threw myself on my bed. I covered myself with my quilt, then I remembered the memory book hidden under the mattress. Papa was going to give that fat woman my bed. I had to move the memory book before my father found it and burned it along with everything else that mattered. Hurrying, I wrapped it in one of my old dresses and put it in the corner of my closet. Minutes later, Papa opened the door of my room.

"Bitsy, we need to move your bed into the living room." I stayed frozen in a mound on my mattress.

"Bits, I'm trying. I am. If we can't keep the house, then I can't keep you. You'd have to move in with your aunt Emmeline. And if you leave me . . ." I felt the bed shift as he sat on the edge.

Peering out from my blankets, I saw Papa swipe his cheeks with the back of his hand. I couldn't stand it. There were too many changes. I crawled from my quilts onto his lap. I hadn't let him hold me since Mama died.

"It'll be okay." He smoothed my hair as I cried. "No more tears. You're a big girl now. You can help me get things in order since Mama's not here."

"Why did you burn her chair?" I wouldn't mention the memory book. I didn't want him to take it from me.

"Oh, my girl, I was so sad." He swallowed several times. "I miss your mama so much. And it was so cold. I'm sorry if I frightened you. I won't let it happen again." He pushed me back so he could see my face. "I'm sorry."

I balled my quilts in my arms. "Where will I sleep?"

"On the floor in here. Or you can join me in the bed I shared with your mama."

I couldn't take the sleeping spot of my mama! I dropped my quilt on the bedroom floor. He hoisted the mattress over his shoulder and carried it into the living room, where I could hear Mrs. Brimley moving about unpacking her small suitcases, talking softly to Redmond.

I snuck into the closet and pulled the dress from around the memory book. I opened it to the last entry and ran my fingers over the page.

August 4, 1931

Today, while Bitsy and I made paper dolls from an old Sears catalog, I told her she will finally be a big sister. This is the longest I have carried a child, aside from Bitsy, so I believe it will really happen this time around. The baby should be born sometime in early December.

There will be a ten-year difference in age between Bitsy and this child, but I hope they will still enjoy each other through the years. Richard and I are thrilled, though we are uncertain about the future of the farm. It is hard to think of providing for another member of the family, but Richard assures me the ones who are really suffering through this Depression are the men with little work ethic. He is sure we'll weather through it. We are blessed to have another child, whatever is going on in the world.

I turned the page. It was a yawning expanse of nothing. There would be no more words from my mama. Where was the baby? Nowhere! And where was my mama?

I smoothed my hand over the spread of white. I couldn't write on the back of her page and rumple her words with my own press of the pencil. But I needed to tell someone of the terrible, awful things happening to me. If Mama wasn't here to record my life, how would anyone remember me, at all? How could I even remember myself? I placed my pencil over the blank page and wrote.

February 1932
I don't like all of these changes, not one bit. It's my papa's fault for losing the farm. And it's Mama's fault for dying and that stupid baby's fault for ripping her open and making her die. And I won't tell anyone else this, not ever, but it's my fault too. I wanted Mama to have that baby. Sometimes I wanted the baby more than I wanted Mama. And now I don't have a mama or a sister. Now I will have a strange woman living in my house, who I don't even know.

And then I didn't mean to, but I couldn't help myself. Turning the page back to Mama's entry, I picked up my pencil and held it over her words like a knife. I dropped the sharp tip onto the fine paper and I covered her entry with my black scrawl. But it wasn't enough. I pressed harder and harder, scratching until the paper curled like peeled paint.

I slammed the book closed. I had really done it now. I'd destroyed a piece of her! I sobbed silently, for I didn't want Papa to hear me. I shouldn't write in it again, because the book wouldn't be full of Mama's words, it would be full of mine. And I would never rip the pages like a spoiled baby! I could make words any day. My mama would never be able to write words, not ever again.

"I don't agree, Richard. You know I think you're a wonderful father, but Bitsy should spend her days with her family, not a stranger who happens to live in your house." I could hear my aunt Emmeline speaking with my father in the backyard. They had stepped out under the cherry tree, because their words were getting too loud.

"She belongs with me, Emmeline. She's all I have left." Papa said this softly, and I had to lean closer to the back door to hear him. "Besides, I'm here every weekend."

"You could see her every weekend and I would just take her during the week. You could even stay with us, you wouldn't need to keep this house." I shook my head silently on the other side of the door. No! I didn't want to leave! This was my home!

"We can offer her a home, with cousins and family," Aunt Emmeline continued. "What does she have here? Who will really take the time to love Bitsy if you aren't around to do it?" she asked. Her voice broke. "Don't you think Cora would want me to be with her?" There was a pause. "I'm sorry, Richard, I didn't mean to weep. I just can't believe she's gone."

I peeked out the door. Papa had his hand on Aunt Emmeline's back. He was patting her as she cried. "I can't believe she's gone, either," he murmured.

They separated and my father spoke again. "I want to keep this arrangement with Mrs. Brimley. You're at the hospital most of the day, anyway. It's not like you're mothering those boys of yours all day long."

"Maybe not all day, but enough," Emmeline replied.

Papa shook his head, looking at the ground. "I've also considered sending her to my sister, Margaret. They went to Arizona in search of work. So far her husband has only found temporary placement here and there. It's no more stable than what I can give her in my own home."

"I miss Margaret," Emmeline said. "Please wish her well when you write next."

Papa nodded. His next words were angry, his jaw was clenched. "I don't understand how you're getting by with all of your children and I can't even support my one." He raised his finger and swung it in front of Aunt Emmeline's face.

She gently took his hand in hers. "Don't blame yourself, Richard, it's not easy." She paused. "You borrowed so much to buy the farm and things have been worse for farmers."

Papa hung his head. "We saved for so long to buy that property, living with your father for all those years . . . and for what?"

There was a loud bang from inside the house. Two of my cousins, Deacon and Blake, slammed open the pocket doors separating our part of the house from the place where Mrs. Brimley slept. They were tugging the wide wood doors, swinging them back and forth and giggling.

"You two aren't supposed to be disturbing Mrs. Brimley's room! Quit it!" I yelled.

My aunt made her way to the back door to check on her boys. I stood still at the edge of the door frame, hoping she wouldn't notice I'd been listening.

"Oh my, Bitsy! You startled me. Are those two boys up to no good?" she said as she walked in.

Aunt Emmeline had five boys, count them, five. And I didn't want to live with them, not at all. My mama would sometimes get sad when her sister would visit, expecting *another* baby. But it would be *another* boy. My mama would remind me that even though there was just me, she still felt blessed because I was a wonderful little girl.

Aunt Em walked back out the door tugging her two youngest by the hands. "Go out there and climb a tree or something, would you?" she said, pushing them through the door.

She beckoned to me from the porch. "Bitsy, you come out too. Have I ever told you about that big old rosebush growing in your yard? The white one in bloom right now?"

I shook my head. "You mean the one Mama called the Emmeline rosebush?"

"That's it. Come out here and I'll tell you how I came to plant it in this yard."

She clasped my hand and pulled me toward the stairs leading into our backyard, when there was a crash and a shriek from near the cherry tree. My papa ran over and scooped up Blake, who had fallen from one of the branches. Blood was streaming from his mouth. "Mama!" he screamed, and reached for Aunt Emmeline. She dropped my hand and ran to my bloodied cousin.

Turned out he drove his tooth clear through his lip when he fell from the tree. Served him right too, for being such a pest. It wasn't long before the whole lot of them left and our house fell quiet again.

That night I opened the memory book to one of the first few pages. I knew Mama had pasted some of the rose petals Aunt Emmeline spoke of on one of the early entries. There it was.

June 12, 1923

Bitsy can crawl, and she is quite a speedy little one. Here's the trouble—she puts everything she can get her hands on directly in her mouth. Dirt, rocks, leaves, no matter.

The rosebush Emmeline planted is in bloom today, and while I wrote this entry, Bitsy smelled the blossom, then stuffed a handful of white rose petals in her mouth. I have fished them from her maw and will fix them to this page when they are dry, as a testament to her non-discriminating palate.

I picked up my own pencil and turned to a fresh white page and wrote the date, nine years after the entry I had just read from Mama.

June 13, 1932
I won't ever leave this house, but Aunt Emmeline came over today and she wants to take me home to live with her. I'll tell you this, I don't like any of her stinky boys and I don't want to live with them one bit. Plus, she promised to tell me the story of the rosebush named after her, but Blake bloodied his mouth and she plum forgot. I'd rather live with fat, old Mrs. Brimley. Aunt Em will never be my mama, even though sometimes when I look at her, I can see my mama's smile.

EMMELINE LANSING

Downington Avenue
1913

"I have a couple of hours before my next class. Where should we walk today?" I called as I approached our bungalow.

Nathaniel was reclined on the front steps, waiting for me after my morning anatomy class. I gazed at him this warm autumn morning, very much present. In two days he would be gone and it made me ache to think of it.

Leaning back on his elbows, he stretched his long legs over several steps. The sun shone on his face, and he spoke without opening his eyes. "Oh, nurse, I've been waiting for you! I'm feeling faint, so I think you should lay your hands on my chest to see if I am still breathing." He raised a brow, a smile playing on his lips.

I knelt down next to him and put my hands on his shoulders.

"You are miles from my lungs, sweet nurse. Lower," he murmured, closed eyes twitching in anticipation.

I slowly slid my hands down over his ribs. He sighed, his chest moving with his breath.

"Rest easy, you're still alive." My heart raced as my fingers skimmed the fabric of his shirt, his chest a solid presence beneath the buttons. I held my palm over his heart, feeling his pulse resonate through my arm. Finally, I slid my hands down and rested them on his waist and lay my head against his sun-warmed body.

"Ahemm . . . excuse me, you two. You're on the *front* porch. And doesn't Nathaniel have some sort of religious commitment making this kind of behavior against the rules?" Nathaniel and I quickly sat up to see Cora's smug smile, her head peeking from the open front door.

Nathaniel stood and put his hands deep in his front pockets. He smiled apologetically at Cora and properly linked his elbow through mine. "I've brought two horses from the family farm today, figuring you may like a ride before the weather turns frigid."

"You didn't!" I squealed. "I haven't ridden since Helper!"

"I did, and I'm glad you're excited! However, these two old gals are nothing fancy," he said as we walked to the backyard. The horses were roped to the shiny new clothesline. "But we may be able to make it to the mouth of the canyon and back before your next class starts."

Nathaniel cinched the saddle on each horse as I caressed their finely boned muzzles. I missed this, the anticipation, impatient stamping of hooves as I prepared to ride. Nathaniel was whispering and nickering to the horses as he worked, patting their flanks. They moved willingly as he pulled on the leather straps. I studied his capable hands while he worked and was surprised how much I wanted them on me.

He finished and stood, brushing his palms on his pants. "Emmeline, are you blushing? Excited for your ride?" He put his hand on my cheek.

"The sun's vivid at this angle," I stuttered, adjusting my hat so he couldn't see me quite so clearly.

In all honesty, I was surprised by our easy intimacy. I wanted those fingers to caress me. I knew he was preparing to serve a mission and I was his temptation. His bishop had told him as much. But I didn't see it that way. He stepped closer to pass me the reins of the bridled mare. I leaned into him.

"Your mount, my lady," he said as he helped me onto the

mare and smoothed my skirts. A familiar thrill coursed through my legs as I readied for the ride. I kicked hard into the side of the horse and we took off, galloping across the empty lots on either side of Downington Avenue. Nathaniel caught up to me and we both slowed to a walk.

"Oh, how I've missed this. Thank you for the wonderful surprise!"

He glowed. "Let's see what you've got, Em, try and keep up! Yah!" He spurred his horse and the two of them raced away.

We galloped hard for several minutes. It didn't take long before we were at the eastern edge of town, where the houses and roads simply stopped and the dry hills rolled continually upward, toward the base of the Wasatch Mountains. The tawny ground was covered with intermittent dry grasses and scrub oak.

"Not bad for a city ride," I panted as we slowed to pick our way through the bushes. Here and there a lizard scampered out of the way as the horses stepped over rocks.

On a crest of boulders, we turned the horses west toward the valley. Wooly in the distance, pines and sage merged into a patchwork quilt of emerald and olive. Westminster College was in the distance, towers rising high into the bright heavens. Beyond that we glimpsed the smokestacks from the brick foundry. To our left ran Emigration Creek, a ribbon snaking its way toward the wide cobbled streets of Sugar House, and farther, squares of farmland, flat and recently harvested, now burnished by autumn.

Near our resting spot it appeared someone had cleared a path toward the creek. Gingerly, we made our way over the crest to water the horses. We were in a small meadow bathed in sunlight. An old sandstone foundation stood in the center of the clearing, its leaning chimney nearly invisible in the brush surrounding it. Stray stones scattered about the footprint. We dismounted and picked our way to the most solid part of the ramshackle cottage.

"I wonder who lived here," I said, pleased with the discovery. "And how long ago? Isn't it lovely right here by the creek, hidden from the world?"

"It doesn't look like anyone's been to this place for ages; the grasses aren't even trampled," said Nathaniel. "Maybe it was one of the first pioneers?"

"Or an Indian! Or a bank robber on the run from the law!"

Nathaniel laughed out loud. "Emmeline, you always know how to cheer me up! I've been brooding about this mission the entire time we were riding." He grabbed my hands. "I'm not sure I can leave you."

"Then don't go!" I begged. "You can stay here with me. We'll get some lumber and build walls on this little place. You can catch fish and I can have babies. No one even needs to know we're here. We could do it, Nathaniel. We could." In my mind I knew I was fooling, but there was truth burning under the casual tone of my voice. I wanted him to stay.

Nathaniel stood and walked toward the chimney, absently kicking at the loose stones as he walked. I followed and touched his hand.

He grabbed my wrist and whirled me to face him. His hands were firm on my waist as he pulled me tight. His mouth found mine and he pressed hard against my face. I backed up slightly and found I was leaning into the rough stones of the old chimney, warm from the sun. They pressed into my chilled body.

Nathaniel moved his lips from mine, drawing a line from my jaw to my clavicle with his finger and following it with his mouth. Never before had he touched me with such urgency. His hands were fire through the thin fabric of my dress as he moved them up and down the sides of my body, from waist to ribs, and back again.

Wrapped in his arms, my body flush from the sun-warmed masonry, I moaned softly. Grasping Nathaniel at the small of his back, I pulled him close. There was heat where our bodies met, his breath in my hair.

His finger hovered above the dip between my neck and collar bone, the Suprasternal Notch, I thought briefly from anatomy class. Under his hand, my heartbeat rose to match his and the pulse between the two of us thrummed in unison. Hesitating for only a moment, he unfastened two pearl buttons and slid his hand through the opening, stopping with his palm over my exposed breast. His fingertips grazed my side as my heart pounded against his burning palm.

Suddenly, his shoulders sagged. His torso still pressed to mine, he drove his hands against the stones of the chimney above my head. Facing the sky, lids still pressed together, he moaned, "What am I doing?"

Without meeting my eyes, he slowly fastened the buttons on my dress. He touched my hair, pulling a lock through his fingers, and brought it to his lips. "Nathaniel," I whispered.

He helped me mount my horse without saying a word and we rode from the clearing.

It seemed only a few minutes had passed when we arrived at my front porch. Nathaniel climbed from his horse and wrapped me in his arms. He touched my bottom lip, lingering for a moment. "I need some time to pray and think," he whispered.

A tear slid down my cheek. He touched it with his thumb. "Oh, how I love you," he sighed.

Mounting his horse, he took the reins of my mare and they walked up the street without looking back. I sat heavily on the top step of the porch and watched his retreat.

A man of his word, Nathaniel decided to go on his mission. A farewell luncheon was planned for him at Brother Conner's. Following the luncheon, Brother Conner would whisk him away in his carriage, bound for the Rio Grande depot. Train, then ship, and Nathaniel would be gone for two years.

As Cora secured the last button of my Sunday dress, I couldn't breathe. Bending over, I put my hands on my thighs, trying to calm myself. Cora rubbed my back. "Are you going to be okay, Em? Who would've thought my sister could get lovesick so quickly?"

"I know. It defies rational thought!" I hiccupped.

I managed to pull myself together for the luncheon. Nathaniel sought me out and secured a spot for me at the long table, which sagged with the weight of the feast: roast chicken, pickles, canned peaches, and pies. But I could hardly eat. Nathaniel talked with the others at the table, but hidden from view, his hand clutched my knee.

Following the meal, Brother Conner led us to the front door where his one-horse carriage stood waiting. It was already loaded with Nathaniel's leather bags. The horse moved from foot to foot, snorting impatiently.

"Before you leave, Nathaniel," he said, "I've a special treat. Sister Conner bought me this Kodak Brownie for my birthday. Stand there in the light with Emmeline, and I'll take a photo of you two so Emmeline will remember you while you're away." He dipped his head under a black cloth. "Now be patient with me," came his muffled voice. "I'm only learning how to work this thing."

We stood awkwardly on the porch side by side.

"Get a little closer. Now move to the left so your faces are out of the direct sunlight."

Nathaniel's hand wrapped around my waist and he pulled me tight against him. Brother Conner was taking forever, fussing around behind the camera, flipping switches and raising his head to peer at us.

Nathaniel's lips touched my hair. "Will you marry me, Emmeline? Please wait for me," he whispered, his voice catching on the last word.

Brother Conner emerged from behind the Brownie. "Got it. I think. I guess I'll know when I have it developed." He stepped away from the camera. "We should probably get you to the station, Nathaniel. Train leaves in an hour."

Nathaniel held my hand loosely, and my fingers stretched to keep contact as he walked away. "I love you," he said, his voice escaping on the breeze.

I mouthed back, "I love you too."

He stepped into the carriage, and was gone.

BITSY ROBINSON

Downington Avenue
1932

October 9, 1932

Today I turned ten. Papa is on a job building a rock wall somewhere. He couldn't even make it home this weekend. I'd like to think he is out buying something nice for me, but in my deepest heart of hearts, I think he forgot. I'm writing in this memory book today because that's what Mama would have done. All of my birthday celebrations have been recorded until now. Here goes . . . this is my version of a birthday entry written by my mama.

Happy Birthday to my Bitsy, a redhead who never smiles. It has not been her best year. Her hair is stringy most days, because she doesn't like to comb it, and I am not at home to help her. She didn't receive a single gift, though a new dress would be nice because the dress she is wearing now is too small and torn at the armpits. I am sad to report that all of the people who loved her when she was a baby are gone. Grandmother—dead, Grandpa—moved, Papa—too busy to care. And me, her mama, well, I'm also dead, dead, dead!

I was shuffling around the kitchen, opening and closing our cupboards, looking for something special to eat when Mrs. Brimley slid the pocket door to her room and bustled herself into the kitchen.

"What's all the clatter about, little miss? Did you get up on the wrong side of the bed?"

I slammed a cupboard. "There's nothing to eat in this house."

"Well now, I'll make you and Redmond some oatmeal. You go get yourself ready for church."

"Don't we even have eggs?" I pouted.

Mrs. Brimley pursed her lips. "Get your best dress on. Meetings start in less than an hour."

I went to my room and yanked my dress over my head. The collar caught on my ears, making them burn. "Not a single soul knows it's my birthday," I fumed. "And I won't tell them. I'll not utter a syllable at church."

And I didn't. I didn't offer to read from the Book of Mormon during Sunday school, even though it was my favorite activity, since I was such a fine reader. I didn't join in any of the songs during Sacrament Meeting, either. I even denied myself taking the Sacrament. Oh, I faked putting the bread into my mouth, so Mrs. Brimley wouldn't punish me. But I was determined to be miserable.

When the meeting ended I zipped out the door and ran back to our house. We kept the front door permanently locked now that the living room was Mrs. Brimley's bedroom, but I sat on the porch swing and stared vacantly out at the street. The trees shading the sidewalk on Downington Avenue were as golden as they were the last year and every other year on my birthday. But this year everything was different. Everything was awful.

I swung the porch swing back and forth until it smacked the porch pillars. Maybe Papa should have burned this stupid swing too, just like he burned Mama's rocker.

The front door opened. I startled. Mrs. Brimley wasn't home from church yet. And if she wasn't in the house, who was?

Papa stepped onto the porch. I tried to scowl at him. He smiled at me. "I wondered who was trying to tear down our porch. But it's only you, my big ten-year-old girl."

His face beamed and his cheeks were ruddy with delight. I jumped up. He remembered, after all!

"Come inside, Bits. I've got a surprise for you."

I followed him into the dining room, sheepishly. If only he knew how ungrateful and angry I had been all day long, he would paddle my bottom.

On the table was a pink bakery box. My mouth started to water, even before I saw the cake. Mama always made my birthday cake. I had tasted a bakery cake only once, at my friend Ruby's birthday party, but that was when I was seven. It was ages ago. My stomach growled.

My papa chuckled. "Open it."

"A store-bought cake?" I said as I touched the box. "How can we afford it?"

"Yesterday was payday, and I can't really bake, now, can I? Besides, it's a special treat for a special girl."

"I didn't think anyone remembered," I whispered.

"Well, I didn't forget and I bet your mama didn't either. I'm sure she's up there in heaven looking at us right now."

I gazed at the ceiling of our dining room, trying to see heaven beyond. "Want some cake, Mama?"

Papa drew in his breath quickly, but when I looked at him, he smiled. His eyes were sad. "I'm sure she wishes she could be here to help us celebrate."

"Me too," I said.

Papa went to the kitchen to get plates for serving. It took him several minutes to return with four, two for us and two for Mrs. Brimley and Redmond. No plate for Mama. He set the dishes one by one on the table, the echo of Mama's missing plate filling the room. We ate the entire cake that day.

The birds were trilling in the yard, bouncing from the bare branches of the apple tree to the cherry tree and back. I was tasked with watching Redmond while Mrs. Brimley made supper for the three of us. Redmond was no climber, but he had somehow managed to hoist himself onto the low branch of the cherry tree and was hanging on precariously. A strong wind would blow him off, and I urged the dark clouds to hasten a gust. It's not that I hated Redmond. But he wasn't my brother or my friend. He was nobody at all, yet he shared my house. He wasn't far enough from the ground to hurt himself, in a serious fashion, but I wouldn't mind hearing him cry if he fell. He was always so quiet. And that bothered me too.

Mrs. Brimley stuck her plump face out the door and called us for dinner. "Bitsy, help Redmond out of the tree and come eat some eggs."

I purposefully approached the cherry tree until I could hear Mrs. Brimley return to the kitchen, then I turned away and slid around the corner of the house. I crouched behind the Emmeline rosebush and waited. Redmond's fingers slipped; his hands were purple from the cold. I smiled. "If you climbed up there by yourself, you'll need to get yourself down."

I gazed at him coolly as he tried to reach the dirt by stretching his leg and pointing his toes. "I don't think your leg is long enough," I called softly.

Redmond switched his grip and tried again. He was really only a couple of inches off the ground when his hands slipped and he crashed, his bottom hitting with a thud. His eyes filled with tears, but he didn't make a sound.

I was instantly filled with guilt. I was a terrible girl. I rushed to him and offered my hand. He shook his head side to side and stood up, rubbing his hip.

Fine. I left him and walked into the house. I clicked the door behind me, holding tight to the handle while he tried to twist it. Mrs. Brimley marched up behind me as I stood at the door. "What are you doing, you devious little girl? Where's Redmond?"

I blinked and turned the knob. "I was just opening this for him," I said quickly.

Mrs. Brimley made a *harrumph* sound. I didn't care. I hated her anyway.

After supper, Mrs. Brimley slid her chair back and crossed her hands across her round belly. Redmond and I sat side by side on the window seat, trapped behind the table. "I've a special treat for you two today. In the corner of my room is something I bet you've never seen. Run in there and look real quick." She slid the table a few inches so we could crawl out. I shoved the pocket door leading from the dining room into what used to be my own living room and entered the quarters of Mrs. Brimley.

And there it was sitting on the floor. A radio! It was the size of Redmond if he crouched into a ball. The dark wood was scratched here and there and the fabric on the speaker was ripped good, but it was a real live radio.

"It's not new, but it belongs to us now. Got it used with the check my son sent. Paid your father for room and board and had a bit left over. It's good to be connected with all the troubles in the land. I got used to having a radio at the last place I lived. Now you two need to treat it with respect, but you can use it too."

I gasped. I'd never used a radio before, though I had seen them in the window of Granite Furniture and had heard the music played by the lady across the street, Mrs. McConnely. I slid my finger over the square button that said *on*.

"Go ahead, push it." I could hear the smile in Mrs. Brimley's voice. Once again I felt guilty for my nastiness to Redmond.

"I'll let Redmond," I said with exaggerated kindness.

Redmond wasted no time. He pushed the button eagerly and there was a low hum from the speakers as the radio came to life.

"Now turn the dial until you hear voices. Adjust it a little bit, back and forth, until you can hear them clearly. The program is set to start in a few minutes." Mrs. Brimley dragged her chair from the dining room close to the radio and lowered herself into it.

At quarter of six, music vibrated the cloth-covered speakers and a bubbly voice found me in the lonely room. "Who's the little chatterbox? The one with pretty auburn locks? Whom do you see? It's Little Orphan Annie!"

I won't say I hadn't heard of the program. All the kids at school played *Little Orphan Annie* at recess. My friend Polly Dogan would usually tell us about the adventure from the night prior. We'd all take a role and act out the escapade. Polly was my only friend who owned a radio, and she never hesitated to rub it in. It made me angry when she bragged about all the new things her family could buy, especially when my family never bought anything new. At least not anymore. But the worst part about Polly having the only radio was that Polly always got to be Orphan Annie. It really wasn't fair.

My mouth must have been hanging open the entire show, because when the program was over, my tongue was rough as sandpaper. Annie's story was *my* story! I was Little Orphan Annie! First, and most important, I had auburn hair. I was cared for by Ma Silo (Mrs. Brimley), I had a trusty dog (well, Redmond), and I was awaiting the return of my wonderful father who was secretly Daddy Warbucks!

Maybe when my papa returned from his job he would be rich enough to get me a real dog named Sandy. I lay flat on my back on Redmond's bedroll and sighed. I needed more of that program. And I needed to get some Ovaltine.

"Could we get some Ovaltine, Mrs. Brimley? This week from the store? The man on the radio said we should drink it every night with supper for our vitamins!" I tried to look convincing.

Redmond finally spoke. "Plus, the announcer said every time we drink it, we help Annie keep her adventures going strong." I rolled over and smiled at him. The kid wasn't all bad.

"Well, I don't know how much Ovaltine costs." Mrs. Brimley smiled indulgently at Redmond. "But I'll check at the market, next time I'm there."

"Please tell me the show will be on every night?" I sighed. Maybe tomorrow at school, I could be Little Orphan Annie at recess. Polly wouldn't be the only one who knew the story from the night before.

Mrs. Brimley tittered. "I imagine it will be. Every evening at quarter of six, like the announcer said. Would you like to listen tomorrow?"

"Oh, yes!" Redmond and I answered in unison.

"Will you play without fighting until then?" Her voice was serious.

I nodded happily. I finally had a friend in my home. And it wasn't Redmond. Her name was Annie.

*   *   *

I was hunting through the pile of blankets and quilts we kept at the bottom of Papa's closet. We were experiencing a cold streak and Mrs. Brimley had decided she could save money and use less coal if she had a cloak to wear around the house while Redmond and I were away at school. She promised to burn extra coal upon our return, so the house would be warm, but only if I could spare a few old blankets out of which she could fashion a cloak for wearing during the day.

Below Papa's abandoned clothing, and behind the stack of neatly folded blankets at the bottom of the closet, was the quilt Mama would drape across her lap while she sewed in the winter, the one made out of Papa's old church trousers—houndstooth, pinstripe, and the like. I hadn't seen the lap quilt in ages. I eagerly pulled it out and shook it to clear the wrinkles.

It seemed stuck in a wrinkled mound, so I pressed my hands against it to set it straight. Right in the center of the quilt was something sticky and stiff. I flipped the quilt to the other side and saw a rust-colored stain the size of a dinner dish. I wondered what had spilled on the quilt. Syrup? A flake came off on the tip of my finger. I pulled it close enough my vision blurred, but when I realized what it was, my breath squeezed from my chest and I threw the quilt onto the floor. I knew what it was. It was blood. Mama's blood, from . . .

I picked up the mound of folded blankets and walked them into the living room, leaving the soiled lap quilt in a discarded heap on the floor of the closet. After dropping the remaining items in a pile near Mrs. Brimley, who sat readying her scissors and needle for her project, I muttered, "Use whatever you like. Nobody needs these things anymore." And I turned away before she could see my tears.

I slipped into my room and found the memory book. I simply needed to read some of the words Mama wrote when she was alive. When she wasn't a stain of blood on a quilt. I pushed my thumb between two pages. The words my finger lit upon would be the words Mama would speak to me today, the words that would bring her to life in my head. I opened the book to my chosen spot. The page was blank! I had opened the book to the empty expanse that told me my mama was DEAD! I couldn't even find her in this stupid book! I couldn't find her anywhere. I slammed it shut and tossed it to the floor.

I remembered Mrs. Brimley's scissors. I raced back into the living room and grabbed them from her sewing supplies. "Where are you going with those?" she called after me as I dashed back into Papa's room.

I picked up the stained blanket. Consciously, I thought I would remove the circle of blood and Mrs. Brimley could use the rest, but as the scissors touched the quilt my throat tightened and my first cut was more of a stab. Ripping and slashing, I made a strange hiccupping sound with each breath. It seemed to take only moments before the entire blanket was in shreds around me.

A muffled gasp told me Mrs. Brimley stood at the bedroom door, her features wrinkled with worry. She came silently to my side and bent to retrieve her scissors. "When you're able, clean up this mess. Sometimes I don't understand you, Elsbeth." She shook her head and returned to the living room.

I swallowed hard and piled the scraps into the skirt of my dress. Holding the hem in my hands so nothing would escape, I walked out the back door and dumped them into the trash. Mama would be so angry at me. This was wasteful. And disrespectful. "Sorry, Mama," I whispered as I returned the lid to the top of the can. I swiped at my runny nose with the cuff of my dress.

Crawling into my closet, I sat on the floor. Maybe I would stay here all day. As I crouched, a strip of quilt no bigger than a worm fell from the folds of my skirt. I picked it up with two fingers. It was blood-stained. I held it to my nose. It didn't smell like anything at all, not blood, not Mama. The memory book lay outside the closet door, where I'd thrown it. It had landed on the wood floor and opened, once again to an empty page. I growled. I wouldn't have it blankly staring up at me like that, blaming me for being a wasteful crybaby. I would fill the empty page with my own words.

January 1933

I'm going to tell you a secret. And I'll never tell it to another soul because they might think I'm seeing a ghost and they might tell me she's not real. But here's the truth: if I stare straight ahead at a blank wall and I let my eyes relax, I can see my mama standing to the side of me. She's right there in the corner of my room. If I turn my head to get a better look, she disappears, and it might take half an hour of staring at nothing to get her to return. So now I keep her there for as long as I can. Trying to see her makes my throat ache and my body shiver, but it's worth it. Today because my eyes were smeary from bawling, it took me only a couple of minutes before she visited. I told her I found the blanket with her blood and that Papa hid it from me and that I wished I hadn't found it. She didn't have anything to say, but she never does. I think from what I could see of her face, she was crying, and that made me cry again too.

As soon as I couldn't see Mama anymore, I wrote this entry and glued the piece of Mama's quilt onto the page. These were the memories that would go into my book now.

March 1933

Polly is not my friend anymore. I will never ever forgive her. Just because her father works for Union Pacific and he still has a job, she thinks she can judge my papa. She says her father says my papa is a no-good hobo. That he isn't working at all. The railroad workers at Union Pacific caught him riding the rails with all of the other hobos. I told her she was just plum wrong and that my papa is working and he sends home money every week so me and Mrs. Brimley and Redmond can eat. And he brought me a store-bought birthday cake that must have cost at least five dollars. And if he is a no-good hobo, he wouldn't be able to afford all of that, would he?

Wouldn't it be something if Papa returned next week and he really was Daddy Warbucks and he had a big fancy car? Kind of like the one we used to have. The one I spit the cherry pits into. And we would drive it to church, be-

cause we could. Polly and her father would see us and they would know we had money to spare and my papa was the farthest thing from a hobo. Why, he was probably helping those hobos on the trains. He was probably handing out sandwiches, so the men could have a decent meal.

My papa is a hard worker and he has always said if a man works hard, he can provide for his family. And that is what he is doing. So Polly is wrong and I hate her. And I always will.

"King me," Redmond said smugly. For a quiet little kid, he sure could talk big when we played checkers.

I examined the board and knew I was done for. I had two men stuck in the corner and he now had three kings that would eventually jump them both.

"Best two out of three. Let's play again after this," I said through gritted teeth.

Redmond nodded, cheeks bright with the certainty of his victory.

"No more checkers until you run the clothes through the ringer. We need to hang them soon, so they'll be dry before dark," Mrs. Brimley called from the kitchen. Redmond and I sat side by side on the window seat in the dining room, tucked close to the table. It was hard to play checkers sitting on the same side, but Redmond insisted we not play on the floor, so here we were.

I sighed and moved my piece into easy jumping position for Redmond. Might as well get this over with. I wouldn't let him enjoy the chase.

After the game, Redmond and I walked into the backyard. The cherry tree was in blossom and the air felt crisp and cool. I took a deep breath and walked into the little washhouse where Mrs. Brimley had left a basket of wet clothing and blankets. I picked up the first item, an apron belonging to Mrs. Brimley, and set it on the rollers. "You turn the crank," I said to Redmond.

We had an electric washer in the basement, near the coal furnace, but we weren't allowed to use it, since it cost so much to run. Mama and Papa had bought it after Mama lost the second baby. It was supposed to lighten her load around the house so she could recover. Every wash day I silently mourned the abandoned machine.

Redmond pushed the crank, his scrawny arms shaking with effort.

"It's going to take you all day at this pace. You put the clothes on, and I'll crank," I muttered.

Redmond fed one of the pillow cases into the rollers and as his skinny fingers got close to the wringer, I spun the handle a little faster to see if I could catch one and pinch it a bit. He pulled away, surprised, but silent. Redmond's trousers were the next to go through and I did it again.

"Hey, you're doing that on purpose!"

"What?" I shrugged. "Put something else through, or we'll never get back to our game."

"You're just sore you lost." Redmond showed his teeth as he smiled.

"I am not," I said, and I spun the crank with all of my might. Redmond yanked his hand back and yelped.

"I'm going to tell if you do it again."

"What am I doing?"

"Trying to pinch my finger."

"Have you been pinched?"

"Almost," Redmond replied, his lower lip pushing out in a pout.

"You've got no proof."

"I'll be glad when we move out and I don't have to play with you anymore." Redmond folded his arms across his skinny chest.

"Today wouldn't be soon enough for me. Now put on the next thing. And mind your fingers," I said.

"We might move today," Redmond replied. "My grandma says your papa hasn't paid the mortgage for two months. She says we're going to move and you'll be evicted. She said the only reason we have food is because my parents are both working and sending money!"

My stomach filled with nervous butterflies, but I was determined not to let it show. "Now I know you're a liar. You probably cheated at checkers too. Put on the next piece of clothing, or I'll tell your grandma you aren't doing your share."

Redmond silently fed one of my skirts through the ringer, taking care to keep his fingers clear of danger. But I wasn't even trying to pinch him anymore. I needed my papa to come home. I hadn't seen him in three weeks.

And then, as if my wishing made it so, he appeared. There was Papa standing at the back door watching as Redmond and I worked on the clothes. I jumped up and ran to him. He pulled me close. I could smell campfire on his clothing. The second thing I noticed was that I could reach my arms all the way around his waist. I knew I had grown, but not this much. The band at the top of his wool trousers, the ones he wore to church each week before he left, hung loose, and his shirt had come untucked.

He grasped my shoulders and held me back so he could see my face. "Let me take a look at my Bitsy. Though you don't seem quite as bitsy as when I left you." He smiled, but his eyes looked ringed with bruise and he could really use a shave. I didn't want to admit it but he looked a little like a hobo. I pushed the thought out of my mind as quickly as it entered.

"Where have you been working, Papa?" I wanted him to answer by reaching into his pocket to pull out a handful of money, so nosy Redmond would be proved wrong.

Papa sighed. "Not so much working, as looking . . ."

My eyes darted to Redmond, who had clearly been listening. He appeared to be intently wringing the next clothing item, but I knew better.

"So are you hopeful?" I said. This time softly. I didn't really want Redmond to hear.

Papa was silent for several seconds. "How about we have a little something to eat, Bitsy? Mrs. Brimley said she would set us out a little bread. I haven't had anything yet this morning."

"You could have my glass of Ovaltine. We each get one glass a day and you can have mine. It has lots of vitamins!"

Papa chuckled and for a minute he was the papa I remembered.

"That's mighty generous of you, Bitsy. How about you drink your glass while I eat my bread and we'll have a visit."

As we walked into the dining room, Mrs. Brimley set a plate of bread and apple preserves on the table and she beckoned for Redmond. She grasped his hand and pulled him into the living room, tugging on the pocket doors to shut them tight.

Papa settled into Mrs. Brimley's chair at the dining room table and I sat on the window seat. "So, how've things been here? It's been some time since I've seen you." He took a mouthful of bread and chewed slowly, savoring the bite.

"I know. I've been waiting for nearly a month for you to come home." I tried to keep my voice free from blame, but it wasn't easy.

Papa nodded and worked his way through the hunks of bread. I watched him chew, waiting for him to speak.

"Polly went down to the Marlow Theater and saw *King Kong* yesterday. She said it was so exciting!" I tried to break the daunting silence.

Papa swallowed his last bit of bread. "Did she now?"

"Did you know her father works for the railroad? I wonder if he might not be able to get you a job there?"

"I wonder." He focused over my shoulder and out the window, toward the mountains in the east.

"Nice view from this room. Mountains look pretty, all greened up for spring."

I twisted in my seat to look out the window, silently fuming. *Take me to the movies!* I wanted to scream. Don't talk about the stupid mountains.

"Uh-huh," was all I said. I put my elbows on the table and settled my chin on my hands.

"Bitsy, elbows off the table while we're eating."

"I'm not eating. My drink's gone and so is your bread."

I gazed toward the closed pocket doors, willing them to open so this awkward silence would end. Even a conversation with Redmond would be better than this.

He focused on my shoulder, saying nothing. I pressed my arm flat against the table and rested my cheek against it.

"So, here's how it is. . . ." he mumbled.

I sat up. Finally.

Silence. "Tell me what you've been learning about in school." He rubbed his hands over the stubble on his chin.

"Mostly long division. Which I hate. Each problem takes forever, or nearly a half hour," I filled the silence.

"Keep working hard, Bitsy. Remember, 'Hard Work Equals a Happy Life.' " He stopped short. "Though at times, I'm not sure it's true. . . ." he mumbled.

I continued, trying to keep things light. "And I've been working on writing my own adventure for Little Orphan Annie. See, she's planning this surprise party for . . ." Papa was holding his forehead in his hands. His fingernails were long and dirty.

"Are you tired, Papa? You look like you could use a bath too," I said.

"I'm just no good, then," he said softly, studying his empty plate.

"What? Yes, you are. Times are tough, Papa. Everyone says so."

"Have you seen your aunt Emmeline lately?"

"Oh, some. She always brings those boys of hers over. They're worse than Redmond." Why was he changing the subject?

"So if I were to leave for a while, say a year, could you tolerate living with your aunt Emmeline and her boys?" His eyes didn't leave the platter of cracked china.

"What about Mrs. Brimley?"

"She's going to be moving on."

"What about our house?" I whispered, but I already knew. Redmond was right.

Papa looked out the window again and smoothed his hand over the table. "We'll let the bank look after her for a while. After I get some money saved, we'll buy her back."

"What if we took in more boarders?" Tears burned under my eyelids. I rubbed them roughly with my hand.

"I'm afraid it's too late for that, what with the farm and the car and . . ."

"But haven't you been working hard?" I was angry. We'd been doing without for almost as long as I could remember. Didn't it do any good?

He didn't answer.

"Polly was right!" I blurted. "You really are a no-good hobo!" I clapped my hand over my mouth. "Sorry. I didn't mean it," I whispered. I waited for him to unfasten his belt and whip me good this time, but he didn't, and that was almost worse.

"There's more truth in what you say than I wish to admit, Bitsy." He smiled, his mouth the only part of his face that seemed happy.

I worked my way off the window seat and crawled into his lap. I pressed my nose into his smoky clothing and his arms wrapped over my back. I couldn't swallow the lump in my throat, but I wouldn't cry either. I wouldn't.

June 1933

Today Elsbeth Dorthea Robinson, new (and only) author of this memory book, will move from the only home she has ever known to live with a bunch of boys out in the middle of a field somewhere. She has no mother or father to move with her. She is being shipped off like a piece of luggage.

She has only three items of any consequence: this book, her baby quilt (torn at the edges), and a not-so-handsome radio, given as a parting gift by Mrs. Brimley. (You should have seen Redmond's face crumble when she said she would give it to me.)

One bright point to this move: I don't have to see Polly or Redmond again. And I don't have to see all those friends at church and school who ask me if my papa is a hobo. He's not. I know he's not. But here is a secret that can't be shared. I am embarrassed by him and sometimes I hate him. And I don't know where he'll go after he leaves me. He might go right back to riding the rails, free of burden. There, I've gone and written my meanest secret in this book. Which makes it true and also makes it wrong. It also makes me a no-good daughter.

There was a gentle knock on my bedroom door. I slammed the memory book shut and prayed it wouldn't be Papa. I sat on the book as the door swung open. In the shadows it was . . . "Mama?" My breath caught in my throat.

"No, Bitsy, it's just me." My aunt Emmeline walked into the room. She tilted her head like Mama when she listened to my stories, but she was taller. And now she was in my room and I could see her face clearly, I would never make the same mistake.

"Are you almost ready?" Her voice had a choking sound mine gets when I'm trying not to cry. She looked at the book I was holding in my lap. I laid an arm across it protectively. "Oh, Bitsy, is that the memory book your mother made for you?" She reached toward it. Her fingers were greedy. "I would love to see what Cora . . ."

"It's really nothing. She hardly wrote in it." I put the book on top of my quilt and folded the edges all around it, securing it like a gift.

Aunt Emmeline nodded. Her nose was red from spent tears. "All right then, what can I help you carry? Your uncle has the radio in the back of the car. Mrs. Brimley said you get to keep it."

I nodded proudly.

"The boys can hardly wait to hear the *Little Orphan Annie* radio program." She paused and I didn't fill the silence. "So I'll grab this suitcase. Is this all of the clothing you are bringing?"

"Nothing else fits."

"I guess we'll get you sewing right away. You'll need some nice clothes when you start at your new school, come fall." Aunt Emmeline seemed nervous. Maybe she didn't really want me either. I watched her as she walked from the room carrying my suitcase. Uncle Nathaniel met her and took it from her hands. He wrapped his arm around her waist.

She leaned into him. He touched a tear that slid down her cheek and pulled her closer. "She thought I was Cora," she said.

I hated she cried about my mama more than I did.

I held the memory book folded in my quilt under one arm. The pencil I had used to punish my papa using my cruel words was still in my hand. I tucked the pencil behind my ear as I looked around my room, trying to memorize the only place I'd ever slept since I was a newborn baby.

I opened the door to my now-empty closet. No memory book hidden there, or dolls or crayons. No clothes either. I slipped the pencil from behind my ear and twisted it through my fingers. Then I gripped it tightly and pressed it into the white-painted wood on the back of the closet door. I braced my foot against the frame so I could use all of my strength. The lead broke, leaving a sharp stick. Using the tool, I carved "EDR" into the paint. My initials. As I forced the sharp end against the wooden surface, the paint cracked. I stood back and blew away the loose flakes. My hand was throbbing. My initials were ringed with ridges and splinters.

I slammed the door and heard a smacking noise deep within the wood. Opening the door I saw the panel I had carved had cracked at the top. I pressed the panel and a gap opened.

"Bitsy, are you coming?" Aunt Em called from the living room. She probably wanted to get her hands on the memory book. I pressed harder against the broken panel, creating an opening an inch wide and who knows how deep. I dropped the book into the dark space. Aunt Emmeline wouldn't know I was a rotten little girl if she couldn't read my words.

By hiding the memory book, I had claimed this room as my own, forever and for always. If Papa really did buy this house back, I would never forget this day. And if he didn't, well, this room would *always* be mine. I threw the broken pencil onto the floor of the closet. I slammed the door again, as hard as I could, and stomped out of my room.

IVY BAYGREN

The frost had settled hard across the lawn. Though I wanted to drive him this frigid morning, Porter was determined to ride his bike to school one last time before the snow descended and stayed in our valley for the remainder of the winter. He was crouched in front of the garage, pumping the back tire. The driveway was shiny with ice and I couldn't help but imagine cars sliding across yellow lines or through stop signs as my boy pedaled doggedly toward the elementary school.

Porter was wearing his navy jacket, hood down and pulled tight around his neck. His back was to me. As I stepped outside, holding his lunch encased in a paper lunch sack, my shoes crushed the frozen lawn, making it crackle as I made my way toward him.

Porter heard and turned slightly my way. "Hey, Mom, could you grab my lunch? I've almost got this."

His dark hair had grown long and it curled slightly as it touched the hood of the jacket. He stooped where Adam always had when he gassed up the lawn mower, bent just so. My son shook his head, and in the instant he leaned in to replace the cap over the tire stem, in that instant, he was Adam—the line of the jaw, the curve of his cheek, the profile of his nose.

I froze, motionless in the center of the icy grass, lunch bag in hand. Porter faced me and grinned. "You read my mind." Adam dissolved, and I was left weak and angry. I thrust the sack into his hands and stomped back toward the house.

"Are you mad at me for some reason, Mom?" Porter called from behind me.

Get a grip, Ivy. I didn't turn around as I dashed back into the house, hollering with as much cheer as I could muster, "I forgot to unplug . . . something. Have a good day at school!"

I slipped into the house and checked out the window. Porter leaned the bike against the garage door, confusion settled heavy across his features. He shook his head, scuffed his toe into the frozen ground, and rode away.

I was losing it! Any of my dozens of self-help books—and Stephen, for that matter—would judge this situation and determine I was *still* not properly managing my grief. Chloe wandered toward me and nuzzled my hand. I was standing near the hook holding her leash. "Okay, fine, girl. Let's go for a walk. I need to get a little perspective." I slipped on my coat and gloves and hooked her collar. She bounced against the door as I collected my cell phone and slipped it into the pocket of my jeans.

We walked purposefully away from the house, up toward the foothills—past the junior high, far from my home. The frigid air burned my throat as I walked, puffs of exhale trailing me. Had the weight of my loss actually grown as time moved beyond Adam, erasing traces of him? Now Naomi's T-shirts and backpack hung in Adam's side of closet, but whenever I opened the door, I visualized my husband's clothing hanging undisturbed. Before, it smelled like a combination of Adam's deodorant and dry cleaning chemicals. Now it smelled like lip gloss.

I'd finished painting Naomi's room blue, but as I turned off her light each evening, I imagined Adam holding a paint roller swollen with petunia pink, the color she'd chosen when she was seven. Sometimes I tried to capture every detail of that day, the light from the west-facing window illuminating the hair on his arms, his work shirt, the Nirvana CD he listened to. And it never brought him back.

Lost in my musings, I found I'd reached a trailhead in the lower foothills of the Wasatch Range, my city stretched wide below me. The trail leading into the mountains was marked with a sandstone pillar built during the Great Depression. Close enough to the city to walk to, yet high enough to offer respite from the furnace-like Utah summers, these marked trails wound through the hills, evidence of hard work done fifty years earlier by men who had no other job options. Trails and tunnels—hopeful markers of desperate times.

I kept walking. Since the trees in the valley had dropped their leaves, the roads and rooftops were newly visible without their shield of green. I could see Garfield Elementary, the school that housed my children day in and day out for years. There was Westminster College, and following the streets, turning corners with my eyes, I found my own house, the black-shingled roof hazy in the distance. Now this was gaining perspective.

My chest ached looking at my little home on Downington Avenue, insignificant from this height. Suddenly, I was exhausted trying to re-create Adam within my walls. My past was filled with memories, a lifetime of precious and sometimes heartbreaking memories. I coddled them, dreamed of them, and filed them away for safe keeping. But in continually looking at my past, was I neglecting my future? I wanted to remember, but I was finding it impossible to relive.

Chloe tugged on her leash. Her tongue was lolling out the side of her mouth. Despite the cold, she was thirsty. "All right, girl. Let's go back."

As I retraced my steps out of the mountains, back into the neighborhood near the zoo, I spotted a Taylor Historic Home Remodel sign standing in the yard of a gray Cape Cod. I crossed the street and stood looking at the sign, pondering. Before I could stop myself, my phone was out of my pocket and I was dialing the number listed. As it rang, I coughed to clear my throat.

A man answered. His voice was warm yet efficient. "Theo Taylor. Can I help you?"

I took a deep breath. "I hope so," I croaked, my words blended with sudden tears.

"Hello?" he said.

"But not yet," I whispered and ended the call, tears streaming down my face.

* * *

The phone rang several times before he answered. I jolted at his voice. "Oh, you're there. I thought I'd leave a message," I stuttered.

"We're on our way to a show," Stephen answered.

"In the middle of a Wednesday? I thought you were at work. I don't want to bother you."

"You think that it's okay to bother me at work, but not on my day off?" Stephen joked, and I could hear Drew laugh over the Bluetooth.

"I was going to leave a message."

"So, start talking."

"I'll be fast, it's just . . . I've made another discovery about the house and I wanted to tell someone about it. But the kids are at school."

"What is it?"

"I was digging a hole in the rose garden. I'm going to replace a couple bushes that aren't thriving—"

"Hold on, you're in the garden today? It's freezing."

"Actually, winter is the best time to plant a bare root. And that's not really the point."

"Sorry, go on," Stephen said.

"So I was digging, and as I sunk my shovel, I heard glass break, so I turned over a big patch of earth, wanting to clear the glass out of the garden, and you'll never believe what I found."

"Glass?"

"Stephen," I grumbled. "I found wine bottles, four of them in all, including the one I broke with the shovel. Two of them are full and all of them have handwritten labels. It's hard to read what they say because the paper is so deteriorated."

"Don't drink them. You're not that desperate and I'll bring an appropriately aged bottle over after the show." I could hear the smile in Stephen's voice. "I also don't think burying a bottle in the ground gives a vintage wine the character you're looking for."

"Very funny, Stephen. Don't you think it's a cool discovery?" I prompted. "Adam would've called this an Easter egg."

"If you found an Easter egg *that* old, I wouldn't eat it either."

"I'm hanging up now," I pouted.

"Ivy, sorry for not taking you seriously. We've already been to brunch and I've had a couple of mimosas. Drew's driving. Listen, we'll stop over after the show to check it out, okay?"

By the time they arrived, I'd investigated the name on one of the bottles. It was a word I didn't recognize, but I could decipher most of the letters, so I typed it into Google to see what happened. I was buzzing with excitement as I answered the door. "Mavrodaphne!" I said as I followed my brother and Drew into the living room.

"Gesundheit," Stephen said as he gave me a hug.

"It's the name of the wine, Mavrodaphne. It's a Greek wine! Do you imagine Eris and her family made wine here? Maybe they served it at the wedding in that photo. Remember?"

"You mean the personal photos you stole from the nice Greek family?"

"Hey, it's not like I snuck into their house. The album was for sale—more or less."

Stephen laughed while he inspected the bottle with the most legible writing and ran his fingertip across the curling paper. "Here's what's most interesting to me—why would someone bury bottles of wine?"

"I've wondered the same thing," I said.

"Looks like the Greek lady had a secret," Drew said. "Perhaps her compulsion to hide alcohol indicates she was a raging alcoholic."

"Very funny," I said, strangely protective of Eris Gianopolous, a woman who was already dead. A woman I'd never met. It was true that Stephen, Drew, and I had engaged in several lengthy and speculative discussions about the Gianopolous family. We'd used the scraps of information I'd collected, and Stephen and Drew had conjectured about typical Greek family dynamics, our ongoing discussions becoming increasingly animated after they read several far-fetched myths from *D'Aulaires*.

"You know," Drew said, thoughtful now. "Every now and then I catch myself wondering if the son, what was his name?"

"Adonis. It said Adonis on the census."

"Yes, Adonis. I keep wondering if he died in the war. I mean he was eighteen in 1944 and V-E Day wasn't until 1945."

"Of course he didn't die," I said quickly. "I'm sure he didn't even fight." I mustered conviction with my words. "Because if I don't *really* know . . . then I get to choose."

"Let the lady have her happy ending, Drew," Stephen said, nodding slowly.

"I deserve it this time, don't I?"

"I believe you do," Drew said, and Stephen put his arm around his partner.

ERIS GIANOPOLOUS

Downington Avenue
1945

The tomatoes were the bane of my existence. I hated them the most, followed by string beans, then peas, then the potatoes. Damn staggered harvest times never gave me a minute of rest. Like a beggar's, my fingernails were continually rimmed with dirt. If the bounty of my Victory Garden was any indication, we'd have beat Japan months ago. As it was, we'd be eating canned vegetables until the day I died.

I'd been picking tomatoes all morning and was starved, but not for another godforsaken red fruit. Hector knew where I stood on the harvest and he'd been bringing home my favorite pastries from the bakery—*loukamades,* baklava, *kataife.* Sweets to keep his wife sweet, but it was only serving to make me fat (fatter). Pinching the pudgy roll surrounding my middle and swearing under my breath, I decided I would go in for lunch. I'd start with a small gooey bite of *kataife,* choke down a couple of tomatoes, and end with my afternoon cigarette. A balanced meal, in my opinion.

The radio in the dining room whirred to life with a pleasant ringing tune. It wasn't quite time for the repeat of Edward Murrow's program, but I would see if there was something lively to listen to while I ate. My favorite announcer proclaimed there was a message from Washington DC and a perky female voice took over the airwaves. Before she spoke I thought: *Please, let it be over. Let her announce that US troops killed General Hideki Tojo, leaving the Japanese army floundering. Let there be a tidal wave, hailstorm, or killer hornets and all the Japanese planes will be permanently grounded. Please let Adonis come home.* Of course, the announcer said none of those things. Shattering my wishes like breaking glass, her voice rang through my newly carpeted dining room. "I'm going to grow my own Victory Garden! For Victory!"

Sweet Jesus. It was a conspiracy. When victory finally came I wouldn't celebrate with a nice can of peas. No, damn it, I'd want to toast victory. A glass of wine or even a stiff drink. "Get sloppy drunk! For victory!" I'd love to hear *that* slogan on the radio. Chest constricting like I'd wrestled a boa, I decided to *start* lunch with my cigarette. Tapping the ash into the sink, I considered digging up the garden. It clearly wasn't winning the war and I hated radio announcers and competitive neighbors bossing me around. Crop yields and canning techniques were all anyone discussed anymore, like we were making a scrap of difference with our rakes and hoes.

Maybe the next year I'd get Hector to build a garage over the top of the garden, but bricks and nails were still hard to come by. Christ, we could hardly afford to drive the car itself. Hector had to work his ass off to get our gas ration sticker changed to a *B* for small business owners, so we could purchase the gas necessary to get him back and forth to the kitchen. For years we'd considered selling the vehicle, but along with the rest of the country, both Hector and I felt like we were paralyzed.

My cigarette spent, I opened the box of *kataife* and shoved several sweet, gooey bites into my mouth, then, tipping the plate of sliced tomatoes into the garbage, I scowled, knowing I must get back to it. Hedging my bets. Gardening for goddamn victory.

There was a persistent knocking at the front door. Crawling on hands and knees, pulling up the starts of morning glory slithering their way like cunning green serpents through our rows of vegetables, I decided to ignore the sound. My hair was wrapped in a scarf and my pits had rings down to the bottom of my rib cage. There was no damn way I was racing to the door.

"Leave it on the porch! Please!" I screamed toward the open back door. But the knocking continued. Finally I stood, both knees popping in protest. "Oh, for Christ's sake, I'm coming," I whispered.

I trudged into the kitchen. On the porch, the silhouette of a capped man was visible through the opaque glass in the front door. Oh, God, a telegram boy! My hand rose to my throat.

"Just leave it," I choked.

"I can't, ma'am. You have to sign for the telegram." So this was how it would end. This would be the final correspondence from my son. The salty taste of tears touched my lips, even as I opened the door.

A kid about fifteen years old stood on the porch, holding a clipboard. He handed it to me, a folded sheet attached to the top. "Sign here. And I'm sorry." I tried to breathe. I knew exactly what would happen if I opened the envelope. In one instant, everything would change.

I signed my name and closed the door. Legs unreliable, knowing what was coming, my fall was cushioned only by the blessed carpet. I rested my cheek on the expanse of blue, comforted by the soft bristle, allowing the plush to absorb some of my pain. Through bleary lids, the postmark swam. Blinking again, I squinted to see that it read: Athens.

I sat up, my mind reeling. Did they transfer him and Hector didn't tell me? I thought he was in the Pacific and all this time he'd been in Europe? Tearing open the envelope, I noticed the handwriting was shaky, written with an aged hand. The signature on the bottom read: Yocasta. Yocasta? My aunt? I leaped to my feet and jumped in place, squealing. Sweet relief whirled around me as I spun through the room holding the unread letter. This had nothing to do with Adonis! Nothing at all!

Finally I focused on the brief scrawl. *Raise a glass of wine for your dear uncle Dimitriou. May he rest in peace.* At the bottom of the note she'd written a Western Union number and, less formally, a scribble in Greek from my aunt, a woman I'd never met. *Your uncle left you a little money.*

A certainty draped over my shoulders like a comforting blanket. Yes, I'd raise a glass for Uncle Dimitriou. I'd raise a glass for victory. I'd tear out the garden and plant a Victory Vineyard, with an abundance of grapes, enough to provide toasts for a lifetime. Conjuring rows of vines leaning heavy on their wooden supports, I could see them spanning the length of the property, plump jewels ready to be plucked. I could almost taste the blood-red wine, fermented with special Greek currants, the celebration wine Uncle Nico served on special occasions. On the eve of victory when Hector, Calliope, Adonis, and I were reunited after the damn war we'd raise our glasses high, brimming with Mavro-daphne.

My back was turned to the driveway when they returned from the bakery, scythe firm in my clenched hand. Many summer days the three of us would go into the kitchen together, but today Hector had taken Calliope extra early to prepare the sourdough starts, leaving me at home to tend to the garden. Probably a bad idea in retrospect. In their opinion. Though I couldn't see them, Calliope's gasp and Hector's curse spilled out the open window as they pulled to a stop on our gravel drive.

Hector ran from the car without shutting down the engine and grasped me by the shoulders. He turned my body toward him and searched my face for the truth. "Is it Adonis? Did something happen?"

"No, everything's fine," I replied. "As far as I know. I did get a telegram, but it was from my aunt."

"Then, for God's sake, Eris, why the garden?" His fingers shook with relief and rage, pressed hard into my skin.

"Because planting a Victory Garden is essentially saying that I fully expect the war to continue," I said. "And I don't sympathize with that anymore. I'm planting something to hasten the *end* of the war—a vineyard so we can make wine and toast a safe return for Adonis."

"But Mama, I'd planned to enter some of the vegetables in

the state fair this year. I told you just last week," Calliope huffed. "You're not the only one who's put in long hours out here in the sun." She picked up one of the wilted tomato vines, red fruit still attached, and held it in front of me.

"Pick the tomatoes off the vine you're holding and enter them in the fair," I replied. "They're not rotten."

"The fair isn't for two weeks. They'll be rotten by then." Calliope dropped the vine and turned so all I could see were her quivering shoulders.

"Haste makes waste, Eris," Hector said. "And you've really done it this time." He walked up and down the barren rows, touching his toe to the wilted plants I'd severed with my unrelenting blade. "Is there anything salvageable here at all?"

"You know I hate it when you use your quotes against me," I hissed at Hector. I touched my hand to my chest and said more softly, "I honestly had a feeling in my heart this was the right move."

"The right move? For whom?" Hector asked.

"Adonis, of course." I needed him to understand. "Until the war's ended, he can't come home. And the garden is a statement that we *expect* the war to continue."

"Convoluted thinking, Eris. And by the way, he's not the only one who matters here." Hector glanced quickly at Calliope staring blankly at the wreck of plants withering in the sun.

I walked toward her, suddenly apologetic, wanting to explain. But before I reached her side, she opened her mouth and started to sing. It was low and slow at first. "Oh, when the saints"—Calliope took a deep breath—"go marching in." I gazed at my daughter, her cheeks smudged with tears. "Oh, when the *soldiers* go marching in." The familiar tune, words enhanced by Calliope, eased my determined scowl. I put down the scythe. "Oh, how I want to be his *mother,* when the soldiers go marching in." She finished the verse and smiled at me.

"Calliope." I took another step toward her as she surrounded me with her voice.

"Oh, when the drums begin to play . . . when the drums begin to play." Hector was faster and had his arm around her now. "Oh, how I'll cheer because he's my brother." Hector was laughing now, starting to sing with our unbreakable daughter. He held out his free arm to me and with bowed head, I slid into his familiar embrace. The three of us standing together in our dying Victory Garden raised our voices . . . to victory.

IVY BAYGREN

I'd waited so long for Bitsy's knock I'd nearly given up, mourning she'd passed before I had a chance to tell her how much her memory book meant to me. Every time Chloe ran barking to the front door, I no longer followed her, peering out the window, because most of the time it was a solicitor, UPS, or one of the kids' friends. As a result, I scarcely heard it when it came. At the faint noise, I glanced out front to see an old woman, round through the bottom, standing on my porch. Who could it be?

The unknown woman turned and planted a kiss on a wisp of a lady who was sitting sedately on my porch swing. Like a child, Bitsy dangled her legs suspended on the wooden slats. She saw me through the window as I approached the door, and winked, her gaze not at all watery like one hobbled mentally by age.

The plump woman introduced herself as Bitsy's daughter, Meg. She asked if she could return for her mother in a couple of hours because she was late to the airport to pick up a friend. In a hurry, the daughter handed a stack of envelopes tied with twine to her mother.

"Give them to Ivy, if you would," Bitsy said, nodding in my direction, her voice clear.

Greedily, I took the letters from Meg's hands. Who were they from? The script had lost the crispness of fresh ink, the font grainy like I was reading each word through a thin layer of sand. The name on the first envelope read *Miss Emmeline Lans-*

ing. Emmeline! As I'd hoped, Emmeline's was the subject of the other stories Bitsy had hinted to in her letter.

Bitsy might not want to answer questions about her own years in my home, but she had information about her aunt she was willing to divulge. My questions about Emmeline renewed their churning in my mind. What happened to Nathaniel? What would force Emmeline to hide away an elaborately embroidered statement of their love? And if he didn't die during World War I as I thought he must have, given the date stitched into the muslin, then what?

"Are they from Nathaniel?" I could hardly draw breath.

"So you found the memory book? And you've read it?" she asked quietly.

"I've savored every word!" I rested my hand on her shoulder. "I really can't tell you how your story affected me."

"I'm glad . . . so glad," she said, looking toward the street.

"Wait here. Or do you want to come inside? I have something to show you."

"I'm fine here. Thank you."

I nodded and dashed to retrieve Emmeline's embroidery. I placed it on her lap and watched as she touched the stitching with papery fingers, light as a butterfly.

"I found this hidden in my attic, tucked into a tiny leather case. I thought Nathaniel must've died in the war . . . or something else awful, for her to have concealed it before it was complete," I said. "But I read your memory book and there she was, Emmeline! And Nathaniel's in it too, and they're married! I've been trying to puzzle it through." I caressed the embroidery as it sat on Bitsy's lap.

Bitsy was gazing at the street, lost in her memories. I watched her face, a kaleidoscope of expression, her eyes focused on the past.

"Ivy, theirs was an uncommon love story," she finally spoke. It seemed she had more to say, but she gazed at the street again, rubbing her hands together to warm them.

"Are you cold?" I asked, though it was unusually warm for

January. The thin sun shone on the porch swing, but it was still winter-chilly. "Do you want to go inside?" She shook her head, wispy gray hair fluttering about her face. "I'll get a lap blanket and a cup of tea for both of us," I said, scarcely able to leave the letters and Bitsy, even for a moment. The anticipation of discovery made my hands shake, but I gently arranged several pillows behind my frail visitor, tucked the blanket around her legs, and handed her a warm mug.

"Their romance was unusual and very real, but I won't say it was easy. In loving each other they made sacrifices and there were consequences, some I imagine they never anticipated." Bitsy sighed, as if tracing the course of action and reaction through the corners of her memory. "They raised me after I moved from this house until I married, so Emmeline was like a mother to me. And Nathaniel a father."

"What happened to Richard, your actual father? The one I read about in the book?" I asked, at once regretting my question, worried I had pulled forth an unpleasant memory.

Her face sagged before she spoke. "It took him some time to settle into permanent work. And when he did, he had remarried. He sent for me, of course, but by that time I was nearly fifteen and comfortable with my aunt's family, so I stayed."

She gazed at the stack of letters on my lap. "Don't worry about me though," she said. "I can see from your face you're fretting."

"Your memory book ended so sadly," I said.

"I was sad. But time passes, Ivy. I've had a wonderful life. My husband was with me for over fifty years. My good memories far outweigh the bad, so enough about me." She smiled. "Let me tell you about my aunt Emmeline."

I slowly removed the twine from the stack of brittle envelopes and touched one of the faded postmarks. "Do you want me to read them?" I asked.

"Your eyes are better than mine, so please. What do you say we read them all now? Do you have time?" Bitsy asked. "Many of Emmeline's letters have been lost, you'll see from the incomplete narrative, but I can try to fill in the details."

After reassuring her I had all day to visit, I sifted slowly through the letters, looking for the oldest postmark. The script varied between feminine and masculine. One had a postmark reading 1913, the rest were later. I pulled out the letter from 1913 and smoothed the pages with my hand.

"Okay," I said, my heart racing with anticipation. "This one is from Emmeline, December 1913." And I started to read.

December 1913

My Nathaniel,
  I write this letter safe in my house on Downington Avenue, while you float in the vast Atlantic Ocean. I can't picture a body of water larger than the Great Salt Lake, and I imagine your ship adrift on the waves without land in sight.
  I can't help thinking of the poor passengers on the Titanic. There was no moon on the night that the Titanic sunk. If there had been light cast by the moon, the captain may have seen the iceberg in the distance. So I have looked up into the sky each night this week, hoping the moon stays bright in the sky over your ship. I know you would tell me to stop being so romantic, but nevertheless, I am feeling a little out of sorts with you gone, so humor my sentimentality.
  As you have probably noticed, I have included the photograph Brother Conner took of us on our last day together. I have a copy for myself as well. He took the photo the instant you whispered to me. I think about those words every day. Now I am sending my response to your words, weeks later. Yes, I will marry you. Even as I write the words, I can hardly believe my pencil has formed them. I always figured I wasn't the marrying type, but you came along and swept me off my feet. So hurry home!

Love,
Emmeline

February 1914

Emmeline,

    Once again, greetings to my future bride! Things are better with Brother Hannon (my companion), thanks for asking. We have grown accustomed to one another's quirks, though I still say he has more quirks than I! To date, we have done several walking tours of the greater Manchester area, delivering meals to the elderly and helping families move from one flat to another. No real interest yet in listening to our teachings, but we are not discouraged. People have been kind and generous, and that is a start.

    I've reread my last paragraph and I see that I sound just like the typical missionary. Here is my attempt to be honest with you: I hate this! No one wants to learn about the church, they only want us to provide them with a meal. Here is the truth: I want to be home with you, Emmeline!

    Enough nonsense! I will resume this letter when I am able to control my willful pen.

    I am writing again, three hours later, and my religious sensibilities have returned. Have you read the news lately? England, and all of Europe, is in an uproar. In brief, Archduke Franz Ferdinand, the leader of Austria, and his wife were touring around the city of Sarajevo, when they were both shot. It's tragic. See if you can find the story in the local news and report back what the Americans think.

All of my love to you,
Nathaniel

May 1914

My Emmeline,
    It has been weeks since I received your last letter. The post is delayed because the whole country is

*preparing for war. The British are taking extra pre-
cautions with their shipping, as it is rumored the
Germans have a new naval weapon called a U-boat
that can easily take down an iron-clad ship.*

*In the middle of all the uproar, we try to teach the
gospel. At the moment, we are teaching a young
German woman named Rosa Lewis. She is married
to an English man named Joseph, who is already a
member of our church. Together, they have a child
they call Dutch. We hope to baptize Rosa and seal
the family for time and all eternity.*

*Teaching the gospel is important, I know, but part
of me yearns to fight the German aggression. And
now I have been given the opportunity. We missionaries in England have been given a choice. We can
continue to serve in England. Or we can cross the
channel into France and minister to injured soldiers
in the field hospitals. Though I am no doctor, they
assure us there is much to be done.*

*Most of the missionaries have decided to go. We
will be crossing the English Channel in a ship
marked with the neutral sign of the Red Cross. This
will keep our ship safe from the German U-boats, so
don't be frightened! I have prayed and I believe this
is the best way for me to serve my fellow man. I
think of you constantly and long for the day when
we can continue our life together.*

Love to you,
Nathaniel

December 1914

Dear Emmeline,
*You will be relieved to know our group of
missionaries and Red Cross workers made it safely
across the English Channel. We landed at Calais and*

*were directed north, into Belgium. Our entire group
is working outside a small town in Belgium called
Ypres.*

*We are situated in a large two-story stucco home,
they call it a chateau. There are probably fifteen
rooms and all have been converted into a hospital of
sorts. Surrounding the chateau there are windmills
and miles and miles of grass. If I look out the window from the second floor, I can see the battlefield,
waving grass crisscrossed with trenches. I can only
wonder who used to live here, and where are they
now, as men bleed on their fine wood floors and die
on their beds.*

*There has been a great battle here. The fighting is
over, for now, but there is so much to do, so many
men are injured. Our work is important, but I'm so
helpless, Emmeline. Boys are dying all around me.
They call out to me, I talk with them, I bless them,
but most of them die anyway. I didn't know war
was like this.*

*I love you, my sweet Emmeline. Write to me
about the rest of the world. Let me know that life is
normal somewhere. I don't know if I will receive
your letters. But it will give me comfort to know you
are writing them.*

Yours always,
Nathaniel

May 1915

My Emmeline,
*I write this letter as a comfort to myself. I don't
know if my letters even reach your hands, since the
whole of Europe is dying around me and scarcely a
person receives the post. I wish you were here to*

*comfort me and I would comfort you, by letting you
know I am still alive.*

*As I write, I am sitting next to Joseph Lewis. We
taught him and his wife while in Manchester. I didn't
know he had enlisted. And the fact I found him is a
miracle. Joe is in grim condition. He cries out for
Rosa and Dutch in his fitful sleep. I rest my hands
on his head and try to send him a blessing. I pray for
him to live, and when I watch him try to draw a
breath, his brow sweaty and his lips blue, I pray for
him to die.*

*The Germans have used chlorine gas in the last
battle and it is slowly killing Joe. I am not even sure
I can write you details of the battle, but I have to get
the words out of me so I can rid myself of their
weight.*

*The battle began with sounds of screaming, rather
than gunfire. Out the window I saw a great low-
lying cloud moving over the battlefield the color
of pea soup. Even through the sealed windows of
the chateau the smell found me, and my eyes and
nostrils burned. After that, there was gunfire
everywhere.*

*Now the battle is over, most of the soldiers we
care for are blind. The gas has scarred their eyes.
And if they can see, most of them can scarcely
breathe. I am writing this, Emmeline, unsure I can
even send it to you. I don't want to fill your mind
with images as terrible as these.*

*Joe appears to be waking, so I will end this letter
here. Know I love you. My memory of you and my
faith in God are all that keep me sane.*

Yours forever,
Nathaniel

June 1915

Emmeline,
  *I write to you with a saddened heart. Joseph
Lewis has died. After my last letter, the fighting went
on around us, finally circling the chateau entirely.
We were ordered to leave, as the British and
Canadian armies could no longer ensure our safety.
We transported our injured patients to another field
hospital created entirely of tarps and tents. It is from
this field hospital I write to you.*
  *I didn't think Joseph could bear the pain of the
transport. He was in such agony simply drawing
breath into his own lungs. The night before our
evacuation, I knelt down beside Joseph's bed and
prayed for God to help him, to give him relief from
his pain or strength for the journey. An hour later,
after I had settled into my own cot, Joseph called
out to me. He called me by name, which he hadn't
done since the first day I saw him. I hurried to his
bedside and held his hand.*
  *He cried over and over, "Nathaniel, take care of
my family. There's no one else who can." And I
promised him, as he lay dying, that I would.*
  *What does this mean, Emmeline? I know you
can't answer me, but I have to write. I am not sure
what I am meant to do.*
  *I am weary. I must contact Rosa and tell her the
terrible news about Joseph. This is not a conversation I want, but it must be done. If the missionaries
have an opportunity to return to England, I will go
with them.*
  *I love you, Emmeline. May God bless you and
keep you safe.*

Nathaniel

August 1915

My Emmeline,

I am back in Manchester now. I have delivered the news about Joseph Lewis to his wife, Rosa. And now she is all alone. A month before I delivered the news about Joe, she heard her brother Gus was also killed in battle. He was her only living relation. And worse yet, from her accent, people in England know she is German. There is much resentment toward the Germans here. She is a woman and the wife of an English man, a British soldier at that. But this doesn't stop the persecution. She has been denied service at the shops and she was taunted and chased home by a group of young boys, who threw rocks at her and called her "Hun!"

Rosa has now officially joined the Mormon Church. My companion and I are hoping other members can offer her safe haven. She is my first baptism and it felt wonderful to finally serve the Lord in the manner I intended.

Now the really good news! My mission will officially end in October! I believe I will be able to come home on schedule. The mission president has indicated he is working on safe passage across the Atlantic, as the waters around Europe are unsafe, even for passenger ships.

My love, I want to share something with you. I have learned a little Dutch from some of the soldiers I attended near Ypres. I wrote this down hoping to send the message to you, someday. "Ik zal zien dat u binnenkort, mijn liefde!" It means, "I will see you soon, my love!" I am counting the days.

Yours forever,
Nathaniel

"That's it. That's the last letter. So he came home and they got married?" I asked. "Why, then, did she not complete the embroidered wall-hanging?"

Bitsy put her hand on my knee. "There's a bit more to the story. I have another letter in my purse." She patted the empty bench next to her. "But I must have left it in the car. And I'm so tired now. To explain the rest, I'll need more energy." Suddenly she looked her age. After several minutes, she said, "Ivy, could you dial my daughter for me? If she's not already on her way, she should come now."

"Yes, but . . ."

"I promise, I won't make you wait so long before I return." She smiled, her face wrinkled with decades of joy. Age had taken away her vigor, but not her spirit.

LAINEY HARPER

Downington Avenue
1980

Like a ghost at the door, like a nightmare, the sensation of drowning arrived, washed over me and left. Two hours of a panic attack left me withered. Waves of fear crashed into me, paralyzing me, adhering me to the couch, my body wedged between the cushions.

I worked my way through my mental checklist *again:* door locked, bathroom faucet off, curling iron unplugged, telephone on the cradle. Sylvie. On a date. Back around ten.

Clutching a pillow, I concentrated on the second hand of the living room clock. Hearing it, feeling it. My pulse thumped through the veins of my neck, constricting, choking me as I sat frozen. Tick—tick. Waiting.

Two-plus hours. Or seven thousand, eight hundred twenty seconds, and the ghost was gone. I pulled myself from the couch and changed my sweat-soaked shirt, so very relieved Sylvie had not been at home to witness my moment of madness.

It had been *so* long since I'd lost control. So long, I'd forgotten something evil lurked in my brain, twisting itself within my happy memories of the past decade. I hadn't missed the darkness at all and I didn't welcome it back. Hopefully it was nothing, I told myself as I swallowed my final dose of lithium for the day. But I knew.

I settled myself into bed to watch *Dallas,* alone. Fragile, so very fragile, I gazed at the empty side of my queen bed, fighting a wave of sadness. But it wasn't the same as the earlier madness. It was a normal, justifiable emotion, as Dr. Yeager called it. It was that *Dallas* night was *our* night. Sylvie on the opposite side of the queen bed, pillows stacked behind us, a popcorn bowl in the middle. Friday nights weren't the same without her. I missed that girl when she went on a date, but she needed to go, and I needed to stop wishing she was young.

The program ended and I turned off the VCR. Sylvie and I would watch the recorded episode together in the morning. Shutting off the light, I lay down. I wouldn't wait up for her. I wouldn't.

A couple of minutes after ten, I heard the key jiggle in the lock.

"I'm sure it's fine if you come in for a second or two. The lights are off. My mom's probably already asleep," Sylvie whispered, closing the door behind her. A wave of cold air reached me in the bedroom as she clicked the lock back into place.

I stayed still. The crack under my door illuminated as someone flipped on the light in the dining room.

"Wow." A male voice broke the silence. The wood floor creaked as Sylvie's date circled the room.

"What?" Sylvie responded from the kitchen. I could hear a gentle fizz as she poured soda into a glass.

"Who got stuck in the seventies?" he said, laughing a little.

"My mom's an artist," Sylvie said, her voice timid, defensive.

"She might want to update her technique. Black velvet, jeez. I haven't seen one of these since I was in the sixth grade."

"Don't be an ass," Sylvie whispered. "I know it's dated. But my mom sold a ton of it, and she still loves it. Painting for her is a form of . . ." She took a deep breath. "She mostly paints for fun," Sylvie finished quickly.

"No offense meant. But don't you get a little creeped out with all of these dopey puppies watching you eat?"

"They're not dopey. They were my favorites when I was little," she said, a little louder now, anger on the tip of her tongue.

"Actually, maybe you should go. We'll probably wake my mom if we turn on the television," Sylvie said as she turned out the dining room light, stopping further discussion. Footsteps and mumbled apologies lingered by the front door and silence.

The next morning the puppies had vanished from the dining room. Playing dumb, I asked Sylvie what happened to the art.

She shrugged. "Oh, I've thought for a while now I'd put them in my bedroom; they kind-of seem like bedroom art, you know." She didn't look at me while she spoke. "I'll hang them next to my bed in a couple of days."

"Okay. Should I paint something else?" I asked, pointing to the expanse of empty wall. I hadn't painted for several weeks and I should. Painting would provide a soothing rhythm.

"Sure. But what if you tried watercolor? Something a little more subtle?"

I blinked. "Subtle isn't really my style."

"Maybe we could leave it empty for a while?" she said, and went into her room. A tiny part of me broke. Sure, I knew the black velvet art was dated, as evidenced by the lack of sales. But it was still beautiful, at least to me. It shouldn't matter that Sylvie was dismissive of it. It was something *I* loved. But it did.

"Sylvie, you missed a good *Dallas*. Do you want to watch?" I asked.

"How about later, Mom?" she called through her closed door. "I've got some stuff to do."

I kicked the snow from my boots and entered the house. I'd walked home from work without fetching my prescribed cup of coffee, because I didn't have the stomach to brave the lines of students jostling energetically for lunch. And I didn't want to run into Sylvie. She was a freshman at Westminster College now (thanks to reduced tuition through my job), and though she always greeted me enthusiastically on campus, I had a sneaking suspicion her slightly crazy mother was a source of embarrassment. It wasn't the black velvet art. It was me.

So I walked home through snow that was no longer white

and light, but dirty and crunchy, without the "one thing I love"—coffee—in my hand. The afternoon sky was the same thick shade of muddy gray it had been all month. Barren tree branches matched the concrete, which matched the horizon, which matched my spirits. There was no sign of sun, just the perpetual fog and smoggy pollution, which disrupted my view of the mountains, or of any distance, for that matter.

Closing the front door, I inhaled the dry heat. My nose felt like it would crack from the cold. I squeezed my nostrils and they froze pinched together for an instant until the warmth of my exhale thawed them. Flopping heavily on the couch, I clicked on the television. My hand quivered as I aimed the remote at the screen.

For a month now, Dr. Yeager and I had been adjusting my medications as we tried to fight the blackness settling in my brain. The panic attack was the beginning of a slide. However, this time there was no week of spectacular. It started with panic and moved to darkness. Sadness had knocked at my door and I hadn't been able to keep it out.

I had done so well for ten years, but the doctor said hitting a plateau on the lithium happens to everyone. However, this was no consolation while it was happening to me.

This last combination of increased lithium and a couple other drugs left my hands shaky and my speech slightly slurred. Dr. Yeager assured me the symptoms would decrease as my body reacted to the corrected dose. In the meantime, I was to do one thing I loved each day, which included coffee. And the doctor was insisting I paint again. I hadn't picked up a brush in well over a month.

Glancing at the television, I noticed a beautiful woman was crying on *As the World Turns*. She was so lovely in her sadness. A close-up of her face revealed her tears left a captivating sparkle. Sorrow made her more beautiful, and it left me puffy-eyed and blotchy.

I drifted in and out of sleep until I heard the music signaling the end of the soap opera. Using monumental willpower, I pulled myself to standing and wandered toward the little television to switch it off. Suddenly, vigorous music filled my ears. The television screen displayed the title of the next program boldly stamped in black and white: *Zorba the Greek*. I reached for the *off* button—I should get moving—but I could hardly lift my feet. I shuffled back to the couch and settled in. One more program.

About halfway through the film I covered my face with a pillow, groaning. This show wasn't exactly what I was expecting. At some point in the middle of the movie, I threw the remote. I had enough misfortune in my own life to be sucked into television tragedy. But I still couldn't turn it off. Watching the film, I prayed for a happy ending. But down deep, I was praying for my own life.

Then at the end (I mean the very end), amid unjustified jubilation, Zorba embraces the madness in his life, allowing him to be free. Apparently, for Zorba, madness was the *key* to enduring calamity.

Not so much for me. Madness wasn't freedom, it was disaster.

The final credits began to roll, and my stomach growled. Though I disliked *Zorba* it gave me an intense craving for Greek food, and anything that moved me these days was worth pursuing. It would be the one thing I loved today. I would make a meal for Sylvie and me—something warm and fragrant to take the bitter edge off a cold day. I grabbed the yellow pages and looked up Greek food. Donning my boots and stocking hat, I made my way to the closest location, Hellas Bakery and Market.

As I stepped through the steam-covered glass door, I was engulfed in a wave of moist, fragrant air. It smelled like thyme and lemon and honey. It smelled vaguely like my home when I moved in years earlier, traces of past meals cooked by Mrs. Gianopolous. I walked straight to the deli case and a twenty-year-old, dark-haired kid sauntered over. He leaned casually against the glass case.

I decided to use a little of the Greek I had heard in the show. "Kalimera."

He chuckled, his fresh unlined grin full of humor. "Kali*spera*, you mean. It's nearly three o'clock."

My cheeks burned red. "Kalispera. Right."

"Can I help you find anything special, ma'am?"

"I'm not sure. I've never cooked Greek food before. But I watched *Zorba the Greek* and they had lamb," I said.

"*Zorba*? Isn't that the movie you made me watch last year, Yia Yia?" He called loudly toward a closed door behind the counter.

"Made you? I thought you liked it," an aged woman answered.

The boy shrugged and rolled his eyes. "How many you cooking for?"

"Well, it's just me and my daughter."

"What did they eat in *Zorba*, Yia Yia?" He called over his shoulder.

The voice called out again. "Oh, for Christ's sake, Adonis, start with olives."

He placed several items into a paper bag. "I'll pick out something good for you," he said.

When I left, I had two bags full of things to cook. I had a pre-seasoned lamb shank to put in the oven, olives, feta, and bread. I had a couple of sad-looking tomatoes the boy apologized for as he reminded me it wasn't tomato season in Utah.

Sylvie returned from her classes as I took the lamb out of the oven. She carried the smell of cold on her coat. "It's been a while since you've cooked," she said, putting her hand on my arm. "Are you feeling better?"

I nodded. Who was the mother now?

I took a bite. The flavors danced over my tongue. Sylvie noticed the tear first. "Mom, what's wrong? Did you burn your mouth?"

"No, no. It's just so good, it makes me weep." *How do you feel, Lainey?* Undone.

"Hey, Mom." Sylvie's voice brought me crashing back into my living room.

My easel was perched in front of me, and on it, a canvas covered in black velvet, as usual. I was lost visualizing the moon, low and bright, like it had been the first night Sylvie and I slept outside. Doctor's orders, I was forcing myself to paint again, but my hands quivered unceasingly. So far, this painting therapy had not brought relief.

So, three days ago I flushed my pills. The doctor and I had continued our experiment, trying new combinations of medication, but they hadn't calmed the waves of lethargy covering my every action. I was hopeful I would be better off without any medication at all. However, three days into the "no lithium" experiment and I still felt like I was drowning. Not to mention the side effects, the shaking hands and jittery vision, lingered, making it impossible to paint.

As I sat pondering the moon, I was also monitoring my body, searching for the start of a spin. So far, the only change was I hadn't slept much in the last two days. Fatigue echoed in my limbs, but I couldn't sleep.

Sylvie dropped her heavy school bag on the couch behind me and sat down with a sigh. "I am *so* ready for summer break."

"It's been a tough quarter, hasn't it? Wasn't today your last final?" I spoke slowly, deliberately.

"Thank goodness it *was* my last!" Sylvie said. She sorted through her loaded canvas bag, pulling out old notes and tests, deciding which to keep and which to throw away. Finally, she lay back on the couch, eying my velvet canvas. "You know, Mom, I've always been a fan of the velvet art, but it's kind of dated. I mean, it's the eighties now. Maybe we should take a vacation to get you some new material."

"I'm doing this for therapy." I gave her a wobbly smile. She was so light after finishing a grueling year of college. I wouldn't let her see my darkness. I hid my hands as they vibrated uncontrollably, not trusting my tremulous voice to say more.

"I'm gonna go lay out with some friends at Sugar House Park this afternoon. We might throw the Frisbee around. Would you like to come?" She really meant it. Oh, how I loved her.

"No one needs to see your mother in a swimsuit, honey. I

think I'll stay home and do a little gardening." As I spoke, I was fully aware of each muscle in my jaw as I tried to stop the quivering in my voice.

She kissed me on the head and went to her room to get ready.

There was a honk from the front of the house and Sylvie ran into the living room. "Are you sure?" she said as she headed out the front door. She was the picture of vigorous health in her white French-cut swimsuit, legs long and tanned. Before she walked out the door she hugged me fiercely, holding me together.

"I'll be fine. You deserve a break! Have fun and wear some pants if you go to dinner," I replied, my tongue thick between my teeth.

She patted her bag. "Got them right here." She gave me another kiss and ran to the car full of girls waiting for her in front of the house.

As she closed the door I put my head into my hands. Distantly, I could remember the joy of summer break, the anticipation of long days full of warmth. I could see it was beautiful outside my window, the grass green, the air fresh. But I couldn't feel it.

How could Sylvie tolerate my company? I was awful to be around. This house held nothing but misery and burden for her. And I was the reason. It would be no wonder if she wanted to escape. If I could escape from *myself*, I would.

A soft voice niggled in the corners of my mind. "They're going to take her from you because you're unfit to be a mother." Unable to control the voice, the words collided in my head, echoing and repeating. I rubbed my temples to stop the chatter.

Call the doctor! This is the voice of madness, one shred of my rational brain screeched. *This is a spin!*

But I needed more time to see if being off the medication lifted my mood, I reasoned with myself. I would go out and work in the yard like I told Sylvie I had planned to do. I would masquerade as a woman who was in control.

But before I could start the yard work, I knew with clarity I had forgotten something. And it was important. I paced the living room, thinking. Probably something from the store, but I couldn't remember what it was. I ticked through my typical grocery list, touching my index finger against my thumb as I said each item: milk, eggs, bread, hamburger, garbage bags. I lost track and started over: milk, eggs, bread, hamburger, garbage bags. No! There was something else. Milk, eggs, bread, hamburger, garbage bags! What was it?

I kicked the easel and the velvet canvas clattered to the floor. Wet paint smeared the floorboards and my shin. I didn't bother to clean it, knowing if I got into the car it would come to me. If I drove to the market, I would surely remember. And if I could remember, I could quiet the list that rattled unresolved in my head. I crawled into the vehicle, my unreliable, shaking hands dropping the keys several times before I could start it.

I drove east on Downington Avenue, then down another street. Where was I going? Oh yes, the market. But I continued aimlessly, taking a self-inflicted tour of the neighborhood, the pattern of glare and shadow making me squint. Each house seemed so placid from the car. The lawns were mowed, sprinklers on here and there. I was looking for something, *anything* to reveal the misery that surely must reside within the walls of at least a few of these houses. Or was it only me, harboring sorrow? Was my home the only one engulfed by suffering, unrevealed?

I wanted the fronts of these peaceful-looking houses to sag and weep, so the world would know the tortuous secrets they *must* contain. And why didn't the walls of my *own* home crumble, showing the world what was happening inside?

I drove slowly, too slowly, cars honking at me as I inched down the road, but knew I must drive deliberately because at any moment my traitorous hands threatened to yank the wheel and hurtle me into another car. If I plodded, I could stop myself before I caused any damage. My heart thumped in my chest, knowing I could easily do it. I *wanted* to do it. I could smash the car with one flick of my wrist. Terrified, I shut off the vehicle, not entirely sure how I had landed in the small parking lot at Westminster College. The hourly chimes were ringing. Maybe their tune was the siren song beckoning me here. Maybe I should drop in to see Dr. Yeager.

I stumbled to the office. A note was taped to the door. *Students—Have a Great Summer! I will return to the office in one week.* Right. That's why I didn't have to go to work tomorrow. I knocked on the door a couple of times, peering into the darkened windows. "Please be here," I called softly. *How do you feel, Lainey?* So scared.

I needed to get some sleep. Things would be clearer if I could grab a couple of hours. I had some sleeping pills at home. I hadn't used them for years, but maybe I would take one or two and see if I could find slumber. Pulling into the garage, I remembered I had planned to do some yard work. Maybe a few minutes in the fresh air would bring some clarity or some quiet. It seemed once the bells from Westminster chimed, they'd never stop, continuing to clang in my head, the tune jagged and distorted.

Outside, I put on my leather gloves and took the shears to the rosebush, since it was the only part of the yard still in the shade. The alluring fragrance of the bush was gone, as the petals had turned flaccid. Today the yard smelled like a funeral parlor.

However, the repetitive snip of the shears was soothing. It erased the persistent ringing as the spent petals fell around my feet. The sun worked its way into my shaded spot, bringing moisture to my neck and torso. A small breeze tickled my arms. Nice . . . quiet. The world had a dreamlike quality to it, peaceful, muted. Finally calm. The baked earth seemed to sway as I attempted balance on shifting ground.

Without much thought, I crossed my arms in front of my chest, clasping the hem of my shirt on opposite sides, and in one freeing movement pulled the shirt up over my head. The breeze quickly found its way to my exposed belly and chest. A moment of pleasure. I had been waiting a year for even one pure second of pleasure. However, my bra was still concealing my breasts and keeping in the heat. Unacceptable. I unclasped the back of my bra and dropped it to the driveway, discarded lace on white petals. Chill rushed over me. I put my gloves back on and resumed deadheading the gargantuan rose.

"Lainey?" A voice reached me through the clouds. "Lainey?"

George . . . it was George! I stared at my shirt and bra. Something was wrong. I needed to do something. Then pandemonium! Bells! The bonging and clanging reverberated, threatening to split my skull. I dropped the gardening shears and put my fingers in my ears. I had to get into the house, but how could I move with a locomotive in my brain?

And I was inside. I locked the door. The doorbell chimed, and a pounding echoed through the house, chattering my molars like grindstones. I slumped to the floor, holding my head. "Stop it," I whispered.

"Lainey, are you okay in there?" George yelled through the locked front door.

"No more noise," I mouthed, my eyes starting to water with pain.

He rang the bell again. I pressed my palms into my ears, locking my fingers in front of my forehead. Using all of my strength, I yelled, "I'm fine! I'm going to take a nap. I'll call you when I wake!"

I watched as he tried to spot me through the window. Finally, his long shadow retreated. I retched, the effort of escape collapsing me to the ground.

I needed sleep. After several minutes, I crawled to the bathroom and pulled myself to standing using the counter. Rummaging through the bottles in the medicine cabinet, I found the sleeping pills. I popped the lid off and swallowed three. I lay on my bed, the world spinning. Tears slid down my cheeks, soaking my hair. I had failed. Sylvie would be taken from me, and the hole would open again. And if that happened, I would let it swallow me. I would disappear into the hole, knowing I had lost the only thing worth living for.

I managed to sit up before I vomited again. The sleeping pills lay soaked on my pillow. Now rest would never find me! I stumbled back into the bathroom and shook the remaining pills directly into my mouth. Leaning over the sink, I filled my mouth with water and swallowed.

The jackhammer was in my head, vibrations rattling my jaw. Teeth crashing together, breaking in my mouth. Shards choking me. Wrapping my arms over my head, I pressed my face to stop the throbbing. Cool tubes the size of spaghetti draped across my cheeks. I yanked at them, my hands shaking with the effort.

"Elaine! Stop!" My mother's voice cut through the din. I tried to center myself on her voice, but the pressure was too much. My mother spoke again. "Doctor, she's awake!"

Suddenly there was movement all around my body. People were tapping on the bottoms of my feet, an unfamiliar hand grasped my wrist and held it lightly, and my mother's warm hand tickled the inside of my other arm, comforting me like she had when I was a child.

"Lainey, can you hear me?" It was a man and it wasn't Dr. Yeager. "Just nod if you can, your throat will be very rough, because we've pumped your stomach."

I nodded, the movement rolling like heavy waves against my skull.

"Elaine, what were you thinking? You could've died!" My mother's comforting hand attached itself to my forearm too tightly now.

Tears leaked from my eyes. "I didn't mean . . ." The words felt like someone was dragging a frayed rope up my throat and out my mouth. I could only croak one more word. "Sylvie."

"She's here at the hospital, but she hasn't been in because she's a minor," the doctor's voice offered. "We've called Dr. Yeager. He should be here shortly to determine the treatment for your disease. In the meantime, try to relax."

Relax? I sat up. I had to get to Sylvie. Before anyone could stop me, I swung my legs over the side of the bed and tried to dash to the door. An IV pole, which was attached to me, crashed against the bed and toppled. I felt a stinging yank in my elbow as the needle ripped out of my arm. I reached for the door. I was almost free!

"Sedate her!" the doctor yelled. Strong hands gripped both of my arms. One prick near my collarbone and the world went black.

*   *   *

"How do you feel, Lainey?" This time it was Dr. Yeager asking the question. His vivid blue eyes were bloodshot, creased with worry.

"I feel alive, barely." My voice was as quiet as a breath, and yet the words still tore as they left my mouth.

"You were very lucky your neighbor George Pearson thought to call 911."

I nodded and pointed at the window. "Bars?" I managed to speak.

"You're on suicide watch, at least until we get you level with medication," Dr. Yeager answered.

I shook my head violently.

"What are you trying to say?"

"I didn't mean to . . ." Tears smudged my spoken words. "I didn't."

Dr. Yeager handed me his notebook and pencil. "Write it."

Tell Sylvie I never wanted to leave her. I didn't mean to. I needed sleep so I could get steady. I never intended to kill myself. I took a shuddering breath, already weak from writing these few words. He held out his hand for the pencil. Before I gave it to him I wrote one last sentence. *What will happen now?*

"Let's work on adjusting your medication. And you need to get some rest. You've got hard work ahead of you. The big decisions can wait." The doctor retrieved his notebook from my grip and wrote for several minutes. His eyes filled. "Lainey, I'm just so glad . . ." He cleared his throat. "Let's get you well."

I'd forgotten something. Something important. I ticked through my grocery list—milk, eggs, bread, hamburger, garbage bags—before I realized I wasn't going anywhere. Especially not grocery shopping. I was stuck in the psych wing of the hospital.

I stared at the second hand on the clock in my room, urging it toward eight-thirty, when the nurse would usually check my vitals. I tried the breathing techniques I was learning in therapy. But I still knew I had forgotten something. Something important.

At eight-forty, ten agonizing minutes behind schedule, the

nurse opened the door to my room. Dr. Yeager followed her in. He was dressed in street clothes, teaching today, probably. He was reading from his notebook as he walked. Before he looked up, I yelled, "I've forgotten something!"

His scrutiny centered on my forehead, like it always did when he was trying to decipher my illness. His face relaxed. "It's Sylvie's birthday today. We talked about it yesterday."

Sylvie's birthday. I instantly slumped back in the bed. Something important. Sobs burst unbidden from my chest. What kind of mother was I? I was in the hospital. I forgot the birthday of my only baby.

"Lainey, you've made great progress, but memory loss is a common side effect of your treatment. It will come back. Be gentle with yourself." He handed me a tissue. "In fact, go fix yourself up. I'm here early today because Sylvie is coming this morning. She invited me to join you two, and your parents, for a little ice-cream cake. She made it herself. Three flavors, she said, chocolate, strawberry, and chocolate chip."

My daughter made her own cake and invited my *doctor* to the party at the *hospital*. I wanted to crawl under my bed and hide for the shame of it. My face must have betrayed my thoughts.

"Lainey, she's a wonderful girl. You've done a great job raising her. This is a day to celebrate, not to fret, so get dressed and put on a smile."

So I did, and we all huddled around the tiny table in my room. Sylvie served the cake on Styrofoam plates from the hospital cafeteria and we ate with plastic forks. The day wasn't perfect, but the cake was delicious. The doctor was right. There was much cause for celebration. Down deep, I knew it.

Sitting in the backseat of my parent's car, I felt like I was twelve again. However, when I was twelve, my parents' shoulders were not quite so hunched with age and worry. My father's bald spot was not as pronounced, and my mother's hair wasn't gray.

"Well, you look good." My mom spoke without looking

back. "You've got color in your cheeks I haven't seen for quite some time." She spoke slowly, meandering from subject to subject.

I'd responded to each of her questions and comments with only a word or two, feeling fragile. Feeling free. Not a word escaped my father's lips. Hadn't we said everything that could be said while I was in the hospital? Now, none of us in the car knew exactly how to address each other on this momentous occasion. I was coming home.

After a month, in the crazy house trying to stabilize, I was coming home!

Soaring above my head, limbs of the gigantic ash trees traced the sidewalks along Downington Avenue, creating a golden arch of autumn splendor. I recalled the day I had discovered my home, how the cool shadow of the street tenderly embraced me that day as it did now, leading me, cradling me. Each tree on our route was bound with a brightly colored yellow ribbon. I swallowed and tried to hide the sudden prick of tears.

"It was Sylvie's idea," my mom said. "She and George have spent the morning tying them." She glanced back now, a gentle smile on her face.

And there was my house. The porch swing hung expectantly on the wide front porch. The lawn was green and freshly mowed. Sylvie was on the swing set, her legs outstretched as she pulled her full-grown body to the sky. Her blond hair flew behind her just as it had when she was eight.

At the sound of the car door, she opened her eyes and jumped. I gasped as she sailed through the air, landing on her feet, just like she always did.

She greeted me like a child, throwing her arms around me, clinging to me. I wrapped her in my embrace and touched the tip of her nose with mine. It was easy. She was as tall as I was. "Mommy," she whispered. "I'm so glad you're home."

The following Valentine's Day, at dusk, I was on the porch plugging in the Christmas lights. Sylvie opened the front door and sat on the porch swing. "Mom, do you know what day it is?"

"Valentine's Day." I sat down next to her and put my hand on her knee. "Happy Valentine's Day, my love."

"Happy Valentine's Day," she replied. "I only mention the date because George told me Louise wondered if we would be taking down the Christmas lights this year."

I gazed at the colorful lights, sparkling against the dusky gray sky. They had plenty of chiaroscuro, contrasting light and dark. They filled the night sky with color, reminding me of my paintings of the aurora borealis. They delighted me.

"I think I'll leave them up a little longer. I love them," I said, knowing Sylvie understood that loving something was important to my gradual recovery. "Do they bother you?"

"No. I love them too, Mom." Sylvie grinned. "And that's what I told George."

"What did George say?"

"He said he's fine with them. But Louise was bugging him to ask you." She shrugged. "You know Louise."

"I do. And I love her too." I stood and adjusted some of the lights that had started to sag. "How about this? Tell George to tell Louise I'll remove the lights as soon as I see blossoms on the cherry tree." I grinned wickedly. "I also *love* the cherry tree."

Sylvie laughed. "That's months from now. Poor Louise will have a heart attack."

Sylvie held up one end of the lights while I tried to reach the nail the cord had slipped from. "Did you remember Dave is taking me out for a Valentine's dinner in about an hour?" she asked, her voice sparkling with the adventure of young love.

I nodded.

"Maybe you should get yourself a Valentine this year," she continued. "You're not too old to find a sweetheart." She tried to make her words light, but I could hear she was worried I would be lonely. I also knew she would be relieved at my news.

"It's funny you should mention getting myself a Valentine." I smiled. "I *also* have a date." As I said it I blushed, feeling a little like Sylvie, flush with the possibility of love.

"You do? Why didn't you tell me?" Sylvie squealed.

"He called this afternoon."

"Who? Who is it?"

"His name is Dennis and he's a fellow lunatic." I giggled. "But he's pretty cute. We met while I was in the asylum, and he's recently finished his tour on the crazy train. So we're perfect for each other. When he's properly medicated, he is a mechanic. I don't know what will come of it. We'll see," I said.

"You know, Mom," Sylvie said as I finally secured the twinkling lights, "you're not like any of the other moms."

I remembered her saying these exact words to me when she was a child. "I'm not sure if that's a good thing."

"It's a good thing, don't worry." She laughed softly. "And it's not because you keep the holiday lights up through February—however, that's part of it."

"I'm not sure I agree," I said, joining her on the porch swing. "You're the one who brings light into this house, not to mention stability. I'm an anchor to your star, dragging you down. All I wanted to do was be a good mother, and I continually rocked your world with my own problems. And yet, you've always landed on your feet. As much as I've tried to help, I think you've raised yourself."

My chin quivered, but I kept talking. "I don't deserve you. And at times I don't know why anyone trusted me to keep you. Even now, I wake up at night wondering when you'll be taken away from me." I swiped at my face with the back of my sleeve. "Oh, God, I am a mess. They're going to put me back in the crazy house."

"Even if they do, Mom, guess what? I have good news."

I raised a hand to my throat, wondering what she had to tell me.

"You, of course, remember I had a birthday while you were in the hospital?" she asked.

"Yes, your momentous birthday when you had to make your *own* cake and bring it to my padded cell." I shook my head at the memory.

"I turned *eighteen,* Mom. I'm an adult and I get to choose where I live. No one can take me away from you now, so that's off your list of worries." She touched my hand. "I choose to live with you."

I nodded, letting the tears roll down my cheeks, unable to speak.

Wrung dry, calm settled over me like a warm blanket when I realized she was right. Really, all I hoped to accomplish was to be her mother. I clung to each day in an attempt to be stable. Despite the ups and downs, time had brought me here. I was sitting with my *grown* daughter. I had made it!

I gazed at the Christmas lights filling the Valentine's Eve sky with color. I loved so many things. I loved my daughter and she loved me back. I would live simply, day to day, because today was all I could be sure of. I knew that now.

How do you feel, Lainey? I asked myself. I took a deep breath. I felt joy.

IVY BAYGREN

I planned to pierce my dark mood with a candle. The vastness of the evening was heavy because it was Saturday night *and* it was Valentine's Day. Both Naomi and Porter had secured a sleepover, leaving me alone in the house. I'd tried to convince them to have their friends to our place, to no avail. And in searching for a prick of light in this darkest of all February nights, I settled with lighting a candle.

The flickering light would set the mood for my evening with *The Bachelor*, the closest I'd come to romance since Adam died. I had the latest three episodes saved on TiVo. Naomi also loved the show, but for some reason, the fact *I* watched it seemed desperate, so I usually watched it alone—or sometimes with Drew, if Stephen was working a double.

Shuffling through the saved programs, I spotted *The Sixth Sense* in the list of recorded movies. God, I loved that movie when it didn't hit so close to my heart. Almost without meaning to, I pressed play and sunk bonelessly into the couch cushions. That's when I noticed my sweater was red. Okay, I had put it on for Valentine's Day, but the fact I was watching *The Sixth Sense* and I was wearing my *red* sweater surely must be a sign.

I paused the movie and ran my hands over my forearms. It *was* unusually cold in here. I exhaled forcefully through my mouth to see if the vapor from my breath was visible. It wasn't.

"Adam?" I whispered.

The candle I'd placed on the television flickered.

"Wedding video!" I said out loud as I dashed to the trunk where we kept the bulky VCR tapes. The woman in the movie was watching their wedding video when Bruce Willis visited!

Throwing old tapes of *The Simpsons* and *Barney* to the ground, I dug into the depths of the chest and there it was: Adam and Ivy, Wedding 1995. The candle winked encouragingly. This was it. I lit several more candles and turned off the overhead lights as I slipped the wedding video into the player, praying the machine still worked. It had been years since we had watched a video tape.

I leaned back in my red sweater and watched the recording my uncle made as a wedding present. The first shot of Adam, standing with a beer in his hand, waiting for the guests to arrive, took my breath away. I crawled toward the television and touched it as his face appeared again on the screen. "Adam?" I said again and rubbed the shiver bumps on my arms.

This time the candle remained stolid and I was certain it was *not* colder than the last time I tried for frozen breath. More red, I thought deliriously as I stopped the video. I squeezed into my scarlet miniskirt along with the sweater, cursing it was the only other red item I had. Why didn't I have a shawl, a gauzy burgundy skirt, or even some stilettos? I found Adam's wedding ring in the underwear drawer, cupped it tightly in my palm, and returned to the couch, checking the thermostat on the way to the living room. I turned the set temperature from seventy degrees to sixty, figuring maybe I could hasten the chill. Then I sat on the sofa, ring in hand, red miniskirt, red sweater, and red wine. Red wine!

Before I pushed play, I poured myself another tall glass. I rationalized my insanity with the fact it was Valentine's Day. And on a day made for lovers, lacking a lover, I was allowed a little hysteria. I leaned against the cushions, took a lengthy swig, turned on the video, and watched. I looked younger, decades younger than I felt. Adam was on the screen, his hands in mine. I held my palms up, their position identical to the one I assumed during the ceremony. "Hold my hands," I said to the screen. Nothing.

Twenty minutes of wedding video and my glass was empty. I exhaled into the living room and saw no vapor. "Give me a sign!" I yelled at the television. "If you're here, anywhere, show me and I'll wait! I'll wait forever, but I need a little something . . . real." I slumped onto the couch.

The telephone rang and I knocked the empty glass to the floor. Glass shattered over the hardwood as I staggered to the telephone. "Hello?" I said cautiously. Would I hear him speak?

"Mom? Do we still have power?" Naomi's voice was jarring.

"Power?"

"Yes. The power's out at Amber's and we're right in the middle of the last episode of *The Bachelor*. Can we come over and finish? It's going to kill us if we don't know who Sean picks! Her mom says she'll drive us."

I gazed at my ruby-red miniskirt riding high on my February white thighs. On the television, Adam and I were leaving the reception, moving toward his little Toyota, the windows written on with lipstick.

"Come home!" I gasped to Naomi or Adam, I wasn't sure. I stood and blew out the candle. What was I doing? "Please, Naomi, please come home."

"I'll be there in a few minutes," Naomi said, her voice indicating she'd heard the sadness in mine. "Are you okay?" she asked. "I'll come without Amber. We can watch the last episode together, if you want."

I heard Amber's muffled protest on the end of the line. "I'm fine. Bring Amber," I replied softly.

"She says her stomach hurts anyway, so . . ."

I could tell Naomi was lying, but I argued no further. I wanted her home where I could breathe in the essence of her, my daughter. So very real.

A couple of frigid weeks later there was a knock at the door. It was forceful enough to make me jump and, coming through the muffled, snow-filled sky, it dropped my stomach. We'd scarcely finished dinner, but this time of year it was already dark, blinds pulled against the black crystal night. I peered through a gap near the window frame, trying to recognize the figure on the porch. A man stomped his feet a couple of times to keep circulation and blew a smoke ring of condensation through the frozen air. Though I'd only seen him once, I knew him immediately. What in the world was Theo Taylor doing on my porch?

It was fine to open my door to this stranger. *I know him,* I rationalized as I swung the door open and invited him in from the cold, abandoning my usual reserve. "Come in!" I said. "You have no idea how often I think about you."

He chuckled, his eyes flicking to my left hand. "What would your husband have to say about that?"

I dropped my hand to my side. "Not much. We haven't spoken for a while." I was strangely emboldened by my evening glass of wine.

"Oh?"

"He died almost nine months ago." I swallowed the tears that usually surfaced when I mentioned Adam's death. Why was I so quickly divulging this closely guarded secret to Theo Taylor? Why did I want him to know what defined me?

"I'm sorry," he responded, looking at his feet.

"No, I'm sorry for spilling. Some days I'm more scattered than others." I took a breath, pulling myself together. "What I meant to say is, I've been researching this house and I've made some interesting discoveries I thought you'd appreciate since you're in the business of studying old houses." I swallowed. "Plus, your signs polka-dot my neighborhood; they're hard to miss."

With a touch of hesitation, he said, "Speaking of that, I have something to add to your research, I think." He blushed when he said this, and I realized he'd thought about me too.

"What is it?"

"A newspaper clipping listing local boys killed in service during World War Two." He kept his attention on the newsprint as he handed it to me. "I almost hope this information isn't applicable to your home, but I think you were researching a family by the name of Gianopolous when I ran into you at Rio Grande?"

"How did you know?" I mumbled, gazing at the page.

"I noticed the name after I knocked the copies from your hands. It's the last name of one of my neighbors, so it stuck in my mind. My neighbors claim no relation to your Gianopolous, but I found this article when I was researching for another client. I traced the name to your address and the rest is history, so to speak."

The page I was clutching was more a list than a story. LOCAL BOYS: WWII SOLDIERS HONORED AT MEMORY GROVE. Theo Taylor watched me as I found the name I was looking for, my heartbeat sluggish as I read it: Adonis Gianopolous—Died Pacific Rim 1945.

"No!" I cried, sudden tears smearing the word.

"I guess you didn't know about this," Theo said softly. I assumed Theo learned about births, deaths, and weddings all the time. To him, it was probably just information, but this was more personal to me.

I shook my head. He studied my face as I tried to pull myself together. "His poor mother," I finally gasped. "I have a son. I don't know . . . I've grown attached to the Gianopolous family, knowing we've all lived in the confines of the same walls." I gestured to the living room, cozy in the golden lamplight, books on the mantle shelves, the walls freshly painted a warm mossy color, and Lainey's masterpiece hanging behind the couch. I pictured the yard as it had looked full of friends and family during the backyard wedding. Did Eris Gianopolous find comfort in familiar surroundings where she'd enjoyed time with her son? Or was she haunted by her loss, searching for him in the empty corners he'd once occupied?

During my careful inspection of the photos we'd taken of the Gianopolous album, I'd found a date written in one of the white margins surrounding the image. It was faint and I'd taken a second photo of the first and used the zoom feature to read the script. September 1960. The wedding occurred fifteen years after the Gianopolous family lost their son in the war. Mrs. Gianopolous clawed her way from tragedy to celebration within the walls of my home.

Theo's voice was grave. "You know, I search for information

on these historic homes all the time, but when I find something like this, evidence of a long-ago tragedy, it always gets me. Even if the people who mourned for this boy are gone themselves, it still gives me pause." He took the paper out of my shaking hand. "I have a son who's twenty. If he'd lived during World War Two, this could have been his name and my loss. It's hard to think about." He paused and touched my cheek with the tip of his finger, catching a tear.

Startled at his gesture, I said, "What would your wife say about you comforting a blubbering widow." I laughed nervously.

"No wife." He held up his left hand. "Just the one boy. I'm sorry though, I don't know why I did that," he stuttered, a blush rising from his collar.

I ran a finger under each eye, checking for the inevitable rivulets of mascara. "So we've both embarrassed ourselves," I said. "Would you care to join me for a glass of wine?" I gestured to my mostly empty glass. "I could show you my historical discoveries and I promise not to cry."

"Well, I'm off the clock, so sure, I'll join you for some wine," he said, glancing into my living room. "I can see why you like this old place. There's a good vibe in here—history, but not heartbreak. You'd be surprised how many houses I walk into where there's a heaviness that permeates the walls themselves."

"I'm quite certain there's been a bit of heartbreak in this home." I smiled gently, and held up the article.

"I believe that," he said. "But there's a difference between heartbreak and heart*broken*. This house doesn't feel broken."

I poured him a glass of wine, and as I handed it to him our fingers touched. There was a charge between us and we both glanced at the glass, aware and suddenly nervous. "So, how long have you lived here?" he asked, leaning against the kitchen counter with forced nonchalance.

"We moved in almost fifteen years ago. The place was in shambles. But Adam, my husband, enjoyed fixing things up. He was always the one looking for evidence of past owners while he remodeled. And after he died, I don't know, I started to do a little research myself." I shrugged. "It allows me to look at my day-to-day struggles with a wider lens, if that makes sense."

"It makes absolute sense," he said. "Every house I remodel and every person who lived there had a story. When I stop and take a minute to consider, it makes me feel less significant and somehow less—"

"Alone." I finished his sentence.

We settled on the couch and I showed him the photos of Calliope's wedding, taken during Eris's time in the home. Finally, I lifted Bitsy's memory book from its regular position on the coffee table. Sliding closer to see the faded script, his elbow pressed against my side as we read together. He asked questions and we laughed at my retelling of each entry. He gasped where I gasped and our sighs mingled as we finished the final entry.

He felt the story, like I did. He understood. Unlike my friends who avoided uncomfortable conversation, or my children, who I must be strong for, or my brother, who always approached me like a doctor treating an ailing patient, Theo knew only me. He understood this part of me. It was strangely freeing that to Theo, I wasn't part of Adam.

"Well?" I said, holding up the memory book.

"Enchanting," he replied, looking at me. His eyes were green flecked with gold, the exact color of Adam's. His face, however, was entirely different. I didn't search for traces of Adam in it while we talked, because I knew he wasn't Adam and I wasn't sad. Realizing this fact thrilled me and pained me in equal measure. Was I betraying my love? Theo's elbow rested across mine as we sat side by side, our proximity no longer required to grasp Bitsy's memory book, but neither of us moved. His warm touch soothed me. His physical presence on my couch, the very weight of him felt like a break in the clouds after a storm, like throwing back my hood to absorb the heat of sun on my face.

ERIS GIANOPOLOUS

Downington Avenue
1960

"There you are. I've been looking all over for you. I even went into the basement, wondering if you were going to drink all of the toasting wine before the wedding got underway." Hector lowered himself carefully onto the porch swing next to me. Between our two rounded bodies, we spanned the width of the wooden seat.

"I've been here for a while, enjoying the calm before the storm." I sighed as the swing cradled me. From the porch we could gaze at the Victory Vineyard, grape vines sagging with plump bobbles. Hector had helped me scour the morning glory between the rows and we had cleared some ground in the center of the vines for a ceremony tent and chairs. For me, there was no sadness in cutting it back; while the Victory Vineyard seemed to promise rich harvest, the fruit made god-awful wine. Perhaps the grapes continually soured, the soil tarnished by loss, knowing the end of the war had not been a cause for celebration in our home. No glass of Mavrodaphne was raised. Our cups were filled with tears.

Using determination born of grief, Lord knows we still tried to make it work. We experimented with oak barrels, sun fermenting, and five different types of grapes; regardless, the wine was barely palatable. We had about a dozen bottles left, which I insisted we use for the wedding toast. And that would be the end of our wine-making. Next summer, we had decided to pull out the rest of the grapes and plant grass. Hector and I were getting too old to keep up the vineyard, especially since we couldn't even *give* the wine away. Oh, sure, in a desperate moment I could be found drinking the swill. But there was a liquor store in Sugar House now, where I could get good wine, so I suggested we put up a swing set for grandkids, when (and if) they came along.

"It's going to be a beautiful day." Hector put his hand on my leg.

I sighed. "I never thought this day would arrive. Calliope settle? She's got delusions about passionate love. Operatic theme isn't a lifestyle. You've heard me tell her as much, haven't you?"

Hector laughed softly. "I have. And as we both know, life isn't a tragedy or a comedy."

I put my hand on top of his. "No, it's both, isn't it?"

"I wish he could be here," Hector said softly after several moments, his voice wavering. "He should be part of this celebration."

Unbidden, a tear slid down my cheek. "He should be."

"He'd probably be married himself, by now," Hector continued. "Maybe he'd have a child or two. He'd be dressed in a nice suit, hair slicked back. He'd probably give the toast . . ."

Hector and I had played this heartbreaking game of *What would Adonis be doing now?* several times a week. It was how we kept him with us. Most days were a guess, but today would have been certain. He would've been part of Calliope's wedding, no question. And so his absence, though softened by the years, was especially vivid today. For both of us.

"It's a hole in our lives," I said, pulling a tissue from my pocket. "A space that can't be filled."

"We have Calliope," Hector replied. "She's enough. This is her day, a cause for celebration."

Hector cleared his throat, controlling his emotion. "I have a quote." He paused, seeking my permission. "It's quite fitting."

"Well, go on then," I said, humoring him.

" 'May you have enough happiness to make you sweet, enough trials to make you strong, enough sorrow to keep you human, and enough hope to make you happy.' "

"Who said that?" I asked.

"Unknown," Hector said. "So I'll take the credit." He hummed quietly to himself. I enjoyed the movement of the swing and the familiar depth of his voice.

A car door slammed, jerking me from my reflection. Calliope extricated herself from her new metallic blue Chevrolet Corvair. She wore an alarmingly loosely belted pink bathrobe, her dark hair piled high on her head encircled with a wreath of baby's breath. Her face was shiny with sweat and she was cursing.

"I'm late! Jesus Christ, you would have thought the stylist figured the ceremony started at midnight, not seven o'clock. I haven't even put on my makeup. Mama?" Calliope called.

"I'm here. What do you need me to do?" I yelled from the porch.

"Get the dress from the trunk. My makeup is in the pink bag next to it. I've got to wipe my face and cool off before I try to squeeze into that damn thing. I'm going into the house!"

Reaching into the car for the trunk release, I was engulfed by the smell of Calliope, part sugar, part musky perfume she loved. An empty Mister Donut bag was crumpled on the passenger seat. I pulled Calliope's dress from the trunk. The pouf lace sleeves stood out from the plunging neckline like shoulder armor, and if I stood the bodice on the ground it would likely stand at attention like a sequined flak jacket. The whole dress was heavily beaded and reminded me of the costume she wore when she sang *Aida*. It was perfect. I couldn't imagine Calliope choosing a subtle, simple dress. Not our Calliope.

I wrapped the train around the back of my neck, so it wouldn't drag over the freshly cut lawn, and I hobbled my way up the front stairs. Hector opened the door for me.

"Good Lord. Is that the wedding dress?" he said, closing the door.

"Yes. I'm taking it to Calliope. Where did she go?"

"She's in the kitchen, head in the freezer, so her sweat won't mess up her hair."

Calliope's body was in a partial back bend, her head fully engulfed in the dark opening. Frozen air swirled around her face. Her robe had come mostly untied and I could see the swell of her belly through her full-length white slip. God knows her belly had never been flat, but the roundness was new.

I touched her above the navel, very gently, and found it firm under my fingers. Calliope's eyes snapped open and she knocked my hand from her stomach. "What are you doing, Mama?"

"Are you . . . ?"

"Jesus, Mama, I'm not a virgin."

"That's not what I'm asking." I knew I should be angry—I mean, this child was conceived out of wedlock—but all I felt was joy.

She smiled sheepishly. "Surprise."

"Oh, *padimou*, I wish—"

Her fingers stiffened protectively over her stomach. "If you say you wish Adonis had the chance . . ."

I blinked, surprised. "I was going to say I wish you as much joy in motherhood as I've experienced," I said somewhat defensively. "But of course I wish Adonis had the chance to have a child. Of course, I wish he could enjoy the undeniable joy of raising a family. But that's not what I was going to say."

"I'm sorry, Mama, it's just sometimes it seems all conversations lead back to Adonis and . . . I mean, I miss him too, but sometimes, I want things to be only about me," she said, her anger dissolving into quick tears. "Oh, God, that sounds so selfish, and now I'm going to smear my mascara."

"Oh, Calliope, I guess I'm compelled to talk about Adonis because I'm afraid I'll lose him if I don't. He's not here to fight for my attention, and I can't stand the thought of him disappearing from my thoughts," I whispered, handing her a tissue. I was fighting the aching uneasiness that always settled into my bones with the candid discussion of feelings. I was much better at destroying something to show my love.

I kissed my palm and cupped it over her round, soft cheek, where it fit just right. "My girl." It was all I could say. I loved her so. Having her near me gave me such peace, but did I say it to her? I didn't. It was easier to talk about Adonis, who wasn't looking me in the eye as I spoke. Could I focus on those who surrounded me, rather than those I had to do without? Maybe I should try.

Waiting for the ceremony to begin, a relaxed hum filled my head, like those first precious moments when the wine softens the edges of the day. I had promised Calliope she could tell Hector about the baby, but I couldn't stop twitching.

"You look like the cat that swallowed the canary," Hector said, taking the chair next to me.

"It's a lovely day. That's all." I could scarcely keep from bursting with the news. "Sit down," I diverted. "I can't see."

Though we faced west, the evening glare was blocked by the full leaves of the cherry tree, bathing the yard in the indirect golden glow of sunset. The tiny white lights we had paid so much for nicely framed the wide arch of the rented trellis and disguised the brand-new garage Hector had built for me.

I told Calliope a September wedding would be too hot, but tonight a cool breeze found us, rolling gently from the Wasatch Mountains, cooling my neck. This late in the summer, evening held the first kiss of fall, a certain crispness to remind us the seasons were fleeting. The moment summer seemed too hot or winter too long, the next season slipped in one evening, and then another. And the monotony was broken.

Each chair was full, friends and family dressed in their wedding finery. Calliope's magnetic confidence had served her well. I laid my hand in Hector's. He squeezed. There was a tap on my shoulder and I turned to see George and Louise Pearson settling behind us.

"You two sure got the yard prettied up nice," George said.

"Thanks," I grumbled, elbowing Hector. He hadn't finished his whole honey-do list, but it was too late now. He nudged me back, unconcerned.

"And I saw Calliope dash into the house in her robe," Louise added. "That girl looks like you did, when we moved in all those years ago."

"I know. She can look forward to all this," I said, patting my middle.

"Hush now, Eris. She's a lucky girl." Hector squeezed my knee.

Calliope's groom, Dale Cresconi, walked to the front of the crowd and looked expectantly at our back door. Seeing no movement, he shrugged at the audience, letting the crowd laugh with him, knowing once again, Calliope was late. He was a good man for our daughter, coming from an Italian family that had been in Salt Lake for several generations. Solid in more ways than one, he was nearly a foot taller than Hector and probably seventy-five pounds heavier; his voice, even when speaking, was audible in all rooms of the house. He and Calliope met while performing at the Utah Opera House. A baritone, he was loud enough to quiet Calliope when her voice rose in anger, and large enough to make her feel feminine.

All at once, there was a pause in conversation, a collective inhale from the crowd, and the atmosphere quivered as one melancholy note floated from the house, timid and fragile. I wondered what instrument could paint such emotion. Holding my breath, the sound resonated, filling me, surrounding me. I turned. Calliope stood at the top of the stairs, the sun glinting off the sequins on her dress. Slowly, all heads turned to her. She was calling for her lover in Italian. Dale echoed her call from the vineyard, weaving her notes with his sonorous voice. One by one, friends in the audience joined the chorus. An opera, a love song of their making, was being performed in the backyard of my humble home.

Calliope glided down the stairs, the train of her dress stretching feet behind her, and took her place by Dale. The piece ended as it began, one note shimmering in the air; a note complete and perfect, a gift from my daughter. Dale wrapped his arm around her and kissed her on the lips. The crowd, still haunted by the melody, burst into applause.

My precious child stood in front of me, carrying the next generation of this family. Years had drifted away like the trailing note of the song, leaving my home empty, but my heart full. The melancholy beauty of it all squeezed sobs from my chest. Hector handed me his handkerchief. I blew my nose more loudly than I had intended. Calliope kissed her index finger and blew it to me.

"Before we begin the ceremony," she said to the quiet crowd, "we want to share with you another joy. A secret we have been harboring for a few months now."

Dale's shoulders were thrown back, savoring the moment. "We will be a family of two tonight, but a family of three by February," he boomed, kissing Calliope again. He placed his hand on her stomach. The crowd rose, clapping once again.

"And"—Calliope paused while her friends took their seats—"I know he is with us today looking down from heaven, so I wanted to tell my brother, Adonis . . ." Tears ran down Calliope's cheeks. "Sorry," she said as she regained her composure. "Like my father would always say, 'Tears are the words the heart can't say.'" Dale handed her a tissue and pulled her close.

"I wanted to say that if it's a boy," she continued, "the baby will be named after his uncle Adonis, who I remember every single day. And if our child is a girl, we will name her Mitera, which means *mother* in Greek, in honor of my own mother." She found me in the crowd. "I love you, Mama."

"I love you," I whispered as Calliope turned back to Father Apostolou. Hector pulled me close as we took our seats. "It's the very best day," he murmured in my ear. I leaned into him, unable to speak.

My life, despite my numerous missteps, despite the ache of loss, was rich and full of joy. I had enough hope to make me happy and enough sorrow to make me human. I let myself cry, because like Calliope said, tears are the words the heart can't say.

IVY BAYGREN

As promised, Bitsy had returned. In a wheelchair now, her grandson and I lifted her feather-light body into the living room for our visit. "I shouldn't have told my grandson I had this one last thing to do before I die," Bitsy said, smiling at me from the couch as I closed the door behind the not-so-young man. "He very nearly turned the car around, figuring he could delay my last days by not allowing my final wishes."

"Don't talk like that," I argued. "You could have years yet."

"Silly Ivy. I don't want years. I only need to tie up a few loose ends," she said, handing me a solitary envelope. The writing was Nathaniel's and the postmark said New York City! I slipped the letter out of the envelope. It was a long one. I flipped through the pages, four of them. This was as long as anything he had written from Europe. A romantic expression of love long waiting. Finally!

December 25, 1915

Dearest Emmeline,
  *Merry Christmas, my love. I am writing to you
from New York. We have been here for nearly a
week and this whole week I have been willing myself
to write you. I have started this letter so many times,
and even now as I write, my hand is shaking.*

*If I tell you anything at all, I have to tell you
everything. So please keep reading. Please try to understand why I have done this. I did what I had to
do, to save her. Please remember I love you. I love
you, Emmeline. I can hardly write these next words.*

*Emmeline, I am married. I have married Rosa
Lewis and have brought her and Dutch back to the
United States with me. . . .*

I dropped the letter, which fluttered to the wood floor.
"What?" I glared at Bitsy, angry at the deception. "How could
he do this?"

"Keep reading, Ivy. Then we'll talk. Love stories are fitful,
unpredictable," she said serenely. "Surely you know by now
that real-life fairy tales don't stop at 'They lived happily ever
after.' "

"I was hoping at least *this* one would," I mumbled as I gathered the pages, my hands shaking with rage. How could he?

*. . . When I told Rosa about Joseph, she fell into
my arms, heartbroken. Things had been hard for her
after Joe left. She had been so worried about his
safety. She had waited for a letter or some word
telling her that he was alive. I know from your
letters you have felt the same fears. I know this part
you will understand.*

*As I wrote in an earlier letter, I was the one who
baptized Rosa. I hoped her baptism would provide
her with protection from her brothers and sisters in
the church. And I also wanted her to be protected
by the Lord. But things continued to get worse,
Emmeline. As I was preparing to return to the
United States, someone broke into her flat while she
was sleeping! They broke her dishes and painted on
her walls terrible, threatening things, in blood. She
and Dutch hid under their bed, and they were
unharmed, but Rosa was inconsolable.*

*As I attempted to comfort her, I couldn't shake
the image of Joseph as he lay gasping in his bed. As
he was dying he asked me to save her. You see,
Emmeline, he asked me to save her and I said I
would. How could I save her if I was leaving? So I
prayed, and very quickly I knew what I had to do. I
had to bring her to the United States with me, where
she could start fresh. So I tried. I bought her and
Dutch tickets for passage on my return ship, but
when we tried to leave the country, they wouldn't let
her travel. She didn't have the proper papers. They
accused her of not being Dutch's true mother. They
said they were going to send her back to Germany
and keep Dutch in England. The officials at the port
told us the only way she could leave England for the
United States was if she was my wife, the wife of an
American.*

*And so I married her. I believe the Lord called me
to be her husband. How could I deny the signs that
God had a hand in our union? Now she is saved.
She is my wife and Dutch is my son and my
responsibility. I am trying to do what is right. I
am trying to keep the promise I made to Joseph,
as he lay dying. His wish and my promise were his
only comfort as he drifted into the arms of God.*

*But Emmeline, my heart is breaking. You are my
first love and I need you. I don't know what to do
now. All I know is I need to see you. I will come to
you as soon as I return to Salt Lake City. Please
don't turn me away.*

*I love you, Emmeline. I love you so much and I
am so sorry.*

Nathaniel

EMMELINE LANSING

❦

Downington Avenue
1916

I dropped his letter. The pages swirled to the floor, an innocent flutter of paper butterflies. I stepped over them, opened the front door, and walked, unaware of the cold, unaware of the time. I didn't shed a tear as I trod evenly away from everything that was once real.

What could this possibly mean? Married? After a couple of blocks I rounded, running back toward my home, back to innocence. I must have misread his words. It couldn't be true. He couldn't possibly be married! As I ran, an evil claw gripped my heart. I doubled over with pain, gasping for breath that wouldn't come. He wouldn't have married someone else, would he? Soft snow touched my cheeks. There were no tears. I stumbled and my knees hit the frozen earth.

It could have been hours later when a voice roused me from my stupor. A familiar voice, it came from within me and from all around me. "Please," it cried. "Please, please, oh my Heavenly Father, please!" I put my fist to my cold lips and suddenly the world was silent. Still binding my plea, I became aware of a hollow ringing in the distance. The bells at Westminster tethered me to reality by announcing it was five o'clock. As the chimes pealed, I was able to stand and find my way home.

My father and Cora were in the kitchen preparing the evening meal. They were startled by my ghostlike appearance. Cora came toward me with open arms. I shook my head, forbidding her words. Denying myself her touch. In my room, the letter was neatly folded on the bed. I put it under my pillow, crawled under the covers in my muddy dress, and fell into a dreamless sleep.

The house was silent when I woke. As I slept, someone had removed my shoes and closed the curtains. Cora had slept in the bed next to me, but I didn't remember her coming to bed, or getting up, for that matter. Looking out the window, the sun was high in the sky. It was Sunday, my family was at church, and I was alone. I walked into the living room holding the letter. The fire was still smoldering. Crouching on the hearth, I held the letter toward the red coals. The pages quivered in my hands from the rising heat and I glimpsed his signature at the bottom of the last page.

Something broke inside me, and sobs racked my body as I gave in to their power. Through blurry eyes, I gazed again at his signature. I ran my thumb over his beloved name, feeling the pressure from his pen on the paper. These past two years I had longed for his words to reassure me he was still alive. All I prayed was he would stay safe and return to me. Half of my prayer had been answered; he was safe. Would I rather have him dead and gone from the world forever? No! If he had died it would be unbearable.

This time as I read, I saw evidence of his suffering. His pain was spread across the page as plain as his words. His steady script shook. The writing was too heavy in places and too light in others. I could hear his pauses and his struggle as he reached for words to explain.

Less than a week later I heard a knock at the door, and I knew. I remained frozen, sitting tensely on the edge of my bed. Cora cracked the door. "Em, it's him. Are you going to see him?"

I tried to move. I wanted to see him. I wanted to hurt him. But I slowly shook my head. Tense conversation and Cora's raised voice came from the front door. I lay down on my side of the bed facing the window, staring at nothing. Suddenly he was standing outside my room behind the frozen pane, his figure dim in the dying light. His arms were tightly folded against the blowing snow. He shouted something, but all sound was carried away on the wind.

I walked toward the window, placing both hands against the cold glass. I could hear him plead, "Please, Emmeline."

I shook my head and mouthed the words so he could read them as they escaped my lips. "I can't."

He nodded and shoved his hands deep into his pockets and turned away. His familiar silhouette was lost in a swirl of snow.

The next morning there was a note tucked through the crack in the front door.

> *Emmeline,*
> *My love. Please talk to me, please see me. I will be alone at our sandstone cottage—you know the one— every weekend until I see you. Come to me when you are ready.*
>
> *I love you,*
> *Nathaniel*

Every Saturday and Sunday for an entire month, I thought of him abandoning his new wife to sit outside our cottage in the secluded meadow. The cottage with no roof and no walls. The cottage that would be bitterly cold. Was he really there? I felt a twisted pleasure knowing he might be frozen and hurting, like me. Sometimes I wanted to go to him. Once or twice, I walked up the bank of Emigration Creek, but my breath would become shallow, my legs weak, until I had to turn back. I pondered sending Cora to him, to tell him he didn't need to wait for me. To tell him I didn't love him, to tell him it was over. But I didn't.

One Saturday at the beginning of March, I rolled over in bed and was aware of sunlight on my face. I shuffled to the window and peered out. Only a dusting of snow remained. The world, like my heart, was thawing. I would walk to him.

Once decided, I was so desperate to see him I ran past the houses and into the open fields leading to the mouth of the canyon. It took longer to reach without a horse, but when I spotted the boulder we had sat on ages earlier, I dropped down to the creek side. Though the trees held fewer leaves this time of year, I knew I was close and I felt a knot rise in my throat. Could I do this?

Finally, there was the old sandstone foundation and the chimney. I put my hand to the base of my throat, remembering his touch on my skin. Was he here?

Then I saw him. He was facing the creek, his back turned to me. Standing, looking into the water, his hands were linked at the small of his back. It was my Nathaniel, lost in thought. He was a little older, a little more contemplative, but it was him. After all he'd gone through. After all *we* had gone through, he was here. I walked to his side and gently touched his shoulder.

He didn't turn his head. "Emmeline?" he whispered.

I exhaled. "Yes."

He took my face in both of his hands, running his fingers over my cheekbones, along the bridge of my nose, through my hair, and along my jaw. He stopped at my shoulders and pulled me into an urgent embrace. As he spoke I could hear the rumble of his words through his chest. "I have waited so long to hold you. Emmeline, can you forgive me?"

And I remembered. It hit me like a wave, and I pushed him away. "You can't touch me like this! You're married! You belong to Rosa. Do you hold her like this?"

He stood awkwardly by my side while I cried, occasionally reaching out to catch a tear. I swiped at his hand. "Don't."

Grasping my elbow, he led me to the rough foundation. "Please sit with me." He had spread a blanket over the cold stones, and I noticed his stack of schoolbooks. I stumbled my way to the blanket, determined to run back to the house as soon as I caught my breath.

"Talk to me, Emmeline."

The anger erupted and I spat the words, "Have you had relations with her, your wife?"

He hung his head. "No."

"Well, you *are* married, aren't you?"

"We are."

"Do you love her?"

"It's complicated. My love for her stems from an obligation to protect her and Dutch, but she really *is* wonderful. She is kind and grateful and accepting." He paused. "So, yes, I am beginning to love her. But it's different than my love for you. Our love, Emmeline, bloomed in the innocence of youth. You are my light and my joy. My love for Rosa was born in loss and pain. It's what binds us." He touched my hand timidly. "I don't know how else to explain it. . . ."

I swallowed so I could speak my next words. "Do you still love me?"

He dropped to his knees and laid his head on my lap. "Oh, Emmeline. Yes."

I touched his head, his hair smooth in my fingers. "Does she know about me?" I whispered.

He raised his head. "I've told her everything. I've told her I'll love you forever. And she accepts it. She's experienced so much suffering in her life, losing Joseph and her family . . . she says she feels safe with me. She asks for nothing more."

"If you really love me, ask her for a divorce. She's safe here now, as you've said. Leave her and choose me."

"I've thought of it. . . ." His voice cracked. "I have. But I can't. I can't go back on my promise to protect her."

I closed my eyes, my hands still cradling his head. "I don't know what else to say. What can possibly be left in our relationship, when you're married to her? Tell me, Nathaniel, what do we do?"

He was silent and I let my fingers continue to move through his hair, tracing the contour of his face, savoring this last caress.

He whispered at first. "Marry me, Emmeline." Then, as if the reality of his own words reached his conscious thoughts, he quickly sat up and took my hands in his. "Marry me!"

"What?" I stuttered. "What are you talking about? You've just said it. You're already married!"

"I know, but it could work. Don't you see? It could work. We could still be together!"

I slowly shook my head. "You mean share you with another woman? Do you mean become a polygamist?" I shouted. I thrust his head from my lap and stood. "I can't share you. I can't stand the thought of you loving another woman."

He grasped my hand and pulled it to his chest. "We can make our own rules, Emmeline. This is the right thing. Please, I know it is."

"The right thing for who? For you? You get to have us both, just like your father?" I jerked my hand from his, freeing myself. "Go back to your wife, Nathaniel. I'll be fine without you!" I turned and ran up the wooded creek bank, clawing at branches and roots to help me to the top. My palms were bleeding as I entered my home, tears streaming, chest on fire.

"Emmeline, today is Easter Sunday and it's been weeks since you've been to church." Cora sat on the edge of the bed and pulled the covers off my face. "Actually, it's been weeks since you've been anywhere at all."

"That's not true," I said, and pulled the covers over my head. "I've been to work at the hospital." I savored my time working as a nurse. It was the only place I felt at peace. Giving comfort to others somehow helped me hold myself together when I felt I might shatter at any moment.

"I mean somewhere social, somewhere fun. You're still alive, you know?"

"Amazing a person can go on living with a broken heart," I muttered.

"Now don't be melodramatic," said Cora, smiling. "You pulled me up when I was down. Get up and get dressed, I've got a surprise for you."

"Cora, please. This situation isn't the same. I'm not ready to go anywhere." I moaned and pulled the covers up again, pinning them under my head.

"Richard and Levi will be here in an hour to take us to Easter service. . . ."

"No!" I yelled.

"And Father said if you won't go to church then you can't go to work at the hospital either," she said, and scurried from the room.

How could she get my father involved? I seethed. I pulled my pillow over my head and tried to return to sleep, where in my dreams I wasn't tortured by thoughts of Nathaniel, but slumber escaped me. Cora was right: I wasn't dead. Though many days I wished the opposite. Easter service was appealing; maybe it would give me some inspiration to resurrect myself.

As the service ended, Levi asked if I would walk with him. "Let's give the lovebirds some time alone," he said, and winked at Richard and Cora, who walked the opposite way, hand in hand.

"I think I'm ready to get home. I've work tomorrow," I said.

"Give me a few minutes. The weather is balmy; it seems a shame to rush back," Levi pleaded.

"We can take the long way," I conceded.

We were silent for several minutes when Levi said, "So, Nathaniel left you for a German girl, did he?"

I gritted my teeth. "It appears so."

"It's a shame. You were so faithful to him, only dancing with me one or two times, and then ignoring me all together."

"Levi, I don't want to talk about this. You can leave me here. I'll walk the rest of the way by myself."

"I'm sorry. That was uncalled for. I was only thinking maybe a guy like me could have a chance with you now." He smiled and shrugged his shoulders.

I returned his smile. "I don't think I'm ready yet. But you can finish walking me home," I said as we continued to stroll.

Ahead of us on the sidewalk walked a young family dressed in their Sunday best. They moved slowly, holding the hands of a toddler. As we got closer, I gasped.

"Oh no! No . . . turn this way." I grabbed Levi's hand and crossed the street away from the family of three.

It was Nathaniel. He raised his hand, his face lighting up with recognition. The woman inspected me as a smile played across her lips. She was lovely.

"Is that . . . ?" Levi started.

Before he could finish I grabbed him around the waist and pulled him to me. I found his mouth. His teeth cut my lip, but he returned the kiss, his hands tracing my spine through my dress.

I blinked and found Nathaniel staring at us, his face creased with pain. He put his hands in his pockets and turned away. The woman and little boy followed close behind.

I shoved Levi away and straightened my hat.

"Whoa, I can't believe Nathaniel would give up on a girl who can kiss like that," Levi crowed. He wrapped his arm around my waist.

"Please don't," I said, and pushed his hand.

"Did you kiss me to make him jealous?" Levi asked, his mouth set in a grimace.

"I don't know. Maybe," I stuttered, knowing it was exactly what I'd done. "This whole thing is wrong! I told Cora it was too soon!"

"You may think it's wrong, Emmeline, but you know what's wrong? You! You need to face the facts," Levi cried. "I may not be Nathaniel . . . but I'm not married, either!"

"I think he's going to ask me to marry him today!" Cora squealed as I tied the bow at the back of her dress.

"What makes you say that?" I responded, trying to keep a straight face. I knew. I was in on the surprise. It was the Fourth of July, and Richard was going to propose to Cora at the Independence Day Celebration at Liberty Park. When the timing was perfect, he told me. What it meant, I wasn't sure. My job was to get her to the park and tag around after them to witness the momentous event.

"I don't know, he's been secretive . . . making sure I could go today, but noncommittal about our plans." She was squirming with anticipation.

"Well, for his sake, I hope he doesn't disappoint you," I said.

The park was crowded. Richard, Cora, and I visited the salt-water taffy booth and the tug-of-war arena. Levi refused to join us today, since I had refused to accept his calls after our disastrous Easter outing, so I had plenty of time to scan the crowd. I was looking for Nathaniel. I'd searched for him in every crowd since Easter. I was angry at myself for yearning for him. And I was heartbroken he hadn't come to call. But if he *had* called, what would I have done?

Our group of three made its way to the creek that meandered through the park, in an attempt to cool our feet. Richard elbowed me in the ribs.

"I think this is it," he said, bouncing on his toes.

"Do it! This is perfect, she'll never expect it here," I whispered.

"Cora," he said, grabbing both of her hands in his. He knelt on one knee, and I could see the soggy ground surrounding the creek had soaked his pants.

"Yes?" Her face glowed.

"Will you marry me?" Richard continued, kissing her hand. He slipped a thin gold band out of his pocket and held it out to her.

Cora clapped her hands. "I will, I will, I will!" She squealed each time her hands met.

Richard stood and swept Cora back for a lengthy kiss. The gathering along the creek broke into applause. Across the water, where no one had stood moments earlier, was Nathaniel. In his arms was a blond boy with tossed curls and wide blue eyes. The toddler was clapping with the crowd and laughing, his chortle accompanying the orchestra of onlookers. Nathaniel fixed me with his eyes, a careful smile emerging. I couldn't move.

As the clapping subsided, he leapt across the shallow creek, using flat stones to keep out of the water, and landed directly in front of me, the child still in his arms.

"Emmeline, your face is as flushed as Cora's," he said. "You look lovely."

"Hello, Nathaniel. Fancy meeting you here," I said briskly, ignoring his compliment.

"The engagement is exciting. For nearly an hour, Richard has been pacing around the park like a caged bear. I wondered what he was planning," he said.

"How is it you watched Richard, and I didn't notice *you?*" I asked, knowing I had been desperately searching faces as we meandered through the park.

"It was easier for me to gaze upon you unnoticed." He smiled recklessly. "I didn't want you throwing yourself at the next man you saw for an unbidden kiss, just because you knew I was near."

My face flashed hot. He had such nerve, I thought. And I realized he knew I had kissed Levi only to make him jealous. Both things made me furious.

"Why should you care?" I huffed. "Surely now you receive kisses of your own."

At my words, the little boy Nathaniel held in his arms kissed him on the cheek. Nathaniel startled, then smiled at the boy. "Who's that, Papa?" the little boy asked, pointing at me.

Nathaniel turned to the child. "This is Miss Emmeline," Nathaniel said, his voice laced with the longing I felt. "She's very important to me."

Unwanted, butterflies flew in my stomach.

"Emmeline, this is Dutch," he continued.

"Your stepson," I whispered.

He nodded.

"Where is your lovely wife?" I sneered, angry I cared.

"Em, please don't be like that." He put his hand on my arm.

"How would you suggest I behave, given these circumstances?" I said, retrieving my arm from his touch. I tried to ignore the heat from his hand.

"Emmeline, I wanted to tell you I talked to my father about the question I asked you. . . ."

"You what?" I spat. "I'll have nothing to do with your father and the life he leads."

"Wait . . ." Nathaniel grasped my arm again, pulling me toward him so he could speak quietly. "That's exactly what I was trying to tell you. Please listen."

"That awful polygamist Brother Redding, who tried to marry Cora. And your father . . . it's not who I am. It's not what I want," I stuttered, but I didn't move away.

"That's just it, Emmeline. It's not who *we* are. I want you to understand my proposal has nothing to do with God. It was not the proposal of a polygamist man following a higher calling. It has to do with my love for you," Nathaniel pleaded. "I want you as my wife, but I am not asking you for the reasons my father marries his wives. I was worried somehow at my core, I was like him. But I'm not. I love you, Emmeline, and I want to marry you. There will be no more wives."

"Except Rosa," I said, hardly moving my mouth.

"You and Rosa. Because I made a promise to keep her safe. But she understands how I feel about you. Please, Emmeline. Please come meet her."

"Meet who?" Cora had finally joined me.

"His wife," I whispered. Cora inhaled.

"So this must be your son," Cora said. "He is truly a beautiful child, Nathaniel. I'm glad you are happy. However, I can't help but wish you were happy with my sister."

"You're not the only one." He touched me lightly on the arm. "Emmeline, please come meet her."

"Nathaniel, I can't do this." My voice broke. I blinked hard to erase my tears.

Looking at my sister, I said, "Cora, congratulations! But I'm leaving. I need to go home now."

"Em, please stay, the fun here is only beginning," Cora pleaded, a scowl aimed at Nathaniel.

"Stay, Emmeline, we'll leave," he said, and turned away. Dutch clung to Nathaniel's neck, his thumb in his mouth. The boy waved to me, thumb invisible, four chubby fingers extended. Nathaniel picked his way through the crowd, legs long, back strong. Watching him cradle a child that wasn't mine made me ache.

Nathaniel glanced back one time, the corners of his eyes wrinkled with worry, but he raised his hand in farewell. I yearned to run after him. "I won't do this," I whispered and headed for home.

*   *   *

"Did you know Richard was going to propose?" Cora asked. Returning late from the festivities didn't stop Cora from turning on the lights to talk.

I sat up in bed and stretched, a smile spreading across my face. "Of course I knew."

"You kept a good secret," Cora said, gazing at her ring. She held it in front of her, angling her hand back and forth so the overhead light could catch the reflection.

"But wasn't it much better that way?" I asked.

"The whole day was perfect. . . ." Suddenly her face creased with worry. "At least for me."

"Well, I'm thrilled for you! But I'll miss you when you move! Who will wake me in the middle of the night to gloat about her engagement?" I teased. The truth was, I would miss Cora desperately. I pasted on my widest smile so I wouldn't smother her joy.

"I know what the solution is. . . ." Cora said.

"What is the solution?" I responded, touching the gold band. "It really is lovely," I said. Cora grinned.

"We need to find someone to take your mind off him," she said. "Someone who can give you a ring of your own. Is there a doctor at the hospital, or anyone else you find remotely interesting?"

I shook my head slowly. Should I tell her what Nathaniel had asked? The unspeakable question that haunted me day in and day out? A solution to my heartbreak so awful, I hadn't told a soul. And yet, I couldn't help but ponder it.

"What, Em, tell me! I can tell by your silence you're hiding something—a secret lover, perhaps?" She giggled.

"Cora, you can't tell anyone this."

"What? There *is* someone. Tell!"

I took a deep breath. "Nathaniel asked me to marry him."

Cora frowned. "But he's already married."

"I know. He asked me to marry him too."

Cora gasped. "You don't mean . . . you're not really considering this, are you, Em? Please tell me you aren't!"

"I'm not. No. I'm not. It's just . . . I ache for him. I close my eyes and all I see is his face." I tried to control the tremor in my voice while I explained to Cora. "I'm trying so hard to stop loving him. But it's not working. Nathaniel should be *my* husband. That German girl is living my life and I can't breathe!"

She was quiet for several minutes. "Won't he leave her?"

"No. He says he made a promise he won't break," I said. "I want what you and Richard have. And I want it with Nathaniel."

"Marrying Nathaniel isn't as awful as being the fifth wife to Brother Redding." Cora grimaced. "But it's not right either. Sharing your husband, imagine. It would be worse than not having him at all. Besides, you'd be excommunicated." Cora was dismissive. To her, the option was impossible.

"I know." I sighed, resigned.

"It would be better if you didn't keep seeing him about town, though," Cora said as she took off her shoes and stockings, readying herself for bed.

"I know," I replied, somewhat guiltily, knowing I searched for him wherever I went, hoping to glimpse his face.

Cora stretched out beside me and yawned wide. "I wish he had made the right choice," she said quietly as she drifted to sleep.

"I do too . . ." I whispered, sinking into the dark, knowing he would be there, dancing behind my eyelids, grinning at me like he had when he was mine. I loved that he waited for me here so I could hold him as I drifted to sleep. As I found slumber, his arm looped around my waist. I imagined leaning my head into his shoulder. In my dreams, we walked together side by side.

I wandered the aisles of the Success Market in Sugar House, arms loaded with the groceries my father had asked me to purchase on my way home from the hospital. The market was crowded; excited voices rang through the aisles. A couple of men were stopped, blocking my progress. "Excuse me," I said. "I need to grab a loaf of bread, behind you. But, if you don't mind me asking, what's all the excitement?"

The men apologized and slid away from the shelves full of baked goods. "The Brits have used their tanks," they said loudly.

"The war could be turning around! We Americans may not even have our chance against the Huns."

I wordlessly reached around them and stuffed a loaf into my satchel. The war. I felt like I had already lived it.

Rounding the shelf where I stood, a tiny blond boy streaked past. He stopped and reversed several paces to inspect me. He had the bluest eyes. "Hello, Miss Emmeline."

"Hello, Dutch," I breathed. "Who are you here with?"

"Mama," he said, and dashed away.

Rosa! I could finally see her up close! My heart raced in my chest.

I crept after Dutch, determined to watch her unnoticed. Two aisles over Dutch stopped in front of a blond woman, a head shorter than me with wide-set eyes as blue as her son's. Dutch tugged on her skirts. She shifted her bag and picked him up. He twirled a finger in one of her ringlets and popped his thumb in his mouth. She kissed him on the cheek, whispered something in his ear, and put him back on the ground.

I slinked after her as she filled her bags and walked to the front of the store. As she placed her items on the counter, Dutch bumped a glass jar of honey, which crashed to the ground. Rosa blinked. "I am sorry," she said, her English heavily accented. "I will still pay for it."

The shopkeeper's face hardened. "You're that German girl," he sneered. "We don't sell nothing to Huns!" He pulled her items off the counter and put them behind him. Dutch whimpered. Rosa picked him up and whispered to him as she walked toward the door.

"Wait," I cried. "She's a woman. The war isn't about her."

"Of course it's about her, she's German," the clerk snapped without looking at me.

"I'll buy her items and my own," I said, and I made my way to the front of the line.

The shopkeeper was Brother Dixon, a man in my ward. His face flushed. "Sister Lansing," he stuttered.

"Brother Dixon." I nodded. "Charge me for everything together, and include the honey."

He rang up the items without another word, and I left the store. Rosa was waiting outside. "Thank you!" she said.

"Thank you, Emmeline," Dutch echoed his mother.

"Emmeline?" Rosa whispered.

I nodded, and pushed her groceries toward her. I couldn't trust myself to speak.

"You are Nathaniel's Emmeline?"

"Not anymore. I should go now." I turned away.

"Please," she said, grasping my wrist. "I have wanted to meet you."

"Well, here I am." I pulled my hand from her gentle grip and stepped back several feet.

"He talks about you."

I wouldn't turn around. I couldn't do this. I walked faster. She ran to catch up, touching my elbow.

"He cries out for you as he sleeps. I hear him from my bed."

I faced her. "He does?" I whispered. "How do you stand it? He's your husband."

Her fragile shoulders fell. "How do I stand it? Knowing my husband loves another woman?"

I nodded.

"I also love another, my husband who is gone. There is nothing to understand. It is part of him. His love for you, his loyalty to me, it is what makes him Nathaniel." Her face was kind.

"It's wrong," I whispered.

"It is not wrong or right, Emmeline. It just is."

I had to get away! I ran with a hitching stride, my heavy satchels banging against my hip as I fled.

"Bye, Emmeline," Dutch called as I dashed toward home.

Tears slid down my face as I ran. Why couldn't she be awful? I wanted her to be old and ugly and mean. And I could gloat that Nathaniel got what he deserved.

Or if she had been jealous and spiteful, there would be some pious relief that I was the better person. But she wasn't awful in any sense of the word. She was gracious and forgiving. She revealed Nathaniel calls out for me, rather than jealously protecting her own marriage.

She was trusting. She was kind. I could understand why Nathaniel felt he needed to care for her. Even in buying her groceries, I wanted to protect her. She needed nurturing.

She was a good person, and though I wanted to hate her for living my life, I just couldn't.

I was exhausted. I gazed out the window at the end of the wide hospital corridor. The mountains seemed to rise close to the building, a black cliff against the silken moonlit sky.

I had been taking extra hours at the hospital, trying to keep busy enough to forget about Nathaniel. Because of my commitment to the profession, I had recently been promoted to head nurse for most night shifts. When I was looking for a silver lining, I credited the lack of a husband for not distracting me from my nursing duties. And I welcomed the mind-numbing fatigue of my schedule. Nursing was the only thing to fill my mind and hands, even when my heart ached emptily.

One task remained before I could leave for the night. I yawned. Sunrise was fast approaching, the eastern horizon changing from pitch to charcoal. One final basket of syringes to fill with morphine before I could sleep. The corridor of the hospital was deserted, so it was easy to hear approaching footsteps at the end of the hall, opposite my view. The footfall was jarring in the hush of the early morning, as it was clearly not the hesitant shuffle of a patient.

"Nurse?" a voice called.

"I'll be with you in a minute," I hollered back, and returned my attention to the syringe. It was precise work.

Defying my attempt at delay, the clip of the footsteps increased, moving quickly toward me. "Did you check in at the desk?" I called nervously, finishing the measurement and capping the needle.

"Emmeline."

I wheeled around. Nathaniel was standing ten feet away, his arms spread, his palms facing me. He smiled and his face creased with the confident energy I had fallen in love with.

"Nathaniel! You startled me. . . ." I set the syringe onto the service cart. "What are you . . . ?"

He walked swiftly toward me, opened his arms, and engulfed me in their steady embrace. He kissed my eyelids, my cheeks, my nose; I found his mouth with mine. Tasting him was like cool water in the desert. He met my gaze and suddenly I was anchored, certain, alive.

"What am I doing? I'm so tired, I'm not thinking clearly," I panted. I pushed against his chest, but his hands were locked tight at the small of my back.

"I've come to ask you again. . . ." He held both of my hands in his, searching my eyes. "Marry me, Emmeline. Please. You can make your own rules. You make your own decisions. Every hour you're not with me is torture."

"You're being dramatic," I said, resisting him. But I knew how he felt, because I felt it too.

He seized my shoulders and pressed me again to his chest. "I need you so badly. Doesn't this feel right?"

"Loving you is wrong," I said quietly. "And marrying you would be so hard."

"But what feels right?" he asked again.

I hesitantly leaned my head against his shoulder, considering the question he was asking me. What sacrifices would I make to be with him? And I knew. Nothing I would give up was worth more than his love, his embrace. Nothing. Not my community, not my religion. Surrounded by his strength and warmth, I felt at peace. I would be tested, but it felt right. Perfectly right. "You do . . ."

"Emmeline?" Nathaniel whispered. He leaned toward me. "Will you?"

"I will." I sighed the words, resigned. His mouth found mine. And I didn't push him away.

My secret sustained me through slumber, dreams of Nathaniel no longer gilded with pain. Melancholy engulfed me as I rolled from bed. As usual when I worked the night shift, Cora and my father had gone before I woke. I had solitude this late morning to pack my possessions. I would leave my home on Downington Avenue today to start anew, taking schoolbooks, Nathaniel's letters, my clothing, and not much more. My family would return as usual to share an afternoon meal, but until that time, I could prepare in silence. I could fully consider the impact of my decision.

I scooped Nathaniel's neatly folded letters into a satchel and found, tucked deep in my dresser drawer, the little leather suitcase I received at age eight on the day of my baptism. I intended to pack it with a few of my smaller things—needle, thread, a broach given to me after my mother died. Originally, the case had carried my Bible and Book of Mormon to and from church, which it had, for five years, until the leather handle came unstitched.

Opening it, I found it wasn't empty. Tears filled my eyes as I discovered the embroidered wall-hanging I'd worked hours on, announcing my marriage to Nathaniel. I'd pulled my last thread the day he'd written from New York. Not so long ago, but I didn't remember putting it in the case. Forgotten completely in my grief, Cora had likely hidden it from me to spare me the sadness of throwing out hours of fruitless work. This carefully stitched tapestry was a manifestation of what may have been.

I lightly ran my fingers over the fine stitches. There was an empty spot at the bottom of the fabric, a void I had eagerly anticipated filling with the looping stitch I had chosen for the other letters on the sampler. Right below *Sealed for Time and All Eternity* would be the date announcing the marriage of Emmeline and Nathaniel Barlow. Now there would be a marriage, but it couldn't be in the Salt Lake Temple. And it wouldn't be recognized by the law or by God.

I caressed the stitching again, folded it, and placed it back into the little broken case. This was my decision, so I would leave this case and embroidery, this evidence of a road I would not travel, behind. I locked the clasps and knew immediately where I would hide it. I found the wooden stepladder and used it to reach the trap door leading to our attic. On the top step, I precariously reached into the dark cramped space and tucked the case behind one of the roof beams, out of sight from the door. Suddenly, the sound of footsteps resonated on the front porch. I closed the door and quickly returned the ladder to the kitchen. My family had arrived and I knew I must talk with them.

As I spoke, my father turned his back toward me. He stepped to the window, staring blankly, shoulders shaking with anger. Cora slumped on the window seat, her hand over her mouth.

Without turning around, my father said, "You are succumbing to a lifetime of pain. Marriage is not a whirlwind romance, Emmeline. It's hard work—even when one husband and *one wife* are committed to each other. How committed is he to you, when he willingly marries another?"

"It was the war," I said softly. "The war changed everything."

"I knew you were hurting," he sighed, mostly to himself. "But I didn't know what to do. If only your mother were still here . . . she would've known. I've failed you."

"No. This is my decision. It has nothing to do with you. You've been a wonderful father, all Cora and I have ever needed." I touched his shoulder.

"Listen to me now." He faced me, fresh anger lining his face. "Here's what happened. He fell in love with Rosa when he was in England. He married her and is telling you a desperate story so he can have you both. Plural marriage is against God's word, Emmeline. It's a sin!" His voice echoed as he spoke.

"I don't believe loving him is a sin. Who made these rules? I make my own rules and I choose to spend my life with him!"

"But he didn't choose you." My father's words were clipped. "You think he's the only one for you, but you're wrong. He has a wife now, and that wife isn't you. Would you willingly give up your community and your salvation? Would you willingly give it *all* up for young love?" He turned to the window again. His voice was softer now. "You should pray, Emmeline. Ask God if this path you are choosing is the right one."

"I have prayed," I responded. "And I've never received an

answer to any *one* of my prayers. Not even when I was frightened because Nathaniel was in Europe. And when he returned and he held me, the only thing I felt was him. His hands were warm around mine and it felt right. *That* is the answer to my prayer." I took a deep breath. It strengthened me and gave me peace. "I can't love another man like I love Nathaniel. Even if I gave him up and married another, that man would always be my second choice. Always. Nathaniel is my first choice. I want him to be my husband."

"You're old enough to make your own decisions, as foolish as they may be." My father collapsed onto the window seat next to Cora and pulled his hands through his hair. When he looked up, there was fire in his eyes. "But I can't let you bring him here to visit. I won't support your polygamist marriage."

"No!" Cora stood. "We can't abandon her!"

I gasped. "Are you saying I won't be welcome in your home?"

My father stared at his hands, so tightly clasped on his lap his knuckles shone white.

Cora's voice wavered. "Oh, Emmeline, are you sure?" She walked to me and held me in her arms.

I nodded. "I love him."

Cora whispered in my ear. "You will always be welcome in *my* home. Stay close to me, my dear sister."

"I won't be so far away, blocks really, at least until Nathaniel finishes his schooling," I pleaded.

Cora nodded silently.

"Nathaniel and Rosa are coming to retrieve me now. Please, will you see them?" I begged my father.

"No, Emmeline," my father answered. "You're making this decision alone."

With a leather satchel on each shoulder and the wooden crate in my hands, I let my tears fall freely. I was willingly leaving my family, like I was leaving the small leather case, full of a life not mine. But I was leaving for Nathaniel, and my love for him was so certain it stemmed my tears.

Cora opened the front door for me. She rested her hand on my shoulder. "Oh, Emmeline. Is this really what you want?"

"Yes," I said. And I knew it was.

She smiled and gently touched my lashes, erasing the streaks of tears. "Let's get you looking your best, then."

"Thank you, Cora. I love you so much, my sister," I said as I stepped onto the front porch and gazed down the street.

Nathaniel walked toward me, his stride long and confident. To his right, holding the hand of little Dutch, was Rosa. Her face was calm, and her arm was extended toward me, her fingers outstretched. My heart surged. I knew where I belonged. I knew where I could find my joy. I stepped off the porch and walked toward them. Nathaniel met me halfway.

IVY BAYGREN

⌒✦⌒

Stephen came in the back door, his steps somber like those he would take when walking into a funeral parlor—hesitant, dreading what he'd see, knowing he must enter. "Ivy?" He whispered rather loudly. He wanted my attention, but he would also give me a minute to pull myself together.

But there was no need. Yes, it was the first anniversary, and I'd admit to a fair amount of sobbing in the shower, but as Stephen walked into the dining room and saw me in front of my laptop, calmly typing, he exhaled loudly. This wasn't a funeral after all. "You had me panicked. It's so quiet in here. Where are the kids?"

"We went to breakfast, then Naomi wanted to teach Porter how to play tennis. She's been taking a class, so I dropped them at the high school courts on the way home." I smiled at him now, sedately.

Stephen pulled up a chair next to me. "A year, huh? God, it seems like it could have been yesterday. I almost expect him to walk into the room."

"I know. I do too. But here's what I've learned over the last year." I took a deep breath. "Even if you wish, even if you beg, even if you visualize . . . he can't come back." I choked on a sob as I admitted these words, mostly to myself. "But I'm okay. I have my memories, and if I don't dwell there indefinitely, I'll be okay. We'll be okay."

Stephen stood behind me and put his hands on my shoulders,

the weight of them soothing me. A doctor's healing hands. My brother's healing hands.

"So what are you doing in here, so diligently working?"

"I'm summarizing that list we made. Writing down the steps I've taken so I can cross things off. You know how satisfying list completion is to me." I smiled up at him. "Today feels momentous, like my progress should be noted." I glanced at the piece of stationery sitting next to the keyboard, glowing like a beacon from the reflective light of the computer screen. Stephen picked it up and slowly read it aloud, considering the words.

1: If one glass of wine isn't enough, pour another
2: Surround yourself with things you love
3: Find a deeper meaning
4: Get the dog to sleep on his side of the bed
5: Never forget
6: Get your house in order
7: Understand there is a little sad in every story

"Today I'm working on several steps. Case in point." I stood and picked up a vase of roses sitting in the center of the dining room table. Refracted light created a brilliant pattern on my hands as I lifted it. The vase was pinkish, pre-Depression-era cut glass, a gift from Bitsy given to me by her daughter as I left Bitsy's funeral. This morning I'd filled it with snowy Emmeline roses, creating a sinuous cloud of lavender and molasses, the fragrance filling the room. "As you can see, I'm surrounding myself with things I love. Step number two, roses."

Stephen buried his face in the mounds of cotton puff petals, then jumped back, a thin line of blood welling at his jawline. "It bit me," he said, and walked into the bathroom to assess the damage, returning with a tissue held to his chin.

"I know. Look." I held up my forearm lightly crisscrossed with scratches. "Happens every time, even when I wear the leather gloves, but it's worth it." I touched a creamy blossom, and a petal of the Emmeline rose fell into my outstretched palm. I held it to my nose.

"The roses don't love you back," he said, looking pointedly at my arm. "The wicked thorns are a striking contrast to the beauty."

"Yes, beauty in spite of the thorns, that's it. Without the thorns the beauty would be too easy. It would be underappreciated. Rose and thorn, you can't have one without the other, and that's what makes them so precious."

"I think I hear . . . Which step was the one about finding deeper meaning?" He picked up the list again.

I barked with laughter, "Oh my God, you're right! I hadn't even thought of that, seriously. I was convinced finding a deeper meaning was the only step I'd completely failed." I took the list from his hands. "I've read books, tried meditation, deep breathing, half smiles, and I still haven't found a deeper meaning, or a good reason, for Adam's death." I picked up a pen lying on my desk. "However, this will work. Rose and thorns," I said, drawing a large X over step 3. "Good enough. I'm *so* calling this one done."

"So, despite the thorns, you love roses. What else have you surrounded yourself with?" My brother was smiling. The lines surrounding his eyes that had become more prominent since Adam died were smooth as he asked me the question.

"The vase reminds me of Bitsy. So, I love the vase. And Earl Grey." I pointed to my empty mug. "And my home."

"Speaking of things you love." Stephen winked and lightly socked me in the shoulder to minimize his words. "Do you plan to see Theo again?"

Theo had taken me to the Historical Society several times, helping me research the women who'd shared my common ground. The last couple of times we'd followed our excursion with dinner and wine. It left me with a nervous flutter in my heart, like the almost-sick feeling before getting on a roller coaster, thrilled with the possibility. Would this ride result in grave injury or the time of my life?

I tamped down a milder version of butterfly nausea as I spoke about Theo to my brother. "We're going on an art gallery stroll this Friday, maybe dinner afterward, I don't know."

"Are you legitimately interested in him, Ivy?"

My cheeks betrayed me. I could hide the jitters, but I couldn't hide the flush. "Well, tomorrow I'm going shopping for a new dress with Naomi, something a little sexier than the cotton T-shirt dresses I wear most days, so I guess I am."

He smiled gently, aware of the strength it took to admit my feelings out loud. I took a breath before speaking again. Not because I felt uncertain or weak, but because the next statement was wrapped around my heart. "But today is Adam's day. Today belongs to all the people who surround me, and yet are gone." I held up the list. "I know there is sadness, amid the joy, in every story."

ROOT, PETAL, THORN

Ella Joy Olsen

About This Guide

The suggested questions are included
to enhance your group's reading
of Ella Joy Olsen's
Root, Petal, Thorn.

DISCUSSION QUESTIONS

1. *Root, Petal, Thorn* is written from the perspective of five different women, their stories bound loosely by their common ground. Was this connection enough to pull the stories together? Did you relate more to one character than the others? If you could meet just one of the women, whom would you choose and why?

2. At its core, *Root, Petal, Thorn* is an observation of the permanence of place and the impermanence of people. How have you been affected by your home and/or neighborhood? And what have you done to make your home your own?

3. Much historical fiction illustrates a famous place or person, but every person (and every place) has a history, regardless of recorded significance. Is a story about normal people and typical struggles more relatable? Or less interesting?

4. *Root, Petal, Thorn* is an illustration of the bittersweet passage of time. Are you a person who looks forward with anticipation, or back at all that has passed? Would you go back to a particular period in your own life? If so, when, and why?

5. *Emmeline*—If you were in Emmeline's position, understanding the culture and time, would you have married Nathaniel? Why or why not? She's a consenting adult when she decides to marry him. Does that fact make this type of marriage okay? Compare this type of marriage to marriage between consenting same sex couples.

6. *Bitsy*—Written memories or journals have always been important documents, recording personal history and significant events. These days there is so much personal

information recorded—vlogs, blogs, tweets—all meant for public consumption. Is this a truer representation of life, though the intent is to be widely shared? Or is social media a glossy image of the truth? And does so much information dilute the significance of each word? Finally, were the sections labeled "Bitsy" more about Bitsy or about her mother, Cora?

7. *Eris*—Eris does what she thinks is best for her son, Adonis, in the face of possible danger, regardless of his anger, and at times sacrificing the happiness of other members of her family. To what lengths would you go (or have you gone) to manipulate a circumstance that might be dangerous to your loved ones?

8. *Lainey*—Mental illness is an especially challenging affliction, in that it has no obvious outward symptoms, like a cast or a cough. Yet it can be a lifelong disease. Many think it can be cured by simply pulling up the old boot straps. And yet it contributes to suicide, drug use, and homelessness. Have you personally experienced mental illness, mild or severe, in yourself or your family? How should this condition be treated?

9. *Ivy*—Ivy is the character who searches for stories as part of her healing process. Do you believe the stories in this novel are her imagination or the truth? What do you want them to be? Have you ever imagined the people who occupied your home, before you?

10. *Ivy*—The stories of the other women who lived in Ivy's home don't fix Ivy's loss or bring her husband, Adam, back. Is understanding that you're not alone in your pain enough? Or would it have been more healing to have faith in a higher power, or a belief that Ivy will see Adam again? Did you want him to give her signs he was still an active part of her life?

Coming in September 2017

WHERE THE SWEET BIRD SINGS

by

Ella Joy Olsen

Though she has a loving husband, Emma Hazelton is adrift, struggling to rebuild her life after a tragedy. But one day, a simple question and an old black-and-white photograph prompt Emma to untangle the branches of her family tree, where she discovers a legacy of secrets.

Where the Sweet Bird Sings is a beautifully written companion novel to the novel *Root, Petal, Thorn,* exploring the meaning of family and identity. What connects us to another? Is it shared history? Is it ancestry? Or is it love?

Connect with Us

Visit us online at
KensingtonBooks.com
to read more from your favorite authors, see books
by series, view reading group guides, and more.

for sneak peeks, chances to win books and prize packs,
and to share your thoughts with other readers.

facebook.com/kensingtonpublishing
twitter.com/kensingtonbooks

Tell us what you think!

To share your thoughts, submit a review,
or sign up for our eNewsletters, please visit:
KensingtonBooks.com/TellUs.